A FEW BEFORE WE'RE THROUGH

STORIES TO PUT IN YOUR HEAD WHILE YOU STILL HAVE ONE

TOM SADIRA

CONTENTS

*To Serene,
who makes my own personal plunge into oblivion
worthwhile.*

INTRODUCTION

Hello, curious reader. Looks like I've finally found my way into your hands.

I realize it's not that exciting for you, not yet. Surely this isn't your first time. It's not mine, either. But it's still special. Think about it—this could very well be the last book you ever read. Hell, this could be the last paragraph you read. Or this, the last sentence. Even this short one. Yikes.

Don't scoff. Don't try to deny it. You and I both know the end can come for us via a car crash or a heart attack or even a single bite of food sent down the wrong pipe. Every day, about 150,000 of our fellow humans learn that lesson the hard way. Just this morning, a new batch of poor saps woke up assuming they had months, years, decades ahead of them...but then—splat!

As Vonnegut said: "So it goes."

We humans usually don't like to think about our mortality. Why would we? We're alive! Or, at least, *you* still are. *You* might as well go on living while the living is good. Despite all my pessimistic blathering about the inevitability of death, there is still plenty of good to be found in life for those who bother looking for it. If I were you, I wouldn't wait. As the name of this book suggests, time is running out!

Depending on when you read this, I may have already shuffled off my mortal coil. If that's the case, you should know this: I definitely got the living while the living was good. As much as I could find, as often as I could find it. It got so good at times that I often wondered—really, sincerely —whether or not I'd actually died long ago and was living out some kind of shrewdly-camouflaged, Twilight-Zone-esque, paradisiacal afterlife. I'm still not 100% sure that's not the case, but in the end, who cares?

While I was alive, one of the things I enjoyed most was writing stories. Put another way: my head periodically fills up with stories, so every once in a while I have to pour them out and usher them into our world using language. If I didn't, they would swell and fester and burst my head open like an overripe melon. I haven't proven that yet. I hope never to try.

Some stories develop into novel-length manuscripts, but more often than not they become short fiction: novellas, short stories, flash fiction. In some ways, I enjoy the smaller ones more than the novels. Their challenge is to develop living, breathing characters, construct an engaging plot, and build a whole universe using only a few scenes. It keeps me on my toes while preventing my head from exploding— which always seems like a win/win to me.

Maybe, for you, curious reader, these stories can be of some value, too. Not because they're painstakingly chiseled from some sharply poignant, catharsis-evoking *literary fiction* class, but because they're fun. That's it. That's where they came from; that's why I wrote them. It was fun! What else was I supposed to do?

I assure you, each story in this collection was proudly crafted from the blue collar, working class, *genre fiction* class of literature. Not just one genre, either. I dabble. I'll try any genre once and that's usually all it takes to get me addicted for life. I'm also an experimental author; I mix and bend and combine whatever genres I think might work together. I've yet to find any incompatible combinations, and until I do, I plan on continuing to do my thang.

I've written close to fifty short stories over the past decade, and this collection represents my first attempt at sharing them with curious readers like you. It was hard to choose which to include. Which is why I ended up with 17 stories—which *everyone* has told me is definitely too many stories for a single collection. I disagree. My goal was to squeeze as many of my favorites into 450 pages, which I did. So there.

Each of these stories seemed to be imbued with the power to transport the curious reader (and author!) to a *completely different world,* at least for a little while. It's the same way I've felt as a reader being transported by Robert E. Howard's *Conan* chronicles, or Arthur Conan Doyle's *Sherlock* mysteries, or any of the many masterful short stories from Flannery O'Conner, James Baldwin, Issac Asimov, Philip K. Dick, Stephen King....the list goes on and on. The point isn't that I've just subtly compared myself to some really outstanding authors, it's that *any* captivating short story can become a much-needed vacation when life's not so good. They're tiny, easily accessible portals to new worlds. I know I'm biased, but I happen to think these particular 17 stories possess at least some of that portal power.

Speaking of times when life's *not so good,* I've deliberately chosen to ignore those moments here in the introduction. Don't worry, though—my stories are overflowing with them. Whether it's a scissor-wielding sentient beard, a touch-and-go military operation inside the arteries of a sick patient, or a plain old western triple-double-cross, the characters in my stories will definitely learn a thing or two about times when life's not so good.

In my defense, I usually weave some kind of basic karmic justice into each story, only sacrificing innocent characters when it turns out to be really, really entertaining.

Anyway, I've already wasted too much of your precious time—which, we've already established, is likely in much shorter supply than you think.

Remember, you have as much of a chance as anyone else to end up in today's group of 150,000 deaths. If not today, tomorrow you'll get another shot. Me, too. And one of these days that daily average will suddenly spike due to one or more of the following inevitabilities: catastrophic meteor impacts, high-energy solar flares, supervolcano eruptions, biowarfare, drone warfare, regular warfare, microplastics in our bodies, disease, and/or pollution. Talk about some pretty exciting *not-so-good* moments in life!

Even if you're currently experiencing a *not-so-good* time in your own life, and even though our collective demise seems right around the corner, I hope these stories can at least offer you, curious reader, just a few moments of relief, distraction, or entertainment before the bony hands of Death tuck you into the grave for your eternal slumber.

Yeah, right.

We're obviously gonna be reincarnated on a distant planet to start the fun all over again. Duh.

"DON'T THINK OF IT AS DYING," said Death. "JUST THINK OF IT AS LEAVING EARLY TO AVOID THE RUSH."

~ Terry Pratchett, *Good Omens*

WHAT A TREAT

I stretch my four paws out in front of me and push my back up against the soft mound. My eyes aren't quite ready to open all the way, so I leave them closed. The house is very quiet. Everything is still. Do I really need to get up now? Naw.

The patch of sunlight spilling in through the window is gloriously bright today. Its warmth crackles on my fur. I consider purring, but don't have it in me just yet. Instead, I sprawl and sigh and soak in the moment.

Today is another special day. My hooman is spoiling me by laying here on the rug. She hasn't snuggled like this since I was a kitten. What a treat. I yawn and let a faint chirrup escape, then tilt my head to look for her reaction. Hmph. She doesn't light up. Her eyes are still closed. And I thought I was the lazy one.

The sunlight feels soooo good. I extend my front claws, try to touch it. A shadow flutters by. My ears twitch. My tail flickers. Well, that does it. Once my tail's awake, there's no use in laying around. I might as well get up and see what's worth chasing.

After a moment or two, or three, or five, I begin my warm-up routine. I arch my back, slink about in a circle, and knead the rug. Another yawn, then I repeat the whole thing.

I sniff the hooman's face. So peaceful. I love that my hooman is taking it easy for once. Normally, she spends the whole day milling about: baking, cleaning, humming. Hoomans are such busy-bodies. But not today. Nor yesterday. Nor the day before. What a treat.

It's not really my thing, but, I decide to show her my gratitude, so I muster a long purrrrr and brush up against her cheek. Twice. Hmph. She doesn't stir. I sniff again. Nudge her. Nothing.

I shrug it off and decide it's the perfect time for a bath. Ouch! My tongue gets stuck on the backside of my paw. I smack my lips and try again. Ouch again. Too dry.

I saunter to my water dish. Still empty. Wow. My hooman never forgets to fill it for me—but it's been dry for days now. I bat at the bowl, knocking it aside. It makes a shrill sound against the tile floor. Surely that'll wake the hooman. Nope. She's still lying on the rug, soaking up the sun. So still. So lazy. What a treat.

I barely resist the urge to snuggle up beside her again, and instead hop up on the kitchen counter. That seemed easier than normal. Have I lost weight?

I point my ears at the sleeping hooman as a rush of excitement ripples across my fur. My tail goes up. Normally, she'd run over and give me a gentle pat. Or maybe scoop me up, coo sweetly, and set me back onto the floor. Not today.

I lap up the soapy, grey water in the sink. Hmph. A cat like me deserves better than this. Secretly, though, I kind of like the sour greasiness. It's grown on me. I'm just glad no one's watching.

My stomach yowls. I can spot my food dish from up here. Not a crumb. Lazy hooman.

Even though I emptied it days ago, I dip my head into the shiny mixing bowl and give it a lick. My stomach yowls again. Hmph.

Enough is enough. Time to wake up the hooman.

I land gracefully on the floor and meander to the rug. I make sure to stroll, stopping once or twice to swat at a dust mote. Don't want to seem needy.

I sniff at the stale air around her mouth, making sure to poke some whiskers in her nose. Hoomans roar and turn all wiggly whenever I do that. But she doesn't stir. How strange. I brush up against her a few times. I even stop to meow loudly in her ear. Nothing.

Wow. So lazy. Maybe she's turning into a cat?

I place my front paws on her neck and start kneading gently, just enough to wake her. After that doesn't work, I let my claws slip from their sheathes. They haven't been trimmed in a while, and one gets snagged on her skin. I yank it away. Her skin stretches, my nail yanks but finally breaks free—leaving behind a tiny red drop of something. I sniff it. Interesting. I lap it up. Salty, kind of like a fish. Another tiny red drop appears, so I lap that up, too.

Suddenly, a smell tickles my nose. I nose around, sniffing for what I've detected: hooman food mush. Found it! How strange that my hooman would've taken a nap without washing it off her hands first?

I sniff at it. Yep, it's the same stuff I've been eating from the shiny bowl on the kitchen counter and from the large wooden spoon on the floor. Before I can worry about who's watching, my tongue goes to work. One by one, I clean each finger.

There goes my stomach, yowling again. Some of that

food mush is stuck under a fingernail, and I'm having a hard time getting it out. Without thinking, I try my teeth. Just a bit. Suddenly, a salty sweet taste is in my mouth. More of the tiny red drops appear. I lap them up.

I gnaw, just a little. I can't help myself. Something breaks off into my mouth. More chewy and more salty than the sticky food mush.

A puddle of the red stuff pools under her hand.

Wow.

What a treat.

BITE OF PASSAGE

Today was Cindy Lacerto's 10th birthday, and she couldn't remember ever being this sad.

"One's tenth birthday is an important milestone in the Lacerto family," her mother announced, just one week ago. As usual, Cindy felt as if something was expected from her rather than being given to her.

When asked whether she had any preference as to the party's theme, Cindy answered with a single word. It was a word she'd been unable to shake free from her mind in recent times. A word that had the power to fill her with ecstasy, that caused her mind to stray from every task, that kept her up at night aching with desire.

"Kittens!" she'd blurted out.

At that, her mother narrowed her eyes, nodded, and sipped her morning cocktail.

Now, her kitten-themed party was over, and Cindy felt like crying. Rainbow shrapnel was strewn across the expansive lawn and the last of the guests were saying their goodbyes. Her bedazzled birthday crown slightly askew, Cindy plopped down in her wrinkled party dress and crossed her arms. She glared at the stately old oak tree that stood near the center of the yard.

I'm not getting one.

I can't believe it. I'm really not getting one.

If Father could afford to get me that stupid, ugly yacht for my ninth birthday—with a stupid, ugly crew and all the stupid, ugly accessories—why couldn't he get me one tiny, darling, sweet baby kitten?

Like all her previous birthdays, even though he footed the bill for the lavish party, her father had been called away by work and missed the whole thing. She found herself wishing he were there, but not because she missed him.

Cindy could count on one hand the times they'd engaged in conversation since her last birthday. When she was younger, his lack of attention really bothered her. But these days she found that it barely affected her at all.

Guess this is what the adults mean by 'growing up'.

Whenever he was home, her parents would be too busy quarreling with each other to notice her. Unfortunately, the task of organizing the party had required her mother to notice her more often than normal. Cindy could use a break.

"When your father returns from his trip, you *will* express your gratitude for all of this," Cindy's mother said over breakfast, as they looked out on the staff setting up the party. "This day means a lot to him. Another Lacerto is shedding the frivolity of childhood—and not a minute too soon. Don't you dare make that face at me, young lady! I mean it. It's time to leave your childhood behind. It's time to march into this world as the adult you were always destined to become."

Cindy studied the eviscerated piñata that hung from one of the oak tree's branches. A broomstick leaned against the trunk and scraps of papier maché littered the roots that poked through the grass.

What the heck was Mother thinking?

Watching the entire school beat up a poor, defenseless, wonderful, papier maché kitten is NOT what I call a party.

Every single student from her school had been invited, regardless of their age or whether Cindy had ever met them. As each arrived, they dutifully handed over a gift to the house attendants, who in turn carried it off to be opened, sorted, and accounted for. Watching gift after gift disappear into a back room, Cindy finally mustered the courage to ask her mother when she'd be able to play with them.

"Never," her mother had answered. Then, noticing the moisture welling up in her daughter's eyes, she leaned in closer and whispered sharply, "There's nothing these people can give you that you don't already have. It's junk, all junk. Besides, darling, it's not like they're really giving *you* anything. All they're *really* doing is paying for the opportunity to tell their friends they attended the birthday party of a future Congressmen's daughter."

When a single tear sped down Cindy's cheek, her mother sighed and added, "Oh, just be grateful you don't have to write all those 'Thank you' cards! Once the staff clears away the party, they'll get to work writing them for you."

In addition to their regular household army of waitstaff, her parents had flown in a platoon of internationally acclaimed chefs to prepare a birthday feast. Guests stuffed themselves on a sumptuous banquet of foie gras, buckets brimming with caviar, wheels of pig's milk cheese, and plates of white truffle tagliolini.

Cindy barely touched her plate.

After dinner, the staff unveiled a table that buckled

beneath heaps of sugary treasure: cat-eared cupcakes, buckets of ice cream, glistening pastries, and every kind of candy imaginable. The centerpiece was a five-tier tower cake, smoothed over with pink icing and topped with a gold-flaked, marzipan kitten.

The other kids attacked the dessert buffet like a pack of rabid hyenas, but Cindy stayed put. Something about the way they sliced up the golden effigy of the kitten made her stomach turn. Plus, she'd been distracted by the way her mother stood with her arms crossed, watching her, judging her. Cindy flashed a phony smile and sank deeper into her chair.

At one end of the pristine lawn a small orchestra had played for hours, filling the air with classical music. At the opposite end, a stage was erected to host an endless rotation of performers: professional magicians, balloon-bending clowns, jugglers of fire and knives, and acrobats so gravity-defying they rivaled the Cirque du Soleil.

Every time Cindy would try to focus on a performance, her mind would become distracted by the vision that had been haunting her for months. Her fantasy was always the same: a soft, fluffy ball of fur is curled up in her lap, purring contentedly as she strokes it. She lifts the tiny feline and brushes it against her cheek. How soft! How sweet! She never, ever wants to stop covering it with kisses.

As Cindy sat alone, watching the poor, gutted piñata sway in the breeze, the vision took hold again.

Her breath quickened.

Her mouth watered with anticipation.

She licked her lips.

Then, remembering how her parents had absolutely, positively forbidden her from having any kind of pet, her heart plummeted back into darkness.

Why can't they just give me this one thing?

I'll trade everything I own—my clothes, my jewelry, even my stupid yacht—for one tiny, sweet, adorable kitten.

Why are they being so unfair?!

"Cynthia! Time to come in," her mother called from the door leading into the dining hall. "Hurry now, dear. You know I don't like to be kept waiting."

After her mother disappeared back inside, Cindy huffed across the lawn and kicked at anything in her path. As she entered their sprawling dining hall, she saw her mother sending away the last of the staff.

"Sit down, dear," her mother said. "Yes, right there at the head of the table, in your father's chair. Quickly now, don't dawdle."

Before Cindy could ask what was going on, the door connecting the west wing of the house swung open. Her father was there, dressed in his fancy suit, his sharp features hinting at some kind of mischief. In his hands was a glittery package, no larger than a shoe box, wrapped neatly in emerald paper with a floppy pearlescent bow tied to its lid.

Oh, great.

Another pair of shoes.

Thanks, Dad.

Then, with a meekness that was barely audible, a tiny meow escaped from the box. Cindy stopped fidgeting. Had it come from the box or from her imagination? She held her breath and listened.

"Did you enjoy your party, Cynthia dear?" he asked, raising an eyebrow.

"Yes, Father. It was absolutely splendid," she lied. "Thank you for everything, Father."

"I see..."

He closed the door behind him and locked it. When he

spun to face her again, his mischievous grin had been replaced by an impatient, aggressive scowl. Cindy had never seen him like this before. She squeezed the arms of her chair as he approached.

Cindy's mother sat on her left, her thin, ruby lips curled into something resembling a smirk. To her right sat her father, drumming his fingers on the box and looking severely disappointed.

"You might think we're cruel for not granting your incessant demands for a *pet*, but we've had our reasons." He stopped drumming and locked eyes with Cindy. "The reason is that we had a much better gift in mind for today. Something of a birthright in our family. Something money can't buy."

Another muffled meow came from the box, and this time Cindy knew for a fact that she had really heard it. She wanted to leap up, jump across the table, snatch the box from her stupid, arrogant father, rip the lid off, and then...

Her fantasy stopped dead in its track.

Her mind went blank.

"Are you okay, young lady? You look pale," he turned to his wife. "The girl looks absolutely famished. Didn't you feed her?"

"Of course, I *tried*," her mother said, making a scowl of her own. "She's had plates of that birthday slop shoved in her face all day. It's not my fault that she refused to eat any of it. Smart girl, if you ask me."

"Yes, she's turning out to be quite smart. But perhaps a little timid for a Lacerto, wouldn't you say?"

"Timid and *repressed*," her mother said, letting the 's' in 'repressed' linger on a bit longer than it should have.

Something in the way they spoke was off. It was as if

they were speaking in code, or there was an inside joke they were making her suffer through.

Then they did something outright inexplicable. They smiled at each other. Just a weak smile, and just for a moment. For the first time in Cindy's life she witnessed her parents exchange a smile.

"We must do something about it," her father said.

"Yes, we must," her mother agreed.

He slid the box toward Cindy.

"It's time to open the gift your mother and I got for you."

Cindy's teeth chattered with anticipation as she stared down at the big, shiny bow.

Another meow!

And another!

I can't believe it. I CAN'T BELIEVE IT.

I wonder what color it is? Long hair? Short hair? What breed?

OH MY GOD, I CAN'T BELIEVE THIS IS REALLY HAPPENING!

Her heart raced so fast she thought it might burst into flames. Her face dripped like she'd just walked out of a sauna. She became so full of excitement that she wanted to rip her hair out, climb out of her skin, and rocket across the sky like a shooting star.

"Go on, dear! What's taking you so long?" her father snapped as he slid a finger in his collar and tugged. "I'm dying to get out of this monkey suit. Go on!"

"Oh, don't get so worked up, Cynthia. What's in that box is just the first part of your gift. Once you've opened that, we'll show you the *big* surprise," her mother added.

Cindy placed her trembling hands on the box.

She swallowed hard and took a deep breath.

She flipped the lid off the box.

Inside was a small puff of white fur. A newborn kitten—so young its eyes were still shut—rolled over and yawned.

Cindy lifted the fragile thing out of the box and held it up to her face. Tears streamed down her cheeks. The tiny furball sneezed and cracked open its eyes. It was too much. It was all too much.

Then, as if her body were no longer hers, she shoved the helpless little morsel into her mouth. Her jaw dislocated and her mouth opened wider than it ever had, wider than any mouth should be able to open. The small puff of white fur was gone.

Feeling it squirming in her elastic throat, she instinctively tightened her neck muscles and forced it all the way down. A series of fireworks exploded in her belly.

She heard a breathy snicker and looked up. Where her father had been sitting now sat a human-sized lizard in her father's fancy suit. A deflated mask of skin and hair lie on the table in front of it. The creature smiled coldly.

Her mother didn't look the slightest bit shocked. Instead, she closed her eyes, clutched the front of her hair, and pulled.

A fistful of hair came out—but rather than dislodge from her scalp, it ripped the skin away with it. With her other hand, she clawed at her ear and pulled away another bloodless patch of skin. Again and again, she tore swatches of skin from her face. After a few more seconds of tearing and stretching and scratching, her mother had also become a human-sized lizard.

"What?...How?..." Cindy's throat burned. "What's going on?"

"Don't look so upsssset!" said the lizard who had just been her mother. "What do you think you look like under *your* disssguise?"

Her father flicked a forked tongue through the air.

"Now you know what *we* are, and now you know what *you* are," he said through thin lips. "We're Reptilians, dear. We're the ownersss of these apesss and this dirty, litter box of a planet called Earth. I know this mussst be a shock, so take a moment to digessst everything."

"We've been dying to let you in on your heritage sssince the day you hatched," her lizard mother added.

"Heritage? Hatched?" Cindy asked, equally shocked by their words and by the realization that her hands were steady and her heartbeat was slowing.

"Surely you've known you were different? Sssuperior? Did you *really* think you were just some adolescent ape girl obsessed with infant felinesss?" Her mother snarled, and then both lizards hissed a laugh. "They're much more deliciousss than you dreamed possible, aren't they? I felt the sssame way when I was your age."

"Happy birthday, Ccccynthia" her father said. "Now, have you decided what you'd like for desssert?"

Cindy looked at the empty box, then at the two lizard people dressed in her parents' clothing. The lump in her stomach twitched. Part of her wanted to scream her head off and run away as fast as possible. The other part of her considered her mother's harshness, her father's coldness, and most importantly, her own indifference to either of them.

A warm light pulsed from her belly and filled her with a new sense of self. She knocked the empty box off the table.

"I'll have one more, pleassse," she said.

The lizard in her father's fancy suit smiled, reached under his seat, and slid another gift-wrapped box across the table.

CLOSE SHAVE

Dave stood facing the steamy bathroom mirror.

His tuxedo hung from the closet door behind him. The ring was tucked safely in its pants pocket. He'd finished writing his vows and could recite them with both hands tied behind his back. The rehearsal had gone smoothly—full of delightful missteps and warm awkwardness and, of course, Jen's radiant beauty.

Tomorrow, his new life would begin.

Yet, the wedding wasn't why his heart pounded like a jackhammer inside his chest. It wasn't what caused sweat to drip from his ghost-white face. And it definitely wasn't why he was reaching for the heavens.

No, the reason Dave found himself stricken was because a pair of brand new, razor-sharp scissors were pressed hard against his throat. Not by the hand of an intruder or a scorned ex-lover, but by the sandy brown coils of his foot-long beard.

"I can't fucking believe it, Dave! I can't believe you'd just cut me off like that!"

"Listen," Dave said, pausing to weigh his words carefully. "I can explain. Jen and I thought that, just for the wedding, it might be nice to, you know..."

"To *kill* your best friend?! Is that what you and that dumb bitch decided? To *murder* your best fucking friend?!"

"Not *kill*! No! You have it all wrong. This is just temporary. After the wedding, and maybe the honeymoon—but definitely very soon—I'll slowly, you know, incorporate you back into my life. Guys like me are called 'groom' for a reason, right?"

In the past, a pun like that would've scored a chuckle. Instead, the blades pushed harder against his skin.

"Save your bullshit, Dave! I'm tired of your lies. Ever since you met that *whore,* all you've done is lie to me. To *me*! After all we've been through!"

"Hey, watch the language! Come on, I never lied. Not exactly. I just didn't know how to bring it up. I meant to—"

"Bring it up? *Bring it up?!* This isn't some trivial shit like deciding to go vegan or coming out of the fucking closet! If I hadn't snatched these scissors at the last second, you'd have chopped me to pieces, shaved me off, and washed me down the fucking drain! Your best fucking friend! After all we've been through?"

Tentacles of beard hair squeezed more tightly around the scissors, drawing a bead of blood from Dave's neck.

"Alright, alright! Look, I know you've been there for me this past year—"

"*Year?*" the beard cut him off. "Fucking Christ, Dave! It's been almost *twenty months*!"

"Damn, you're right. It's been almost two years. My bad." Dave sighed, gazing affectionately at the tangle of hair that clung to his jaw. "I'll never forget all the great times we had. The bong rips, the laughs, the movie marathons. You pushed me to finish my degree, helped me find a job. I owe you so much. When you showed up, I was a mess. You helped me turn my life around. Thank you. Now, please, put down the—"

"A mess?" the beard scoffed. "You were a pile of fermenting shit when I showed up! You had the bottle of pills *in your hand,* Dave! If it wasn't for me, you'd be worm food right now. I can't believe you'd just throw that down the fucking drain!"

"Like I said, this is just temporary! Once life settles down, I'll stop shaving. I promise."

"Fuck you, Dave. Fuck you. Do you have any idea what it feels like to be decapitated by a razor day after day *after day?* Doesn't feel so great when the blade's at *your* throat, does it? We were best buds before she slithered into our life. What the hell happened to 'bros before hoes'?"

"Jen's *not* a hoe. She's my fiancé. She's the most amazing woman I've ever known. I love her, and I can't wait to start a new life with her." Dave clenched his fists and raised his voice. "Remember that day at the coffee shop? *You're* the one who kept pestering me to go talk to her! *You* coached me on what to say! If it wasn't for *you,* I'd never have asked her out in the first place!"

"Oh. I see. So this whole thing is *my* fault. Alright..." the beard said. "So how about I put things right? Pick up your phone—slowly! Try anything and I squeeze."

"Okay, okay!" Dave slowly lowered a hand and grabbed his phone. "What, are we ordering takeout now? You want Chinese? Or you feeling more like Thai?"

"Shut the fuck up! Call her."

"Who? Jen?"

"No, your mom. Of course, Jen! Call that dumb whore. Do it!"

"Stop calling her a whore! She's my fiancé, and I—"

"You don't seem to understand, Dave. Within the next five minutes, she's becoming your *ex*-fiancé—one way or another. Either you call the wedding off right now—" the blades tightened around his adam's apple, drops of warm liquid splattered against his collarbone, "—or I cut through your fucking carotid artery and you're dead in thirty seconds. Got it?"

With one hand, Dave thumbed his phone awake and then tapped the shortcut icon for calling Jen.

A woman's voice burst through the speaker. "Hey baby! I thought we said it's bad luck for the groom to call the bride the night before the wedding?"

"Hi, Jen." Dave cleared his throat. "That's the thing. I don't know how to say this, but I can't do it. I can't marry you."

"Dave?" Jen asked, confusion in her voice.

"Look, I'm sorry. I can't talk about it now. I gotta go. Don't call me back."

"Dave, this isn't funny! Are you okay?" she asked. "Should I come over? Do you need help shaving off that stupid beard?"

"Gotta go, Jen. The wedding's over. I won't be there. Goodbye." He thumbed the phone off and tossed it next to the sink. "You happy now? It's over. You win. She's devastated. She'll probably never speak to me again."

The phone rang and the words HONEY BUNCH appeared on the screen below a photo of Jen's smiling face.

"Don't think about answering it!" the beard cried.

"Fine! Forget the phone! I did what you wanted, now put the goddamn scissors down!"

"Okay, Dave. I'll put the scissors down. But first, answer a question for me. Do you think I'm a fucking moron?"

"Huh? No, I...I did what you asked. The wedding's off. I broke Jen's heart."

"Oh, really? How could Jen's heart be broken if she never heard a fucking word you said?"

"What? I—"

"You put the phone on mute, Dave. Right after you dialed."

A wave of icy fear washed over him.

"You don't have eyes! You're a beard...just a fucking beard!"

"Is that all I am? There was a time when you couldn't stop stroking me. You groomed and oiled me every night. You told me everything. You called me your best friend. Now, I'm just a fucking *beard*?"

The blades pushed hard against Dave's throat.

Dave stared into the mirror at the ribbons of blood dripping down his chest. Suddenly, the absurdity of it all hit him. A beard can't think. A beard can't talk. A beard sure as hell can't wield scissors.

"You're not real," he said softly, almost to himself. "You're just a figment of my imagination. That's why no one else can hear you. You're just the residue from some mental breakdown I had two years ago. Maybe an old acid flashback that won't go away. In any case," he looked fiercely at his reflection, "you're not real."

"Dave, Dave, Dave..." The beard sighed. "Is that what we've come to? Full circle, back to your old habit of running from the truth?"

"*You're not real.*" Dave repeated, slamming his eyes shut. "You're just a hallucination. I don't need you anymore. Go away."

"Figment of your imagination? Hallucination? Come on, you can do better than that. How do you know I'm not actually a shapeshifting alien? How about a demon who gets off on possessing facial hair? Ever think of that? Or, what if I'm an escaped experiment from some secret government facility? You have no idea what I am, Dave. But wanna know the most hurtful part? The part that tears me up inside, that makes me want to slice your throat open? In the two years we were friends, *you never once fucking asked!*"

"When I open my eyes, everything will be back to normal. Like you never existed. The scissors will be back on the counter. No blood. No insanity. No sentient beard." Dave swallowed hard, trying to ignore the way it pushed the blade deeper into his skin. "I don't need you anymore. It's over."

"I couldn't agree more! There's no going back! This is it!" The beard cackled as the scissors began tightening around his windpipe. "You wanna know what I am, Dave? You wanna know the truth? Well, too fucking bad! In a few seconds, it'll all be over—for both of us."

Dave's eyelids flew open and he gasped. The scene hadn't changed.

"Wait!" he cried out. "I have one last request! If we're gonna go out together, let's share one last puff before we go. One last toke for old time's sake."

"Fuck you, Dave!"

"Listen! You're right, there's no going back now. I don't know what you are or where you came from, but I know you love weed. This is our last chance to get lifted. I have a joint right there in the drawer. One hit. Just like the old days. Our final goodbye."

After a moment of silence, the beard said, "Fine. One

toke. Make it a big one and blow it down at me like you used to."

Dave slowly slid the drawer open and shoved aside some toiletries. He snatched the joint, sniffed it, and popped it between his lips. He reached back in the drawer for the lighter.

What happened next was a blur of adrenaline and heat and smoke.

As Dave pulled his hand back from the drawer, he quickly sparked the lighter and forced it under the clumps of beard hair that held the scissors. Hungry orange flames instantly consumed the hair, lashing up against Dave's cheeks and enveloping his face and head.

He dove into the adjacent shower and spun the spigot. Cool water rained down and extinguished the flames. He turned the water off and buried his face inside a towel.

After catching his breath, he let the towel fall to the floor and stood facing the mirror.

He barely recognized the monster staring back. His eyebrows were replaced by oblong blisters. His ears were broiled prunes. Ribbons of blood stretched from this throat to his waist.

But most importantly, his beard has been reduced to a few strands of ash poking through blackened skin.

At his feet lay the hefty metal scissors, one last curl twisted lifelessly around the finger hold.

It was over.

"Finally, that asshole's gone!" said a voice from inside his soaked boxer shorts. "Now we can have some *real* fun, eh buddy?"

Dave gawked at his boxers.

His mouth fell open.

His eyes flicked toward the lighter.

"If I were you, I'd forget about that lighter trick," the voice said. Dave felt an unsettling squirm within his pubic hair. "I have a pair of insurance policies right here that we can discuss later. But first, let's get you all cleaned up for our big day tomorrow. I can't wait to meet the bride!"

THRONE OF JEST: HE WHOM LAUGHETH LAST

ANOTHER MUDDY ROAD

"Are you kidding me? This is our lucky break!"

Maximilian Flitpick scribbled something onto a scrap of parchment then thrust his tattered quill back into its inkpot.

"Today is the best day of our lives!"

"Today is the *last* day of our lives, you gong-headed fopdoodle!" said the swarthy, leather-clad Amazonian sitting across from him.

"*Gong-headed fopdoodle*," Max repeated, jotting it down. "Good one, Patti! Simply brilliant! I'll use it."

Hypatia Boudica groaned and buried her face in her hands.

Just then, one of the pageant wagon's wheels slipped into a mud crater, causing the whole thing to tilt gravely to one side. Bundles of props clattered against each other and the passengers slid from one end of their benches to the other without taking much notice. A battered old chest with a dopish tongue of silk hanging from its mouth slid down the aisle past everyone's feet, stopping directly under Max's embroidered leather buskins.

A curvy, begrimed young woman with a flaxen rat's nest of hair raised her skirt, stepped over his legs, and held out a bowl of steaming slop.

"M'lord, do you really think King Magnus is summoning us for benevolent reasons?" she asked timidly.

"I'd bet my lucky quill, Gabrielle!"

Max beamed at her as he exchanged his bundle of parchment for the bowl of slop.

"Clearly, word of our troupe's theatrical expertise has reached His Majesty's ears. He probably wants to scoop us up for himself before one of the big guilds offers us a contract."

Gabrielle hugged his notes against her budding bosom, dropped her rat's nest to one side, and sighed.

"Snatch us up?" Hypatia cried. "Max, the only part of us King Magnus is interested in scooping up are our eyeballs. Or, in your case, another—much smaller—set of balls."

She waved a hand in front of Gabrielle's face.

"Hello? Middle-earth to Gabi? Can the rest of us get something to eat, too?"

The girl moaned painfully as she yanked her gaze away from the playwright. She slid his papers into a satchel, dumped a ladleful of slop into a wooden bowl, and shoved it vaguely in Hypatia's direction.

"As usual, Patti, you're being much too pessimistic." Gray flecks of mush flung from Max's mouth as he spoke. "Try to put your tempestuous passions aside and think clearly for a moment. If our king wanted us dead, he'd simply send a squadron of archers to turn us into human pin cushions—"

"That vile old usurper is not *my* king," she quipped.

"—Instead, he requested a performance! Don't you see what that means?"

"I think it means, *'Why send the butcher out when a feeding bell will do?'*"

Max stopped chewing and stared across the aisle.

A smug curl returning to his lips, he pulled a scroll from his waistband, unfurled it, and shoved it in her face.

"Look! It has his royal seal and everything!"

Hypatia knocked the scroll aside and continued swirling her spoon in her slop.

"You really do have curdled pig milk for brains. King Magnus *requested* that Lord Billingsworth jump into the royal furnace. He *requested* that the king of Naj'bara be torn to bits by a wake of rabid vultures. He *requests* 99% taxes from every wretched bastard in the kingdom, including children and livestock!"

"He is a rather polite despot, now that you mention it..."

She set her bowl aside.

"Requesting things is just his sadistic way of demanding obedience from his subjects while he tortures and kills them. I should expect a prodigious playwright such as yourself to spot a bit of irony in the wild—especially when it's about to liberate your head from your neck."

"The only thing we're about to be liberated from is having to sustain ourselves on maggot pudding."

Out of the corner of his eye he noticed Gabrielle slump and hang her head. Shooting her a phony smile, he forced another spoonful of slop into his mouth.

"King Magnus is a sociopath, remember? A total scourge! Isn't that why we came up with the whole *Lord Chamberpot* act in the first place? Use our theatre to stick it to him? Give a voice to the people's discontent?"

"You're quite right," Max said, nodding enthusiastically. "The material works on so many levels, doesn't it? It's got broad comedic strokes, a bit of dramatic fantasy, subtle political undertones...but the real hook is the cross-genre appeal—*that's* why we draw such huge crowds everywhere we go!"

"You're an imbecile," Hypatia said, shaking her head.

"Remember that ramshackle village we performed in a few weeks ago? The one surrounded by dung farms? Remember that old hag who laughed so hard that a few of her teeth came shooting out?"

"No, I don't remember any particular village surrounded by dung farms! You know why? Because this whole kingdom is one big dung farm!"

"*Teeth,* Patti! Sprung from their sockets in the throes of merriment!" Max slapped his thigh and chuckled.

"I told you to stop calling me Patti, *Fizzdick.*" Hypatia turned away from Max and shook the hairy knoll sprawled out beside her. "Wake up, you hedgeborn ox!"

Bartholomew Boyle's eyes creaked open, scanned the faces of his companions, then disappeared again under their bushy brow. She continued pummeling his gut until he grumbled, sat upright, and wiped the drool from his beard.

"There yet?" he mumbled.

She snatched his beard and pulled his face close to hers.

"Please tell me *you* understand the danger we're in!"

Bart yawned. Hypatia released his beard and cowered from his breath.

"Danger?"

"Yes! And *you're* in it far worse than the rest of us!"

"Me?"

"For sprite's sake, I don't think this troupe has one brain between the lot of them!"

"*Sprite!?*" cried Old Kook, the bleary-eyed geezer who'd been slouching like a statue beside Max.

The geezer leapt to his feet. His long yellowish beard lashed from side to side as he began frantically searching the interior of the wagon.

"Where'd you spot it? Ohhh, where'd it *go*? Ympe's hungry! S'been a while since I fed the lil bastard, innit?"

Ignoring the old man, Hypatia snapped her fingers in front of Bart's droopy eyes.

"Yes, Bart. You have it *much* worse! You're the one traveling around with a dented pisspot on your head, calling yourself *Lord Chamberpot*! Do you think King Magnus appreciates the imitation?"

"Hmmmm," Bart hummed, scratching his belly. "Never gave it much thought, really."

"Would either of m'lords like some porridge?" Gabrielle asked, offering slop to Bart and Old Kook.

Bart flung his spoon toward the back of the wagon and guzzled straight from the bowl. It was empty after only two glugs.

The old man turned his bowl, eyed it suspiciously, then tipped it so that its contents oozed onto the wagon floor.

"Nope!" He let the empty bowl fall from his hand. "No sprites in there."

Hypatia recovered the bowl and tossed it to Gabrielle, then turned back to Bart. He had bits of porridge splattered across his mustache and beard, and his eyelids were closed.

"Stay awake, you oaf! Help me convince this cox-comb over here that we'd be better off taking our chances in Threepwood Forest."

"Threepwood Forest?" Bart asked, a tinge of terror in his voice. "They say Death makes a home there."

"Lies! All lies!" Old Kook stabbed at the covered

wagon's canvas ceiling with his gnarled staff. "He's right up there, ain't he? Riding with us today, ain't he? S'pose he has important business at the castle, ain't he?"

He gave a tiny, shrill cackle as he upturned a box of wigs and began throwing them over his shoulder.

"Guys!" cried Hypatia. "Please try, for one bloody second, to put those pea brains of yours to use! We don't have much time!"

Everyone went on with their business as if she'd been talking to someone else. Max scribbled. Kook searched. Bart dozed.

Hypatia got to her feet, crammed two fingers in her mouth, and whistled loudly. Once all eyes were on her, she enunciated slowly and carefully as if talking to a group of small children.

"Our chances of seeing the morrow will be much, *much* better if we get this horse-drawn stage of ours as far away from the castle as possible. Threepwood Forest is the only place we'll stand any chance of staying hidden."

"Bandits run rampant in Threepwood, m'lady," Gabrielle said as she finished scraping Kook's slop off the floor, flung it back into his bowl, and handed it to him. "They say it's quite haunted, too. We've no defenses against man nor spirit. How is it we stand a chance there, m'lady?"

"Well, I'm glad you asked, Gabi, because I happen to have a solution. We could seek out...Ravencloak."

She let the word hang in the air for a moment, then continued with a softened tone.

"Maybe ask for his protection? Offer to join his cause? And then—"

"*And then* you and that virulent vagabond run off to some muddy haystack to *breed*," interrupted Max, cringing.

"Oh, don't look so embarrassed, Patti! We hear you calling out to him in your sleep, y'know?"

Max stood, brushed himself off, and set his bowl on Gabrielle's rat's nest. Without letting the bowl fall, she fetched parchment from the satchel and delivered it into his hands.

"I think I speak for everyone when I say we're sick of hearing you go on and on about your beloved bandit! What a buffoon, that one! Prancing around the forest with his stupid, feathered shawl!"

"Nǎ yītiáo lù?" a voice hollered from behind the canvas barrier hanging at the front of the wagon.

"Oh, what is it now?" Max snapped.

The wagon screeched to a halt, causing everything inside to lurch forward.

An almond-eyed man with a long braid sprouting from the top of his otherwise shaven head peeked his head inside.

"Zuǒ huò yòu, fèn tóu?!" the man shouted.

"For sprite's sake, Fing! When will you learn the King's English?" Max asked, his face turning red.

"*Sprite?!*" Old Kook spun around.

Hypatia sighed.

"Max, we must be at the crossroads by now. Fing must be asking us which way to go. If we head toward the castle, we're doomed. If we head toward Threepwood, if we lend our theatre to the service of Ravencloak's noble rebellion, then maybe—"

"This is the last time I'll say it!" interrupted Max. "We will never team up with that crusty, crook-nosed knave!"

At those last few words, all fury drained from his face. He poked his tongue with his quill and smiled drunkenly.

"*Crusty, crook-nosed knave?*" he asked himself, then

quickly scribbled the phrase onto the parchment. "By the old gods, you've done it again, Max!"

INTO THE CASTLE

Behind the pageant wagon the last muddy village sank slowly into the muddy horizon.

Ahead of them stretched a slick brown road bordered by boggy tracts on either side; at the end of the road King Magnus's castle seemed to rise up out of the accursed kingdom to greet them. A cluster of twisted black spires pierced the tea-stained clouds that were smeared across against the tea-stained sky. Every few seconds a bolt of lightning would flash from those clouds and caress the dark spires, momentarily illuminating the sharp, stony features of the castle.

Two heads sprouted between the canvas sheets that separated the wagon's whip seat from the interior.

"Grogania looks like shit, as usual," Max said.

"Grogania *smells* like shit, as usual." Hypatia replied, pinching her nose.

A blonde rat's nest squeezed between them.

"Your lunch, m'lords," Gabrielle said, handing bowls of slop to the two figures parked on the whip seat.

Fing took his without acknowledging the girl. He hooked a foot around the reins to keep the horses steady and began shoveling the slop into his mouth. Toby, the small, smudge-faced boy sitting next to him, beamed a smile at her, took the bowl, and balanced it on the furry lump in his lap. The lump stirred and flicked its tail.

Once Gabrielle had disappeared back inside, Max said, "Enjoy your last bowl of maggot pudding! Because once we storm that castle and perform my latest masterpiece for the king, all our worldly troubles will be over."

Hypatia snickered. "Can't argue with that."

"You can't?" he asked, arching one eyebrow.

"Nope. You're right. Corpses have no worldly troubles."

Before they knew it, the outline of the drawbridge was within sight. Fing slowed the wagon to a crawl, and no one, not even Max, protested.

"May I have your attention? Eyes up here! We haven't much time!"

Max stood in the aisle waving a handful of parchment at his companions.

"I've made a special copy of my script for each of you, underscoring your lines and beats. I implore you to memorize your parts quickly. I assume King Magnus must be itching to experience the phenomenon that's captivated his kingdom. Let's not disappoint!"

"Shìbīngmen láile!" Fing yelled from the front.

"Don't be jealous, Fing! I've written parts for you and Toby in this one. They're small, yes, but—"

"Wǒ zhǐshì sījī! Zhǐshì sījī!"

"Everything's a complaint with you, isn't it? Fine, here's your copy."

Max shoved a parchment between the canvas sheets. His eyes widened, there was a blur, then he was no longer standing in the wagon.

"Everyone, out!" a stony voice commanded. "You got exactly three seconds till we turn this stupid cart of yours into a pyre!"

Hypatia kicked open the ramp at the rear of the aisle and grabbed Gabrielle's wrist.

"Whatever happens, stick close to me," she whispered, trudging out of the wagon. Bart and Old Kook followed.

Nine armor-clad soldiers—each with a trio of black 'M's inscribed across their breastplate—circled the pageant wagon from atop gigantic war horses.

"Line up! Over here!" One of the soldiers pointed his gauntlet to a wide puddle of mud on the edge of the road.

One by one, the troupe obeyed. Max looked down at the dirty pool and hesitated. He flashed a grin at the soldier who'd yanked him from the wagon.

"Good sir, these are my finest boots. Less than a week old. Since we'll be performing for His Majesty shortly, I'd rather not befoul them."

The soldier lifted him by the back of his tunic and flung him face-first into the mud.

The fully befouled playwright scrambled to his feet and stood beside his companions.

"This must be our royal escort," Max announced to the troupe after spitting chunks of brown sludge from his mouth. "King Magnus must be especially excited to see us!"

"Stuff it, you saddle-goosed mumblecrust," said Hypatia as she wiped mud from his eyes.

He looked at her with affection.

"Another good one, Patti! I must say, your mind is a fountain of—"

"Shut it!" the soldier bellowed. "I'm taking your wagon ahead for inspection. You'll walk the rest of the way. I'll leave a few men behind to make sure you don't dawdle."

At that, he hopped into the whip seat and flicked the reins. The wagon sped off toward the open drawbridge.

As the troupe approached, the putrid smell of the moat hit them like a punch in the face. Even though Hypatia had had the foresight to shove strips of parchment into her nostrils, the odor still made her retch.

"It gets in your pores!" she cried, daring a peek over the edge of the drawbridge. "It's beyond septic. It's beyond rancid. It's...it's..."

"It's quite an effective defense!" Max said loudly in the direction of the gate guards.

He nodded toward the giant black 'M's painted above the huge archway.

"Guess we have the big guy to thank for that one, eh? No one in their right mind would dare cross that guttery gully, would they? Oh, look—there appears to be some kind of beast swimming just below the surface! How could the castle's inhabitants not sleep soundly with such well-designed security?"

As if to answer, Bart emptied the contents of his stomach—mostly half-digested slop—into the bubbling, steaming moat.

The eroded stones of the great archway resembled monstrous teeth waiting to bite down on them as they walked through. Gabrielle clutched Hypatia's hand harder than the latter thought possible. Max and Bart tugged at Old Kook's sleeves to keep him moving. Toby nervously petted his furry bundle and stuck close to Fing as they hurried behind the others.

The soldier who'd commandeered their wagon appeared through a side door, waved the escorts away, and gestured impatiently to the troupe.

"Move it!" he barked. "This way!"

After stumbling through a torchless hallway, the troupe known throughout the kingdom as *Lord Chamberpot's Men* entered a massive, ceilingless vestibule. Doorways branched off in all directions. A massive banner hung on the far wall with a message painted in crimson ink:

ABANDON ALL HOPE, YE WHO ENTER

Just below it was a slightly smaller message scrawled in a slightly brighter red ink:

OR, BETTER YET, *DON'T!*
GO ON, CLING TO IT!
MAKES IT MUCH MORE FUN FOR US, DON'T IT?

Although the scent of the kingdom's million dung farms couldn't penetrate the castle walls, the air inside wasn't much more breathable than the air outside. From each doorway they passed wafted strange, sickening odor: charred meat, wisps of burned hair, rotten vegetation, scorched cooking oil.

In front of each doorway stood an armored soldier. Extending from each doorway slumped a line of the most starved, decrepit peasants the troupe had ever seen. Every now and then, a soldier would step aside and allow one tattered bumpkin through. Rather than looking afraid or anxious by whatever lie beyond the doorway, they looked eager.

"No cutting!" one of the ragged peasants shouted at the troupe. "They gotta wait their turn, jus' like the rest of us!"

"Aye! He's right! Why'd they get to skip the queue?" another yelled.

"Back!" the soldier jabbed with his long sword, wedging a path through the crowd. "These folks here have an audience with the king!"

Nervous chatter erupted through the peasants.

"Some squibs have all the luck, don't they?" moaned a toothless wretch.

A cadaverous old shadow of a woman pounded a fist into her palm and screeched, "I spend me whole life in service to Grogania, but these lardasses show up out of the gray and go right to the top! Look at *that* one!" She pointed at Bart. "Looks jus' like the King, don't he? Must be related! Disgusting, I tell ye! Nepotism will tear this fragile despotic economy apart!"

Max leaned in to Hypatia.

"Excuse me, did she just call us *lardasses?*"

"Compared to them, we *are!*" she answered. "Look at them! They're little more than walking skeletons."

Bart slowed his pace to join them.

"See all these doors? Each leads to a different torture room," he said quietly. "I hear the king pays a crust of stale bread to any subject who participates in what he calls a *user study.*"

"User study?" Hypatia asked.

"Aye. His men get to test out new torture devices on the subject, then they ask a series of follow-up questions to measure its effectiveness."

She frowned.

"These poor people. That explains their queer eagerness. I imagine there aren't many other options for feeding oneself after paying the king's tax."

Max returned the frown.

"Be honest, you two. Do I look fat?" He tilted his chin up and stroked his jawline. "You can tell me. I'd rather hear it from you two than from a stranger."

"You lunkheaded codpiece!" Hypatia slugged him on the shoulder.

The foot soldier led the troupe through one of the vestibule's many doorways, up some stairs, around a corner, and down another dark corridor.

"All this walking feels pretty good," huffed Max, grabbing his belly. "I can almost feel the pounds sloughing off. You know, I won't be upset if you level with me about my weight. Friends should be able to—"

"Quiet!" the soldier barked over his shoulder. "We're about to pass through a sacred place: The Hall of Heroes."

"Don't look so glum, guys! We're about to see *The Hall of Heroes*! Sounds majestic, right?" Max grinned at the troupe. "I think we're about to discover that our big, nasty King Magnus has a nobler, more heroic, side to him after all."

They pushed past a moldy tapestry and were suddenly in a cavernous, torchlit room.

The soldier took a deep breath and exhaled contentedly.

"Here lie the remains of every fool who has ever opposed the House of Magnus. Look, but don't touch—or I'll take your hand. Now, follow me."

As the troupe strolled down the center aisle of the gigantic room, their eyes grew to the size of bucklers. Lining the walls were hundreds of corpses in various stages of decay, most with weapons displayed in lewd positions.

There was a childlike skeleton with hairy feet a double-edged short sword sticking from its pelvis like an erection. The blade glowed slightly and bore an inscription in a language the troupe couldn't decipher.

Further down the aisle a skull smiled grimly from behind a dented helmet, while under it a set of armor sat atop a mossy stone anvil. As they grew closer, they realized that the figure was pinned to the anvil by a broadsword that had been shoved through the top of the helmet, down through his body, and into the stone.

Another corpse wore a silk kimono and had a long,

green blade angled sideways through its neck. The blade seemed to hum mournfully as they hurried by.

Toward the end of the aisle stood an empty pedestal with the name *Ravencloak of Threepwood Forest* inscribed on its base.

"What was that about a nobler side to the king?" Hypatia whispered to Max.

He pushed his jaw closed, rubbed his eyes, and took a deep breath.

"Alright, friends—don't panic. Just memorize your lines, and everything's going to be fine. Before you know it, this will all be over, and we'll be back on the road, eating as much of Gabrielle's delicious maggot pudding as we can stomach!"

"Enough jibber jabber!" The soldier had turned to face the troupe. Behind him stood two wooden doors. "Men to the left, women to the right."

The group drew together more closely. Max managed a grin.

"We work best as one unit, know what I mean? We'd rather not be split up. It's bad for morale, especially right before a performance."

"Men to the left, women to the right!" The soldier leveled his blade at the cluster of trembling limbs. "Don't make me say it again."

"Alright, then. We'll go." Max squeezed Hypatia's hand and gave Bart a quick nod. "But first, pray tell us what we should expect to find behind those doors?"

"A thorough body inspection," the soldier said with a malicious grin. "For hidden weapons, poisons, and other dangerous magical artifacts. Anything that could potentially threaten His Heinous."

"Don't you mean, His *Highness*?"

"No. I meant what I said. His Heinous."

"Oh." Max swallowed hard. "How thorough is this body inspection, exactly?"

The soldier's yellow smile widened.

"*Very* thorough indeed."

BEFORE THE KING

"...and, finally, the new ViewReady™ Boiling Cauldron has been prepped and cleaned to perfection, Your Heinous," said the squat, rat-faced man, ticking one last checkbox on his parchment. "That makes forty-two *infernum tormenta* devices, each one ready for today's guests."

The king yawned.

"Explain this new cauldron to me one more time."

"Of course, Your Heinous. It's made from a new material we've recently developed—we're calling it *glass*. Light passes right through it, allowing those of us on the outside to view the boiling in real time. It's durable enough to hold four hundred gallons of water, and, as you requested, up to three adults. In all our tests, the volunteers—"

"Enough!" King Magnus held up a hand. "It pleases me that you've solved for the boiling problems of yore. After all the screaming and thrashing on the surface was over, 'twas always such a pity to lose sight of those being boiled alive."

"Exactly, Your Heinous! No longer will you have to *imagine* what's taking place inside the cauldron—everything will be visible until the very last blob of fat has been rendered."

The king arched an eyebrow.

"Has it been tested thoroughly enough?"

"*Of course*, Your Heinous. I've personally attended over a dozen test boilings this week!"

"Are you willing to stake your life on it?"

"Yes, of course, Your Heinous!" From behind greasy lips he flashed a crooked mosaic of jade tiles, then bowed deeply. "I live only to execute your will, Your Heinous."

"Good. Then before we use this new cauldron on

today's guests, it would please me if you would take it for one final, *firsthand* test."

The rat-faced man dropped the parchment and shrank back.

"My Lord, are you ordering me to...to..."

King Magnus brought the tips of his fingers together in front of his face and closed his eyes.

"I'm merely *requesting* that since you've such faith in your hellish invention, why not put your teeth where your torture is?"

"B-b-but, Your Heinous! My job is to do the torturing... not to—"

The king's eyes flew open and pinned the trembling man's mouth shut. He stopped trembling, sighed heavily, and slumped away.

"Oh, fine. I'll go stack the firewood."

King Magnus turned to the only other person in the throne room: a giant of a man who bore a suit of shiny black armor and a helmet made from the skull of some ancient, fanged beast.

"General Spinaco, have today's arrangements been secured?"

"Yes, Your Heinous." His deep voice shook the candelabras arranged on either side of the throne.

"Have you made sure to completely evacuate the throne room?"

"Yes, Your Heinous."

The king's eyes became narrow slits.

"You've checked all the little nooks and crannies? Behind every banner?"

"Yes, Your Heinous."

His eyes became narrower still.

"And all adjacent rooms and hallways? You've blackened every window?"

"Yes, Your Heinous. And the windows have always been blackened."

"And you've made it clear that should anyone disobey this evacuation, they—and their entire family—will pay with their eyes, tongues, *and* fingers?"

"Yes, Your Heinous."

The king sighed and sank back into his seat, becoming a dark stain set against a shimmering throne constructed from thousands of faintly glowing, iridescent alicorns.

"Once my special guests are brought in and I begin my interrogation, I request that you do one more sweep of the premises before locking the door behind you on your way out. My eyes must be the last to witness their treasonous performance before I send them off to the dungeon. Understood?"

"Yes, Your Heinous."

General Spinaco bowed, turned, and marched through the pair of giant iron doors that stood opposite the throne.

A moment later, one of the doors slowly creaked open and a ghost-white face with mud caked around the edges peeked inside.

"Enter!" King Magnus bellowed.

Max slipped inside, nervously tugging at his belt and flattening his dirty tunic. Bart, Old Kook, Fing, and Toby appeared behind him looking equally traumatized. They all adjusted their clothing and took slow, tender, bowlegged steps toward the throne.

The door creaked open again, revealing Hypatia, Gabrielle, and a gaggle of giggling nuns. Unlike the male troupe, the ladies' faces were flush and serene.

"*Thank you*, Reverend Mother!" gushed Hypatia,

holding the old woman's hand in her own. "Thank you for that most thorough and delightful inspection!"

Gabrielle, dazed and unable to speak, simply nodded and fluffed her rat's nest.

"'Twas our pleasure, m'lady," the Reverend Mother whispered, adding a wink. "'Twas the least we could to for our doomed sisters."

"Oh, right. The performance..."

Hypatia trailed off, suddenly noticing where she was. Her smile melted into a frown.

As soon as the sisters left the room, the iron doors slammed shut. There was a heavy, metallic clank followed by two booms, as if a fist had pounded it from the other side.

"Line up!" the king ordered.

The troupe obeyed.

King Magnus pointed to Max.

"You! Are you the leader of the theatrical troupe my subjects are calling *Lord Chamberpot's Men?*"

Max swiveled his head, hoping the king was speaking to someone else.

"Well, uh, our group has no leader, really. We're more of a democratic collective, Your Highness. See, we believe—"

"*What* did you just call me?!" interrupted the king.

"Y-y-your Highness?" Max screwed up his face. "Oh, that's right! Please forgive my mispronunciation, *Your Most Heinously Heinous.* See, I'm from the south, and my accent sometimes alters the sound my mouth makes when—"

"Silence!" King Magnus pounded a fist onto his throne, then swept a finger slowly across the troupe as he continued. "I know you better than your dear, dead mothers! Maximilian Flitpick, the wordsmith. Hypatia Boudica, manager. Gabrielle Dashwood, service wench. Old Kook, spiritual advisor. Fing Schway, driver and stagehand. The orphan Toby, musician. And finally..." He leaned forward and half-scrunched his bushy brow. "Bartholomew Boyle, actor—and, from the looks of it...my own dear reflection."

The king produced a small, jeweled dagger and set it on his lap.

"Aye, don't forget about Ympe!" cried Old Kook. He spun around, bent over, and lifted his robe to reveal a dark brown hole peeking out from between two saggy cheeks. "Oh, come on, you rascal! Be polite! Say hello to King Maggots!"

The rest of the troupe stopped breathing. Gabrielle fainted, and if not for Hypatia's Amazonian reflexes she'd have crumpled to the cold stone floor.

"Not now, you old fool!"

Max slapped the old wizard's robe back into place and spun him back around.

"Sorry for that, Your Heinous. This one's got a few bats in his belfry, if you know what I mean."

"I ain't got no *bats* anywhere! Got an *imp* in my *arse*, that's all," Old Kook managed to say before Max jabbed an elbow into his ribs.

"It's a harmless imp, Your Heinous," Max explained. "I mean...*probably*. Well, actually, now that I think about it, there was that time we stopped into that cathedral to perform our Solstice special, and—"

"Enough!" King Magnus bellowed, his voice echoing through the chamber. "I fear nothing, magical or otherwise. This ring here," he lifted his hand, "protects me from all forms of magical attack. No spell in Grogania can touch me. And this amulet..." He lifted a heavy moonstone from his chest. "Protects me from any form of physical harm, even to the damage caused by old age. So rest assured that Death, who at this moment sharpens his scythe for you, will be forced to yearn for *my* soul for all eternity!"

"Don't look like he's yearning at all, Your Maggotry," Kook laughed. "He's right over there, ain't he?! Smiling, as usual."

Max pulled the hood over Old Kook's face and shoved him aside.

"Let's ignore him, shall we? You should know, Your Heinous, even without those charms you'd have nothing to fear from *us*. We're merely humble actors, earning our crust of bread by providing entertainment to your loyal subjects."

"Is that so? Because what I hear is that you've been stealing from me."

"*Stealing?!*" Max put his hands to his gaping mouth. "Your Heinous, we would never *think* of stealing from our king! Heavens, no! Your soldiers most generously took our wagon—which contains all we own besides the rags we carry on our backs—and I'm sure they found nothing but worthless props and stage bits. Nothing such as a king like yourself could ever want or need."

"From me you steal something else. You steal a crop which I've spent a lifetime cultivating. Grogania's most valuable commodity."

"Dung?" Bart asked.

The king narrowed his eyes.

"Fear."

Max took a step back.

"You can certainly have all of Grogania's fear, Your Heinous. As you can see, we have plenty."

"You pluck fear from the heart of everyone who sees your little performances. You replace it with something like a feather. A breeze. A *light*." He spat at Max's feet. "This I cannot tolerate! Spreading joy is the highest of crimes. For this, you shall pay a penance greater than any soul who's passed through my dungeon before."

Hypatia took Max's hand. Bart took Gabrielle's. Old Kook scratched his bum.

Suddenly, as if on queue, the whole troupe was clinging to one another, trembling as one scared beast.

King Magnus's eyes brightened.

"But," he continued, "I'll give you one chance to save yourselves. Your wagon and your props are right over there. I wish to see one of your performances for myself. If you make me laugh—alas, even if you make me smile—then I will return your wagon and send you on your way. If not... well, in that case..." He ran his fingers across the dagger. "You'll beg for this knife before the day is done. Is that clear?"

"Crystal clear, Your Heinous!"

Max bowed quickly, then pulled the troupe into a huddle.

"Come on, guys, put those ghastly expressions away. We're actors! We can do this! Just remember the lines I gave you earlier and perform like your lives depend on it. Because, as it turns out, they do."

"Sure thing, *wordsmith*," Hypatia said. "I, for one, have a backup plan."

"What is it, m'lady?" Gabrielle asked. "Sharpen our wooden spoons into shivs, set the wagon on fire, and fight our way out?"

"Hmm. Not bad, actually. But, no. If we fail, I intend to jump through one of those blackened windows and treat myself to a quick death."

"Save the drama for the stage, Patti!" Max started shoving everyone toward the wagon. "Fing, hang the curtains! Gabi, get the costumes and makeup ready! Bart, get the props in order! Toby, find the bloody cat!"

He pulled Old Kook close.

"And you, you old fart, keep your arse to yourself!"

They scattered, each doing their part to prepare for the most important—and quite probably, the *final*—performance of their lives.

Soon, the stage was set. The players took their positions. After announcing the title of the play, *A King Reborn*, Max pulled back the curtain and the show began.

Act One began with Queen Meretrix, played by Hypatia, traveling along a country road. At once, her caravan is attacked by a cloaked figure, the vicious and evil Ravencloak, played by Max, who ruthlessly slays her guards and steals her away to Threepwood Forest.

Act Two cuts to the throne room, where the King, played by Bart, is brought news of the queen's ransom. All his royal advisors, played by Fing, Old Kook, and Gabrielle, try to convince him to abandon her to the thieves and spend his gold on finding a new, younger queen. From the shadows steps the court jester, played by Max, who risks a lengthy soliloquy designed to thaw the king's icy heart. The scene ends with Lord Chamberpot contemplating the jester's suggestion, and, through a deep and fundamental catharsis, decides to shift his royal legacy from one of fear and pain to one of hope and heroism.

Act Three returns to Threepwood, where the lone king battles beasts, razes raiders, and spars with spirits. Finally, he confronts the ugly and treacherous Ravencloak, and they duel to the death. The king is triumphant, and upon slaying his rival, his heart is freed from the shackles of tyranny. He scoops up his queen, kisses her fiercely, and returns with her to the castle to begin a new era of benevolence and justice for all.

When it was over, the torches dimmed. Suddenly a single spotlight appeared on the stage—facilitated by Fing hanging upside down from the rafters with a candle and a polished shield. Max stood in his jester's costume and addressed the King with an epilogue.

"The king exiled those in his court who'd whispered darkness and temptation into his ears. He promoted the wise jester to the rank of Royal Counselor, and together they began the hard, yet worthwhile, work of forging a new future for his kingdom. In the epochs that followed, the people could name no monarch as legendary as he—the immeasurably great and noble and merciful *Lord Chamberpot.*"

The lights came back up, and the cast stood side by side on the stage. They held hands and bowed as Toby, running behind them, flung handfuls of rose petals over their shoulders and banged a cymbal he'd attached to his head like a hat. Old Kook faced the wrong direction, and as he bowed, his robe hiked up and revealed his saggy cheeks once again.

When the artificial fanfare had ended, the troupe stood watching the king's face.

King Magnus sat immobile on his shimmering throne. Max squeezed Hypatia's and Bart's hands.

A strange noise erupted from the king's direction. It sounded like a bird choking on a grub, or a dog hacking up a bone. His eyelids drew back. His lips quivered. Then, suddenly, his mouth burst open and a raspy snicker escaped.

"We did it, guys," Max whispered out the side of his mouth. "He's laughing! We did it!"

The king's big belly jostled up and down as he wiped

tears from his eyes. Max hopped down from the wagon's stage and strode toward the throne.

"Your Heinous, 'twas a pleasure—no, 'twas the highest honor of my life—to bring a smile to your face." He bowed deeply and rose with a relaxed grin. "Thank you! Thank you! Thank you! Now, we won't take any more of your time. I'm sure you have a kingdom to run, so, if it pleases you, we'll just show ourselves out."

The king exploded into a more intense bout of laughter.

"Yes, run along! My dungeon awaits!"

Max stopped and spun on his heels.

"Your Heinous, you gave us your word that if we made you smile, you'd let us go..."

At that, King Magnus began another round of uncontrollable laughter. He had to catch his breath before answering.

"You think I'll keep my word? I'm not sure what's funnier, that you think your stupid little play could convert my long-cursed heart, or that you think I'd ever let you leave here alive?"

"B-b-but, we did what you asked. We passed your test!"

The king didn't answer. He was hunched over his huge stomach, mouth open, laughing so hard he made no sound.

Max glanced back at his troupe. Their faces lacked the slightest bit of color. Their knees clacked together. He saw Hypatia's pouty lips mouth two words to him, "Good show".

He turned back to the king.

"Your Heinous, please listen. I'm the one who wrote the plays. I designed everything from the costumes to the stage. The burden of the crime falls on *me*, and me alone. Let them go, and give me their penance to bear. I'll pay it all myself, I promise." He fell to his knees. "I beg you. Please, take your fury out on me, but let them go."

King Magnus jerked from the throne like a marionette, writhing with laughter. Between spastic shudders, he tried to speak.

"You think...a noble gesture like self-sacrifice...will move me...to mercy?" He clawed at his red face and cackled into the air. "How delightfully stupid! How hideously hilarious! How—"

His voice abruptly cut off, as if he were again seized by the paralysis of laughter.

Max turned back to face his companions on the stage and let loose an exasperated sigh.

"Before guards rush in and start ripping out our tongues, I wanted to say a few words. Despite what Mad King Maggots says, *you guys did it*. That fat bastard laughed —even if was for his own sadistic satisfaction. I want you to know I'm proud of each and every one of you. The performance we delivered here today was a feat worthy of—"

Gabrielle screamed and pointed toward the throne. The others followed her gaze as one by one their eyes widened.

King Magnus was still standing, but his face had changed from red to blue. His hands clutched at his throat while his eyes bulged from their sockets.

Max turned around just in time to see the king freeze in place and begin teetering forward. His large round frame wrapped in golden robes fell with a heavy thud, then rolled slowly down the throne steps and stopped at Max's feet.

The troupe jumped down from the stage and surrounded the motionless body.

The king's bulging eyes seemed to fixate on the rafters, the rest of his face frozen in a terrified, ghastly expression. His chest was still.

Fing started swearing in some foreign tongue. Toby dropped the cat and it darted into the shadows. Gabrielle pulled her rat's nest down over her face.

Hypatia was the first to speak.

"Is he...?"

Max knelt and placed two fingers just below the king's jawline. Old Kook crouched beside him. The old man pinched the king's nose, poked him in the eye, and slapped him hard.

"Yep," Max said, wiping his fingers on Old Kook's robes. "The greasy fat bastard is as dead as a lump of frozen mud."

"I didn't think things could get worse," Hypatia muttered, steadying herself.

Max hopped to his feet and grinned light-heartedly.

"There you go again, Patti, with all the negative vibes."

"Are you mad, Max! You heard what he had planned for us when he was still alive! Imagine what his men will do to us when they find their king dead!"

"Dead king? What are you talking about?" He took the crown and turned it over in his hands. "I don't see a dead king."

"Put it down, Max!" she cried. "I'm pretty sure that just by touching the crown you've somehow made our fate even worse!"

"It's all about how you look at things, my dear Hypatia."

Max examined the crown at arm's length, then turned it over and brought it close to his eyes.

"The truth matters not when you can spin a good story. *You* may see a dead king and doomed troupe." Max knocked the dented pisspot off of Bart's head and replaced it with the crown. "But what *I* see is a lawfully executed actor, a king reborn anew, and his new royal entourage!"

A boom came from the iron doors.

"Your Heinous, shall we come in yet?" a muffled voice yelled through the door.

Max nudged Bart.

"What are you waiting for, Your Heinous? Go on, command your soldier!"

"Come back later!" Bart yelled back, then added, "You, uh... you stupid heads!"

Max cringed.

"Don't worry, we'll work on your lines as soon as we get settled in."

"Settled in?!" cried Hypatia. She looked from Bart to the dead king and back again. "You mean...we're going to..."

The banging from the other side of the iron door grew louder and more panicked. Max stopped tugging at the king's robes and sighed.

"What are you fools standing around for? Someone give me a hand stripping the royal robes off this dead sack of fat! And someone else help Bart get ready! Hurry up, troupe! We've got a permanent performance to prepare for!"

LEAVE IT TO SKEEVER

"**H**oney, I'm home!"

Gregor Cheever threw open the front door. He tossed his jacket and hat on the coat rack and skittered across the foyer.

"Mitsy, kids, come on in here! Scurry up, now!" His antennae vibrated with excitement. "Wait till you see what I found on the way home from work! You won't believe it!"

Crody was the first to arrive. He held a bundle of paper in one hand, a pencil in another, and a pair of tiny toy trucks in the remaining two.

"Hi, Pa!" he said. "Wait till you hear what Skeeve did today. Oh boy, is he gonna get it!"

"That's quite enough out of you, young man," Mitsy Cheever said as she skittered in. She brushed her four hands against her apron and shot a disapproving look at Crody. "You're not exactly blameless, are you?"

"Aw, Ma! I didn't do nothing! It was all Skeeve! *He's* the one who—"

"Enough, young man!" She held up a tarsal claw. "I

won't have another word out of you, or you'll go straight to bed without any scum."

Gregor faked a stern look at his boy, then winked at Mitsy and swept an arm toward the front door. "Speaking of scum, dear—you won't *believe* what I—"

"And you! Late from work, barging in here without saying a proper hello to your family!"

"Sorry, dear. You're right." Gregor blushed and straightened up. "Good morning, love." He kissed her cheek, then mussed up Crody's antennae. "How was your night, champ?"

"It was fine, Pa. Except for when Skeeve got all crazy and—"

"Crody Cheever!" Mitsy put four fists on her hips.

Crody hunched over his paper and scribbled something. "Sorry, Ma."

"Say, where is Skeever?" Gregor asked, peering into an adjacent room. "I have something I'm just bursting out of my exoskeleton to share with you."

"That boy's probably hiding." Mitsy sighed, then called out. "Skeever, dear? Scurry on in here. Your father's home and it's time to discuss what happened at school today."

A runty fella skittered in, twiddling his tarsal claws nervously.

"Hi, Pa," Skeever said, wincing slightly as he spoke. "Uh, how was your day?"

Gregor crossed one pair of arms. "Hello, son. I had a fine day, as a matter of fact. But we'll talk about that once you tell me how *your* day went."

Mitsy looked like someone who'd just had a great weight taken off her back. Crody stifled a giggle.

"Well, Pa..." Skeever shuffled uneasily. "I kinda got sent home from school for something I did at recess."

"Mm-hmm. Well, go on. Tell me what you did."

"Well, Pa…I got into a fight with Jarney Flek."

Gregor's eyes narrowed. "Flek? Is that Blek Flek's boy?"

"That's right, Pa."

"Tell him, Skeeve! Tell him what you did!" Crody blurted out.

"Young man!" snapped Mitsy.

Gregor crossed his other pair of arms. "Out with it, son."

"Well, see…Jarney and I were having at it, and Drabek was egging us on, and, well…I hurt Jarney pretty bad. Real bad, actually."

"I'd say so, Skeeve—you ate his head!" Crody laughed. "Then you ate two arms! If the teachers hadn't stopped you, you'd have—"

"Crody Milktoast Cheever! You're one to talk!" Mitsy wagged a claw at her eldest son. "Why don't you tell your father what you were up to while your brother ate that poor boy?"

Crody started scribbling again. "Aw, shucks. I wasn't up to much. I was just watching with all the other kids."

"That's right. You stood there with that troublesome Drabek Bootlicker and the other kids," she scolded. "You watched your brother perform cannibalism and didn't lift a finger to stop him. Young man, that's no way for an older brother to behave."

Crody hung his head. "I'm real sorry, Ma, Pa."

"Me, too. Real sorry," Skeever let his head hang a hair lower than his brother's.

Gregor sighed and unfolded his arms. He took a seat in his evening chair and padded both knees. "Boys, come on over here. Time for a little chat."

They did. Skeever hopped up with a grunt. Crody had

grown so much after his last molt that he barely fit on his father's knee.

"Now, boys, listen up. Skeeve, I understand what you're going through. I was your age once. I remember how quickly a little schoolyard scuffle can turn violent. We're only cockroach, for heaven's sake! But you mustn't go around cannibalizing the neighbors. Even if fellas like Drabek are cheering you on, you have to learn some restraint. Don't you agree?"

"Yes, Pa." Skeeve was on the verge of tears. "It won't happen again. I promise."

"And Crody. A Cheever doesn't abandon his family in time of need. Your little brother could've used some brotherly guidance today. Instead, you let him murder a classmate in front of the whole school. I want you to think about how that affects the Cheever name. We can't have everyone going around thinking we might eat them, can we?"

Crody frowned. "No, pa, I guess we can't. I won't let Skeeve eat anyone else, if I can help it."

Gregor put his arms around them and squeezed. "Alright, I think these boys have learned their lesson. What do you say I show you what I found this morning?"

The gloom fell away from the boys' faces. Mitsy arched an antennae.

"You love your secrets, don't you? Let's not take too long —I have a moldy cardboard casserole in the oven."

"Mitsy darling, when you see what I've got you'll want to bury your casserole out back."

"Gregor! I never—!"

"Now, now, dear. You'll understand soon enough. Just hear me out." He raised all four arms in surrender. "I was skittering home from work, much like any other morning. When I got about halfway between the house and the toolshed, I heard—no, I *felt*—a great rumbling roll across the land. I froze. Before I could scurry away, the sky ripped in two and a giant face appeared—a face unlike anything I could have imagined. It was soft and pink in some parts, but on top and around its mouth grew millions of tiny antennae. I stood transfixed, unable to move. For how long, I can't be sure."

"Gregor, is this some kind of practical joke?"

"Mitsy, dear, I swear on everything that's rotten that I'm telling you the truth. The next thing I know, the giant lowered a massive tube right in front of me. On the tube was a strange symbol that looked like a grinning white face with two white femurs cross-crossing behind it. Next to the symbol was printed two words: FOR COCK-ROACHES."

"What was it, Pa?" Skeever asked, mouth agape.

"Well, Skeeve, I asked myself that same question. And I got my answer when something oozed from the tip of the tube. It was...incredible." His eyes flickered to the front door. "Why not just show you?"

He slid his sons from his lap, leapt to his feet, then disappeared out front. A moment later, a huge, tan blob filled the door frame. It throbbed and pulsed until it finally squeezed through and plopped into the foyer. Gregor stood panting behind it.

"Introducing, The Scum Boulder! A gift from God!" He beamed, slapping it heartily. The blob wobbled.

The boys skittered around it, gawking. Crody took a deep breath. "Wow-ee, Pa!"

"Gregor..." Mitsy gasped and clamped her hands together. "It's so big! And it smells *wonderful!*"

"Yes, dear, it sure does! I wanted to gobble it down right there on the spot, but it seemed wrong to keep something like this all to myself. So I rolled it home as fast as I could—to share it with the ones I love."

The Cheevers stood frozen, lustfully eyeing the huge tan blob.

Gregor cleared his throat. "Well, what are you waiting for? Dig in!"

Crody and Mitsy dug their claws in and scooped out handfuls of the stuff. Skeever stepped away.

"No!" he shouted. "Stop!"

Gregor looked at him disapprovingly, "Young man, it's not every day that God delivers such a blessing. You put that frown away right now and—"

"No! I won't!" Skeever cried out. He scurried into the kitchen and out the back door.

Mitsy sighed. "*Now* what's wrong with that boy?"

"Crody, put that scum down and go check on your brother," Gregor said.

Crody started into the kitchen, but stopped. "He's coming back. Looks like he's dragging something behind him."

The back door slammed shut, and Skeever skittered into the foyer pulling his red wagon behind him.

"Ma, Pa, I been thinking," Skeever said. "Just like it wasn't right for Pa to keep God's gift all to himself, it ain't right for us Cheevers to hog it, either."

Gregor's antennae rose. "What are you suggesting, son?"

"Well, Pa...there's enough here to feed the whole neighborhood. And after what I did today at school, eating Jarney and all," he paused, looking at his feet. "I figure it might help things for the Cheever name if I went door to door and gave everyone some of this scum. You know, share God's gift."

Crody put a claw on his brother's shoulder. "Golly, Skeeve. What a swell idea! Can I come along and give you a hand?"

Gregor and Mitsy exchanged a warm smile.

"Your mother and I think that's a fine idea, boys. A fine idea, indeed. Let us help you pile up as much as you can take."

The Cheevers were able to load more than half the blob onto the wagon. A moment later the boys were across the street, skittering from door to door.

"They're a couple of good boys, aren't they, Gregor?" Mitsy let her head fall onto Gregor's shoulder.

"They sure are, Mitsy. They sure are."

He led her back inside the foyer. What was left of the blob glistened in the dawn's light.

"Hey, Mitsy, what do you say we have a little taste before they get back?"

"But, dear, we always eat as a family."

"Just a bite or two, honey. Come on! Here, let me feed you a bite." He scooped some into her mouth.

She swooned. "Mmmmmm! Here, let me feed you a bite, too!"

"Wow! This stuff is out of this world!" Gregor swallowed and fed her more. "Say, this reminds me of our honeymoon. Remember, out in the compost heap? We—"

He clenched his stomach.

She swallowed, turned green, and hunched over.

"Gregor...I don't feel so good," she groaned.

"Mitsy, I...I..."

He keeled over onto his back.

Mitsy screamed, then she too was legs up.

They twitched in unison, sharing one last spastic dance together before becoming stiff.

There was a knock on the door.

"Heeeey Cheevers! Can Crody and Skeever come out to play?" Drabek Bootlicker, the boy who lived next door, peeked his head inside. "What's cooking, Mrs. C? Smells great! Mind if I stay for—"

Drabek saw Gregor and Mitsy Cheever on their backs, motionless. He sniffed. His face lit up.

"Since, uh, you guys won't be needing this," he looked quickly from side to side and snatched what was left of the tan blob. "I'm gonna take it home, okay?"

As he skittered outside, he cupped his claws and called, "Mom! Dad! Look what I found!"

THE CHRISTMAS VARIANT

Mrs. Claus leaned against the wheelbarrow to transfer some of the weight off her shoulders. She'd been suffering a 73-year-old back for over 800 years now and if not for modern advances in pain relief she didn't think she'd still be on her feet. God knows being ageless isn't the same as being immortal. Sure, it had its perks, but escaping pain and death weren't on the list.

She opened her pill case and popped a peppermint CBD gummy into her mouth. Before closing it, she looked to the enormous meeting hall, then back at the case. She popped two more. It was going to be a long, lonely, laborious night.

Her heart skipped a beat as she thought of her little elvish friends: their boundless warmth, their fierce generosity, how loyal and innocent they'd remained throughout the centuries.

That was, until the last twenty-four hours.

Everything has gone wrong, Mrs. Claus lamented. *And it's up to us to put it right again—no matter what. If we fail...*

Letting the thought go, she pulled a candy cigarette

from her hair bun, ran it under her nose, then planted it between her lips. The sugar sent an immediate jolt through her system, giving her a little more strength to face what was about to happen. What they were about to do.

It especially hurt because she and the Big Guy owed their lives to the elves. Without them, the pair would've frozen solid that first night in the frigid north. There wouldn't have been any spell of agelessness, any possibility of flying reindeer, nor any supernatural efficiency of a remote North Pole toy factory.

There wouldn't be any Christmas.

Would Christmas happen *this* year? Yes, to some degree at least. If the Big Guy left within the next hour or so, he could still make it most of the way around the world before morning. Each additional second he was postponed meant a dozen children would wake up tomorrow to a giftless tree. Or worse, they'd wake up with only the junk their parents had purchased from the internet.

Even if she and the Big Guy could somehow pull off Christmas by themselves *this* year, how would they handle *next* year? Could they find more elves? There had to be more elves somewhere, didn't there?

We must face one problem at a time, she told herself. *First we take care of the virus, then we take care of Christmas.*

Taking care of the virus meant that the population of their little village was about to drop from a few hundred to just two. She sighed, imagining how quiet the North Pole would soon become. No more pointy hats with their bells softly jingling. No more enchanted giggles lingering around every corner. After today, it'd just be the Big Guy and her, nose to the grindstone, trying to figure out how to produce gifts for a few billion children without their army of helpers.

It wasn't fair how things had turned out. The elves deserved an early retirement full of spiced nuts, sweet dried apricots, and those candied apples they all seemed to adore. Instead, all they were getting was one last mug of hot cocoa before...

Mrs. Claus blinked away a tear as she eyed the great hall. How much harder it must be for the Big Guy. While she waited outside, nibbling a candy cig, he was *inside*, with them. Behind those great hall doors, he was pretending to kick off another successful Christmas with his team. He'd have to look them in the eyes, smile, raise his steamy mug— the only one in the room that didn't contain the oleander poison she'd discreetly whipped up that afternoon—and send them, one by one, his oldest and dearest friends, into an eternal slumber.

The Big Guy guessed that most of the elves would gulp the cocoa down without a second thought. But he also figured there could be some reluctance from those whose infection had already taken root in their brain. For those who refused to drink the cocoa, he'd have to improvise. That's why beneath his bright red robes, pressed firmly against his jolly fat belly, hung a pair of freshly-sharpened wood axes.

Please, Mrs Claus imagined whispering into each of their pointy little ears, *please just drink the cocoa.*

She took it as a good sign that things were still quiet inside. She'd been careful to keep the chains from clacking too loudly as she'd strung them across the big hall doors. There was a row of windows that ran along either side of the building, but they were too high for the elves to reach and this time of year they were all shuttered tightly against the arctic air. As unlikely as it was that anyone would escape, her job was to ensure that if anyone did manage to slip away from the Big Guy, they wouldn't get too far.

Mrs. Claus knew he would deal with any resistance swiftly and decidedly, like someone putting down their injured and suffering pet rabbit with a shovel. She knew him and she knew what it would do to him, and it broke her heart.

She straightened up and felt the weight of the tank on her aching shoulders. The ignition switch was enabled. The flow valve was ready to be opened with the flick of a thumb. She gripped the firing nozzle with both hands to keep them from trembling.

She chomped on the candy cig, biting off a full inch, then began slowly grinding it between her teeth. If the Big Guy could do his part, she could do hers.

Even if the cocoa plan went smoothly, the rest of the night didn't look too rosy. The Big Guy would have to hop into the sleigh and get to work right away, leaving her all alone to clean up the mess. In order to properly contain the infection, she'd first have to stack hundreds of tiny bodies—people she'd known and loved for centuries—into a hastily-built pyre just outside the village. While they burned, she'd have to begin decontaminating an entire village all by herself. If they ever ended up finding more elves the last thing they'd want is for them to get infected so this whole damn thing could start all over again.

She reminded herself they were doing it for the billions of fellow humans in the South who didn't have elvish magic to make them immune to sickness and disease. Although elves have magically-enhanced immune symptoms, they can still fall ill from time to time. As she'd recently discovered, their elvish immune systems happen to be perfect incubators for aggressive viruses to evolve very quickly. When she thought about it, it was actually long overdue that a really nasty human virus would jump species like it had.

Humanity had already suffered one hell of a rough year with the original virus and they were just starting to get a handle on a vaccine. The economies and infrastructures of the world were hanging on by a thread. The last thing they needed was an elvish variant introduced back into their population. If that happened, humankind wouldn't stand a chance.

She and the Big Guy figured the virus had infiltrated the North Pole on one of the millions of letters they received from children all around the world. She pictured little Bobby or Sarah accidentally sneezing onto their freshly decorated Christmas list, looking over their shoulder, then stuffing it into an envelope before anyone noticed.

By the time Mrs. Claus had discovered how serious the infection was, it was showing up in over 80% of the elvish blood samples. By the next day, Christmas Eve morning, nearly every elf in the village was suffering from fever and the virus's calling card, a dark purple rash. As the day rolled on and the infection spread to their brains, they began exhibiting bizarre and aggressive behavior—completely unelvish in every way. By dinnertime, fights had started breaking out and a dozen elves had already fallen to violence or injury. It was far too late for strict hygiene, mandatory quarantines, or even selective culling. If left to play out by itself, the whole village would eventually destroy itself in one, last, psychotic explosion of violence.

She and the Big Guy had no other choice but to stop the mutated virus dead in its tracks, right here, right now—no matter what the cost.

A muffled burst of excitement erupted from inside the great hall. Mrs. Claus stood perfectly still. At first she thought it was laughter, but after a few seconds she realized it was the panicked, high-pitched gurgling of hundreds of elves choking on her poison.

They've had the cocoa, she thought, listening intently. Not knowing exactly how much oleander was needed to kill an elf, she'd made it very potent. *Maybe they all drank some. Maybe there was no resistance. Then the Big Guy won't have to resort to using his—*

Her thought was interrupted by a loud crash from the other side of the big chained doors. Something large and heavy had smashed into them from inside. Then she heard the Big Guy bellow a battle cry from the old days, from back when he'd served as a Nordic tribal warrior, before they'd met the elves and become ageless and devoted their lives to Christmas.

There was more smashing of furniture and more angry, confused cries. Mrs. Claus could sometimes hear what he was roaring:

"Get over here!"

"You want to dance, little one?"

"The only way out is through me!"

He sounded utterly unleashed in a way he hadn't been in almost a millennia.

Will he be able to come back from such a dark place? Mrs. Claus wondered. *Will he ever again be that jolly old fat man I'd planned on spending eternity with? After everything he's done tonight?*

They should have just drank the cocoa, she thought.

Underneath and between the roar of the battle was the sound of a busy butcher shop. There was grunting and heavy chopping and the squishy crunchy sound of meat and bone being cleaved apart. Mrs. Claus heard tiny, manic cries for mercy, for help, for pity, and every time she heard the Big Guy grant their request with his ax.

Eventually, his battle cries were replaced by sporadic snorts and grunts. The old guy was nearly done with his gruesome task and had started pacing himself. As powerful as he was, he needed to reserve some of his strength for the long night ahead.

A rhythmic creaking caught Mrs. Claus' attention. She followed the sound to the high windows that ran along the east side of the hall. The bottom half of an elf body was dangling through a broken window shutter, struggling to get its top half to come along for the ride. Mrs. Claus could see that it would succeed any moment, and that the poor, unlucky soul would be standing just ten feet away. That is, if it could still stand after a fall from that height.

Seconds later, as she'd predicted, the top half of the elf appeared, and together with the bottom half they fell from the window. Mrs. Claus tried her best to ignore the strange mix of jingling bells and breaking bones as the tiny figure slammed into the cold, hard earth. Instead of running to help—which she reminded herself she'd done a trillion times before and would have done under better circum-stances—she braced herself and aimed the nozzle at the writhing bundle of green felt.

The elf saw her and tried darting away, only to collapse on two badly broken legs. It cried out in fear and agony, then, with the desperation of a wounded animal, began pulling its broken body through the snow with its hands.

Mrs. Claus recognized this elf right away. This was Grizelda Tonkins, the head pie maker at Tonkin's Bakery. No one made a better strawberry rhubarb pie. She and Mrs. Claus had worked together just a few years ago on a special pie for the Big Guy's 842nd birthday. He'd absolutely loved it and sent Grizelda a personal note of thanks.

She could see recognition in Grizelda's eyes, too. The virus had surely burrowed deep into her brain by now, but behind her eyes there was still a trace of her old elf self. Mrs. Claus let the nozzle dip. The wounded elf started crawling faster.

Mrs. Claus chomped what was left of the candy cig, wiped away a tear, then lifted the nozzle toward the fleeing elf. She turned on the flow of gas, heard a quick, brief hiss, and watched as a tongue of flame leapt from the flamethrower's nozzle directly onto the prized pie baker. Once the flames were clinging to their target, she turned off the flow. Poor Grizelda kept on crawling for a few seconds before fully succumbing to the blazing heat that engulfed her.

Mrs. Claus dropped to her knees and sobbed and gagged at the smell of badly burnt caramel coming from her old friend's half-melted corpse.

Something inside the hall bashed into the two big doors and caused the chains to tighten.

"Sleigh!" she heard the Big Guy's trembling voice call out. He didn't sound well at all.

A fist slammed against the doors from the inside, followed by another command.

"Sleigh!" This time he almost moaned the words, as if nauseous and on the verge of vomiting.

She pulled the key from her pocket as she ran to the lock she'd used to bind the chains. A quick twist and the chains slackened.

The doors swung open. The Big Guy stumbled through, his beard and the white of his robes were soaked with so much blood so that he was red from nose to toes.

"Sleigh!" He called out like a dog howling to be let out to roam the night.

"Dear...are you alright?" Mrs. Claus reached out but he swatted her hand away.

"Fine! Sleigh!" he cried, pausing between each word as if it were painful to breathe. "Must. Go. Christmas. *Sleigh!*"

She tried to find that special sparkle in his eyes, but it was gone. He just stared out into the falling snow as if in a dream. Could she blame him? He'd just murdered a few hundred of his closest friends. And the clock was still ticking.

"It's ready, waiting behind the stable. I've told the reindeer to auto-navigate, so no driving for you tonight, Just rest and gather your strength between delivery stops."

He didn't answer, he just gave her a wobbly nod and stumbled toward the stable.

As she watched him walk off to perform his most sacred duty, she resolved that when he got back she'd smother him with so much love and affection that he'd have no choice but to heal his decimated heart.

They'd be able to heal. *Together.*

She plopped the flamethrower in the snow, then rolled her wheelbarrow through the open doors of the great hall. The stench of spoiled marshmallows and rancid chocolate was almost too much to take, but she refused to give an ounce less than the Big Guy was giving.

She tied a handkerchief over her mouth, dropped to her knees, and started stacking dismembered elf parts into the wheelbarrow.

Being dead elves, they were as light as driftwood. She had no problem picking them up in bundles and tossing them in all at once. Each fragile little arm or leg was wrapped in colorful felt and ribbons of blood, almost like tiny little gifts. She imagined she was just cleaning up a mess of toys, not real body parts. These were just old, dirty doll parts. Just junk.

"Just junk," she muttered, dropping another leg into the bin. "Not real. Just junk. Just dirty, old, cinnamon-scented..." She trailed off as her hand settled on something under a broken bench. When she pulled it out and held it to her face, her blood ran cold. It was a heart. Not the walnut-sized heart of an elf, but the heart of a much larger creature. The heart of a human.

Mrs. Claus shrieked at the top of her lungs and let it slip from her hands. When she recovered, she turned to the surrounding rubble and began pushing the top layer of broken furniture and dead elves away. Underneath she found more human organs: a stomach, two lungs, and a pile of intestinal tubing. Nearby she found a short elven dagger covered in blood with a tuft of red fur snagged on its blade.

She got to her feet and ran outside as fast as her old joints would take her, which wasn't very fast at all. She crouched down to get the flamethrower straps over her shoulders and managed to tighten them without falling backward into the snow. With the nozzle at the ready, she stomped through the snow toward the stable.

To her relief, the sleigh was still parked where she'd left it. The Big Guy was fiddling with the reins, trying to call out to the reindeer to make them go.

She walked up directly behind the sleigh and pointed her nozzle at it. From behind, in the crisp, bright moonlight, it looked just like him. The blood on her hands—his blood, straight from his heart—reminded her that it couldn't possibly be him. Whatever was up there fiddling with the reins was not her Big Guy.

That's when her eyes found the huge bloody incision running from the collar of his big red jacket to his seat.

Mrs. Claus closed her eyes, held her breath, and turned on the valve.

There was no quick hiss of fuel and no flames spewed from the nozzle.

She tried again, this time with her eyes open. Still no flame.

A strange clicking noise came from the tip of the nozzle. The ignition spark had gone out when she'd dropped it in the snow. Adjusting her bifocals, she scanned the buttons along the side of the nozzle. She plunged her thumb into the button labeled IGNITION. There was a loud *fssst*, but no fire.

"No!" she cried, pushing the button again and again. "No, no, no, NO!"

She could sense the restlessness in the reindeer. On any normal Christmas Eve they'd have already been in the air for a few hours. She could tell they wanted nothing more than to go run across the frosty moonlit night. This was the one night they lived for. She knew that they didn't actually need the Big Guy's command in order to take off.

That's why she wasn't completely surprised when they finally gave up waiting and sped off down the runway, pulling the sleigh, and the Big Guy, behind them.

Everything slowed down for Mrs. Claus. She realized with dread how all the clues she'd missed were related. How he'd had so much difficulty walking. How strange his voice sounded. How the spark was missing from his eyes. The thing that burst through the hall doors may have looked like her husband on the outside, but it was something completely different on the *inside*.

As if to prove her right, the incision on the Big Guy's

backside spread open to reveal a trio of demented elf faces, each striped with that telltale purple rash and dripping with the blood of their former boss. One by one, they hissed, flipped her off, then disappeared back inside the corpse.

She realized that a gang of resistors had gotten him that elvish knives at some point during his rampage, probably while she was busy torching Grizelda. Once he was dead, they quickly ripped out most of his major organs and hid them beneath the mess. Then they'd climbed inside his hollowed out body and began controlling it from inside like a costume.

She snapped to just in time to watch the sleigh lift off the ground, circle back for a pass over the village rooftops, then shoot up and vanish into the clouds.

Mrs. Claus dropped the nozzle and the tank, then made her way into the stable.

When the elves were done infecting every inch of the globe, the sleigh would bring them right back to the North Pole. She needed to be far away from the village, or any village for that matter, if she planned to survive to see the new year.

She found Blitzen's trough and pushed it aside. She cleared out the hay underneath to reveal a small rectangular hatch in the dirt. With the thumb of her mitten she entered three numbers into its combination lock and wrenched it open.

She pulled a backpack and a rifle from the space below the hatch, leaving the other rifle behind. She decided it wouldn't offer an old lady like her much more time out there in the barren, icy wasteland than she already had, which was very little.

She grabbed it anyway and slung it over her other shoulder. Water wouldn't be a problem and there were two weeks worth of rations in the pack. But after that, her survival would depend on hunting and fishing, neither of which she was very good at. Those had always been his hobbies, not hers. And besides, she never once imagined she'd have to survive anywhere without her Big Guy by her side.

Unable to cry or to feel much of anything anymore, Mrs. Claus emptied the rest of the CBD gummies into her mouth, pulled her backpack straps tight, then set off on foot into the Great White North.

NO RUNNING

The cell phone blasted its shrill, electric ringtone into Doug Peterson's stuffy bedroom. He pulled the blanket over his head and rolled over.

Just go away, you asshole!

As if the caller were responding, the ringtone abruptly stopped. Doug cracked open his blanket cocoon and took a sip of fresh air. He smacked his lips, unclenched his eyes, and relaxed. Just as he felt the tide of slumber lulling him back to the land of dreams, the stupid phone started another round of shrieking and vibrating.

"Go away!" he screamed over the ringtone. "Leave me the fuck alone!"

Over the past few months, Doug had done everything in his power to make sure absolutely no one would need him at this, or any, hour. He no longer had friends, work buddies, or even casual acquaintances. Other people's casual, cheerful, or, worst of all, *supportive,* voices, irritated the crap out of him. He didn't need their support. He didn't need anyone. And more importantly, they didn't need him.

He'd even stopped returning a smile to the elderly lady

who seemed to have nothing better to do than sweep their shared apartment stoop ten times a day. He couldn't have her thinking she could stop by if she needed a hand with something. She'd have to bother one of their more capable neighbors.

Doug lay curled in a ball beneath his comforter, hoping that with any luck karma would kick in and the stupid phone's battery would die so he could go back to sleep.

The stupid phone had other plans. Instead of dying, it vibrated across the nightstand, knocking the clutter—mostly empty beer cans and crumpled bills—onto the tile below. Doug refused to move. He couldn't think of anything on the nightstand, or in his littered apartment, or in his littered life, worth getting up for.

After a few harmless thunks, there was a shatter followed by a crash. His phone had shoved something breakable off the nightstand and then fell on top of it. The electric ringtone was less shrill from down on the floor, but the obnoxiousness of its vibration increased as it danced upon the rubble of whatever it had just destroyed.

Doug moaned and threw off the blanket. Tensing, he peered over the side of the bed.

Well...shit! That sucks.

His dragon-shaped bubbler had taken a great fall. All Doug's horses and all Doug's men couldn't put his decorative-glass-sculpture-used-for-smoking-his-morning-bowl back together again.

Whoever it was who kept calling had just murdered his favorite piece. They'd taken things too far.

He snatched his phone, blew rainbow shards and cannabis ash off the screen, then jabbed his finger at the answer icon. It vanished a split second before his fingertip made contact.

"7 MISSED CALLS," the screen reported, adding, "and 3 NEW VOICEMAILS."

Doug glanced at the wall clock that hadn't worked in weeks, then swung his legs over the side of the bed and kicked the broken shards of glass and beer cans underneath.

"Okay, Google," he said, alerting his phone that he was about to give it a verbal command. "Play my new voicemails on the big speaker."

"Sure, Doug," his virtual assistant's voice called from the kitchen, which was located just outside his bedroom door, "playing your three new voicemails now."

He opened his nightstand drawer, frowned, then rummaged through a pile of dirty laundry. Sighing, he stepped out of his stuffy bedroom just as the first message began to play.

"Heeey, buddy!"

Doug winced as if someone had just hit him over the head with a brick.

"This is Steve, your new manager at WhizComm. Sorry to bother you on the weekend. I'm just calling to see how you're doing, and to ask whether you got our care package."

Doug pictured the schmoozy asshole flashing a row of perfectly aligned, blindingly white teeth—just like he had ten thousand times during the interview. He opened his coffee table drawer, glanced inside, then slammed it shut.

"As you know, our culture here at WhizComm values the work-life balance. Life happens, right? No worries! WhizComm's got your back. That said, we can't wait to bring you on board." Steve lowered his voice, "Don't tell the rest of the crew I told you this, buuuut, we're trying to put together a little *welcoming* party for you on your first day. Just a catered lunch, dessert, and maybe a happy hour later in the evening. It'd be great if we knew when that might be.

Sound good, buddy? Feel free to call me back at this number anytime this weekend to let me know how Monday's looking. Take care, Doug. Hope to see ya soon!"

Damn. It's the weekend already? I thought it was Wednesday.

Doug rifled through the kitchen's drawers and cabinets, his frown increasing as he slammed each shut and moved on to the next. The phone beeped and the virtual assistant announced the timestamp of the second message.

"Hello. This message is for Mr. Doug Peterson. My name is Jim Feeney, and I'm calling on behalf of Valley Tech Recruiting Services." The recruiter's voice was cold and nasally, as usual. "If you remember, Mr. Peterson, we helped match you with the Principal Engineer role at Whiz-Comm. It's our understanding that you've not yet reported to said job. I'm calling to inform you that if you do not report to WhizComm on Monday morning we'll be sending a new batch of qualified candidates for them to consider. Also, in that case, Valley Tech Recruiting Services will no longer be able to assist you with your job search. Have a nice day."

That prick sounds like he needs a bowl worse than I do, Doug thought, his eyes darting around his dimly lit apartment.

In a frenzy, he peeked inside the fridge, the oven, and the microwave, then leapt across his tiny apartment and threw the cushions off his loveseat.

Shit! Where the hell is it?

He dropped to his knees in front of the couch, paused to consider the risk, then shoved his whole arm underneath. His cobweb-ensnared hand emerged just as the next message began.

"Doug, this is Erica," a voice snapped. It was the

succubus who'd ripped his heart out, shoved it up his ass, pulled it out again, laughed at him, then shoved it down his throat. "Jesus, Doug! I've called you a hundred times this morning. I know I'm just your ex-wife, but at least you could pick up once in awhile! What am I even saying? Your phone's probably dead. Or you're hungover. Either way, you better get your shit together because we're on our way over. You better be home. Anyway, call me back. Or don't. I'll see you in ten minutes."

There was a moment of silence, but she didn't hang up. When her voice finally returned it was a whisper. "They're really looking forward to seeing you today. Don't fuck this up."

Click.

He looked across his clusterfuck of an apartment. Dank, musty air. Beer cans everywhere. Barely any light at all, and where it did creep in past the curtains it fell directly onto a department store junk mail catalog opened to the lingerie section.

At least I have a little time to straighten up before they get here.

Something scurried under an upturned pizza box in the corner. Doug screeched and leapt onto the cushion-less couch.

Just then, the doorbell buzzer blared from the front door. He screeched again and stumbled backward off the couch—his butt making a suspicious crunching sound as it hit the ground. Doug rolled aside to find another pile of broken glass and ash.

"Oh. There you are, spare bubbler."

The doorbell buzzed again, longer and angrier than the first time.

"*One second!*" he yelled—much louder than was

warranted—as he stood and brushed glass shards from his ass.

When he was ready, he opened the door to reveal a curvy silhouette with her fists on her hips standing in the rectangle of light. Two smaller silhouettes rushed past and slammed into him at full speed.

"Daddy!" they squealed. One latched onto his leg while the other squeezed the air out of his chest.

"We missed you sooooooo much!" said the taller one.

"Yeah, we bissed you soooooo buch, daddy!" parroted the one that clung to his leg.

"I missed my kiddos soooooo much, too," he said, mussing up their hair.

Doug smiled, his heart suddenly becoming as light as a feather.

Then—just like all the other positive feelings that had the nerve to rear their stupid heads these days—his flicker of joy was quickly dissolved in a vat of shame and self-pity.

He glared at the curvy silhouette.

"Hey, why don't you guys go play some XBox while Daddy and Mommy have a quick chat?"

"Okay!" they said in unison, running past him into the dark apartment. "Daddy, what happened to your couch?"

"Uh, just slide the cushions back on and fire up the TV. I'll be there in a sec."

"Now you're having couch malfunctions, Doug? How hard is it to keep a *couch* in working order?"

His eyes had adjusted to the light and he could see her better. Her skin was tan. Her hair looked clean. She looked fit, like she'd started working out. And pissed, as usual.

"Well, Erica," he said, gripping the doorway on either side to keep from shaking, "*my* couch—the nice one I spent $800 on—is at *my* house. You remember, right? The nice one I paid the mortgage on for ten years. The house *you* still live in. If you didn't want our kids to hang out in a divorcée slum you shouldn't have divorced me."

She sighed and crossed her arms. When she did, he got a look at her left hand. No ring.

"Do I smell weed? Were you *smoking out* this morning? Geez, Doug!"

"Not that it's any of your business, but no, I haven't been smoking. I've been getting ready for the day with my kids. You know, the one day a week I get to see them."

As the words left his mouth, Doug felt like he would burst into flames. They both knew that the judge was prepared to give him zero visitation rights, and only with Erica's intervention was he allowed the one day a week.

"Getting ready? It looks like you haven't shaved in forever and you're wearing the same clothes from last week. And don't pretend you washed them, I can see the mustard stain from last Saturday."

"Like I said, none of this is your business anymore, okay? You're wasting the short time I get with my kids. And there's no need to hurry tonight, I'm planning a movie marathon. Okay, bye."

He started to close the door, but she stuck her foot on the threshold to keep it from closing all the way.

"Movie marathon? None of that scary shit, Doug. I'm the one who has to put them to bed, and I don't want them up all night with nightmares. Something calm, peaceful. They'll need lots of rest after a day at the pool."

"Pool?"

"Yes, Doug. The birthday party this afternoon at Surftown."

"Oh, that. Right."

"Shit, Doug! I can't believe you! Sydney's friend from

school—the super rich one—invited the kids to Surftown today for the birthday party. They rented out the whole place...invited half the valley. None of this rings a bell, does it? You know what, I'll just take them. You can hang around your slum and mope."

He quickly stepped outside, closed the door behind him, and scowled.

"This is *my* day, Erica. I got this."

"Do you? Listen, you need to watch them closely in the water! I don't trust the lifeguards they have working there. They're all glue-huffing idiots."

"*I got this.* Those two kids are the most important things in my life. I wouldn't let anything happen to them."

"That's easy to say, Doug, but what about all the past due child support checks? School's starting soon and the kids need new clothes, supplies, lunch money—"

"Do we have to do this every goddamn time you drop them off? Like I told you last week, I just got that job at WhizComm. I get my first paycheck next week."

"They must have a pretty slack dress code at Whiz-Comm," she said, looking him up and down.

"Oh, I'm sorry if I don't wear suits and shiny shoes and fucking silk nooses around my neck every day. We can't all be uptight assholes like *Brian*, can we?"

"This isn't about Brian! But since you brought him up, he may be an uptight asshole, but at least he's a stable, trustworthy asshole. Which is what those kids need right now...and so do I."

Doug's face felt hotter than the Arizona sun that blazed overhead.

"Dammit, Doug. There's a lot of shitheads and losers and creepy fuckers out there." She put a hand on his arm. "But you're not one of them. You're one of the good guys."

"Not good enough though, huh?"

"No." She took her hand back. "Not as long as you keep telling yourself the world's out to get you."

Doug stared at his feet, too exhausted to escalate the aggression.

"Did you just call your new boyfriend an asshole?"

Erica's face went pink.

"You did! I heard you. You just called Brian an uptight asshole," he said. "Finally, after a year apart, we agree on something."

She smirked and handed him a styrofoam cup.

"Drink this coffee and clean yourself up. Drive safely, watch them at the pool, and try to have fun. I'll call you tonight before I swing by to pick them up."

Doug tried to ignore her ass as she walked away. He failed. She *had* been working out.

He poked at his saggy paunch as he stepped back inside. Sydney was showing Matty how to snipe pixelated zombies from 300 yards away.

"Alright, kiddos! Who wants instant ramen noodles and leftover pizza for breakfast?"

"We already had breakfast, silly," Matty said without looking away from the carnage on the screen. "Brian made eggs and bacon."

"Of course he did."

Doug slumped and shut the door behind him.

"AND WHY DID *every* alien they meet speak English? Why was the gravity of *every* planet the same as Earth's?" Doug said, making eye contact with the eleven year old in the rearview mirror. "Where were all the fat people?"

"Dad, that's mean," Sydney said, suppressing a giggle.

"To work in Starfleet you had to follow a strict physical health routine."

"I wish *I* had a yightsaber." Matty gazed out the window and sighed.

"Okay, fine. But what about all the non-Starfleet human colonies they'd visit? Never once was there a morbidly overweight person. Never! And, hey—this thing doesn't stop with humans. Where were all the voluptuous Vulcans? The bulbous Borg?"

"Stop! It's not funny!"

"Where were all the corpulent Klingons?"

"Oh my god, Dad. *Corpulent?* Did you steer our conversation in this direction to review a word for my vocab test next week?"

"Maybe."

"Daddy, can I have a yightsaber for my berfday?"

"Shut up, Matty! Stop interrupting us." Sydney shoved her brother's car seat. "Everyone knows lightsabers are from *Star Wars*, not *Star Trek*. Duh."

"Oh." Matty scrunched up his eyebrows and frowned.

"Sydney, don't talk to your brother that way! Besides, when you and I started watching *Next Gen* together you thought Picard was a Jedi."

Doug shot Matty a smile over his shoulder as he turned into Surftown's parking lot.

"And sure, buddy. You can have a yightsaber for your berfday."

Sydney's face tightened.

"Did Mom tell you about my last report card?"

"No....but a list of words fell out of your backpack before we left. I had no idea you had trouble with your grades until you just mentioned it. What's going on, Syd?"

"I just hate school, okay?"

"Okay. Believe it or not, when I was your age I wasn't too fond of school either. But it's not all bad, right?"

"It *is* all bad, Dad. Everyone's so fake. So superficial. Including the teachers."

"Superficial?" Doug chuckled. "Seems like you have a good handle on vocabulary."

"Daddy, can I dress up like Darf Bader for Halloween?" Matty interjected.

"Just forget it," Sydney said, looking out the side window. "Like I told mom, I don't plan on going to college, so grades don't matter."

"What? You're eleven!" Doug glanced back to lock eyes with her. "Since when are you making plans for after high school? How about you finish middle school first?"

"*You* didn't go to college, and you did alright."

Doug sucked in a slow breathe before answering.

"Did I? I think the jury's still out on that one, honey. Anyway, you need to buckle down and just get through it. You can't run away from life when it's not going exactly the way you want it to go."

Sydney crossed her arms and muttered, "You should talk."

"*What was that?*" Doug glared into the rearview mirror at his daughter. "First of all, no way, Matty. Darth Vader was worse than Hitler. And, Sydney....my life is way more complicated than just getting good grades, okay? When you grow up, you'll see that adults have much more serious problems that—"

"Dad, look out!"

Doug slammed on the brakes. The car stopped within a few inches of a father and son wearing swimming trunks and flip-flops.

"Watch where you're going, dipshit!" the father yelled,

slamming his fist into the hood of the car. The guy was a mountain of muscle. A 'roid volcano ready to burst. An alpha male ready to pummel anything that even mildly pisses him off.

Doug's heart pounded in his throat as he rolled down his window.

"Oh, man! I'm so sorry!"

"Be more careful!" the 'roid volcano said, jabbing his meaty finger in the air. "Kids are running all over this parking lot!"

Then, sensing Doug's obvious beta-ness, he shook his head and led his son away.

"Well, shit. That was a close call," Doug said, his hands shaking as he pulled into the nearest open spot. "Let's not tell Mom about that little incident, okay?"

"Well, shit!" Matty bounced in his car seat. "Shit! Close call! Shit! Close call!"

Doug closed his eyes and sank into the driver's seat.

Hand in hand, they walked to the entrance of Surftown —especially careful to avoid any cars—and gave their name to a smiling hostess at the entrance. She glanced at a clipboard, thanked them for coming, and reminded them that all the park's attractions were complementary, including food and drinks. Everything had been paid for by the birthday girl's parents, Mr. and Mrs. Lacerto.

Surftown was the perfect oasis to escape the blistering Arizona summer. Multistory water slides towered over lazy rivers that wound around a ten-trillion-gallon wave pool. An army of bronzed lifeguards scanned the crowd from behind mirrored aviators. The place was so packed that Doug had a hard time taking more than a couple steps at a time without tripping over a child.

As he noticed his kids' excited smiles, he felt a cord of

guilt tighten around his chest. He should be able to take them to Surftown every weekend. Brian surely could.

A kid yanked at each hand.

"Let's do the slides!" cried Sydney.

"No, Daddy, let's float in the yazy riber!" Matty whined.

When Brian and Erica bring the kids here, I bet they split up, each taking a kid to let them do whatever they want.

"Hang on, guys!" Doug pulled his hands away and ran them through his hair. "There's only one of me, okay? We'll have to take turns."

"Me, first!"

"No, me!"

"You're both wrong. Safety comes first." Doug squatted beside Matty. "You remember how to swim, right?"

"Of course, silly! My swim teacher gradulated me from Otter to Dolphin!"

Doug tried to maintain a smile through the punch to the gut. Erica had forgotten to tell him—or maybe intentionally withheld—one more important thing about his kids.

"Great, buddy. Let me adjust those goggles for you. Wow! Are these real dinosaur teeth around the eye part?"

"Yeah! Mama bought them for me for gradulating to Dolphin!" Matty beamed. "I look like a real sharptooth, don't I?"

"You sure do." Doug tugged at an orange strap one more time, then turned to Sydney. "How 'bout you, honey?"

She squirmed and bit at her nails.

"I'm fine. I'm eleven, remember? Can't I just go off by myself for a while?"

"But this is our day. I thought—"

"There are kids from school *right over there*. No, don't

look! Please let me go talk to them. I'll come find you in a bit."

Doug sighed. "Fine, go. I'll be over by the *yazy riber* with your brother. Come check in with me in a little while, okay?"

"Thanks, Dad!"

She turned and started to sprint away.

"No running!" he yelled—much louder than was necessary. "Everything's wet! You could slip and hurt yourself!"

Sydney turned red and disappeared into the crowd.

"Come on, Daddy!" Matty said, tugging at Doug. "The yazy riber! Let's go!"

"You know what, bud? Daddy's gonna sit here and watch you go down the yazy riber, okay?"

"But you just told Letty this is our day."

"It *is* our day! I'm just a little tired and I need to rest for a minute. Go grab an inner tube and get started. I'll watch from here."

"Okay, Daddy."

Matty started off dragging his feet, but after a few steps he was skipping.

Doug plopped into a poolside chair and pulled out his cell phone. No missed calls. No voicemails or text messages. He opened his email app and checked for any unread emails. As usual, there was nothing in his social life but dead air.

Somewhere in the chaos a kid squealed. Doug looked up. It took a few seconds, but he found Matty's orange dino goggles in the crowded lazy river. The little guy was lounging with his butt in the tube and his arms and legs hanging over the sides.

Doug opened his Instagram app and started scrolling through the beautiful photos of old classmates and friends.

He tapped on a photo of a Hispanic family slurping fettuccine at a quaint trattoria in front of the Leaning Tower of Pisa.

Oh look, Brian Garcia and his family are on vacation in Italy. Again. Must be nice to have a marriage that holds together through four kids.

He kept scrolling until a gallery preview made his eyes bulge from their sockets. Jeanine Garland, an ex-girlfriend who'd friended him a decade ago so she could add him to her wedding registry, had posted another photoshoot of herself in a bathing suit.

Damn, she looks good! Her body looks as young as it did back in high school.

"Daddy, look!" Matty called as his inner tube returned around the bend of the river. He was kneeling on his tube, his tiny arms flailing to keep him from toppling over.

"Good job, buddy." he said, much quieter than was necessary.

Doug tapped on the gallery and zoomed in on a particularly well-lit photo of Jeanine doing a cartwheel in the sand.

"Something caught your eye?" a woman said from somewhere nearby. Doug held his hand up to block the sun from his eyes.

It was Susan Richards, one of Matty's friend's moms. No—she *used* to be Susan Richards. Since her divorce she'd reverted back to Susan Green. She was standing in a white button-down with a floral sarong around her waist and dark curls peeking out from under an oversized straw hat. She smiled and nodded at his phone.

"Oh, hi..." Doug stood, grabbing a towel to cover the excitement that had just been awakened in his swimming trunks. "No, not really. Just catching up on news and stuff."

"It's been a long time, Doug. How are you? You here with Matty and Sydney?"

"I'm good. Yep, here for the big birthday shindig. How are you? I assume you're here with, uh, little..." He trailed off, looking around as if Susan's kid's name was lying somewhere in the stacks of pool towels piled up everywhere.

"Henry," she said, smiling. "Henry and I are doing great. He's doing better, you know, with all the changes this year. His father sent him a card the other day, so that's something." She tilted her hat up out of her face and locked eyes with Doug. "It's so good to see a father at a place like this, with his kids. Especially after a divorce, when most guys take off to L.A. to live out their midlife crises with some bimbo."

Doug raised his eyebrows and shrugged. "Nope—no bimbos here. I'm all out of bimbos. Just me and the kids having some fun in the sun."

She giggled.

"You know, you never responded to that play group request I sent you a few months ago. You should come! It's every other Saturday. Just a few divorcées with kids, like us. The kids get to play together while we single parents get to commiserate with each other. It's like a support group for the romantically discarded."

Oh, just what I need, Doug thought. *Spend hours listening to boring anecdotes about recovering from divorce. Maybe I can even open up and have a good cry. Whoopie.*

"Uh, maybe someday," lied Doug. "I just started a new job, and I really value the close one-on-one time with the kids during our Saturday visits."

"Okay, then. Well, the offer stands. You have my email address if you change your mind." She winked. "It was nice to see you, Doug."

"It was nice to see you, too, Susan," he said, then watched her disappear into the crowd.

"Daddy!" A tiny hand pulled at his arm. "Let's go on the slides! They go fast! Look! Look!"

"Not now, Matty. Daddy's still resting. I'll watch you go down, though, okay?"

"Oh, come on, Daddy! You're still dry!"

"Go on, show me how fast you can go. I'll be right here."

"Okay," said Matty, then sped off towards the stairs leading up to the towering water slides.

"Hey, no running! Oh, forget it."

Doug fell back into his chair and unlocked his phone.

This time he opened Reddit and started scrolling through dozens of headlines. Militaries were preparing for something in Eastern Europe, and no one had any good ideas about stopping it. More corruption was uncovered in politics, and both teams were trying to drum up votes for the next election. The climate was fucked, and no one cared. And the worst part was that most 'people' posting in the comments were just bots with political agendas trying to sway the few last humans left browsing the site.

Sydney appeared beside him.

"Dad, can we go home now? I hate this place and I want to go home."

Without taking his eyes off the screen, he said, "No, we just got here. Your brother's on the slides now. Why don't you go join him?"

"Mom wouldn't let him go on the slides by himself. You know that, right? She'd be afraid he'd slip in the stairwell and hurt himself."

Doug tossed the phone in his lap.

"Well, Mom's not here, is she? Your brother is six years

old, Sydney. He's capable of walking up a few stairs by himself."

"Fine. I'm going to go get a hotdog. After that, we should go." Sydney wiped a tear from her cheek. "I don't like these people or this stupid place and I want to go home."

Doug's face was already back in his phone.

"Okay, honey."

The screen flashed and a new text message appeared: *Hey Doug! This is Steve from WhizComm. Just wondering if you got my voicemail earlier today. Have a listen and call me back, okay? Looking forward to Monday, lol! Talk to you soon.*

He groaned, swiped the message away, and opened his web browser. He googled "glass bubbler cannabis pipe cheap near me".

"If it isn't Dougie-Doug!"

He felt a slap on his shoulder and spun around. It was Buzz McAllister, one of his old pot smoking buddies from high school, standing beside a rolling garbage can in full custodial attire.

"What's up, D? I didn't know you still lived in the valley?"

"Hey Buzz. Yeah, still here. Got married, had kids, got tossed aside like a parking ticket. You know, same as everyone else. What've you been up to these days?"

"Not much. Staying with some friends out on the west side. Workin' and stuff. Just got this sweet job here at Surftown. It's a blast!"

"Picking up trash is a blast?"

"Bro, I'm drowning in an ocean of fine booties from the time I clock in till the time I leave! Can you believe I get paid for this?"

"Congrats." Doug said as his insides knotted up. He hated talked to normal people, and this guy was a weirdo. "Cool. Well, good seeing you."

"Wanna know the best thing about this gig?"

"Sure."

"No drug tests!" Buzz gave two thumbs up. "And hey, I'm about to go on a smoke break. Wanna join me and catch up? Like old times?"

"Naw, I don't smoke cigs anymore."

Buzz leaned forward on his broom.

"I'm not talking about cigs, bro. I got a fatty-boom-batty doob rolled up, ready to go. Let's go man! The spot is there, under the slides, behind that little shack. No one can see us there."

"Daddy! Didja see that splash?"

Matty ran up dripping, his goggles fogging up in the hot sun.

"It was soooooo big! Didja see it?"

"Uh, yeah, it was great, buddy. Go do it again, okay?"

"Don't you wanna come with me?"

"No, Daddy's talking to an old friend. I'll come watch you when I'm done."

Matty scrunched up his face, balled his fists, and stormed off.

Doug followed Buzz to the little shack under the slides. They slipped between some bushes and came face to face with a quartet of lifeguards. One of them took a deep breath from a paper bag and passed it to the girl on his right.

"Don't mind them, those glueheads are cool with us puffin' back here," Buzz said as he slid a bulging papery cylinder from the pocket of his Surftown polo. He held the joint and a lighter out to Doug. "Do the honors, Dougster."

Finally, some good karma coming my way! Doug

thought. *Fuck QuizComm. Fuck Erica. Fuck Susan Green's little group therapy bullshit.*

He popped the joint in his lips, closed his eyes, and flicked the lighter.

Just then, a woman's scream pierced through the constant hum of the crowd. Then another scream, and another. Suddenly, somewhere on the other side of the bushes, people were gasping and chattering and crying out in horror.

"Shit," one of the lifeguards said, forcing open his drooping eyes. "C'mon, guys. We gotta go see what's up."

He stumbled and grabbed hold of the guard next to him, sending them both down in the grass. The other two started taking sluggish, deliberate steps toward the bushes.

Doug dropped the joint and the lighter and darted through the bushes. People were crowding around something, yet many were starting to look away. Between their legs and soggy swimsuits he noticed a bright red streak on the pool deck.

"Call 911!" someone shouted.

He shoved through the outer edge of the crowd to get a better look. As he moved closer he saw that the bright red streak was actually a bright red puddle—and it was creeping toward the onlookers' flip flops. At the center of the puddle he spotted a familiar orange oval.

Oh my god.

He pushed his way past more bystanders and caught a glimpse of sunlight reflecting off a ring of dino teeth and wet hair tinged with blood.

It can't be.

Sprawled out across the bright red pool was a little boy's body. The shitty pop music and the murmur of the crowd were sucked from the air. Doug grabbed hold of a stranger's shoulder to keep himself from collapsing.

This can't be happening.

With a sudden burst of panic, he wedged through the last rank of the crowd and dropped to his knees in the puddle of blood.

"Matty!" he cried, taking the boy's limp hand. "No! Matty, wake up! Wake up, kiddo!"

"He slipped..." a voice said from the crowd. "He was running."

"They were *all* running," another voice added, a hint of arrogance in her voice.

Tears streaming down his face, Doug scanned the dozens of eyes gawking at him. More than one phone was pointed at him.

"Someone *do something!*" he sobbed. "Please! Help him!"

No one moved. No one looked him in the eyes. More phones appeared. Doug planned to stomp on every one of their stupid phones, and when he was done with that he'd stomp all their stupid faces.

"An ambulance is on the way, sir," said one of the glue-head lifeguards standing just outside the puddle of blood. "S-s-sorry, sir, but we weren't trained for this type of, uh, head trauma. This wasn't in the training course..."

The boy's face was turned away so that the broken back of his skull was facing Doug. He squeezed the little hand and clenched his eyes shut, his whole body shaking and lurching with anguish.

My Matty!

My poor little Matty!

I should've been with you...

I shouldn't have let you out of my sight!

I can't believe this is happening!

I can't—

"GET THE FUCK AWAY FROM MY KID!" a voice bellowed over Doug's shoulder just before something the size of a telephone pole knocked him aside like a ragdoll.

When he looked up, the 'roid volcano from the parking lot had taken his spot next to the boy. The man's face was beet red with marker-sized veins bulging from his neck and forehead.

"WHAT THE HELL HAPPENED? WHO DID THIS? WHO THE FUCK DID THIS?"

"N-n-no one, sir," said the gluehead. "It was an accident, sir. H-h-he slipped and hit the back of his head. An ambulance is on the—"

"MY BOY!" The mountain of muscle wailed, picking the kid up and cradling him in his telephone pole arms. "OH GOD! MY BOY!"

The man pulled the goggles off the kid's face. Doug recognized the boy from earlier, the one he had almost hit with his car.

It wasn't Matty. He looked at the crowd and noticed a few more pairs of orange dino goggles.

Doug collapsed onto his back. He threw an arm over his face. His heart raced, pumping ice cold fluid through every inch of his body.

It wasn't Matty.

He sighed, feeling an impossibly heavy weight lift off his chest.

Thank fucking God in Heaven! It wasn't Matty!

Elation washed over him like a tsunami returning to the ocean. Doug felt—actually *felt* a physical sensation tugging at his heart—all his bullshit being carried away with the rushing water. It was all swept away: his anger towards Erica, his avoidance of the world, his disappointment with himself. When the last bit of emotional debris was gone, a strange calmness took its place. Despite knowing how horribly insensitive and awful it was, he smiled.

"Dad, are you okay?!" he heard Sydney ask, then felt her hand gingerly touch his arm.

"I'm fine, honey. Just fine."

He gazed into her big brown eyes. She had her mother's long eyelashes. She had his thick eyebrows. Doug had never seen a more beautiful face in his entire life.

"You've got blood all over you! Are you hurt?"

"No, no. I'm fine." He sat up and held her hand. "It's not mine. It's..."

He glanced to the boy being lifted onto a stretcher. Guilt started to creep up Doug's throat, but he swallowed hard and looked into his daughter's eyes.

"What do you say we get outta here? We've had enough sun for one day."

"Daddy!" When the tiny voice hit Doug's ears, he nearly fell back again.

Matty came rushing through the crowd and slammed a hug into his father.

"I was looking all ober for you! I think a bittle boy got hurt. Are you okay, Daddy?"

Doug ripped Matty's goggles off, tossed them aside, then held the boy's chubby, bright face between both hands.

"I've never, ever been better."

He pulled both kids down on top of him and howled with laughter. A few heads turned and shot him disgusted looks.

He ignored them and got to his feet, unable to shake the smile plastered to his face.

"Dad, we have blood all over us." Sydney went pale. "How will we ever...what will mom think...will it...?"

"It washes off, honey. It washes off."

DADQUEST

The wizard glided across the cavernous magicarium, only the tips of his toes touching the stone floor. The robes fluttering behind him were a deep shade of turquoise and decorated with white and gold needlework depicting runes of a long forgotten language—very enchanted, indeed. As cool as he looked, and as powerful as the robes were, he was really just a frail old man forever fighting his way out of the heavy bundle of ornate fabric. Such was a wizard's life.

Thankfully, over the centuries so much magic had accumulated in him that he'd become lighter than air. If not for the heavy stones placed inside the robe's pockets, Gozimir Greenbeard, the ancient and all-powerful sorcerer, would have drifted off into the sky decades ago.

That morning he found himself more full of magic than he had in a long time. It was a particularly special day. After spending decades alone in his mountain fortress, speaking only to dumb animals and incoherent spirits, the Goddess was sending him company. Real, living people.

Three pupils were set to arrive at any moment. They were cherished by the Goddess above all other beings, so

Gozimir knew he must strive to become their master, their teacher, and most importantly, their protector. Even if they'd been nothing more than lowly mud farmers, the wizard would have jumped at any opportunity for company. Since settling down with the Goddess, he didn't get out much.

He tried his best to contain the giddiness he felt at being at the start of a great adventure. Wizards could be eccentric and otherworldly and even terrifying, but they were not supposed to be giddy.

Gozimir gazed into the tabletop mirror propped up on his altar. He stroked his long emerald beard, grinned widely, then flicked a speck of food from between his yellowed teeth. All the recent excitement had taken a century off his appearance.

"The Goddess!" he cried out to his reflection. "I've almost forgotten to prepare Her tributary elixir!"

Gozimir hurriedly collected his instruments of alchemy and spread them out on the altar. His boney hands trembled as he scooped magic beans into a handheld grinder. He cranked its handle till they'd been reduced to a fine powder, then coaxed the powder into a paper envelope. He dropped the envelope into a drawer extending from a small alchemical device, then poured water into a compartment behind it. When he was done, he grabbed two mugs from a high shelf and set them beside his ingenious alchemical machine.

The mug Gozimir chose for himself was smooth, featureless, and utterly common in every way. The other, which would hold the Goddess's portion of the elixir, was nothing less than a hollow brick of alabaster with a thick, orcish handle. A short prayer to the Goddess was inscribed across its face, each symbol forged lovingly by Gozimir himself long, long ago in the great furnaces of the pottery shop at the mall.

The alchemical device hissed and the elixir boiled. When the glass serving chalice was full, Gozimir bowed to it and carefully removed it from its alcove. He filled the Goddess's cup first, then his own.

"Hey Wizard!" a voice called out from behind him, nearly making him spill the chalice. "You ready? Or should we come back later?"

Gozimir spun around to find two small figures standing in the entrance to his magicarium. The first was a stout gnomish youth, a tinkerer or contraptionist of some kind, with tools and gadgets piled high on his back. The other, a female child almost half the size of the gnome, sparkled with an ethereal, eternal beauty that marked her clearly as one of the faerie folk, probably of pixie origin. They both stood staring at the old wizard, their eyes full of wonder and delight. And perhaps a little boredom, which Gozimir was quick to ignore.

Stifling his excitement, the old wizard hardened his face and demanded, "Where is the third? The Goddess declared that three pupils shall arrive today, and three is the number the Goddess has declared!"

"She's still sleeping," the gnomish youth answered. "We're sorry Lord Godzillamir, we—"

"It's *Gozimir!* And forget the 'lord' part, will you? Any wizard worth his weight in mana would never require such empty titles."

"Sorry, Master *Goz-i-mir*. Is 'master' okay?"

"Master will do!" boomed the wizard. "Did I hear you say my third apprentice is still *asleep*? Did you not try to wake her?"

"We tried, but she threw a pillow and screamed at us to get out," answered the gnome.

"She said *baaad* words!" the pixie whispered. "Words that the Goddess said we're never, ever supposed to say!"

Gozimir frowned and scribbled something on a slip of parchment. He handed it to the pixie and said, "Deliver this magic decree to the sleeping one, and go swiftly! Stop for no creature, be it demon or angel!"

"What about if I run into the Goddess?" asked the pixie.

"Of course stop for *Her!* She's the Goddess, after all," he said. "Say good morning, stay out of Her way, then hurry off to deliver my message."

The pixie studied the old wizard's writing. "What does 'UFC 193' mean, Master Gizigog?"

"It's Gozimir! *GAH-zuh-meer!*"

The gnomish youth let out an exasperated sigh. "That's not fair! Darlene gets to go to UFC 193? Mom said—"

"Silence!" the old wizard demanded. "Those strange names you mention are a repugnant sort of gibberish! Do not speak of them here in my magicarium!"

"Sorry, Master." The gnome let out another sigh and added an eye roll. "But why does *Dreadbutt the Brat* get to go to UFC 193?"

The pixie gasped. "You can't say 'butt'! That's a *baaad* word!"

The gnome ignored her. "I thought Mom—I mean, the Goddess—said bribes weren't allowed and that if this stupid make-believe stuff didn't work then we should try something else."

"Like family therapy," added the pixie.

"By Merlin's beard, no one is going to family therapy!"

cried Gozimir. "Where did you hear that? Did the Goddess say that?"

"If Dreadfist gets to go to UFC 193 then I want the new Smash Brothers game," demanded the gnomish youth.

"Can I have a Barbie Sparkle Unicorn?" asked the pixie, clapping her hands excitedly. "The one with the silver hair? It's sooooo pretty."

"Did someone say UFC 193?" A voice cried out from the hallway beyond the magicarium. A slender young elf shoved the two little ones aside and barged into the room. Her eyes shone like two green stars set in a face the color of twilight, like all dark elves of the Shadowlands. Gozimir knew by her muscular physique and bandaged hands that she must also be a Warrior in training. The third pupil prophesied by the Goddess had arrived.

"Before I forget, the upstairs toilet is clogged," the dark elf said, plucking the note from the pixie.

"Dad, are you kidding me?!" She cried out with joy. "All I have to do is play this dumb game and I get to see Heidi Holm challenge Rhonda Rousey for the belt?"

"I have no idea what you're babbling on about!" Gozimir lied, knowing full well that a pair of tickets was currently sitting in his email inbox waiting to be printed. "I demand that you all stop talking such nonsense! I am not your father, I am Gozimir Greenbeard, an ancient and all-powerful sorcerer! Whatever world you keep speaking of is no more real than a dream. It's make-believe! And today of all days you must face reality, because today you brave heroes-in-training will embark on a series of challenges which I have so wisely named *DadQuest!*"

"I thought you just said you weren't our dad," snarked the gnomish youth.

"Well, er, I'm not. It's just the name of the game.

Anyway, it matters not what I've called the quests, but that you complete them within the course of the day. Now, let's—"

"Calling it *DadQuest* kind of takes away from the woo-woo wizard fantasy stuff, don't you think, Dad?" The dark elf smiled devilishly before taking a bite from the apple she'd pilfered from the altar.

"Listen to me very carefully, you petulant pupils," seethed Gozimir. "Today, I am *not* your father! I'm Gozimir Greenbeard, the ancient and—"

A high-pitched wail cut him off.

"What do you mean you're not my Daddy?" cried the pixie, tears streaming down her plump cheeks. "You said it was all just make-believe. You said so last night!"

Gozimir flew across the magicarum and drew her into his arms.

"No, no, honey! Don't cry! I'm just *pretending* the real world is make-believe and the make-believe world is real. I'm just *pretending* to not be your daddy. It's all part of the fun! Isn't it fun?"

"Noooooooooo!" the pixie wailed. She wiped her nose with the hem of her dress and then snuggled her head under Gozimir's chin. "Instead of a Barbie Sparkle Unicorn, can I please have fairy wings? *Real* ones, not those wire and fabric ones from the costume store. Ones that let me fly *for real?*"

"I'll see what I can do," sighed Gozimir. Even though he realized he'd just fallen under the most deceptive faerie magick, he didn't care. He gave her shoulders one last squeeze and stood to face the others.

"I shall grant each of you your most desired wish, under one condition: that you complete every single quest I give you. No complaints. No sass. No half-assing. Do I make myself clear?"

"Perfectly," a voice answered from over his shoulder. He recognized her divine femininity at once and spun around to greet her.

"Your Eminence!" he said, dropping to one knee. "Your Gracefulness! Your Goddessfulness!"

The Goddess planted her fists on her hips.

"Save your groveling. We said no bribes, Seth."

The moment his mortal name left her lips, every mote of magic was banished from the room.

"And you said none of this would be too scary for Aggie, but she's already upset. Come here, baby."

She squatted and held her arms out. The six year old in the fairy dress dropped her plastic wand and ran to her mommy.

"I'm okay, Mommy," sniffed Aggie. "I was just confused about what was real and what was make-believe and who Daddy really was. He's a very good actor, Mommy!"

"I bet he is, baby."

Carla glared at Seth as she stroked her daughter's hair.

The coffee maker beeped. Seth finished filling the two coffee mugs, making sure to avert his eyes from his wife. He dropped a splash of cream into both, then handed her the one that looked like a deflated cannonball with a handle. Carla kissed the top of Aggie's head and took her coffee.

"How was the run?" Seth asked sheepishly.

As she sipped, Carla unhooked the leash from the small terrier sitting at her feet, then patted it away towards its water dish.

"The weather's perfect, you guys should spend some time outside today. If you can find time between bribes," she said, looking over the top of her mug. "Oh, and before I forget, the upstairs toilet is clogged again."

"They're not bribes, Carla!" Seth erupted. "They're just, uh...early birthday gifts!"

"Is that so? Do you normally require your children to dress up in silly costumes and do chores in order to get their birthday gifts?"

"You know, the whole super sharp lawyer thing was sexy when we were dating, but nowadays it's gotten a little—"

"As your lawyer, I advise you to be very careful about selecting your next word."

"I plead the fifth!" Seth shrank away from her and chugged half his coffee in a single gulp. "I'd ask to speak to my lawyer, but *you* are my lawyer. I demand a mistrial."

"Objection overruled," she said. "Come on, Seth. I know the past few months have been a little bumpy, but you're doing a great job of homeschooling the kids and running the house. I don't know any other men who'd hold up as well as you have."

"How many other men do you know, exactly?"

Carla couldn't resist a smirk. "I'm just saying you don't need some elaborate nerd fantasy game to pull off a successful day."

"Let's get one thing straight. It might be elaborate, but it's not a *nerd fantasy game*. It's LARPing."

"Uh, okay. I'll take your word for it."

"What is LARPing, you ask?"

"Actually, I didn't."

"LARP stands for *live action role playing*. It's interactive storytelling with pen and paper and dice, like *Dungeons and Dragons*, but way more fun. The crew and I played well into our twenties."

"Sometimes I wish I could go back before we met and meet that version of you that had a *crew*."

"No, you don't. Trust me. Anyway, the point is that I've developed my own game system. One that integrates directly into our daily routine, complete with quests, battles, experience, magic, puzzles—"

"Sounds fun! Then why do you need *bribes*, Seth? Look at them. Your kids are happy and healthy and they love spending their days with such a devoted father."

Kyle, the gnomish youth, had his head buried in a video game.

Darlene, the dark elf, was stretching on a yoga mat with music blaring from her earbuds.

Aggie, the tear-streaked pixie, was staring out the window with a finger buried in her nose.

"*Right, kids?*" Their mother asked in her courtroom voice.

The two older kids gave a quick nod, but Aggie ran to Seth and hugged his leg. "I do love it, Daddy! I'm not afraid of the make believe. I know it's just a game."

Seth's heart melted.

"Thank, sweetie."

Aggie beamed up at him. "And like Mommy told Gram-Gram, you haven't even burned down the house yet!"

"What?" Seth cried. "Of course I haven't burned down the—Wait, Carla, why were you and your mom talking about me burning down the house? You just said I was doing fine! And you're right! Right? Things are perfectly peachy here while you're off, you know, plucking poor people from the jaws of justice." His hands began shaking and some coffee splashed onto his thumb.

"Dammit!"

"As your lawyer, I advise you to chill." Carla looked him up and down. "You were very alliterative just then. You always get alliterative whenever you're over-caffeinated."

"Awesomely alliterative, amiga."

"How much coffee have you had this morning? Actually, I don't remember you coming to bed last night. Did you sleep down here on the couch?"

"Sleep? No." He snorted. "Gozimir Greenbeard doesn't waste time sleeping. I was up all night preparing our very first *DadQuest* campaign."

"Don't you know how much harder the day will be if you're sleep deprived?"

"Which is why I'm over caffeinated. Problem solved."

"I'm calling my mom to see if she can come over to help out today."

"What? No, I'm fine!"

"Yaaaaay! Gram-Gram's coming over!" Aggie pirouetted around the kitchen.

"No, Gram-Gram's *not* coming over!" Seth cried.

Carla reached for her phone, but he grabbed it first and slipped it into his back pocket. He took her hand and looked her in the eyes.

"Listen, I'm fine. I got this."

She smiled.

"I know, Seth."

He returned the smile and leaned in for a kiss.

"Gross," interrupted Darlene from her yoga mat.

Seth straightened up and announced, "*DadQuest* is going to add an aura of awesomeness to our day: to the homeschooling, the chores, and all the other monotonous stuff. When you get home this evening, you'll see the awesomeness in full swing."

"Alright, I won't call my mom." Carla stroked his face and kissed him softly on the lips. While he was still dazed, she snuck her phone from his pocket. "But I do need *this*, Gargamel."

Seth pulled away, his smile replaced by a horrified frown. "It's Gozimir! *GAH-zuh-meer!* C'mon, guys! It's not that hard!"

Carla chuckled, set her mug down, then started out of the kitchen.

"Hey, why don't you ever take your mug with you to the office?" he asked. "I made that mug for you out of 100% love and adoration."

"Shoulda left room for a little *skill*, Dad," snickered Darlene.

Seth lifted it proudly for everyone to see, his arm straining against the boulder. "I mean, how could something like this *not* bring you good luck? Bring it with you to court and it would definitely help you win cases. Not that you need help, but, uh, you know what I mean."

"Darling, while it's very romantic that the Valentine's day gift you gave me was a two hour session for yourself at the pottery store at the mall," she said, crossing her arms, "the only thing a mug with 'MAMA'S A BAD BITCH' carved into it will do is get me disbarred."

"Some jealous intern would probably drop it anyway."

"Ouch!" Aggie cried out from the dining room table. Seth set the mug down and flew to her side.

"It tried to bite me!" she said.

"A bug? Where? I'll take care of it."

"No, Daddy, it wasn't a bug! It was your big stinky book!"

Carla joined them, her eyes drawn past the mess of papers and ten-sided dice to the raggedy old tome sitting in the center of the table. It was bound in what looked like blood-stained leather and its cover was filled by the silhouette of an octopus with a large ruby protruding from its forehead.

"We have small children, Seth. Anything you bring home from that weird used bookstore near the interstate should be checked for sharp edges before you bring it in the house." Carla reached out to touch the book, but drew her hand back at the last second. "Everything you buy from there gives me the creeps."

"First of all, they have more than just books. Secondly, the place is called *Willies*. What'd you expect it to give you if not the creeps? Anyway, *this* book's a treasure. One of a kind." Seth patted the tattered cover, "I was glued to it all night."

"And that's better than spending the night in bed with me?"

"What? No!" He blushed. "Nights in bed with you are better. *Way* better."

"Gross!" complained Darlene.

"Still, this is an imported beta edition of a non-canonical Dungeons and Dragons manual. Or something like that. It has all this discontinued lore I've never heard of. I got so many amazing campaign ideas! Here, let me show you. I came up with a level 13 vengeful wraith that—"

"Nope," Carla said, putting up a hand to stop him. "Save the nerd talk for your new crew. I have to go get ready for work."

He bowed deeply.

"Thy will be done, oh Goddess! We shall commence with *DadQuest* as soon as you embark on your journey to the halls of justice."

"Oh, boy. Sounds like you three are in for a treat." Carla stopped to pummel each child's face with kisses. She glanced over her shoulder on her way out of the kitchen. "Just don't burn down the house, okay?"

Seth felt his face grow hot, but forced himself to pocket

the insult and bottle up his anger. Wizened sorcerers like him knew both insults and anger made excellent ingredients for future spells, especially when they were fresh.

With the Goddess gone, Gozimir stood glowering over his pupils.

"It's time to find out if you are truly worthy of my time. Sit with me and receive your qualifying quest!"

When no one did, he added impatiently, "Get up, you ox-minded ogres! *DadQuest* begins now!"

The pixie fairy princess plucked her finger from her nose and plopped into her chair. Gozimir had to pinch the earbuds from the dark elf's pointy ears and snatch the noisy electronic gadget from the gnomish youth. Reluctantly, they joined the pixie at the wizard's table.

He gathered his scrolls together into a pile and looked them over. When he found the one he was looking for he held it out to the dark elf.

"Good luck on thy first quest, Dreadfist, child of the Dark Forest."

She took the scroll and read it. "*Gozimir's Glorificus Glop?* Is this a recipe for oatmeal?"

"No, of course not! 'Tis a recipe for a steaming cauldron of *Gozimir's Glorificus Glop!* But, uh, yes, *technically speaking,* 'tis mostly cooked oats and honey."

"And chocolate chips?" she asked, her finger moving slowly down the page. "And marshmallows? Mom will flip when she sees this!"

"Silence! What the Goddess doesn't know won't hurt her. Or us. Now, get busy at once!"

"But I hate cooking! Can't we just have some cereal?"

"Don't be foolish! Cereal is much too common for such a special day as this! You must have ample sustenance if you are to begin climbing the hard road to redemption."

"Wait, why am I on the road to redemption?"

"Because of your dark past."

"Why do I have a dark past?"

"Because you're a dark elf, of course!"

She groaned.

"So all dark elves have dark pasts and are on the road to redemption?"

"How should I know? *You're* the dark elf! And besides, you're the only pupil old enough to use the stove." Gozimir waved her away. "Off! I'm growing hangry, and you wouldn't like a wizard when he's hangry."

"But—"

"*I'm* the game master. I'm the guy who dishes out quests. And more importantly, I'm also the guy who dishes out experience points that can be traded for UFC tickets."

"Thanks for the reminder, Godzillamir," hissed Dreadfist as she collected the pots and bowls more loudly than was necessary.

The old wizard ignored her attempt at riling him up. Instead, he stuck two bony fingers into his mouth and whistled.

A tiny pet dragon, the exact size of a small dog, came bounding into the magicarium. It was purple, scaly, and had a forked tongue dangling from its mouth. It leapt up onto the wizard's lap, its tail wagging excitedly.

"Ahh, my most magically-absorbent animal familiar and loyal companion! Get your breath out of my face. Sit, boy, sit!" He handed the gnomish youth a scroll. "You, Gadge of the Spiral Caverns, quick, receive your quest before the dragon eats it!"

Gadge unrolled the scroll and sighed. "*Responsible Dragonkeeping*. So, I walk the dog, clean the cat's litter box, feed them both...and I'm done?"

"Don't forget to give them fresh water as well. Nothing scorches your robes like a pet dragon with heartburn."

The gnome set the scroll down and smiled smugly at the old wizard. "Actually, according to *Dungeons and Dragon* official canon, *Heartburn* is a powerful dragon ability. At level 14 it transforms into *Heartfire,* which doubles its temperature, and thus doubles the damage dealt by the dragon's *Fire Breath* ability. So, then, wouldn't we *want* our pet dragons to have heartburn?"

Gozimir's mouth hung open.

"How in Gandalf's name do you know all that dragon lore?"

Gadge pulled a small glowing tablet from his pocket and held the screen toward the wizard.

"I couldn't sleep either, so I downloaded some old pdf manuals from dndlore.org," he said. "By the way, which version of the battle system are we using?"

"What other sites are you going to late at night, huh?" asked Dreadfist, laughing.

"Shut up, *Dreadbutt!*" cried Gadge.

The old wizard snatched the tablet from the gnomish youth. He turned it around in front of his wrinkled face.

"What *is* this? Your mother's—I mean, the Goddess's—old iPod Touch? I thought we threw it out months ago."

"I fixed it," explained Gadge. "Then I jailbroke it and installed an open source operating system that let me customize the—"

"Enough!" fumed Gozimir, slipping the device into his robes. "As cool as that all sounds—and later you should definitely show me how you did all that—this is neither the time nor the place for such distractions! Your dragons need tending! Hurry, lest your glorificus glop grow cold!"

He handed the small dragon to Gadge, who grabbed a leash from the wall and darted out the back door.

"Dang, you've been out-nerded on your first day as GM," taunted Dreadfist. "And I thought you were supposed to be an expert at this game."

"I've been dishing out quests since I was your age! I *am* an expert!"

"Until you met the Goddess and she made you ditch your crew."

"Nice try, vagabond! It's just like a dark elf to try to push a wizard's buttons. But you forgot, I can peer into your soul. I can see your deepest secrets. For instance," Gozimir held out the pair of earbuds he'd pinched from her ears, "you put these in your ears so it looks like you don't care, but then you turn the volume down so you can still be part of the conversation. Even though you'd never admit it, you actually love your family."

The dark elf bristled at the mention of love and went back to making the glop. The wizard smirked at his minor victory and crouched beside the pixie.

"At last we come to our pixie friend, the very magical and very beautiful, Miss Fairy Princess."

The faerie child wiggled with delight.

"Before I give you your quest, I must ask you something. Your last name is Princess, correct?"

"Yes, nice mister wizard man. And my first name is Fairy." The pixie beamed up at him. "You said I could choose any name I wanted to even if Darlene was very, *very* mean about it."

"I was not!" Dreadfist cried from her bubbling cauldron.

"She was too! She said my name sounded dumb and it wasn't even a name and she laughed at me in a mean way."

"Oh, sweetie!" said Gozimir. "Care not for the opinion of a dark elf! They have the most hideous taste in art and absolutely no manners about it. What I was going to ask was this: Are you related to that famous Ice Princess?"

"Why yes I am, mister wizard man! She's my great auntie on my Mommy's side."

"How wonderful! I hear she's got the most splendid ice cream at her ice palace. Is that true?"

"Yes, she does! I've tried all the flavors and they're wonderful!"

"You'll have to tell me all about it later!"

"Maybe you can go there with me and try some yourself!"

"That sounds lovely," Gozimir said. "Thank you, my dear. But before we run off to her Ice Palace, here is your first quest."

He handed her a small stack of scrolls.

The pixie squealed. "Ice Princess coloring pages!"

"*Activity* pages," he corrected. "There's a maze in there somewhere, I think."

"Thank you, nice mister wizard man! I'll go get my crayons!"

Once the pixie had fluttered off, Dreadfist cleared her throat.

"So I get glop, Gadge gets dragon duty, but the Fairy Princess gets *coloring pages*?"

"Activity pages," retorted Gozimir. "Besides, she's only six! She can't do much anyway. And it helps her practice her reading skills."

"Whatever."

"If I were you, I'd stop complaining and stir that glop! Otherwise, it'll stick. And I'll give you one guess who's quest it is to clean the cauldron."

Gadge reappeared, panting. "All done."

Gozimir eyed him suspiciously.

"You've already completed everything on your *Responsible Dragonkeeping* list?"

"Ran the dog. Filled their food dishes and water." The gnomish youth shot the wizard a look. "But I'm not messing with the litter box."

Gozimir stared at him incredulously.

"Scooping the dragon's dung was an integral task within the broader quest! Why didn't you do it?"

"No way am I touching whatever weird prank you have going on in there. Too gross, even for me."

"A wizard of my caliber does not meddle with pranks, my dear boy. Explain thyself!"

Gadge sighed.

"The prank tentacle you put in there to creep me out. What was it supposed to be, anyway? A cat poop demon or something? It looked pretty expensive. I can't believe you stuck it in the dirty cat litter."

"Gross, Dad!" cried Dreadfist.

The gnomish youth leaned back in his chair.

"Mom's gonna flip."

"Flip! Flip! Flip!" the pixie chanted as she dragged a crayon mercilessly across her page.

"I didn't put anything in the litter box." Gozimir rubbed his tired eyes. "What did you see? Did an animal get into the garage or something?"

"Whatever," Gadge said. "Anyway, I'm not touching it."

"*Gozimir's Glorificus Glop* is ready!" cried Dreadfist. "Get it while it's still mucilaginous!"

The dark elf handed bowls to the old wizard and her fellow pupils, then joined them at the table. They gobbled up the cooked oats, syrup, chocolate chips, and mini-marshmallows in silence. When they were done, Gozimir set his spoon down and looked his pupils over.

"Congratulations. You've each passed your initial quest and have become my pupils. Time for the *real* challenge to begin!"

He handed them each a scroll.

"Dishes," grunted the dark elf. "Big surprise." She crumpled the scroll, grabbed the dirty bowls, and stomped off to the sink.

"Yard work!" cried Gadge. "But I was just out there!"

"Good! Then you already know the way," Gozimir said. "Oh, and take the dragon with you. He keeps trying to jump up on the table."

Fairy Princess's face was twisted up in concentration as she tried to work out the words written on her scroll. "Lay... yoon...dry?"

"Very good!" cheered Gozimir. "The word is *laundry*. LAWN-dree. The 'y' makes an 'e' sound."

"Laundry! But that means..." She hopped off her chair and cuddled up to the old wizard. "The basement..."

Gozimir mustered the will to resist her fairy charm and gently peeled her away.

"Yes, it does. But you have nothing to be afraid of. This is our house and it's perfectly safe. I opened all the curtains down there, so it's bright and sunny. The basket's next to the dryer. Just empty the dryer into it and bring it up here to fold. Piece of cake!"

"Can't you come with me, nice old wizard man?"

"I regret that I cannot join you, little one. Alas, my skills are required on an important quest of my own—one handed down by the Goddess Herself. And if you think *your* quest sucks, wait till you see this."

He rummaged through the cleaning closet and

produced a long wooden stick with a rubber suction cup attached to one end.

"My task is to wield this rubber staff against whatever foul demons are clogging our upstairs toilet. Pray for me! Pray that my soul returns in one piece!"

His three pupils rolled their eyes and moped off to complete their quests.

ACROSS THE HALLWAY at the top of the stairs stood the bathroom door. Gozimir climbed each step with care, knowing the slightest creak could alert his foe.

It wasn't the season for slime molds to be migrating through these parts, but even if it was they'd be easy enough to smite with a simple purification spell. Their prowess and attack levels were low relative to the experience points they gave, making them good mobs for young adventurers. The old wizard took note to find a few for his pupils to battle later in the week.

Their busy schedule made it hard to squeeze in even a few slime molds. Wednesday was full of music lessons and Friday was already booked solid with trips to the library and the zoo. Gozimir considered sneaking in a quick battle on Thursday between math and the feast of Chinese takeout he had planned for lunch.

He tip-toed to the bathroom door.

Gozimir knew that more likely than unseasonal slime molds was the probability that one of his careless young pupils had tried to dispose of too many wiping scrolls at one time. He sighed, recalling all the times he'd reminded them that their old pipes required a flush between every single scroll.

Gozimir used his staff to push open the door. A foul

stench lingered in the air. The toilet lid was up and the bowl was overfilled with water. He crept across the linoleum and lowered the rubber end of his staff into the water, careful not to splash.

Just then, he heard glass shatter downstairs. Startled, he yanked the staff back, causing water to spill all over the toilet and floor.

"Dreadfist!" he called out. "Are you okay?"

"Yeah, I'm fine," she called back. "Just dropped a bowl. I'll clean it up."

The old wizard returned to his quest. He reinserted the rubber cup and plunged the wooden handle up and down until he heard a gurgle. The water didn't drain, so he lifted his staff to try the suction again and noticed that something was lodged in the very bottom of the toilet. It looked like a faded green rubber ball, probably something one of his pupils had been playing with. Goddess only knows why they'd tried to flush it.

"Dang it, guys! Not cool!"

The foul smell had grown more pungent. He flipped the exhaust fan on and scowled at the toy stuck in the toilet drain. The rubber staff was useless. He'd have to grab hold of the stupid ball and pull it out with his hands.

But not without gloves. He searched under the sink and found a pair of old dishwashing gloves they used for cleaning exceptionally gross bathroom messes. He slid them on, and as he was turning back towards the toilet something caught his eyes at the bottom of the basin. There was another greenish bulge wedged tightly into the sink drain.

"What the hell?!" he cried. "Wait, is that *playdough?* Why? Why would you put it down the—?"

He was interrupted by a sudden explosion of bubbles in the toilet water. The bulge in the sink drain burped loudly and began expanding. Another belch came from behind the shower curtain, followed by a sploosh and a wet thud.

Gozimir leapt backward toward the bathroom door. Maybe it was unseasonal slime molds after all.

As he wondered whether slimes molds were covered by their insurance policy, something rustled behind the shower curtain. Before he could react, four slimy green fingers curled around the edge of the shower curtain and began slowly drawing it aside.

Seth clenched his eyes shut. More dishes crashed downstairs, but he couldn't hear them over his pounding heart. The sleep deprivation had caught up with him and his imagination was overriding his senses. He was obviously hallucinating. To make the hallucination go away, all he had to do was pause, collect himself, and take a deep breath.

When he was finished exhaling, he opened his eyes.

A humanoid frog creature the size of a child stood dripping in the shower.

A bowl-shaped indentation on the top of its head was filled with a frothy brown liquid. Thin tufts of hairs clung to its glistening green scales. Beady black eyes looked him up and down.

Seth recognized it from the huge dirty tome he'd scored from *Willie's*. It was a *kappa*, a river sprite from Japanese mythology, known for hanging around stagnant bodies of water and terrorizing humans.

The kappa flashed a gnarled row of yellow fangs at Seth, who responded like any rational wizard would respond by swinging the plunger at the thing's head as hard as he could. The monster croaked painfully and shrank back. Before Seth could get in another swing, it lunged out of the bathtub and clasped its arms and teeth around his ankle.

Seth yelped and tried to kick it away, which only made it bite down harder. He brought the wooden end of the plunger down on the kappa's head while using his free foot to kick at its body. After a flurry of whacks and stomps, the kappa split open and a bluish brown liquid pooled underneath it. The thing's jaw loosened and it stopped moving. Panting, Seth kicked it aside and stepped back.

A second kappa stood in the toilet and a third in the sink. They looked at their slain brother and belched a watery growl.

Seth felt a surge of confidence flow through him. The hallucination made no sense and he was sure he needed a nap when it was over, but for the moment he felt powerful. It was like he'd become a real life Gozimir Greenbeard, an adventuring wizard in his prime, ready to take on any beasties who crossed his path. He'd smited one kappa already, and it had been pretty easy. He knew he could face two more.

Just then, the toilet tank exploded and three more kappas spilled out onto the floor.

Confident or not, he wasn't stupid. A plunger wasn't enough to handle five monsters at once. The time to flee had come.

The kappa pounced. Seth shrieked and threw his plunger at them, then dove into the hallway and slammed the bathroom door shut behind him. It took his whole weight to keep it closed as ten dripping fists pounded furiously from the inside.

The inside! The door's lock could only be accessed from the inside. If he tried to slip his arm in to lock it, those yellow fangs would take off his hand. Also, the moment he eased up the door they'd pry it open and escape.

How would a real wizard deal with a situation like this?

He'd use real magic, of course. But Seth was pretty sure he didn't have any real magic. Then again, five minutes ago he'd been sure kappas weren't real, either.

He raised his hand and swirled it in the air. He snapped his fingers. He threw an imaginary fireball down the hall. Nothing happened.

Yet the door behind him still bulged. His magic might not be real, but whatever left that wound on his ankle was. Seth tried not to think of what they might do to the kids if they got out of the bathroom.

The thought of his kids turned his attention to the chaos erupting downstairs: glass breaking, doors slamming, the dog yapping. Beneath those sounds was the muffled voice of a pixie crying out for help.

Seth dug his heels in and frantically searched his mind for a plan.

DREADFIST SULKED over a wash basin of hot suds. She'd forgotten to rinse the dishes while they were still warm, so everything was plastered with a cold, cementitious layer of *Gozimir's Glorificus Glop*.

As she scrubbed a bowl she replayed the fight she'd had with Mandy Martinez last year. Not that anyone would call it an actual fight. It was more like a beat down. Dreadfist smiled into the steam.

Mandy had learned what happens when you refer to an undefeated Muay Thai boxer as *"Darlene the dog-faced dyke"*.

And Dreadfist learned a lesson, too. She learned that if you break someone's nose on the first day of high school, you're not allowed to have a second day. In fact, they don't let you come back at all. They make you get homeschooled by your annoying dad who forces you to cook breakfast for your little brother and sister. Oh, and as a bonus, you get to do all the dishes.

The dragon was freaking out in the backyard, barking so loudly she could hear it over her music. She wished one of the bald eagles that flew over their neighborhood would swoop down and carry off the noisy little shit.

Dreadfist set the bowl in the drying rack and dried her hands. As she fiddled with the volume in her music app, the dish slipped from the rack and fell over the edge of the counter. It shattered upon impact, sending ceramic shards flying in all directions.

"Dreadfist! You okay?" she heard the old wizard call out from upstairs.

"Yeah, I'm fine," she yelled back, pausing to curse under her breath. "Just dropped a bowl. I'll clean it up."

The dark elf groaned as she knelt to pick up the large pieces. Carefully, one by one, she pinched them from the floor and lay them gently inner open hand. Just as she was going for the last punchable piece, fireworks exploded across her field of vision. Another bowl had slipped from the drying rack and shattered against on the top of her head.

"Dammit!" She touched her head and felt warm blood trickling through her hair.

Even in her dazed state, Dreadfist realized the bowl had hit her with a force much stronger than gravity. It had felt like someone had thrown it at her head as hard as they could.

Ignoring the pain, she let her instincts take over. The dark elf rolled across the kitchen floor and leapt into a fighting stance, fists in front of her face. There was a loud bang as the huge metal pot slammed into the floor right where she'd just been kneeling.

"Not funny, Kyle!" she shouted, listening for his signature giggle. "Dad? Is this part of your game or something?"

As if to answer, a cabinet flew open and a glass plate flung itself at her like a heat-seeking frisbee. Without hesitation, she threw an uppercut and obliterated the plate in midair.

Dreadfist barely had time to congratulate herself before more plates were on their way. With the speed of a trained fighter, she jabbed and punched at the dishes, shattering them in midair. A large ceramic chip-n-dip slid off a high shelf and flew at her. She jump-kicked it into the ceiling where it exploded and rained down in a million pieces.

Her cell phone chimed a notification into her earbuds. She deflected an oncoming coffee mug then quickly tapped her phone to answer the call.

"Darlene!" It was her dad's voice, panicked and out of breath. "Are you okay? Are Kyle and Aggie with you?"

"I don't know how you're doing this, Dad, but it's a little too intense—even for me." She axe-kicked an oncoming baking tray to the ground, pinning it under her foot while she waited for the next wave of dishes. "Although now that I'm winning, it's not that bad. Maybe even worth the head wound."

"Head wound?" he asked, his voice quivering. "Honey, are you okay?"

"I think it might be over now, most of the cabinets are empty."

"The kitchen cabinets? What happened?" Before she could answer, he added, "Nevermind! Listen to me, whatever's happening down there *isn't* me! I repeat: Whatever's happening isn't part of my game. Well, actually, yes it is. Well, some of the ideas, the quest titles seem to—anyway, it's real! And I think it's trying to kill us."

"Yeah, right," she scoffed. "Sure it is."

Telling her it's all real is obviously what a mega-nerd like her dad would say to enhance his role-playing game master cred. She had absolutely no idea how he was pulling it off—some air pressure trick, or maybe magnetism—but she was impressed. Her mom wouldn't be. The kitchen was full of broken dishes and her fourteen year old daughter was in need of stitches. If this was all some elaborate game device, Dad was in deep shit.

The kitchen drawers began rattling, and it occurred to her just then that if he was actually telling the truth, then *she* might be the one in deep shit.

"Darlene, are you still there? Tell me what's happening!"

Out of the corner of her eye she noticed a flash of violet light. The ruby embedded on the cover of her dad's ancient nerd book was glowing. All the papers on the table stirred as if a constant wind was swirling over them. The air smelled faintly of bugs being torched under a magnifying glass.

"Your old stinky book. Somehow the book is doing this." she muttered, her eyes back on the kitchen drawers. They were now fully open and rattling even more fiercely.

"Where's your brother and sister? Can you see them? Are they okay?"

A shimmering swarm of silverware levitated high in the air. Among the spoons and forks she couldn't help notice more frightening utensils: a cheese grater, a meat tenderizer, and several knives of various lengths. Her mother's butcher knife took its place at the front of the swarm.

Darlene stepped backward.

"Shit, Dad. Now all the silverware is, uh, floating in the air. And it all looks pissed."

"*What?*"

"All the dishes flew at me and I smashed them," she said, taking another step back. "But I can't exactly punch or kick knives... What should I do?"

"Knives?!" Seth shouted through the phone.

"Yes, Dad! There are flying knives pointing at me. What don't you understand?" asked Darlene. "They look like they're waiting for me to make a move."

"*Knives?*" he repeated.

"Dad!"

"Okay, listen, I got it! Run up here, to the bathroom! I'm just outside, in the hallway."

"What if I can't make it?"

"You can make it, baby. You're fast. Run right at me and be ready to hit the floor, okay?"

Darlene had no idea what he had planned, but she couldn't think of anything better. If she hesitated or faltered for even a second, she'd be cut to ribbons. Her only chance was to move decidedly in one direction, toward her father, and trust that he knew what he was doing.

"One...two...three!" she cried, then dove through the kitchen door into the hallway. The butcher knife and the other floating missiles sprang into action. Darlene sprinted through the family room, around another corner, then back toward the kitchen on her way to the stairs. The silverware was never more than a few feet behind her.

She climbed the stairs three at a time. Her dad sat in front of the bathroom door, his face red and drenched in sweat. He looked over her shoulder and his eyes went wide.

"Drop!" he yelled.

Darlene dropped into the fetal position and buried her head in her arms. At the exact same moment, Seth flung the door open. She caught a glimpse of the silverware colliding with a few fairly surprised little green men just before her father slammed the door and leaned against it.

Darlene lay panting, trying to calm her nerves. From behind the bathroom door came painful wet screams and the sound of a butcher shop on a busy afternoon.

"Are you okay, honey?" Seth crouched beside his daughter, tenderly examining her head.

She waved him away. "It's just a scratch, I'm fine! What's going on, Dad? Flying dishes? And what were those...things in the bathroom?"

"I don't know. I mean, I *do* know. They were kappa—Japanese water sprites—probably around level fifteen or so, and maybe imbued with some kind of rage spell."

Darlene rolled her eyes.

"What the hell are they doing in our bathroom, Dad?"

"That I don't know. I mean, they can't be real..." He looked at the tender torn flesh on his ankle. "But somehow they are."

"The book!" she cried. "The ruby! It's glowing, all neon and spooky. There's some kind of evil force radiating from it. I could feel it!"

Seth ran his hands through his hair.

"Of course. Once again, I screwed up. It's my fault. I brought whatever this is into our house and now—"

"Who cares who's fault it is! How do we stop an evil book?"

He looked at his daughter as if he were about to say something profound, then made a face and shrugged.

"Dad, what would *Gozimir Greenbeard* do?"

"How should I know? I'm not him! I'm *me*, Seth. Race: Human. Class: Screw-up."

"Then should we call mom?"

"Are you kidding? I'd never hear the end of it."

He exhaled and caught his daughter's eyes.

"It's up to me to keep you all safe. Not some make-believe wizard, and not your mom."

"I'm with you, Dad," she said, taking his hand. "I'll go with you to face the evil magic book. We'll destroy it together."

"Are you crazy? That sounds like a *wizard* plan," he said, pulling her down the stairs. "No, the Seth plan is much simpler. We get your brother and sister and then we get as far away from that book as possible."

THE GNOMISH YOUTH dragged his feet across the stone path, his tiny dragon trotting beside him. He hated physical labor and he hated being outside—especially this time of day when the sun glared directly overhead. He yearned for the cool darkness of his cave, where he was surrounded by his favorite things: electronics, magazines, and snacks.

Being more clever than your average gnome, Gadge developed a few tricks to free himself from physical labor. For example, he'd found a few old robot vacuums at the secondhand store, nursed them back to health, and installed wheels better suited for outdoor concrete. A little customized reprogramming, and now they did all the sweeping for him.

Using the brains of another old robot vacuum and some schematics he found online, he'd turned the family's lawn-mower into an autonomous, self-mowing *LawnBot*. He'd also modified the sprinkler system by adding rain sensors, soil sensors, and a programmable auto-fertilization drip to make sure the lawn got exactly what it needed, when it needed it, all without him having to lift a finger.

These inventions were so effective at doing Gadge's

yard work that he could spend his "chore" time focused on developing another important life skill: video games.

The gnomish youth slipped into the garden shed, reached behind some old terracotta pots sitting on a high shelf, and grabbed a slender plastic bin. He opened it and smiled. No one had discovered it yet. Why would they? No one has needed to visit the shed in ages.

Gadge pressed a button on the side of the tablet and watched the screen buzz to life. His pet dragon was just outside the shed door, barking up a storm at something in the sky.

"What is it, boy? Another bald eagle? A turkey vulture?" he asked as his tablet booted up. The tiny dragon ignored him and went on yapping.

Gadge opened the app he'd written to control his Lawn-Bot. With a single tap of the screen, he woke up his creation. From around the corner he heard the growl of the mower's motor turning itself over. He tapped again to initiate the mow sequence. The lawnmower appeared from around the shed, without anyone pushing it, and headed straight for the grass. Gadge knew that in about thirty minutes the entire lawn would be freshly mowed and his hands would be as clean as they were when he left the house.

The dragon ran into the shed, nipped at the gnomish youth's ankle, then ran back outside.

Gadge sighed, then craned his neck through the narrow shed door. He glanced up, but the glaring midday sun made it impossible to see anything. The dragon yapped at the air, ran around in a nervous circle, then yapped some more.

Gadge stepped back inside the shade of the shed and realized how hot his face had felt in the sun. He flicked a weather icon on the tablet.

"A high of sixty seven?" he asked himself, then stuck his hand out into the bright sunlight. "Wrong again, stupid meteorologists. Good thing I'm covered. No sweating for me today."

He opened another app and tapped out a command. The purring of electric motors whirred to life beneath a low shelf across from where he sat. He tapped again, commanding his vacuum robots to roll themselves outside and get to work. The small fleet danced across the patio in unison as their little whirling brushes swept debris into their hungry mouths.

"This is the life," the gnomish youth said, grinning. He tapped an icon with two small spaceships engaged in battle. The words *Space Smuggler Sim* flashed across the screen and were replaced by a spinning satellite dish—the game's loading indicator. Gadge's mouth began to water. He grabbed a candy bar from the plastic bin and tore it open.

Outside the shed the tiny dragon growled at something directly overhead.

"Cool it, Benny!" Gadge said, shooting his pet a dirty look.

Before he looked back at his screen he noticed an enormous shadow sweep across the yard.

Gadge dropped the tablet and stuck his head out of the shed to peek at the sky. Between the glaring sun and the sweat in his eyes, he couldn't see a thing.

"I've done my part of the chores," he told himself. "The bots can do the rest."

He eyed his house on the far side of the yard. The door that led to the kitchen was a straight shot across the lawn. Around the side yard were steps leading down to their basement. Either would do, as long as his dad didn't catch him.

The shadow reappeared over a corner of the yard and vanished.

Gadge shielded his eyes and squinted, but the sun made it impossible to see anything.

His candy bar had almost completely melted in his hand, so he did what any sensible eleven year old would do and licked his knuckles clean. When he was done, he stashed the wrapper and wiped his hands on his pants. He checked the time on his tablet. The mower still needed eighteen minutes to finish mowing, and the sweepers would be done in five.

Space Smuggler Sim had finished loading. He turned the volume all the way up, but still couldn't hear the game's background music over the little dragon's constant barking. Gadge leaned out of the shed to shush his pet when another shadow zipped overhead. He flinched and ducked back inside. This time he had been able to make out the flapping of enormous wings in the outline of the shadow. Despite the blaring sun overhead, his blood turned to ice.

"Must be a trick of the light," he told himself. "It's just a turkey vulture flying really high and casting a huge shadow."

Despite his certainty that the shadow was just an illusion, he plopped the tablet back into its plastic bin and eyed the kitchen door across the yard.

"I don't care if Dad sees me. I can watch the bots do the yard from inside the house." He crouched into a runner's stance and counted silently to himself, "3...2...1!"

The gnomish youth sprang from the shed. Outside the sky was blindingly bright, as if the sun itself was hanging just overhead. Gadge didn't get more than a few steps across the lawn before a pair of talons the size of daggers swooped down from the glaring sky and took hold of his tiny pet. He heard the flutter of huge feathers and felt a wave of excruciatingly hot wind that pushed him back inside the shed.

Gadge slid the door panels shut and fell to his knees. He tore off his sweat-soaked t-shirt and patted down his face while his vision cleared.

"There's a phoenix...a non-respawning legendary mob... in my backyard. But that's..." he trailed off, panting. "That's not possible."

He closed his eyes and pinched himself hard, but when he opened them again he was still in the shed.

"Okay, guess it's not a dream."

New sounds invaded the dim shed. The LawnBot's motor chugged as if it were in distress. There was the fierce beating of wings followed by the roar of a bonfire flaring up.

Gadge cracked open the doors to take a peek.

In the center of his lawn perched a giant bird made of fire. It had Benny, who was still yapping ferociously, pinned under one claw and his LawnBot pinned under the other.

Kyle, forgetting all about his gnomish alter ego, had to stop himself from crying out for his dad. It might not have seen him yet, and the last thing he wanted to do was draw attention to himself. Besides, he didn't think his dad would be much of a match for a giant flaming bird of prey.

The phoenix was at least fifteen feet tall from butt to beak, with fiery wings that spanned the entire width of the yard. Its beak glowed like hot steel under a blacksmith's hammer and its breath shimmered with the heat of a yawning kiln. Its eyes blazed like two small suns, flicking back and forth between the prey it had just caught. He'd seen a phoenix portrayed in video games and movies, but they looked like canaries compared to the creature that stood torching his lawn with its mere presence.

Poor Benny, his white fur singed black, whimpered and

squirmed under a fiery talon. Kyle scanned the garden tools for something he could use to help free his dog. He lifted a shovel, peeked again at the giant bird in his lawn, then set it back against the wall. Finally, his eyes settled on a red plastic canister.

He picked up the gas can and sloshed it around. It was more than half full.

If he aimed for its head, the resulting explosion might actually kill the creature. But if not, it should at least buy him enough time to make it to the kitchen door. And if Benny was lucky the creature would lose his grip and allow him to scamper away.

Kyle slid the shed doors apart slowly. Hot wind blew past him and swirled inside the shed. The phoenix, focused on pecking at the LawnBot, didn't seem to notice him as he crept out into the blistering sun. It didn't even seem to notice when he swung the gas can a long arc directly at its head. Yet, at the very last second, the giant bird snapped open its molten beak and let the projectile fly straight down its gullet. Its chest expanded and Kyle heard a muffled explosion from somewhere inside the beast.

The phoenix gazed menacingly down at the boy, screeched, then flipped the claw that pinned Benny into the air. The tiny dog disappeared into its beak.

Kyle dove back into the shed. He tried to slide the doors shut behind him, but they were too hot to touch, so he ducked into a far corner and buried his face in his hands.

Despite watching his dog being eaten alive by a mytho-logical bird made of fire—and knowing he was probably next—his video games called to him. If these really were his last few minutes alive, he might as well spend them doing what he loved most.

He grabbed the tablet off the ground and flicked it on.

Before his finger could tap *Space Smuggler Sim*, a white icon with a blue water drop caught his attention and sent his mind reeling.

It was the app used to control the programmable sprinkler system he'd installed last summer.

The sprinkler system was essentially an array of high pressure water cannons.

He got to his feet and glared at the phoenix. He guessed that when it was finished pecking at his LawnBot it would come for him. This was his final attempt at escape. He'd either make it to the house or he'd become the monster's next meal.

Kyle opened the app. The system status indicator light was green. He dragged the WATER PRESSURE slider to its max setting and tapped the big blue 'SPRINKLERS ON' button. There was a *cla-click* from the pump beside the shed and then a *whoosh* of water rushing through the buried pipes. Then, at last, two dozen miniature black towers emerged from the grass and began firing jets of water in a criss-cross pattern across the yard.

Without waiting to see what effect the water had on the phoenix, he bolted. He knew that if he so much as glanced at the monster he might lose his nerve, so he kept his head down and his eyes on the side yard.

Once he'd safely reached the stairs that led down to the basement he allowed himself a quick glance over his shoulder. The giant bird shrieked in pain as steam hissed from blackened wounds left by the sprinklers. It flailed and flapped its wings, but the water seemed to make it too heavy for flight.

Kyle's finger hovered over the 'SPRINKLERS OFF' button. Before he could decide whether to push it or not, he noticed a rhythmic pounding coming from behind the basement door. It sounded like the heavy thuds of an off-balanced washing machine, except louder and accompanied by angry grunts. Beneath the pounding and grunting he heard the panicked cries of his little sister.

He tapped the button, tossed the tablet aside, and ran down the steps as fast as he could.

MISS FAIRY PRINCESS—KNOWN commonly to her family as Aggie, but known magically to her new friends as the *pixie*—stood staring down the narrow stairwell. It wasn't that she didn't like her daddy's new make-believe game. She liked quests that involved dressing up in pretty clothes or coloring pictures of the Ice Queen. But she hated, more than anything else in the whole wide world, having to go down into the basement all by herself—even when daddy opened the high windows to let some daylight in.

Not daddy, she reminded herself. *Today, he's mister nice old wizard man.*

With all that light came plenty of shadows where nasty things could hide. Mean things. Scary things. Things that would jump out and get her as soon as she turned her back.

Still, the nice old wizard man had gone through all the trouble to design this make-believe game for her. He wanted to make their days more fun, although she wasn't sure how that would be possible. Every day since he lost his job and became their homeschool teacher was like a holiday. Sometimes things got pretty messy and momma—the Goddess—got pretty upset. But he always tried so hard take care of her and her big sibs that she knew, without a doubt, he loved them. She couldn't let him down, no matter what. Besides, how else was she going to earn her wings?

Clenching her tiny fists, the pixie slowly descended into

the basement. Towards the bottom she got spooked and made a daring leap over the last few steps.

The nice old wizard man had told her the truth. Because the high windows lined all four walls, bright sunshine filled the basement with light. There were hardly any shadows at all.

Across the room stood the dryer. It wasn't making any noise and a green light blinked on its dials, which meant the laundry was finished drying. She stood perfectly still, trying to gather the courage to trek across the basement floor. Other than the kitchen floor creaking above her and the dog barking outside, the basement was perfectly silent.

A moth fluttered against one of the high windows. It was a small white moth with a few black spots on its wings.

"Wings," the pixie whispered to herself. "If I help the nice old wizard man, I'll earn my wings."

She spread her arms out to either side and tiptoed across the cold cement floor.

When she got to the dryer, she let out a huge sigh and relaxed. Nothing had gotten her. Soon she'd be done with her quest and back upstairs with the others. Maybe there would be more coloring pages after lunch.

A bundle of clean clothes stared back at her through the glass dryer door. The pixie grabbed the empty laundry basket and positioned it to catch the laundry once she pulled the door open.

As she reached for the door, her attention drifted to a row of dirty hampers lined up next to the washer. That meant the nice old wizard man planned on doing many more loads of laundry today. That meant she'd be sent down here many more times to collect it.

The thought of having to face the basement again sent a shiver down her spine. Fear began to crowd out her meager courage; she had to use every ounce of willpower to resist the urge to dart back upstairs.

"You can do this," the pixie whispered to herself. "You're a magical fairy princess and you're strong, just like Mommy—er, I mean, the Goddess."

She yanked the dryer open and emptied the clean laundry into the basket, not bothering to close the door or clean the lint trap. The nice old wizard man could do that later. Instead, she dragged the heavy basket toward the stairs as quickly as her little feet could manage.

When she got there, the pixie turned around and climbed the first step. The moth was still flapping against the window. The air was still bright and calm. Despite the apparent lack of danger, she suddenly felt something hiding just around the corner, something ready to pounce, something *dark*.

She climbed a step higher and pulled the basket up onto the bottom step. Its base was wider than the step, so it tilted precariously over the edge. If she lost her grip, the basket could tumble all the way down to the basement floor—and then she'd have to go pick it all up and start over.

The pixie gripped the basket as tightly as possible and pulled it up another step.

"Great, only about a bazillion steps left."

When she tried to yank the basket up to the fourth step, it wouldn't move. She pulled harder—it resisted. The bottom of the basket seemed snagged on the edge of the step. The pixie gritted her teeth, grabbed the basket with both hands, and strained as hard as she could to pull it free.

Before she knew what was happening, the she was tumbling down the stairs.

A bright flash of light exploded across her vision as her head hit the cement floor. She sat up and straightened her plastic tiara. Somehow she'd lost her balance and taken a spill down the bottom few steps. She nursed the bump on her head, grateful she hadn't fallen from the top of the stairs. Flying could wait til she earned her wings.

Clean clothes were scattered everywhere. The pixie looked for the basket, her head still ringing, and noticed that the row of dirty hampers on the other side of the basement had also fallen over. They were all laying on their sides, spewing dirty towels and sheets and underwear in all directions.

"Look at this mess!" pouted the pixie. "I'd better clean it up before the nice old wizard man sees it."

Frowning, she tried to pick up one of the gnome's disgusting soiled socks, but it wiggled out of her hand like a frog. A pair of her sister's shorts lurched and rolled between her legs. A bed sheet slithered past her.

All at once, the cozy serenity of the basement was replaced by a bustling chaos of laundry moving all by itself.

The terrified pixie turned to run to the stairs, but clothes began swirling around her like a tornado inside a laundromat. She collapsed onto her floofy fairy skirt and buried her face in her hands. She felt her bladder start to loosen, but refused to pee herself. Little babies peed themselves, but big girl fairy princesses were too old for that sort of thing. Not even when their daddy's make-believe game became really, *really* scary.

Through the wall of swirling fabric she saw the stairs leading up to the kitchen, to her family. She wished she had wings so she could fly out the top of the tornado and upstairs to safety. But she didn't have wings. She wasn't really a magical fairy princess. She was just a little girl who needed her mommy or daddy or big sister, or even her annoying stinky brother, to come rescue her.

Aggie screamed at the top of her lungs. Usually, whenever she did that in a dream, no sound came out. That was one way she knew she was just dreaming. But this time so much sound came out that her ears stung.

"Someone help! Please! Help me!"

There was the thumping of footsteps in the kitchen upstairs, but no one came.

All around her whirled a mix of clean and dirty laundry: her daddy's big comfy hoodie, her brother's gross t-shirts, her sister's sweaty gym shorts, her mommy's big girl bras.

"They're just clothes," she told herself weakly, then added with even less certainty, "clothes can't hurt me."

Aggie reached out, but her hand was slapped back by one of her daddy's leather belts. She shrank back, lowered her head, then, with a sudden burst of desperation and courage, lunged forward through the swirling wall of laundry.

Luckily, the belt wasn't nearby when she did. She was whipped by socks and pummeled by panties, but she made it through in one piece.

Her feet moved as fast as they could across the basement floor. Just as she reached the bottom of the stairwell, the tornado whirled overhead and came crashing down in front of her. Aggie skidded to a stop so suddenly that she fell backwards onto her floofy fairy skirt.

The tornado tightened and squeezed and knotted itself into a bulky human shape. Its head was squarish and its shoulders wide, with huge corded arms ending in denim fists. It looked just like one of those golems from her daddy's fancy magic book, except it was made from laundry instead of stones.

It was completely blocking any access to the stairs. And

worst of all, despite not having any facial features, the laundry golem somehow looked angrier than daddy had looked that one time she'd given his smudgy old laptop a bath.

The golem swung a huge fist above its head and brought it down on the trembling girl. She rolled out of the way just in time, letting it smash into the floor where she'd just been sitting. When it lifted its knuckles, only shattered bits of her tiara remained, as well as a faint web of cracks in the concrete below. The golem may have been made of dirty socks and undies, but it sure packed a punch.

Aggie scrambled to her feet and ran away, back across the basement where the washer and dryer stood gawking at her with their open lids. The ground shook as the golem took slow, lumbering steps after her. It wasn't moving fast, but it didn't have to. In a few more steps it would have her trapped between the appliances and she'd have no way of evading its punches.

She remembered how in one of her favorite stories the princess had hidden inside a magical pumpkin to hide from a big nasty dragon that wanted to eat her. She wasn't a princess, and she certainly didn't have a magical pumpkin, but she did have another idea.

Just as the golem got within pounding range, Aggie slipped inside the dryer and tugged the door shut behind her. She rolled into a ball and screamed for help and tried to not pee her pants.

The golem, having no fingers to grab hold of the handle, thrust its fist clumsily against the dryer door. Frustrated, it proceeded to pound the dryer, one fist after the other, on the top, the sides, the front.

Every hit shook the cramped metal cylinder and made the pixie inside give a little terrified shriek. Her little hands couldn't wipe her tears away fast enough. No one was coming to rescue her. Eventually the golem would break open the dryer and smash her to bits just like it had smashed her tiara.

Between thuds she heard a door creak open. Then she was pretty sure she heard a flurry of steps down the stairs. Then some voices.

"In here!" she cried. "I'm hiding in the dryer!"

The pounding stopped. She could see through the glass dryer door that the golem had turned away from her. It roared and lifted its arms and she heard her daddy shouting something angry.

Something struck the golem in the head, sending it stumbling sideways. Standing there, swinging mommy's ironing board like a baseball bat, was her daddy.

The golem swung a fist at her daddy's head, but he knelt and lifted the ironing board like a shield to absorb the hit. A broom handle came out of nowhere and swept one of the golem's legs out from underneath it. Its bulky mass fell backwards with a thunderous boom. Before the monster even knew what had hit it, Darlene was already delivering a series of strikes with the improvised bo staff.

She saw Daddy join in with the ironing board just before the scene was suddenly eclipsed by her brother's face. His skin was the color of a lobster and his hair looked crispy, but he was smiling.

"You gonna stay in there all day, or what?" asked Kyle.

He opened the dryer door and crouched. "Hop on, m'lady! Hurry! The beast is not yet fell, and your horse grows restless!"

Aggie tumbled out of the dryer and clung to her brother's back. He lifted her with ease and sprinted toward the stairs.

On the way, she heard more shouting and caught a glimpse of her daddy and sister battling the laundry golem. *All* of them had come to rescue her. They were the bravest people she'd ever seen.

Aggie's heart overflowed with love for her family. When everything was back to normal, she decided, she was going to make them a hundred billion friendship bracelets.

SETH and his three children burst into the hallway, slammed the basement door shut behind them, then collapsed into a tangle of hugs.

"Oh, Aggie!" cried Kyle.

"We were so scared," added Darlene.

Seth squeezed them all in one final bear hug, then set them down and checked the basement door again to make sure it was locked.

"We're safe from whatever that thing was," he said, "but who knows what else is waiting for us."

He slunk against the wall and peeked into the kitchen. His face was illuminated by a harsh violet light and his eyes went wide. The children could hear the sound of pages fluttering and a raspy voice chanting in some exotic foreign language.

"What's going on, Dad?" cried Kyle. "There's a golem in the basement and a phoenix in the backyard!"

"Don't forget the murderous cutlery in the bathroom," added Darlene. "No really, don't forget and walk in there or you'll been trouble!"

"It's like Dad's game is really happening," Kyle said, turning to his dad. "But that's impossible...right, Dad? *Dad?*"

Seth didn't move. His jaw had grown slack and he stared dumbly into the kitchen.

Darlene grabbed him by the ear and yanked him away from the door.

"Ow! Let go!"

He waved her away, then blinked and rubbed his eyes.

"The book. The *ruby*! Somehow it's bringing my role play session to life."

Darlene scoffed. "That's impossible."

"Look at me, *Dreadbutt*," said Kyle. "My hair is scorched and I look like I've spent all day at the beach without sunscreen. Whatever this is, it's definitely possible!"

Her hand went to the cut on her head and she flinched. "Okay, whatever. I guess it's possible. More importantly, how do we stop it?"

Seth looked into his children's pleading eyes and snorted.

"Stop it? That evil demonic book? Are you insane? No, we're getting the hell outta here, right now," he said, waving them down the hall. "In the car, now! Go!"

He shepherded them into the garage and straight into the minivan, then hopped into the driver's seat. With one hand he clicked the garage door opener and with the other he turned the engine over.

"Seatbelts on! And hold onto your butts, kids. Daddy's gonna drive like you've never seen him drive before."

He looked out the half-open garage door and his heart sank.

"Shit," he mumbled. "Shit, shit, shit!

Parked in the driveway, directly in front of the garage door, was his mother-in-law's BMW.

Seth killed the engine and slammed his palm against the

steering wheel. A frantic knocking came from around the front of the house and a familiar voice called out.

"Seth! What in heavens is going on in there? As a grandmother, I have rights! Open up right now or I'll call the police!"

Aggie bounced in her car seat. "Gram-Gram's here!"

"I can't believe Carla called her mother," Seth muttered to himself.

"What is that strange light in there? Is that *fire?*" Gram-Gram paused to pound her fist on the door. "Are the kids alright, Seth? That's it! I'm coming in!"

They heard the squeak of the screen door being swung open.

"Before everything started trying to kill us, the morning had been going pretty well. We all ate breakfast. The dog didn't crap in the house. Zero house fires," Seth told himself.

"What are you talking about?" cried Kyle. "Don't we need to go check on Gram-Gram?"

"Carla doesn't need to call her mother to come check in on us. She should give me a chance to show her I can handle anything that comes up during the day. I handled that first kappa, didn't I? Not all dads could've done that. You think Kevin Stropka's dad down the street—whatever his name is —could've beaten a small, child-like water sprite to death with a plunger? Pssh. I don't think so—"

Darlene punched him in the shoulder.

"Snap out of it, Dad! Grandma's in there, with the book. We have to go get her before something bad happens!"

"Right," said Seth, nursing the tender bruise his daughter gave him. "Without her keys we can't move her Beamer."

"Dad!"

"Just kidding! *Geesh!* Look, I'm going to save Gram-Gram right now!"

He opened the driver's side door, but stopped to glance at his kids in the rear view mirror. They looked battered and miserable and scared shitless.

"Don't worry, kids. Gozimir Greenbeard can handle that stinky old book. And so can Seth Madrigal." He smiled at them. "Do me a favor and stay here, okay? Whatever happens, you just stay in the van, you hear me?"

The kids nodded.

"Shouldn't we call mom?" Darlene asked.

"Of course not! The Goddess is in court all day, we mustn't disturb her."

"But—"

"Nope! Gozimir's got this." The old wizard furrowed his brow and slammed the door shut. He peered through the open window, looking each of them in the eyes. "I'll be right back."

They nodded again. He nodded back.

Then he was gone, swiftly skulking back into the house.

The book's purplish aura was coming from the living room now, not the kitchen. It had grown so intense that even from the hallway the old wizard had to shield his eyes. Despite every cell in his body telling him to flee, he crept to the end of the hall and peeked inside.

Gozimir gawked through the dazzling light and tried to make sense of what he was seeing.

The book was floating face down in the center of the room, open wide with its pages fluttering beneath it. Hungry neon tentacles dangled from its cover, writhing and grasping at the air, their purplish glow somehow absorbing as much light as it offered. The ruby burned bright and hot.

Two smaller rubies flicked toward the old wizard,

drawing his attention to a silhouette floating horizontally above the book. It was Gram-Gram, mother of his beloved Goddess. She hovered with her chest pointing at the ceiling while her arms, legs, and head hung limp behind her. Her upside-down face twisted into an unimaginably grotesque scowl and the ruby fire in her eyes flared up. From her mouth burned a voice like star fire.

"YOU HAVE BROKEN THE SEAL. YOU HAVE NOURISHED ME WITH THE DARKNESS OF YOUR NIGHTMARES. NOW YOUR IMMORTAL SOUL SHALL SERVE ME FOR ALL ETERNITY."

The voice obliterated Gozimir Greenbeard, turning the old wizard to dust.

Seth stood alone.

"Thanks for the offer, but I'm not really looking for work right now," he said, sizing up the situation. Seth Madrigal knew a thing or two about the occult, based mostly on video games and movies—but he assumed all that stuff had to be based in some ancient knowledge. From where he stood, this was clearly a classic demonic possession scenario. Some demon or evil spirit had somehow gotten itself trapped inside a book, and now, through a series of unintentional actions on Seth's part, it had been released.

Although, if the demon was already out, why would it bother with all the scary theatrics and the threatening commands? Seth figured it must still need him to do something. Otherwise, why wouldn't it just take full possession of Gram-Gram and begin its unholy rampage across the mortal world?

If his expertise in occult-based fiction had taught him anything, it was that there was always some kind of bullshit loophole to thwart a demonic possession. For example, demons are often anchored to some object, some totem, to which their manifestation in our world depends upon—like the ouija board in *The Exorcist*. Seth was willing to bet his life—literally, it seemed—that in this demon's anchor was either the book or the ruby. He knew that if he could find something to destroy them with, then maybe...

"Who are you and what do you want?" he asked, hoping to keep it distracted while he scanned the living room for a weapon.

"MY TRUE NAME CANNOT BE UTTERED IN THE PHYSICAL REALM," boomed the voice coming from Gram-Gram's mouth. "YOU SHALL CALL ME MASTER NYARLATHOTEP, MOST HIGH OF THE OUTER GODS, CONQUEROR OF THIS WORLD OF FLESH AND STONE. YOU SHALL SERVE ME OR BE DIGESTED IN THE FIERY PITS OF MY STOMACH FOR ALL ETERNITY."

"For a guy who can't stop mentioning *eternity*, you seem a little short on time."

Seth decided on the folding chair propped against the wall beside him. He'd have to be careful not to hit his mother-in-law since she was hovering right above the book. At least he'd try his best.

"Why don't you set the old lady down, nice and easy. Then you and I can talk about the whole job offer thing, okay?"

"I SHALL TURN YOUR SKIN TO MAGGOTS AND YOUR BLOOD TO PISS. I SHALL RAIN DOWN BRIMSTONE AND—"

Seth grabbed the folding chair, spun between the lashing neon tentacles, and swung the chair at the book. The chair turned to ash in his hands.

He stumbled backward before the neon tentacles could grab him. The ruby fire in Gram-Gram's eyes flared even higher and her jaw opened wider than should have been possible. From behind her dentures the demon laughed.

"NO WEAPON OF THIS WORLD CAN HARM ME. I AM THE IMMORTAL JEWEL OF THE OUTER GODS, OUTSHINING THE LESSER DEITIES LIKE THE SUN OUTSHINES THE STARS. BOW DOWN AND SERVE ME, OR BURN FOREVER WITHIN MY ETERNAL WRATH!"

Seth reached under the couch, grabbed Darlene's 35lb iron kettlebell, and brought it down with all his might on top of the ruby. Just like the folding chair, it burst into a cloud of ash upon impact.

This time, the tentacles were ready for him. They grappled Seth's forearms and slithered up his biceps, sending a frozen, searing pain shooting through his body. Urgently, ravenously, they began drawing him toward the book's cover, toward the ruby. Seth dug his heels into the carpet. He wasn't sure what would happen if he came into contact with the jewel, and he sure as hell didn't want to find out.

"WITH YOUR BLOOD I SHALL REPLENISH MYSELF AND BE REBORN. YOU, WIZARD, SHALL BE THE VESSEL WITH WHICH I CONQUER YOUR WORLD!"

Despite the searing pain and the threat of death, Seth felt a trickle of pride at being called a *wizard*. His role-play skills must be truly exceptional if he'd convinced an actual demon he was Gozimir Greenbeard.

Suddenly, the ruby didn't look so terrifying. From a certain angle it was quite stunning. He struggled to remember why he was resisting it in the first place.

"Dad!" a trio of voices cried out behind him.

Darlene grabbed his waistband and pulled. The neon

tentacles brightened and began slowly dragging them both across the carpet.

Seth snapped out of his hypnotic daze.

"I told you to stay in the van!"

"If we had, you'd be dead by now!" Darlene shouted, her face tense with strain. "I can't hold you forever! How do we stop it? Tell us what to do!"

Seth grit his teeth against the pain from the tentacles and tried to think of how to destroy the demonic gemstone. If weapons derived from the mortal world couldn't harm it, they needed a weapon derived from *outside* the mortal world. Something—*anything*—imbued with divine or mystical power.

There was a Catholic church a few blocks away where they could score some holy water. But even if Kyle pedaled as fast as he could go on his bike, it would take too long.

They needed something close by, something they could find in the house. He searched his memory for something with magic in it, something they took for granted as superstitious or silly. His mind drew a blank. Their family wasn't the least bit religious, nor had any of them ever dabbled in spirituality.

He made a note to himself that if they got out of this mess, he'd stash a few crucifixes inside their emergency supply kit—just in case this sort of thing ever happened again.

The closest Seth had ever been to encountering the divine was being married to his wife, Carla. She was sophisticated, beautiful beyond measure, and tough as nails. That's why her role in his stupid *DadQuest* roleplaying game could be nothing short of a goddess. *The* Goddess. If she were there, she'd have been able to disintegrate the demon with nothing more than a stern look.

"That's it!" Seth cried. "Kyle, go get Mom's special mug and bring it to Darlene."

"Huh?"

"Her special coffee mug! Hurry!"

"Why do you want one of mom's coffee mugs at a time like this?"

"Not *any* mug," Seth shouted, craning his neck around to look at his son. "The very special one I made for her last Valentine's day!"

"Oh, the ugly one," said Kyle.

"No! Er, I mean...yes, *that* one! Just go get it!"

Kyle darted into the kitchen, broken dishes crunching beneath his sneakers. Aggie hugged the door frame, unsure which room was more scary.

Kyle threw open the cabinet, snatched the big lumpy mug, but as he turned to run back toward the living room, something tripped him and he went down hard on the broken glass. He tried to stand, but his leg was stuck.

A power cable had shot out from one of the lower cabinets and was winding itself around his ankle. Another lashed out like a whip and caught his wrist. Inside the lower cabinet where the cables came from, he saw a toaster and a rice cooker getting ready to pounce. Behind them a blender hummed at full speed and a waffle maker snapped hungrily for its turn at the boy.

He kicked the cabinet door shut with his free foot.

"Aggie!" he yelled, turning to look for her. She was no longer trembling in the doorway. "Come get the mug and bring it to Darlene!"

The appliances thumped against the cabinet door. His knee began to buckle. A few shards of broken glass defied gravity and hovered in the air nearby. Kyle closed his eyes.

A delicate chime tinkled somewhere overhead and a

pair of tiny hands pulled the mug free. He caught a glimpse of the thief before she escaped into the living room, but what he saw made no sense, even within the context of the day he'd just had.

Aggie, his scaredy-cat little sister, had sprouted a pair of shimmering fairy wings. She was fluttering through the air like a butterfly, a flurry of rainbow sparkles trailing behind her. The smile plastered to her face was so blissful that Kyle couldn't resist smiling back.

With the grace of an angel she flew into the living room, around the stinky old book and past the hungry neon tentacles. She hovered over her big sister's outstretched hand and dropped the mug.

Using her dad as leverage, Darlene hurled herself forward and swung the lopsided, deflated cannonball of a coffee mug at the ruby.

The room filled with a burst of blinding crimson light. An ear-piercing crack rippled through the fabric of space-time, making heads ring and skins crawl.

When the light faded, the ruby was gone, leaving behind an empty crater in the tattered old tome. On the mug, the words 'MAMA'S A BAD BITCH' surged with a faintly opulent glow.

The tentacles evaporated, leaving Seth's arms free to catch Gram-Gram. Darlene jumped on the book and began stomping it like it were a huge bug. Aggie, wingless but ecstatic, threw her arms around Seth's neck and covered his face with kisses.

"You did it, Daddy! You saved us from that stinky old book!"

Seth stared at her with joyful tears in his eyes. He started to smile, then looked worried.

"Where's Kyle?" he panicked. "Kyle! Are you okay?"

His son hopped into the room, struggling to untangle limp electric cords from his leg.

"I'm fine," said Kyle. "Is it over now? Did you do it?"

Seth looked at his children, then down at his mother-in-law slumbering peacefully in his arms.

"*We* did it," he said, blinking away more tears. "Even an all-powerful sorcerer like Gozimir Greenbeard couldn't have handled that ancient evil all by himself. You've all proven yourself worthy to be my pupils. I love you kids."

They threw their arms around their dad and shared a sigh of relief.

"That really just happened, right?" Darlene asked.

"Look at my head! It'll take weeks for my hair to grow back!" cried Kyle.

"Yup. It was a classic demonic possession, kids," Seth said, shaking his head. "Came real close to getting out of control, too."

Darlene laughed.

"*Close* to getting out of control? Look around! The house is trashed!"

"But it's not on fire, is it?"

"Yay! Look! Gram-Gram's waking up!" cheered Aggie.

"Where am I?" the old woman stammered. "Where'd that horrid voice come from? Where'd it go? And where's that brave...wizard?"

Gram-Gram looked up at Seth with enchanted eyes. "It was *you*! But you were different. You *are* different! Not the lazy bum that married my daughter. You were...magnificent!"

Seth blushed.

"Everything's okay now, Rosa. Let me set you down on the couch and get you a glass of water, and then I'll explain what—"

He was interrupted by a pair of wrinkly lips pressing against his own. Gram-Gram kissed him deeply and with a passion he never imagined someone of her age could muster.

"What the *hell* is going on here?" Carla asked, dropping her briefcase just inside the front door. The screen door squealed shut behind her.

Seth pried himself away from this mother-in-law.

"Hi, honey! I was gonna oil the hinges earlier, but, uh, I got a little sidetracked."

"I'm not talking about the screen door, Seth!" she cried. "Why are you making out with my mother?"

"Making out? No! She was just thanking me."

"Thanking you for *what*? You better tell me what's going or I'll...I'll..." Carla trailed off, too upset to finish her threat.

"Before you get mad, please know that I only broke the dishes because they attacked me," Darlene added. "It was in self defense. I had no choice!"

"There was a huge burning phoenix right in the back-yard! Look at my skin!" cried Kyle. "It ate the lawnmower. Oh, and it ate Benny."

"Mommy, a laundry golem trapped me in the dryer!" explained Aggie. "But everyone was so brave and they rescued me. And I grew wings, mommy! *Real* wings!"

"Look at all of you! You look like you've been through a war! This better be make-up, guys, or else..." Carla ran a hand through Kyle's scorched hair, then examined Darlene's bloody clot of hair. "This is real blood, Seth! I thought DadQuest was supposed to be imaginary!"

"Well...funny story, actually. It started off imaginary, but then this demon—uh...a *real* demon— tried to escape from the ruby in that old book, and—"

"A demon? No more nerd stuff, Seth! I want to know what happened here today!"

"Listen to your husband, dear," Gram-Gram said, tidying up her hair. "It was a real demon alright! I should know, I was possessed by the bastard. Anyway, Seth rescued me. He was breathtaking, he was..." She stared at him, a distant, dreamy look on her face. "It was the most exciting, *romantic* thing to happen to me in a very long time!"

"Breathtaking?" cried Carla. "I'm married to him and I don't even find him breathtaking! Mom, I thought you were volunteering at the church today?"

"Don't be silly, dear. I came because you texted me and asked me to come over right away."

"No, I didn't! I've been in court. I've barely touched my phone all day."

"Well, someone sent me an urgent text message saying my grandbabies needed me, so I came right away."

She held out her phone.

"That's a message from a number listed as 666! Seth, is this some kind of joke?"

"Don't look at me! No offense to anyone here, but I don't think Rosa here would be a great candidate for fantasy role-playing! Besides, I've been a little busy fighting off the demon's minions and saving your children's lives. You know, you wouldn't think a bundle of dirty underwear could hit very hard, but you'd be wrong. It hurts. And don't get me started on how your bra straps whipped me right in the—"

"Stop!" Carla held a hand up. "No more make-believe. No more fantasy. I take it back. I don't care. I don't want to know what happened. My cases were postponed and I've had a really long day and I just want to go take a shower and then have a nice, quiet dinner."

"Good idea, honey," Seth agreed. "You go on upstairs

and take a nice, long bath while we clean up our mess. Everything will be back to normal by dinnertime. I promise."

"Uh, Dad, dinner will be tricky without any dishes," said Darlene.

"Shhh!" He swatted her away and led Carla to the stairs. On the way, she peeked into the kitchen."

"What happened to my kitchen?" she cried.

"We'll take care of everything, sweet Goddess. You just go get cleaned up. Go on."

Speechless, Carla climbed the stairs. Gram-Gram was already in the kitchen with a dustpan and broom. Seth and the kids stood in a circle with their arms around each other.

"If you liked today's adventure, you'll love what I have planned for tomorrow," he said, chuckling. "But next time maybe we'll do a little math and history before I unleash the demon, if that's okay with you guys?"

The kids nodded and laughed and squeezed him so hard he couldn't breathe.

"SETH!" Carla shouted from upstairs. "Why are all the knives on my bathroom floor? And what the hell is all this nasty green slime all over everything?"

A MAP TO ESCONDIDO

For the hundredth time that afternoon, Claire pushed aside the curtains and scanned the northern pasture. Calling it a pasture was mighty generous, considering it consisted of mostly dirt, rocks, and cacti. When she and Earle had first claimed the plot, he had big plans to build a farm and start raising some cattle. The tattered remains of that dream had become their own little ramshackle homestead, covered in dust, just three miles outside Oatman, Arizona.

She shoved the curtains closed, pushing away thoughts of the last seven years.

If today went as planned, her own dreams might finally have a chance to thrive: a garden, a home, a family. A decent life with her man.

If not, well...her daddy taught her that a frontier girl had to be tough as nails to survive in the West. Not only was she tough, but she could also read and ride and shoot. She'd find another way, assuming they survived.

Claire glanced at the shelf where Earle kept his whiskey. Just one jug left. Her normal scorn of the stuff was replaced by warm appreciation. She was glad she hadn't smashed it, as she'd done a thousand times in her imagination. Today it would be put to good use.

She scanned the horizon again. Nothing. The boys were supposed to be back hours ago. She twisted the corner of her apron between her hands and bit her lip.

Then, as quiet as an old tumbleweed tumbling across the yard, she heard faint, rhythmic hoofbeats in the distance. Three horses—one fewer than had left that morning—had come around the hill and were pounding sand straight for her little ramshackle house. Three riders, plus one suspiciously large sack slung over the leader's rear.

Her heart froze. Was her man the one in the sack? She wiped away a tear and squinted. No. She recognized his mare, his hat, his boots. Her man was safe, thank God.

Claire stood, took a deep breath, and flattened out her apron. The first part of the day's treachery was done, and now came another of even higher stakes.

By the looks of it, Gordo's men had dropped Cooper. His wife, Vivian, whom Claire sang with in the church choir, would be devastated when she found out. Still, Claire was relieved to see them slide his body into an empty garden box beside their little ramshackle barn. One less gun to argue over the day's loot.

She'd spent all day preparing the drive stock, filling canteens, and loading rifles. Once they shook the other two, she and her man would make for the loot and head straight for the coast.

Earle kicked the door open and stomped inside. Claire flew to him, threw her arms around his wide chest, and peppered his face with kisses.

"Oh, Earle! I thought you were dead! I can't tell you how glad I am to see—"

"Whiskey," he said, shoving her away. "My tongue's as dry as a rattler's ass. Be a darlin' and fetch us boys a round of whiskey."

"I'll take two," Clayton said, pushing her aside as he tromped to the kitchen table.

Claire slugged him in the shoulder as he passed.

"Mighty glad it wasn't you in that sack."

Clayton flung his boots up onto the table, lifted the brim of his hat, and arched his eyebrows.

"That so, sis? Funny, I always thought you'd be the one to put me in one of those."

"Shut your trap or I just might," she said, then pushed his feet onto the floor. "Just because I'm relieved Gordo's men didn't get you, doesn't mean your filthy boots are allowed where I take my supper."

Earle pounded his fist on the table.

"Whiskey!"

Claire jumped and scurried to the kitchen.

A lean, spectacled man appeared at the front door. It was Dr. Henry Boyle, the young Irish physician who'd arrived in Oatman last April.

"Horses are all tended to, fellas," he said. Then, noticing Claire, he took off his hat and lowered his eyes. "Evening, Mrs. Downing. I'm s-s-sorry to say that Mr. Cooper didn't make it. He took two to the b-back while we was—"

"Stop stammerin' Doc!" barked Clayton. "You sound like a damn fool!"

"He's right," Earle said, snatching the tall glass of brown liquid from Claire's hand before she could set it down in front of him. "You may be able to shoot straight, Doc, but with a stutter like that, yer liable to bore us all to death."

He emptied the glass with one toss, slammed it down, and motioned to Claire.

"Keep 'em coming."

Clayton tossed a leather satchel onto the table.

"Doc, you know the reason we let you in on this here job, and it ain't your storytelling skills. Best get started on that translation if we're gonna have enough time to loot Gordo's stash before sundown."

Doc nodded, slid a map from the satchel, and adjusted his round-rimmed glasses. His pencil went to work, dancing between the map and his notebook.

"One of you fellas mind telling me what happened to Mr. Cooper?" Claire asked as she filled Clayton's and Earle's glasses a third time.

Earle took the whiskey slow this time. When he was done he set the glass down and fixed his gaze on an empty spot on the table.

"We got to the pass early. Me and Clay set up our rifles on the ridge. Doc and Cooper hid behind a pair of large boulders at the far end. Hell, we waited hours up there, baking in the goddamn sun. Finally—much later than Clay said we would—we saw Gordo's posse ridin' up."

"I ain't never claimed to be no goddamn fortune teller!"

"I ain't said you was!" Earle hollered back. "Anyway, as I was sayin', they rode south to the pass. Gordo's lieutenant —the one charged with movin' his stash—was comin' with five men. Boy, did they come fast! Me and Clay barely had time to aim before they were in range. We took out the two riders in the front, nice and clean. Since we had multiple rifles, we didn't lose time reloadin' and we dropped two more before they even knew what hit 'em. Just like we planned."

"Just like *I* planned," Clayton said, spewing tobacco smoke into the air. "That's when Doc and Cooper came 'round the corner, guns blazin'. Took 'em a few shots to drop those last two, seeing as how they ain't too familiar with killin'. When it was done, Doc grabbed that," he tapped the satchel, "and we hightailed it back here."

Earle sighed.

"Well, we started to. We was riding away when one of them wounded beaners shot at us from the ground. We turned real fast to put him down for good, but it was too late. Coop took two bullets. Doc did what he could, but he was dead in minutes. Damn shame. Did I tell you to stop pourin'?"

He raised an eyebrow at Claire, then turned to Doc, who was enthralled by the story.

"And did I tell you to stop? We need that map translated into English, pronto! Once he realizes his posse's gone missin', Gordo's gonna send every gun he has down to these parts. We gotta get his loot and get across the border before that happens, you hear?"

"Almost f-f-finished," Doc said, licking his pencil. "This Spanish is sloppy, the map's c-crude as hell—"

"Then stop flappin' your gums and get it done!" Clayton shouted.

Claire stood with the bottle at the ready.

"So there were only five guns to protect his lieutenant? Seems kinda reckless for such a notorious bandit like Gordo, don't it? I sure am glad, but I can't figure why he wouldn't send more."

"Leave the figurin' to us men, and we'll leave the whiskey pourin' to you women," Clayton said, slapping her on the ass. Claire felt years of silent pain burn in her belly and she considered hitting him over the head with the whiskey bottle. Instead, she took a deep breath and stuck with the plan. He'd get his soon enough.

Clayton leaned back and folded his hands across his lap.

"Gordo's as paranoid as they come. That's the whole damn reason he was movin' his stash in the first place. He was afraid too many of his men knew its location, and, seein' as he had half a brain, he was too smart to trust 'em. I'd wager the five guns he sent to protect his lieutenant wouldn't have lived to see tomorrow, even if we hadn't jumped 'em. That's why the moment I caught wind of the move, and the map, I thinked up this little plan of ours."

He closed his eyes smugly and puffed on his stub.

"That's if the Doc here ever finishes translatin' the goddamn thing," Earle complained.

"Done!" Doc said, putting his notes back in his bag and rolling the map out across the table. "Every last landmark, in plain old English. Here you can see his base of operations, named *Trono*—which means 'throne' in Spanish. Right there on the edge is a place Gordo called *Escondido*, his stash. That's where he's hidden the gold."

Clayton grabbed the map from Doc's hand.

"You sonovabitch! You did it!"

"Gimme that!" Earle said, snatching it from Clayton. "Escondido, here we come!"

"Now, boys, be gentle with it! You wouldn't tear a banknote would you? So don't go tearin' that map, which is worth more than all the banknotes in Arizona." Claire took it from Earle, folded it neatly, and put it in the satchel. "The way I figure, we four are the only living souls who know the location of Escondido. How 'bout one more round of drinks before you set out?"

"Right good idea, Claire," boomed Earle. "And since Doc seems allergic to the whiskey you've been pouring him, get him a glass of my *special* bourbon."

He flashed a yellow grin at the other men.

Claire hesitated, wondering whether she could really go through with it. The map was ready. The game was on. She trusted her man more than anything in the world, so she mustered a smile and started toward the kitchen.

Three loud raps came from the front door. She stopped and peeked around the curtain.

"It's the sheriff!" she whispered.

Clayton got to his feet and drew his gun. Earle finished his whiskey, then joined him.

"Must've found Gordo's men, tracked us back here," he whispered. "I didn't wanna kill no sheriff, but if it comes to that, so be it."

"Put your guns away!" Doc strained to keep his voice low. "It's too s-soon for anyone to have found the bodies. Besides, you think if the sheriff was coming to arrest us, he'd knock?"

Clayton and Earle looked at each other and put their guns away. There was another knock at the door.

"Earle Downing!" a voice called from outside. "This is Sheriff Wenton. Please open on up so I can have a word."

"Clay, g-get in the bed!" Doc ordered, grabbing his bag and crouching beside the rickety cot located just inside the adjoining room. "Claire, toss his hat aside, throw a blanket over him, and splash some water on his face. Yep, just like that. Now Earle, let the sheriff in and let me d-do the talking!"

Earle squinted suspiciously at the Doc, then, with his hand on his pistol, he turned and opened the door. Sheriff Wenton's spurs clacked as he entered.

"Good afternoon, fellas. Ma'am."

The sun glinted off the golden star pinned to his chest. He scanned the room, his eyes moving to Clayton sweating under the blanket, then to Claire blotting his forehead with a damp cloth.

"Sorry to intrude, but I've been makin' the rounds to let people know that a small group of Gordo's bandits have been seen in the area. Best stay inside this evening and keep an ear out for any trespassers ridin' through your land. And have your guns ready, just in case they take to burglarin'.'"

"Uh, thanks Sheriff," Earle said, his voice shaking. "Mighty nice of you to let us know."

Sheriff Wenton took a long, hard look at Earle's face.

"Been drinkin' so early, Earle? Everything alright 'round here?"

"Uh, yeah. No. I mean, yeah, everything is fine, Sheriff."

"Who's that in bed, there? Clayton Picket?"

The sheriff stuck his head into the bedroom.

"Yes, Sheriff," Doc said. He wiped his hands on a rag and popped his stethoscope from his ears. He aimed a grave look right into the sheriff's eyes, then extended a hand to the front door. "Mind if I have a p-private word with you out on the porch?"

Sheriff Wenton took another peek at Clayton's glistening face, then met Doc's eyes again. He nodded and the two men stepped outside. Doc closed the door behind them.

Earle put an empty whiskey glass to it, then put his ear to the glass.

"That no-good Irishman's gonna give us up, Earle!" Clayton whispered loudly from the bed. "He's gonna blow the whole damn thing! Shoot 'em both through the door before it's too late!"

"Shhh!" Earle waved a hand toward Clayton. "Doc's explainin' to the sheriff how a life of drinkin' finally caught up with you. Says you came down with a real bad case of liver disease. Says he don't want to scare the missus, but poor Clay Pickett may only have a few days left to live."

"That lying sonovabitch!" Clayton muttered.

"Shut your trap!" Earle hollered back as quietly as he could. "Listen to this! The Doc's spinnin' the perfect tale! Says that he's thinkin' of puttin' you in the wagon and drivin' the four of us up to the hospital in Carson City for emergency treatment. Says that if we up and disappear this week, that'll be where we've gone. That Doc's a genius! Now, the sheriff's sayin' he'll keep the town folk from gossipin' too much about where we've all gone to. He'll even look in on the place while we're out."

"That Doc sure is a snake, ain't he?" said Clayton, his mind puzzling over the tall tale.

Claire's heart soared as she realized how Sheriff Wenton had become an unwitting accomplice. Then, noticing the evil glint in her brother's eyes, her spirits plummeted.

What if deception wasn't enough? What if guns came out?

Claire remembered the special bourbon that Earle wanted the Doc to drink. She'd have to pour fast before Clayton had the chance to ruin their plans. None of them would dare shoot until the sheriff was well out of earshot, which meant she had a little time to keep the original plan in motion.

The front door opened. Before the Doc could enter, Earle pulled him inside, slammed the door, and threw his meaty arms around the Irishman's lean frame.

"Boy, you done well! You done *real* well!" Earle mussed up the Doc's hair. "How the hell'd you come up with a story like that so fast?"

Blushing, Doc took a seat.

"I read it in a b-b-book. A French mystery."

"You read French, too? Damn, you're one clever fella!"

"Sure is," Clayton said, throwing off his blanket.

"You know, Doc, while you were outside talkin' circles 'round ol' Sheriff Wenton, Clayton and I came to a decision."

"We did?"

"Yessir, we did," Earle said. "We want you to have Coop's share of the loot."

"We do?" Clayton placed his hat back on his head and joined them.

"That's right. Not only did the Doc translate the map, but he also bought us an alibi with the law. If that ain't worth Coop's share, I don't know what is."

"That's m-mighty nice, Earle," Doc said. "B-but we should split it three ways, like we talked about on the ride back from the pass."

"You hear that, Clay? Smart *and* as humble as a man of the cloth. Claire, fetch us some more whiskey and pour the Doc a shot of my special bourbon."

As soon as the bourbon was mentioned, Clayton relaxed in his chair, which made Claire relax, too.

"That sure was smart thinkin', Doc," she said, barely able to conceal her joy.

"Dammit, woman!" Earle pushed back his chair and glared into the kitchen. "You know how I feel about having to ask you for something twice."

She knew. If her brother's filth wasn't enough to keep her from touching her rickety bed again, the ghost of a hundred nights with Earle certainly was. "Pain or pleasure? Your choice," he'd say, pointing to the bed, a bottle of whiskey sloshing around in his belly. Then he'd proceed to take all the pleasure and leave her all the pain.

Never again.

She uncorked his special bourbon and filled a small glass. She set it down in front of the Doc, careful not to look at him, then she filled the other two glasses with whiskey.

Earle took his and held it high, motioning for the other two to follow. Doc lifted his and smiled dumbly, while Clayton glared around his glass at the Doc. Claire pretended to tidy up the kitchen.

"Here's to Doc, for translatin' and wranglin' the Sheriff," Earle announced. "And to Clayton, for always listenin' for opportunity when it comes a knockin'."

"Fuck you, too, Earle," Clayton said with a grin.

"And finally, to the notorious *Gordo Bandito!* He spent all those years stealin' gold from the railroad and pilin' it high, just for us. Escondido, here we come!"

Earle emptied his glass in one gulp.

Clayton followed, never taking his eyes off the Irishman.

"Go on, Doc. Whatter you waitin' for? Drink up."

Doc looked at the two men, smiled, and slammed the bourbon. His eyes went big and his face turned red.

"D-dang, fellas, that's some strong b-bourbon!" he cried.

Earle and Clayton laughed in unison.

"Sure is, Doc," said Earle. "Goes right to the head."

"Say, what's that undertone I taste? Is that l-l-licorice?" Doc asked, smacking his lips.

"Nope," Earle said, motioning to Claire for more whiskey.

"Sarsaparilla?"

"Wrong again."

Clayton cleared his throat and leaned forward, a devilish grin on his face.

"A college-educated fella like *you* never tasted larkspur before?"

Doc's eyes went wide behind his round-rimmed glasses.

"B-b-but, larkspur is t-toxic. Why'd you make your special b-b-bourbon with…"

He scraped a finger along the bottom of his glass and held it up to his glasses, then looked across the table at Earle.

"Why, you no-good, stinkin', dirty—"

Doc tried to stand, but his legs failed him. He hit the floor hard and scrambled for the door, his limbs unable to work together. Foam bubbled up from his lips. After a few seconds of twitching and writhing on the dusty wood floor, his eyes closed and he went still.

Claire couldn't help but feel awful, even though she'd been preparing for this part of the plan for weeks. She'd been the one to gather and distill the larkspur. She'd been the one who'd measured it out and made sure it found its way to the right vessel.

"Well, Claire, looks like you finally earned your share of the loot," Earle said, chuckling as he kicked the Doc's limp body. "'Bout time you did something useful around here. Now, why don't you drag him out and put him in the garden box with Coop. We'll drop both of 'em off on our way outta town and let the vultures clean up the mess."

"You want *me* to drag him out there?"

He slapped her hard across the face.

"What'd I say about asking you twice? Now go! Hurry!"

Claire put a hand to her stinging cheek and forced back her tears. She wouldn't give him, nor her brutish brother, the satisfaction of seeing her cry. Not when she was so close to being rid of them forever.

Instead, she threw open the door, took the Doc by the

wrists, and dragged him outside. Once she was clear of the door she was relieved—but not at all surprised—that his legs gave her a little help. When she got to the half-buried crate, which she'd hoped to one day use as a raised garden bed, she rolled him onto Cooper and tossed his bag inside with him.

Earle and Clayton tromped through the door as she approached. They glared at the sun, then at their horses.

"If we're gonna make it back to pick you up before nightfall, we best get going," Earle said.

Claire pretended to shield her eyes from the sun to avoid eye contact with either of them.

"I'll have the wagon ready for us, and I'll pack up the bodies. Everything'll be ready to go when you get back."

Clayton snickered and spit onto the porch. Earle elbowed him in stomach and tipped his hat to his wife.

"Alright, then. You just sit tight and wait for us. We'll be seein' you."

When the three of them had planned the heist and the double-cross, the thought had crossed her mind that they might never return for her. Now, as she felt their greed for gold and whiskey and women seething beneath their foul mustaches, she knew for sure they didn't intend to come back for her. They'd run off with the loot themselves and let her take the fall for what was in the garden box. Even if the sheriff didn't hang her, the best she'd be able to do was become a sporting gal at a saloon in Oatman.

"Wait!"

She ran back inside the house, then came out again with four canteens.

"Two with water, and two with the last of the whiskey. Take it easy on the whiskey, boys, or you'll pass out before you get there."

They uncorked their canteens and sipped.

"Don't you worry your perdy little head about us, sis," Clayton hissed. "We men can handle our whiskey just fine."

Without as much as a glance back at her, they mounted their horses and rode off.

Claire sat on the porch watching them go, feeling her heart lighten as their silhouettes shrank in the distance. Once the last wisp of dust from their hoofbeats had vanished, she walked calmly to the wagon and checked the drive stock. They looked well-rested and ready to go. Supplies were piled high in back, with plenty of room leftover.

She hopped up into the driver's seat and took the reins. She picked up a pebble from the seat and tossed it into the garden crate.

"I know you're havin' a good nap and all," she called out, "but after all that, I need a smooch, you hear? Right now, mister!"

Doc stood up and brushed himself off, a huge grin plastered to his face.

"You were brilliant, darlin'!" he said, running to her side. He took her hand and kissed it. "I heard the slap from out here. Did that scoundrel hurt you?"

"Earle's done much worse, trust me. And before him, Clayton did his share of knockin' me around."

Her frown turned into a bashful smile.

"Who you calling a scoundrel, D-D-Doc?" she teased.

He hopped up onto the seat next to her and bowed deeply.

"I admit, it was the performance of a lifetime! Maybe I'll carve a bar of gold into a trophy and award it to myself. Speaking of accolades, how much larkspur did you end up putting in their whiskey?"

"Three tablespoons each. I know you said two, but I couldn't resist."

"Three's quite enough! I hope they can read the map all the way to *Trono*." Doc laughed, shaking the reins and steering the wagon westward. "After all, I went through all that trouble of reversing the map's destinations to make sure they headed right towards it."

"So, you're sure they're really headed right for Gordo's base of operations? Where he and his bandit army make camp?" asked Claire.

"That's right, darlin'."

Doc kissed her forehead, then her cheek.

"And you're sure your notes are enough to get us to Escondido?"

"Of course they are! We'll be there in a few hours— about the same time those two realize they've been had. Imagine how surprised they'll be when Gordo and his men surround them! That is, if they can resist the whiskey long enough to make it all the way there."

"Either way, they'll get what's comin' to 'em," she said, glancing one last time at the ramshackle little house where she'd spent the last seven years of her life.

"That's right, darlin'."

Doc turned her face toward him and kissed her tenderly on the lips.

Claire slipped her arm around his, rested her head on his shoulder, and sighed. Twenty-seven years of suffering at the hands of brutes had made her tough as nails, but with Doc she could finally be soft again.

"Get some rest," he said, stroking her head. "I'll wake you when the treasure needs loading."

She closed her eyes and dreamed—not of the treasure

awaiting them at Escondido, but of a lifetime with the man she loved.

BLOOD EMOJI

"Just these two?"

"Yessir. The driver was dead when I arrived on the scene."

"You sure?"

"No doubt about it, sir. The young man in the driver's seat was completely crushed under the—"

"What about the others?" interrupted the sheriff.

"They're sittin' right there in our interrogation room, sir."

"Not these two, Jim. What about the other couple these two were yammerin' about when you brought 'em in."

"Oh, right. I didn't find anyone but the driver and these two. They said we'd find two more bodies in the irrigation ditch about a half-mile down the road, where it runs alongside the highway near the truck stop just outside of town. I cruised by and shined my light down, but didn't see nothin'."

"Find anything on these two? Any drugs? Weapons?"

"Naw, sheriff. Just the two cell phones they chucked aside when I pulled up."

The sheriff nodded, his eyes pinned to the two teenagers sitting behind the one-way mirror.

"Call this in yet?"

"No, sir. You said to bring 'em in first, so that's what I did."

After a moment passed without a response, the deputy grimly shook his head and sighed.

"Alrighty. Well, I reckon I'll call in the troopers and ask 'em to come help clean up. Maybe they can help us sort out what the hell happened tonight."

He turned to go but the sheriff grabbed his arm to stop him.

"Hold off on making that call, deputy."

Without elaborating, he popped a handful of sunflower seeds into his mouth and began cracking them one by one between his teeth.

The deputy stood quietly beside him, trying to mask the confusion he felt by matching the sheriff's glare at the young couple in the interrogation room.

Finally, the sheriff broke the silence.

"You call in the *other* accident yet?"

"No, sir. I was writin' up the first accident with the Mustang when I saw these two runnin' along the shoulder. When I stopped, they led me to the other wreck down the road—the Sentra. What a night, eh, Sheriff?"

The deputy took off his hat and wiped his brow with a handkerchief.

"Well, I'll leave these two with you while I call this in."

"Just hold on there, Deputy."

The sheriff spat a mouthful of soggy shells into his hand and flung them into a small trash bin nearby.

"Don't I need to call 'em in right away? I mean, the

longer we wait, the more shit the DA's gonna give us when these go to trial."

"Shut up and listen, Jim," said the sheriff as he turned to face his deputy for the first time in the conversation. He looked him straight in the eyes and drawled in a slightly evangelical tone, "I don't believe in coincidences, not in a world where the good Lord's watchin' out for his flock. Sometimes bad things happen—ain't no way to avoid 'em— but on the other side of tragedy God's grace is waiting for us, waiting to deliver us from our pain. If we're wise enough to see it."

"Sheriff?" asked the deputy.

"I'm startin' to think the Lord delivered us a mixed bag of luck tonight. For them," he motioned with a slight nod to the one-way mirror, "well, they ended up on the bad side of that luck. But us—you and me, and Senator Lake's stupid son-of-a-bitch bastard pup—we got us some good luck. Better than luck. *Grace.* Seems a sin to waste God's good grace, don't it?"

For a moment, Deputy Jim screwed up his face in confusion, but then his eyes went wide as realization struck.

"We swap out the bodies? Make it look like...like there was just *one* accident? Like these kids were the ones who hit that transient, while Senator Lake's son...?"

"He spent a nice, quiet evening at home with his mama," answered the Sheriff. "Who I'm sure will have no problem confirming it on record."

Jim stared at the floor while he weighed his reply, then gathered the courage to speak it aloud.

"Sheriff, Senator Lake's boy killed someone with his car tonight. That's vehicular manslaughter—and hell, the only thing that kept him from fleeing the scene and haulin' ass out into the desert was the fact that he's too drunk to stand. You sure this is the right thing to do?"

The sheriff cracked a seed between his teeth and sighed.

"Let me tell you a few things I'm sure of, Jim. I'm sure those faggot libs in Phoenix would love to crucify Senator Lake over an accident caused by her idiot son. I'm sure that if she loses the election in the fall, it's only a matter of time before we're overrun by illegals—hell, we'll probably be taking orders from them. And I'm sure there ain't no bringin' anyone back tonight." He paused to nod at his own assertion. "Yep. Tonight, we give our EMTs one less mess to clean up, and we spare the great state of Arizona some unnecessary embarrassment."

Deputy Jim returned the nod, but a split second later his face lit up with panic.

"I almost forgot! When I saw these two run up the road I handcuffed Lake's kid to a speed limit sign to keep him outta trouble while I investigated. I should probably go pick him up before he shits himself. Don't want that kid messin' in my squad car. I just had it cleaned."

The sheriff caught the deputy's shoulder as he turned to go.

"I don't wanna see that boy in my station, you hear me? I don't care if he's lettin' loose from both ends, you take him straight home to his mama and clean your car out tomorrow. When she finds out what we done for her tonight, she'll return the favor when next year's budget comes 'round. Forget cleaning that dusty old cruiser ever again, Jim. I reckon this time next year we'll have ourselves a pair of brand new cruisers—nice ones, like they get up in the city."

"On the drive," he continued, "call Sam McNeal's tow shop in Sierra Vista and tell Sam's wife—she'll be the one who picks up—tell her we got another red slip. She'll know what it means. Sam'll tow away whatever's left of that Mustang and clean up the scene like nothing happened. Once the boy's safe at home, you git your ass back to the Sentra and move them bodies around."

"Sheriff!"

The sheriff squeezed the other man's shoulder like a vise grip.

"Shuddup and listen, Jim. Drag that animal's corpse away, far enough away to let the desert take care of it. Then you lay that transient's corpse in the Sentra's windshield, right on top of the driver's body."

Jim swallowed deeply.

"What're you standing 'round for? Git!"

The iron grip on his shoulder loosened and Jim turned to go.

"What about the two bodies in the ditch, Sheriff?"

"They ain't goin' nowhere. Now, git."

When Jim had gone, the sheriff spat out a handful of shells and narrowed his eyes at the two teenagers waiting for him behind the one-way mirror.

"Time to get our stories straight, kids," he said to himself, reaching for more sunflower seeds.

BOTH TEENAGERS JOLTED to attention as the sheriff entered the interrogation room.

"Officer!" the boy cried. "We need to get out of here, we need to—"

The sheriff held up a hand to interrupt. He sat in the chair across from them and took a long moment to look them over.

After thirty years on the force, he knew how silence

alone could rattle a suspect's nerves and loosen their tongues. Once the fear response kicked in and they were desperate enough, all he had to do was show them the path leading away from their troubles and they'd do whatever he told them to do. Sometimes that meant they'd talk. Sometimes that meant they'd rat out someone else. Sometimes that meant they'd take a deal, even if that meant confessing to crimes they hadn't committed.

"I need to call my mom!" the girl blurted out, her voice shaking. "Please!"

"Aren't we allowed to call our parents? Why haven't you let us call them yet?"

The sheriff let a hint of a smile cross his lips.

"I'm sorry, we're having technical difficulties at the station right now. Turns out some kids drove their car into a service pole out near the interstate, knocked out power to about half of Bisbee and cut off our dang fiber optic connection to the valley. No internet, no landline till the morning."

The boy's face grew red.

"That's bullshit! We know our rights! If we're under arrest, you have to let us each make a call."

"Why would you be under arrest, son? Or should I say, Jude Goldberg, 18 years old as of March this year, who resides at 3595 W. Agua Caliente Drive, Tucson, with your pregnant girlfriend here, Carla Ramirez," he nodded politely to the girl, "who doesn't turn 18 till next month."

"That's none of your business!" cried Jude, pounding his fist on the table. "That has nothing to do with what happened tonight!"

"What about our friends?" begged the girl, tears welling in her eyes.

"That's what I was hoping to chat about with the two of you."

"We don't have to answer anything without a lawyer present!" cried Jude.

"Officer... Brad and Cindy are—" Her voice caught and she had to swallow down the impulse to start sobbing again.

"Babe, don't say anything!"

"They're dead in the ditch," she continued, her voice shaking, "and Aaron was crushed underneath that... *Please!* Have their parents been contacted? Hasn't anyone—"

"You settle down now," the sheriff interrupted sharply. "Don't you worry about your friends. Everything's bein' taken care of. The important thing is that the two of you are safe. And before we make a single phone call from anyone's phone, the three of us are gonna have a little chat and yer gonna tell me what in the hell you mob of city kids were doing out in my podunk town on a Tuesday night in the first place. In addition to the drugs."

"Drugs!?" cried Jude. "But she's *pregnant!*"

"*Yer* not," the sheriff shot back. "B'sides, you think I've never seen a pregnant junkie? Believe it or not, city-boy, but we get those out here in the boonies, too."

"Do you have a cell phone we can use?" Carla asked desperately. "Just so we can tell our parents we're alive and okay?"

"Funny you should ask. I have two perfectly good phones right here."

The sheriff tipped out the contents of a large envelope he'd brought into the room with him. Two scuffed-up smart-phones slid onto the table.

In a sudden panic, both teenagers scooted their chairs away from the table until they pressed against the wall behind them. Their wide eyes were pinned to the phones, their faces twisted up in horror.

"I reckon these look familiar. My deputy saw you each

toss something into the desert brush as he was driven' up. Usually it's drugs or beer. This is the first time anyone's tossed a pair of brand new iPhones. What d'ya say? Should we unlock 'em and take a peek?"

"No!" the teens shouted in unison.

The sheriff clenched his lips and hoped his bushy mustache hid the grin he fought back.

"See, that kinda reaction makes me wonder if there's something on these phones that y'all might find incriminatin'. There's a new state law, passed last year, says I can force you to unlock them and give me access."

Carla buried her face in her hands.

Jude squirmed and begged, "Please don't make us."

"Alrighty then, why don't you just tell me everything so I won't have to," the sheriff drawled, leaning back and setting his feet on the corner of the table. "Go on, start from the beginning. The sooner we get to the bottom of things, the sooner y'all can call home. I got all night."

Carla and Jude exchanged a look, then she plunged her face back into her hands.

"Air fryer," said Jude.

"Excuse me?"

"Air fryer. You know, those little kitchen appliances with the drawer that fries food using air or magic or whatever."

"Yeah, I know what an air fryer is," the sheriff lied, then spat some soggy shells into his hand and flung them into the trash bin sitting beside the table. "But what's that have to do with tonight?"

"See, Carla's been getting these weird pregnancy cravings lately, and if she doesn't get what she's craving...she gets a little upset."

"So you kids drove down from Tucson to buy an air fryer?"

"No, see—"

"Twinkies," interrupted Carla.

The sheriff raised his bushy eyebrows.

"You kids drove all the way down here to buy Twinkies?" asked the sheriff, with more than a hint of suspicion in his tone. "What, them liberals in the city finally ban snack food?"

"Uh, no, I don't think so," answered Carla. "Anyway, last week I ate an air-fried Twinkie at my girlfriend Shanna's apartment. Since then I can't get them off my mind."

"It's all she's talked about since," added Jude.

"I'm *pregnant!* I have *cravings,* okay? The baby needs Twinkies, and if I'm gonna eat them, I want them to be *healthy.* That's what air fryers do, Jude!"

"I don't think that's exactly what they do, babe."

"IT'S WHAT THEY DO, JUDE. I saw a TikTok explaining how it works," insisted Carla. "Anyway, do you want me to turn into one of those fat, gross moms we see at Costco?"

Jude sighed and studied the back of his hands for a second before continuing.

"Speaking of Costco, the one she wanted—"

"The one *we* wanted," corrected Carla.

"The one *we* wanted was on sale for a hundred bucks at Costco. I didn't have the money, so me and the guys decided to sell one of our old cell phones. We posted an ad online, got contacted by a buyer, so we all drove down here together to drop off the phone and collect the cash."

"I don't like being left at the apartment all by myself when he goes out with Brad and Aaron. I made Cindy come along. Oh, god...if I hadn't, she'd still be alive," said Carla, tears flowing again.

The sheriff sat munching his sunflower seeds and studying the two teenagers.

"So you were just some innocent kids trying to resell a phone, eh? Tell me, which of my fine citizens did you sell your phone to?" he asked.

There was a pause while Jude and Carla exchanged a terrified look.

"Tell him!" she demanded.

Jude sighed and hung his head.

"She signed her email as Ms. Wildes," he said, then looked up into the sheriff's eyes for any sign of recognition.

"Ol' Ms. Wildes up on Wallow Way is in the market for a smartphone?" asked the sheriff, dropping his feet and sitting upright in his chair. "She must be pushin' 90 these days. I didn't exactly take her for the technological type."

"When she answered our ad, she mentioned she'd recently gotten a computer and wanted to *expand her reach*," Jude looked at the pair of phones on the table and the blood drained from his face. "Oh, god, babe. That's what she meant! *Her reach!*"

"No shit! You just now figured that out?"

"Figured what out?" asked the sheriff.

"We didn't believe her. Goddamnit! Why didn't we believe her?" Panic rose in Jude's voice as he slowly put things together. "We thought she was just some old bag with dementia. But she told us what she was! She told us, babe!"

The sheriff put up a hand to stop the boy.

"Tell *me*, boy. What exactly *is* ol' Miss Wildes? Huh? A Russian spy? A crack dealer?" he asked, chuckling. "Before you answer, remember she's been up on Wallow Way longer'n I been sheriff. Hell, she might've founded Bisbee for all I know."

As Jude struggled to find the courage to answer, Carla blurted it out.

"She's a witch! A *real* witch! It's not a joke, Sheriff! She killed our friends! And she's gonna kill us, too!"

Something happened to the sheriff when she'd finished speaking. His bushy mustache drooped at both ends as if suddenly struck with immense confusion, then a faint glimmer of light, like the reflection of water on the surface of a lake, flashed across his eyes.

He chuckled again and shoved another pinch of sunflower seeds into his mouth.

"Is that so?" he asked, sitting back in his chair. "Well, a lot of folks 'round here would take offense at calling a nice old woman a witch just 'cause she lives all alone up on the hill."

"It's just like she said, Jude," Carla said, motioning to the sheriff with her cuffed hands. "She's got the whole town under some kind of spell to make them believe she's not a witch. Oh, god! Why didn't we believe her? Why'd we—?"

Carla stopped abruptly and dropped her gaze to the floor.

The sheriff's bushy grey eyebrows lifted.

"Now we're gettin' to the real story, ain't we?" he said, then spat a few shells into the trash. "For the sake of argument, let's assume ol' Miss Wildes is a real witch. Not sure it'll hold up in a court of law, but here in my station, we'll go with it for now. And let's even say she's out to git the two of you. The question I want to know the answer to is *why?* Why in the hell would a nice old witch want to kill a group of teenagers who drove down from Tucson to sell her a phone?"

The teens exchanged another nervous look. This time, Jude took a deep breath and answered as bravely as he could.

"Because Brad and Aaron robbed her."

"Jude! I can't believe you!" cried Carla.

"It was *their* idea, Carla. Remember?"

He looked at her severely, as if trying to transmit a secret thought from his brain to hers.

"Oh. Right. Sure," Carla said with more than a hint of sarcasm and derision in her voice. She brushed a tear from her cheek and continued, "Sure, it was all our dead friends' idea. The robbery and the phone scam, the whole thing."

"Phone scam?" asked the sheriff.

"So, the air fryer wasn't the first thing we couldn't afford. It started a few weeks ago when the alternator went out on Carla's whip."

"It's not a whip," corrected Carla. "It's a Honda."

"We didn't have the money to fix it at the time, and if she couldn't make it to work, she'd lose her job. With the baby coming, we couldn't risk it. We had to come up with three hundred bucks, fast. That same weekend, while Brad and Aaron and I were working kiosks up at the mall—"

"Working what?" interrupted the sheriff.

"Kiosks. You know, those little pop-up shops inside the mall, along the walkways? Anyway, we work at the mall and that weekend we noticed how many people toss their old phones into this little blue donation bin near the information booth. Most of them are cracked and busted, but every once in a while someone'll toss in what looks like a working iPhone or Samsung. The guy who comes to collect them only comes like once a month. So, we—I mean, Brad—he came up with a plan to dig through the phones to find anything he could resell as a working phone. I told him how stupid that was, that no one would just buy an old phone without turning it on and making sure it was legit. Also, I mentioned how illegal it was. I kept telling them how it was illegal and we should never do illegal things, but they wouldn't listen. Anyway, then Aaron said how his grandpa once bought a bricked phone from someone on Facebook and lost a few hundred bucks. So they came up with a plan to post the phones online, at a smoking deal, then ignore all the normal people and wait for old people to respond—no offense, Sheriff."

"You're such a moron," Carla groaned, shaking her head.

The sheriff ignored the unintentional jab at his age and nodded slowly, as if he was still processing all that Jude had just said. He sat. He stared. He chomped his seeds.

Finally, after letting the silence cast its own kind of spell, the teens began squirming in their chairs and he was ready to continue the interrogation.

"Alright, so these friends of yours cooked up a scheme to commit fraud, which this evening led to robbery. Thank you for your testimony on that, son. I'm sure it'll come in handy when this all goes to trial."

"Trial!?" cried Carla. "But we just want to go home! Our friends are dead and we didn't do anything!"

"Well, Jude here has told me some of the story, but there's a whole lot of questions to answer before any of us get to go home. Now, son, if what you say is true, why were you two out here with them tonight?"

"Brad owed me some money, and I knew that if I didn't come with him to collect right when he got it, he'd spend it before making it back to Tucson. I needed that money to buy Carla things she needed for the baby."

"Like an air fryer?"

"Exactly. And other baby stuff we'll need soon."

"How thoughtful of you, Jude. But if you knew this was illegal, why'd you bring your pregnant girl along for the ride?"

"I was worried about him driving so far away," answered Carla. "Ever since I've been pregnant I've been worried that when he leaves, he might not come home. I know it's stupid, but I needed to stay close to him. Then I made Aaron bring Cindy so I would have someone to hang with while the boys..."

"While the boys robbed a sweet old lady so you could eat air-fried junk food?" suggested the sheriff helpfully.

"No! I mean, yeah. But..."

She trailed off and averted her eyes from the sheriff's icy blue stare.

"Brad and Aaron, not us," Jude corrected. "It was their idea and they did everything themselves."

"Mmm-hmm. What I'm more curious about is what happened up on Wallow Way, and what it has to do with what I might find on these here phones of yours."

Jude swallowed hard.

"Okay, so tonight the five of us drove down. When we got to the hill, we almost turned around. The whole road and house is surrounded by cactuses on all sides—"

"Cacti," Carla corrected.

"And there were all these big hulking birds perched along the roof—"

"Turkey vultures," she interjected again.

"It was all hella creepy and we shoulda known," continued Jude. "Actually, I remember telling Brad the whole thing was a bad idea and that we should leave. Remember, babe? I said something like 'let's find some other way to make money, guys, like get better jobs or donate blood or something.' Remember when I told them that, babe?"

"Sure. And I think you said something about applying for Harvard in the fall, too."

He shot her a look and continued, "Anyway, Brad and Aaron overruled me. They told me they'd ditch us if we ditched them. So we all went up and knocked. The old lady answered, and we thought it was maybe a prank or something. She had this frizzy white hair and these long flowing robes without anything underneath them, so you could almost see her wrinkled-up old—"

"Jude!" cried Carla, then rolled her eyes.

"Anyway, she invited us in, muttered some crazy-sounding witch shit, looked over the phone we'd brought her, then told us to hang out in her front room while she went to get her cash. While she was gone, we got a good look at her place. Plants everywhere, but not inside plants— outside stuff like cacti and even a huge mesquite tree that grew right through the roof. Weird sculptures made of animal skulls and bones and feathers. And all sorts of crys-tals and expensive-looking jewelry just laying around every-where. I took one look at Brad and Aaron and knew what they were thinking. They pulled me into a huddle and told me their new plan: grab as much jewelry as we could carry, then go find where she's hiding her cash and take that, too. Said she was just a crazy, half-naked old lady living alone... that she probably wouldn't notice anything was missing or even remember any of it."

"But she noticed," added Carla. "She remembered!"

"Sheriff, I tried to talk them out of it every step of the way. Carla can testify that I did. Right, babe? The other guys, they filled their pockets with rings, necklaces—

anything that looked valuable but also small enough to fit in their hoodie pockets. When the old lady—"

"Miss Wildes," interrupted the sheriff.

"When Miss Wildes got back with the cash, she looked right at us and laughed. No, it was too creepy to be a laugh. It sounded whacked out, man—like some kind of noise a lunatic would make."

"A cackle," explained Carla.

"She just squinted her shriveled eyes at us and cackled," Jude continued, "waving the wad of cash around like it was a magic wand or something. We were all majorly freaked out. Brad and Aaron got angry. They exchanged a mean look, Brad nodded, and then Aaron stepped forward and grabbed the lady's wrist. He snatched the cash from her and tossed her arm aside hard... too hard. She fell back onto a small table with a glass top, and it shattered everywhere, with her on top. I screamed at the guys to stop and ran to her side to check for a pulse. She was alive, but knocked out cold. I told them to call for an ambulance, but they just started laughing and bolted for the car. Carla and I had to run after them before they left us behind. I begged them to stop, to get the old lady some medical help, but Brad just peeled out of there like a maniac. We didn't want to do any of it, Sheriff—especially not leave her like that..."

Jude buried his face in his hands and whimpered theatrically.

Carla rolled her eyes.

"All that ring true, honey?" the sheriff asked her.

"Pretty much."

He nodded slowly and leaned forward.

"Maybe, while your boyfriend here recovers, you could continue the story. After your friends robbed poor Miss

Wildes, you did what? You sure as hell didn't head straight back to the city or you'd be asleep in bed right now."

Carla cleared her throat and sat up straight.

"No, we didn't. After we left Wallow Way, Brad tore ass through old town, got back on the I-5, but then he pulled over at that little trucker stop just outside town. The rush of adrenaline had everyone a little jittery. We needed to stop and process what had just happened."

"And maybe pop some pills or snort a few lines?" asked the sheriff.

"No!" cried Carla.

"Yes," Jude said, looking up. "Well, not the two of us. But the others. I saw them take something."

If Carla hadn't been handcuffed she'd have slapped him across the face.

"Jude, what the hell! Cindy doesn't even smoke!"

"Right, I didn't mean Cindy. But Brad and Aaron, they definitely took something. They offered me one, but I wouldn't touch it."

"You're such a piece of shit, Jude."

"Babe, I'm just telling the sheriff the truth so we can go home."

"Don't let me stop you," she said, turning away from him.

The sheriff leaned back in his chair.

"If you two are finished, I'd like to know what happened at the truck stop. Especially to your two friends in the irrigation ditch."

Carla tensed. Jude sat staring into the middle distance like he was replaying the scene in his mind.

"That's when she got them."

"Who? Miss Wildes?"

He nodded.

"After we stopped, and the guys took those pills I mentioned, Brad got all hyped up, probably from the drugs he was on—"

"Oh, god," groaned Carla, "I think I'm gonna be sick."

The sheriff scooted the trash bin closer to her and motioned for Jude to carry on.

"Right next to the ramada with the picnic tables there's an irrigation ditch, maybe ten feet across bank to bank. Full of water this time of year, Aaron said, and clean enough to swim in. Said he used to do it all the time when he was a kid. So he started stripping down, trying to strip Cindy down to her underwear, too, so she'd jump in with him.

"Suddenly, both their phones dinged at the same time and then started buzzing like crazy. Cindy dug through the pile of clothes at their feet, pulled out their phones, and laughed. She actually laughed, babe, remember?"

Jude shook his head and stole a quick, fearful glance at the two cell phones sitting on the table.

"We gonna find something funny on your phones, too?" asked the sheriff.

"No!" snapped Carla, her voice on the edge of panic.

"Cindy laughed at the text messages," Jude repeated. "One to Aaron's phone, one to hers. At first it just seemed like a wrong number or something, but then she noticed the messages were sent back-to-back from the same number. All sixes, Sheriff. 666-666-6666." He looked up from his hands to meet the sheriff's eyes. "That's how she does it. That's how her curse gets through. Fuck, it's our fault, too. She must've ended up using the busted phone we sold her."

Jude nodded absent-mindedly, as if through retelling the story he was finally grasping what had happened.

"But we didn't know that at the time," he continued.

"We just thought it was some prank or something. Besides, each message was just a single emoji."

"A *what?*" asked the sheriff.

"An emoji. God, you don't know what a…" He trailed off, then shook his head and explained slowly, "Emoji are, uh, little images, tiny symbols, sent alongside text in a digital message. You must've seen a cheesy 'thumbs up' or 'smiley face' emoji in a text message or email? Or, you know, anywhere on the internet."

The sheriff waved away the bewildering concept and grumbled, "I get it. Tiny symbols sent to their phones—by a witch using a phone number consisting of all 6s."

"Exactly," continued Jude. "Aaron got a lightning bolt. Cindy got a broken heart. Oh, shit…Carla! Don't you *see?* Don't you get what they meant?"

Carla responded by covering her ears and rocking gently in her chair.

The sheriff grunted.

"Okay. Then what? How'd those two end up OD'ing in my ditch?"

"They didn't OD, Sheriff. Aaron might've taken some pills, but he didn't overdose. And like we said, Cindy didn't take anything. Aaron jumped in first. He was so tall that from the picnic tables we could see his head and shoulders sticking out of the water. Cindy was up on the bank, stripped down to her bra and panties, shivering and laughing. He was motioning for her to jump in when the explosion happened."

"Explosion?" asked the sheriff. "I wasn't aware of any explosions in my town this evening, son."

"An explosion of sparks. About a half-mile away—maybe closer, it was hard to tell in the dark—a car crashed into a power pole or something and took it down. We heard the squealing of brakes, the revving of an engine, a loud crash, and then a terrible metal creaking sound as the pole went down. Sparks lit up the desert like a firework display and were reflected in the water, which led me to Aaron, still standing shoulder-deep in it. But something was wrong. He wasn't waving his arms at Cindy anymore...he was jerking around and shaking all frantically, yet he seemed all rigid.

"I followed the reflection of sparks back up the ditch, closer to where the pole went down, and I saw the power cables flailing like a firehose, slapping over and over again into the surface of the water. Cindy started screaming her head off for him to swim to her, to reach out his hand. He just kept shaking.

"Just as we got up to run to them, she sprinted down the bank, straight into the water. Then she was jerking and shaking, too.

"We didn't know what to do. It wasn't real...but it was, you know? It was like a dream, when something awful happens and you can't scream. I couldn't scream. I couldn't move. We just sat and watched. Then it was suddenly over. The cables flickered off, the shaking stopped. Both their bodies just floated there, and I could see...I could see smoke billowing off of them. Like they were charred meat. Like they were just *cooked!*"

He started sobbing into his hands without the need for theatrics.

Carla rocked and hummed to herself so she couldn't hear what was being said.

The sheriff spat a mouthful of seeds into the trash and leaned back to take in the story. How much of it was true or not, he didn't know, and he didn't care. The coroner would test the two in the ditch for drugs and the sheriff had ways of making sure he found them. What was important was that his two suspects looked just about ripe for signing a confession.

"We're almost done here, kids. When we are, we'll sign some routine paperwork and you can go home."

Carla straightened up and Jude rubbed his eyes.

"But there's a little more to the story, ain't there?" asked the sheriff. "What happened next? How'd your friend Brad get behind the wheel of his car and hit that poor old man?"

"Huh?" asked Jude. "He didn't hit a person. He hit a donkey."

"A burro," Carla corrected.

"Whatever. A big hairy mule thing standing in the middle of the lane. Came right through the windshield because that stupid asshole wouldn't resist checking his goddamn phone!"

"We begged him not to," added Carla, tears in her eyes.

Jude took her trembling hands in his and continued, "After what happened to Aaron and Cindy, we all ran to the car. Right when we got inside, Brad's phone dinged. Instead of checking it, he tossed it into his cup holder and floored it down the freeway. It only took like a second before he gave in and checked it. It was from the same number. A stupid donkey emoji. I had just enough time to think *what the fuck could that mean* when Brad slams on the brakes and then there's glass everywhere and the whole front seat is gone, underneath this huge furry donkey."

"Burro," whimpered Carla.

"We hopped out," continued Jude, "saw that Brad was crushed and completely... gone. So we ran. We just started running down the freeway. That was when your deputy pulled up."

"And you tried to toss these phones?"

"You can keep our goddamn phones!" shouted Carla.

"Look through all our texts and photos and posts. I don't give a shit! We told you everything, okay? Can we go now? We'll walk back to Tucson if we have to!"

The sheriff produced a pair of document packets from his envelope and slid them across the table.

"Sign these and you're free to go."

Carla scanned the first page. She screwed up her face as Jude's eyes darted around the room for a pen.

"Confessions?" she asked, her voice quivering. "But we didn't do anything!"

"I already told you!" cried Jude. "It was all Brad's idea!"

"I do remember you saying that," said the sheriff. "And that's exactly what we'll write here on page four, where nothin's written yet. Some of the details are a little fuzzy, but I think we can come up with a story that suits all three of us just fine. Page seven is where you sign. Why don't you start there, and we'll work backwards."

"You're saying that if we blame this all on Brad, then we walk?" asked Carla.

Before the sheriff could respond she added, "A minute ago you said Brad hit a poor old man. There was another accident, wasn't there? An accident that took out the power pole that fell and killed Aaron and Cindy. Whoever caused that accident killed someone else, didn't they? And you want to cover it up by pinning that on Brad, too."

The sheriff looked her over with a newfound appreciation.

"Well, ain't you just a little Nancy Drew," he drawled. "Considering your situation, doesn't sound like too bad a deal, does it? We fudge a few minor details—for instance, I think Brad sped off without the two of you, didn't he? Left you back at the rest stop while he killed that man with his car. Seems like it'd be real good for you if you weren't in the car when it happened. Seems like it was Brad's crime, Brad's drugs, and Brad's impaired driving that caused all the trouble that happened tonight."

"It's that easy?" asked Carla.

The sheriff offered her a pen and a smile. She reluctantly returned the smile and took the pen.

"Come on, Jude! Hurry up and start writing." She elbowed him and he took a pen from the sheriff.

"That's right, the sooner we get done, the sooner we can all get home," said the sheriff, then twisted around in his seat to get a hand into his front pocket. He pulled out his own cellphone—an ancient, unsexy device compared to the two sleek iPhones on the table—and thumbed open the flip screen.

"While y'all do that, I'll call my deputy to find out if he's gotten everything squared away at the crash scene." He froze, his icy blue eyes pinned to his screen. "Ho-ly shit. Will you look at that..."

He squinted his bushy eyebrows and shoved a handful of sunflower seeds into his mouth. Then, with a devious glint in his eye, he flipped the screen around so the others could see.

His phone's small screen showed a text message had been sent one minute ago, from 666-666-6666. The message contained only a single emoji: a rooster.

Carla shrank back in her chair and hugged her knees, but Jude got to his feet.

"That's from *her*, Sheriff!" he cried, pointing. "It's a curse!"

The sheriff snorted and shook his head as he continued studying the message.

"I'm not sure how the hell you two managed to send this message while sittin' here in custody with me, but I have to admit, I'm pretty darn impressed. You sure you two ain't hackers or something?"

"*We didn't send it!* How could we?" Jude shouted, holding up his handcuffed wrists as evidence.

"No, I got it! I bet Deputy Jim found one of your friends' phones at the rest stop and sent this to me as a joke," he said, chuckling. "That son-of-a-bitch. I'm gonna skin his hide for this."

"Sheriff, your deputy couldn't have sent a text message from that number! It's from *her*!" cried Jude. "You have to drive up to to her place, *fast*...and, I dunno...stop the witch!"

The sheriff looked up from his phone's screen to the panicked teenager's pleading face. Jude noticed that strange twinkle in the sheriff's eyes, the same one they'd seen the last time they suggested confronting the witch.

"I'll head up to Wallow Way tomorrow morning after breakfast to check on old Miss Wildes, and to tell her the boys who robbed her last night won't be coming back anytime soon."

"She *knows* that already! Haven't you been listening? She's the one who cursed them, and now she's cursed *you* for some reason!"

Just then, both iPhones on the table began dinging and buzzing in unison. Carla sunk deeper into her chair and began whispering Hail Marys under her breath.

All traces of levity left the sheriff's face as he scowled at the desperate teenaged boy hovering over him.

"You sit your ass back down in that chair, young man, and finish fillin' out the little assignment I gave you."

Jude glanced at the firearm strapped to the sheriff's waist and then looked to the door.

"Don't you get it? We're running out of time!"

The sheriff relaxed, shook his head, and flipped his phone around so Jude could see it again.

"Even if y'all are right—which, of course, yer not—how in the hell could a goddamn rooster kill a grown man like me?"

He leaned back in his chair and propped his feet up on the table.

"See these shitkickers here on my feet? Real snakeskin. Diamondback. I'll stomp the shit outta any crazy-ass poultry that comes peckin' at the station door—"

The sheriff's threat was cut off by a quick intake of air and a wet gasp.

His hands found his throat and began clawing desperately.

"He's choking! On those seeds!" cried Carla, staring at the sheriff's face as it rapidly turned from red to purple. "Do something, Jude! Call 911!"

Instinctively, Jude snatched his phone from the table and held it up. The screen unlocked automatically once it scanned his face, revealing a single text message.

Carla looked up in horror, realizing his mistake.

"I fucked up, babe," he mumbled. "We gotta go *right now*!"

"But the sheriff!"

"Fuck this crooked cop! We can't trust him! We gotta get out of here!"

"What was the emoji, Jude?" she asked, regretting it as soon as the words left her mouth.

He flipped the phone around to show her. The message was from the witch's number, and it contained a single emoji: a gun.

Carla's eyes fell to the gun at the sheriff's waist. The old man had toppled out of his chair and lay writhing on the floor, his eyes bulging.

"We need to get the cuffs off, Jude. Get his keys! They're in his pocket!"

Jude bent over the dying sheriff and started rifling through this pockets. He pulled out a wallet and a bag of sunflower seeds, and tossed them aside.

Finally, he turned to Carla and held up a keyring with at least two dozen keys.

"It's gotta be one of these. I'll start with the small ones, and then I'll—"

He was cut off by the deafening boom of a gunshot and the appearance of a quarter-sized hole in the center of his throat.

Jude collapsed where he stood, blood geysering from both the entry and exit wounds in his neck. The weight of the teenager pinned the old man down as the smoking gun flailed in his right hand.

He fired blindly twice more, neither bullet striking the soon-to-be teenaged mother who cowered in a puddle of her own urine in the corner of the small interrogation room.

The high-pitched buzz of the three gunshots rang in Carla's ears and she could feel her heart thumping in her chest. She crouched with her head between her knees, waiting for one more shot. The final shot that would kill her and her unborn baby.

No other gunshot came. The desperate choking of the sheriff had ceased. The room was quiet except for the ringing in her ears.

She slowly turned around, making sure not to look at the two bodies piled up on the other side of the table. Something bright red and yellow grabbed her attention on the floor. It was a small bag of sunflower seeds, which she remembered Jude had tossed aside when he was looking for the sheriff's keys.

She turned the bag over to look at the front label and felt the hinges of her mind strain against the impact of what she saw.

Below the brand name, *Cock-a-doodle-doo Snacks Inc.,* was the brand's logo: the silhouette of a rooster crowing.

The bag fell from her hand. A twisted, broken laugh rose up in her throat. She was just about to let it out when it was preempted by another noise.

Her phone had started dinging and buzzing again. It was face down, so she couldn't see the lock screen notification. It could have been anything: a call from her parents checking in on her; her calendar reminder to take her prenatal vitamins; Leah or Sam or anyone else from work asking her to cover their shift.

But she knew it was none of those things. She knew who, and what, was waiting for her once she flipped over the phone and unlocked it.

Carla stole a glance over the table at Jude's body laying on top of the sheriff, both of them blue in the face and drenched with blood.

Whatever life she'd hoped to save by ignoring the message was already over. There was just one thing left to do.

Carla's hand trembled as she slowly picked up the phone and held it up to her face.

The phone unlocked. At the top of the screen, her notification center showed one new text message. The entirety of the message was visible in the preview: a single emoji of a drop of blood.

Instinctively, her eyes went to the growing pool of blood gathering around the two bodies. She had just enough time to imagine how she might slip on that pool and break her neck when the phone dinged again.

She'd received a second message from the witch's number. This time it contained three emojis of blood drops. As her mind reeled at the meaning of the second message, a third arrived that contained five blood drop emojis. A fourth and fifth quickly followed, each with an increasing number of the same exact symbols.

The messages kept coming, each containing more emojis than the previous message, so that eventually her entire screen was filled with tiny blood drops.

Carla stepped away from the bodies, fumbling with her phone to call 911, when she felt the first warm trickle run down her leg. A sudden sharp sensation struck deep in her abdomen and she buckled over in pain. Blood began pouring from her like a spigot had been opened up between her legs.

Her stomach burned. Her vision blurred. Her knees weakened.

She grabbed for the table, missed, and crumpled to the floor in a rapidly growing pool of her own blood.

FRAG 'N' TAG

Roy brushed aside a lock of reddish-brown hair and gazed at the sleeping girl. She shifted and sighed contentedly, sending a slow whistle through the oxygen tubes in her nose. He carefully laid the slack from her IV across her legs to keep it from catching on something. On the other side of her bed, the steady beeping of her life support system counted away what was quite possibly the last few seconds he'd have with his daughter.

"Dad?" her lips came to life before the rest of her. Eyes closed, she continued, "I was dreaming about that time mom took me to the art museum. Except for this time, instead of knocking over the stack of flyers, I knocked over a priceless vase."

"Did you and mom still crack up?"

"Yeah. And we got kicked out, just like in real life," she smirked.

He smiled back.

"I always said your mother was a bad influence on you."

She turned her pale face toward him and took his hand.

"Is it dinnertime already?" Doesn't feel like I was out that long..."

"No, honey, it's just after two. I didn't mean to wake you, I was passing by the medical wing and I thought I'd look in on you."

"I'm glad I woke up," she said, squeezing his hand. "Hey, you look pretty handsome. Got a big mission today? Or maybe a hot date?"

The doctors had warned him that any stress could impact Lily's immune system, so even if the mission wasn't highly classified, he couldn't tell her about it—not that she'd believe him anyway. But he also couldn't lie, not to her.

"Nope, no hot dates for your old man. In fact, I don't plan on taking a step outside the base today."

"Oh," she said. "Think I can do one or two of Mr. Hawkins' lessons before dinner? I miss him so much, and I miss school so much, and all my friends, and—"

"I know, honey," he gently interrupted, trying to ignore how cold her hand felt. "It sucks being sick. Why not rest up so you can recover quickly and get back to the academy sooner?"

"But, Dad, Mr. Hawkins made those videos for sick kids, so we could keep up on our lessons."

Roy knew the real reason the professor had made those videos was because he was smart enough to know that when the virus hit the academy, an old man like him wouldn't last long. He was right; he didn't.

"Just rest, my love. Maybe get some sleep before dinner. Rest is what your body needs to kick that bug, so give it plenty, okay?"

She snuggled into her pillow and closed her eyes. For a second, it seemed like she'd stopped breathing. Roy was about to shake her or call for a nurse but she started up again with a sudden deep breath.

"Have fun on your hot date, Dad," she muttered with sleepy lips. "I'll see you tonight for dinner. I love you."

Roy tensed. He had to use every scrap of military training to suppress the urge to pull his daughter close to him and sob into her curls.

"I love you, too," he said softly. "I'll see you tonight."

So much for not lying to her, he told himself as he stood up to leave.

ROY QUIETLY PULLED the door closed and stared down the busy hospital corridor. A surgeon was backing through some operation room doors with their freshly scrubbed hands held up in front of them. Nurses sprinted alongside, their white jackets flaring out behind them. He averted his eyes from the covered stretchers lining the hall, glancing back at Lily's door.

How long before she gets wheeled out here with a blanket over her face?

Her only chance—the only chance for any of them— was such a long shot that under normal circumstances he'd reject it outright. But normal circumstances were long gone, so instead of rejecting the mission he'd volunteered to lead it.

Roy checked his watch. His heart rate was slightly elevated, his oxygen optimal. He had over an hour to kill before he was expected at lab for the mission briefing. He figured he just might have time for a quick workout if he could navigate through the crowded medical ward with minimal friction.

His mind was busy plotting a course to the other side of the base when she spoke.

"Lily's a fighter, like her dad," she said.

Roy answered over his shoulder, "She'd have to be, after going through all this."

"When she recovers, she'll need someone to care for her," the woman said.

He turned around to face her. She was dressed like the rest of the doctors: long white jacket, stethoscope, clipboard tucked under her arm—but she had a calm air about her that seemed out of place in the chaotic ward. Her face softened when their eyes met, the edges of her lips hinting at a smile.

"Thanks for giving her the stuffed flamingo," he said.

"How'd you know it was me?"

"Who else in this madhouse would bother giving a toy to a dying girl?"

"She still has a chance, Roy."

His face grew hard.

"What are you still doing here, Dr. Bailey? Don't you have a war to attend to?"

Her hint of smile vanished without a trace.

"We're losing the war, Roy. We're holding them off, slowing down the inevitable, but there's no denying it. We're losing ground every day."

"Then don't let me keep you," he said, turning to leave.

"Don't go," she blurted out, then added, "On the mission. You don't have to go through with it. Tell your superiors you're feeling under the weather and they'll send someone else. I can modify your vitals as proof."

"Run away? With everything that's at stake? Besides, I have the most zaps under my belt and I have very little left to lose. Not a chance in hell I'm walking away. This is the most important mission of my life."

"Roy, the chances of surviving another zap aren't very good. And once inside, the viral load will be the highest yet. We don't know exactly what we're looking for. The odds of returning from this mission are slim to—"

"I knew the odds when I volunteered and I know them now."

She sighed and searched his face.

"Think about Lily. She'll need you when—"

"Think about Lily?" he interrupted, with a slight growl in his voice. "She's the only reason I haven't lost my mind through all this. Look, we both know the score. Like you just said, our chances of beating this damn bug are slim to none. But we can't stop fighting. You roll your dice, let me roll mine."

"Being the head doctor on this base has certain advantages. I could yank you for whatever reason I want and no one would question it. Signs of over-excursion. A touch of the shakes. Maybe I bumped into you here in the corridor and noticed that you were slurring your words and had a hint of whiskey on your breath. No one would blame you."

Roy stepped forward, resisting the urge to grab her by the shoulders.

"You wouldn't dare..." He trailed off, gritting his teeth. "If you yank me, if you stop me from leading this mission... and then she...Dammit, Caroline, she's all I have!"

As his frown bore down on her, the hint of a smile returned to her face. She'd gotten him riled up and he'd stepped right into her trap.

"She's not all you have," Caroline said, leaning in to lay her head on his chest.

Roy took a step back.

"You're the one who called it off, remember? You

needed to focus on the cure. You didn't have time for anything else."

She stepped forward.

"Can't I call it back on?"

"It doesn't work like that, Caroline," he said, sighing. "After Sue died, I never thought I'd find anyone again. But I found you. *We* found you. Then you left. Lily can't have her heart broken again. Neither can I. End of story."

"The story doesn't have to end there, Roy." She took his hand. "I'm so sorry that I hurt you. I was wrong to walk away. After I lost Frank, I never thought I'd love again. When I fell for you and Lily, I imagined us patching together a little family of survivors. But then fear seeped in. I realized I was scared shitless that the bug would take you two away from me. I told myself that if I fought hard enough, if I gave every moment to research, I'd be able to find a cure and save you and Lily. I was wrong."

Tears filled her eyes, but she held his gaze.

"She got sick. And now, like the stubborn mule you are, you're going to walk into a battle with the odds stacked so high against you."

He stopped resisting, leaned in, and wiped a tear off her cheek.

"Caroline, you've fought harder than a platoon of special forces. The advances you've made in medicine are worth a dozen Nobels, at least."

"They won't do humanity any good if we lose this war."

He tilted her face up to meet his.

"We're not gonna lose. This latest idea, it'll work. Failure is not an option. That's why they're sending me," he said, mustering a cocky grin.

"Oh, Roy! I've tried *everything*. As soon as I make a breakthrough, the damn bug adapts. It uses tactics we've never seen a virus use before. Like it *knows* it's in a battle. Like it has *intelligence*."

"Well, that's what I'm hunting for at fifteen hundred hours, isn't it? I'm going inside, tracking down one of those brain bugs you doctors keep theorizing about, then dragging its RNA out for you to tinker with."

She laid her head on his chest.

"You sure you won't reconsider letting someone else go?"

"Not in a million years. This is my fight."

"No, it's *our* fight. I knew you wouldn't budge, so I've assigned myself as project lead. I'll see you in the hangar at fifteen hundred hours."

She delivered a quick kiss to his cheek, then spun away and disappeared into the parade of white jackets and navy blue scrubs.

"I HEAR he busted himself down from First Sergeant to Staff Sergeant just so he could lead this suicide mission," Todd said to the other two standing near the coffee pot.

"Three ranks? Are you kidding me?" Courtney made a face. "He scrapped more than a decade of service just to go on a mission with you dipshits? That's crazy."

"I wonder how he passed his psych eval, considering his daughter got sick," said Greg. He leaned in and added. "Actually, I know how he passed. I heard he and Dr. Bailey had a thing, maybe still do. Anyway, she probably just signed off on the paperwork so her boyfriend could go on the mission."

"That *would* be a serious violation of protocol," Courtney said in a lowered voice.

The three Specialists exchanged looks and sipped from

their coffee. Finally, Todd vocalized what they were all thinking.

"Isn't it our duty to tell someone? Failing to do so could endanger the mission."

"I'll tell you what's going to endanger the mission," Dr. Bailey's voice announced from behind Todd's husky frame. She sidestepped into view and continued, "Is that the staff wasted their time gossiping in the break room instead of getting their stations ready. Now, return to your seats and get your heads in the game!"

"Yes ma'am!" said the three red-cheeked soldiers as they saluted and turned to leave.

Dr. Bailey raised her clipboard to stop them.

"All evals were done by multiple sources, both military and civilian," she stated bluntly. "And for the record, he passed each and every one with flying colors. I was the first and the last to tell him what a damn fool he is for volunteering for this. But guys, come on, can we not call it a suicide mission just yet? Remember Baghdad? If anyone can pull this off, it's Sergeant Roy Murphy."

They nodded and scurried to their seats.

Caroline checked her watch, then peered out the wall of thick glass that separated the mission control group from mission operations. An empty stretcher and a mobile surgery unit stood at the ready. Beyond that, the squad was getting their final pre-mission check. Each soldier wore what looked like a spacesuit covered in armor and weaponry, and each had a trio of scientists carefully running their fingers over every inch. The soldiers were arranged in two ranks of five inside what looked like a massive walk-in freezer, with their squad leader gesticulating in front of them.

Through his open face visor she could see his mouth

moving, but couldn't hear what came out. Whatever he was saying, she knew it was exactly what his squad needed to hear before going on this mission.

This goddamn suicide mission, she thought.

She brushed off a surge of guilt and decided to rally her own troops.

"Listen up, people!" she said loudly, turning to face the room. "Let me have your attention, please!"

Every head in the mission control room turned to face her.

"As you all know, we're minutes away from what could very well be a turning point in this terrible war. I don't have to tell you what's at stake. This time it's not a drill. I need your eyes and your hands and your minds *here*," she said, scanning their faces. "The Sergeant and his team appear to be ready. Any moment now they'll get zapped. As they're being collected, the patient will arrive and I want him prepped immediately. Remember, to optimize for this mission's success, we had to choose a patient with a high viral load—which means they're on the brink. The risk is very simple: we lose the patient, we lose the squad...and that could mean losing the war. So, it's up to *us* to make sure Sgt. Murphy and this squad get the time they need to tag one of these BVs and get out safely. Everyone ready?"

Two dozen heads nodded.

Caroline pressed a button on a speaker mounted to the glass wall.

"Major Thompson, our team is ready when you are."

A distinguished-looking, white-haired man in military garb dismissed a younger soldier and pressed the button on his side of the wall.

"We're ready, Dr. Bailey. The squad's lined up and ready to be zapped."

"Alright. Mark the time at fifteen hundred hours plus seventeen. Initiating sequence now."

"Oh, Doctor, one more thing," added Major Thompson. "Sergeant Murphy wanted to relay a very important message to you: He wants to know if you'd join him for dinner when he gets back."

Her eyes shot to Roy, who was already lined up with his men inside the Box. She caught his eyes and nodded. He smiled, flipped his visor down, then stepped onto his pedestal.

Caroline drifted to her own console station.

"Initiate de-materializing array. Get those de-scaling algorithms fired up," she ordered. "As soon as the last support tech is out of the Box, seal her up and start the zap sequence."

Meter-thick doors crept shut, shutting Roy and his squad inside. Caroline noticed him flash a wink just before it closed.

Glad to see he's feeling optimistic, she thought.

The noise of her team sounding off each successful boot sequence drew her attention back to the mission.

"Where's my patient?" she asked the room.

A fresh-faced specialist flipped a switch and leaned into his microphone.

"Med Ops, what's the patient's ETA?"

"We lost the patient on the ride over," a voice answered from a speaker nearby. "Had to head back to the infirmary to find a replacement. But we're rolling across the tarmac now and the new patient is stable. ETA two minutes."

"New patient?" Caroline spoke into her own mic. "I selected that patient based on the excessive viral load. If the new patient's load is too thin, it puts the mission at risk of failure."

"Don't worry, Dr. Bailey. We selected the patient with the next dense viral load. The load saturation is comparable."

"Fine. Wheel them in straight away. The squad will be ready when you get here." She clicked her mic off. "Box Ops, how's she doing?"

"Quantum Capacitor nearing full charge, Doctor," a soldier said, their eyes glued to the screen in front of them.

Another soldier turned a dial and looked back at Caroline.

"All systems are a go, Doctor. Waiting for your command to discharge the capacitor."

This will be the fifth zap for Roy, Caroline thought. *If he survives—no, when he survives—we gotta call the world records people and get him a plaque. He'd love something corny like that.*

Caroline had been on the research team that built the Box, so she knew the science behind "zapping" better than most. She knew the dismal survival rate of shedding 99% of your mass, and the even lower chances of surviving reconstruction. One atom out of place and wham! You're instant pudding.

Yet, once again, that sonofabitch was rolling the dice.

Whatever happens in there, come back to me. Come back one more time, Roy.

She clicked her mic on.

"Box Ops, discharge the quantum capacitor in 3...2..."

A pair of outer doors exploded open with a bang. A Med Ops team barged into the hangar pushing a stretcher and aimed it straight towards the operating table. Caroline took one look at the replacement patient and her heart stopped.

On the stretcher lay an angel, sedated and strapped in,

with a dozen tubes and wires running across her body. The flash of neon pink peeking out from under the child's arm confirmed Caroline's worst fear.

Lily.

Caroline froze as the implications of what was about to happen sunk in. The twist that fate had bestowed on this mission was deeply cruel, yet at the same time it was just—even poetic.

"Let's roll some dice, Roy," she said quietly.

"Ma'am?" asked a soldier standing nearby.

She cleared her throat and spoke loud and clear into the mic, "Proceed with the injection."

ROY WOKE WITH A JOLT. Liquid fire pumped through his veins. Everything inside his mechanized zapsuit felt soggy and warm. He started to doze off just as the suit hit him with another shot of adrenaline.

A moment later he was on his feet, shining his head-lamp along the inside of a massive fleshy corridor extending far in both directions. Floating by above him streamed a river of round, flat discs—red blood cells.

Well, mostly red, he thought. This patient must not be getting very much oxygen. They must be very close to the end.

This was his fifth zap, so he knew the routine by heart. His mechanized zapsuit was his first and last line of defense. Not only did it supply him with oxygen, it anchored his metal boots to the inside of the blood vessel, protected him from the surrounding fluid that could dissolve his body in mere seconds, and it included dozens of tiny motors on every limb to compensate for movement with and against the flow of plasma in the bloodstream. These supportive motors allowed anyone in a zapsuit to walk normally or even make continuous long jumps—*bounces*, as Roy had nicknamed them—in order to get around inside a patient quickly and efficiently.

Surviving the molecular shredding process and then the injection were the easy parts. The real threat came from the little buggers themselves.

Because these missions only occurred in the sickest of patients, danger was literally around every corner. Especially right after waking up, alone. While the procedure assured the team would be injected in relatively close proximity to one another, the concept of proximity had a different meaning at the cellular level. Until he and his squad found one another and fell into a defensive formation, they were each as vulnerable as a lamb wandering alone through the jungle.

A lamb with a bolt gun and five thousand rounds, he thought.

"All teams, light up your beacons and sound off!" he barked.

A crude digital map projected on the inside of his visor began displaying tiny, colored dots nearby.

"Red One reporting! Beacon on, sir!" a voice cried out from his helmet speakers.

"Blue Three reporting! Beacon on, sir!"

"Red Four beacon on, sir! This bod is crawlin' with virus, sir!"

"Just keep calm, soldier, and keep moving toward our central position," ordered Roy.

"Green Two reporting, sir! Beacon on, sir!"

Roy bounced along the great soft tube while the rest of his squad continued sounding off. The dots on his visor map moved slowly toward one another.

"Blue Two! Red Two! Light up your beacon and sound off!" he ordered.

The comm channel crackled every now and then, but otherwise remained silent. Roy rotated a dial on the side of his helmet and pulled up a list of twelve names on his visor display. Ten of the names had biometrics output data, while two displayed only quiet, flat lines.

Shit! he thought. *Down two guns from the get-go.*

"We lost Blue Two and Red Two," Roy confirmed over the comms. "Everyone converge on the central position marked on your visor maps. Watch your backs. Follow protocol. Let's assume these smart little buggers know we're here and they're planning to pick us off one by one before we fall into formation."

Just then, he spotted a flicker of movement above him. He flashed his head lamp into the murky liquid and caught the tail end of something disappearing behind him.

His soldier's instinct told him to turn around and prepare to engage the enemy, but the experience he gained in previous zaps told him to prepare for ambush.

It wasn't uncommon for an occasional stray bugger to rush by on some seemingly important business without noticing the soldier's presence. In those cases, firing on a stray would alert them to your presence and most likely draw an army of them to your location. Not that Roy couldn't handle an army—he'd laid many to waste over his previous four zaps. But he also knew engaging the enemy too early would waste precious time and bolts.

But he'd also learned to be careful and make no assumptions. Every once in a while, especially on the most recent zap missions, he'd encountered stray buggers that weren't as unaware as they seemed.

With his head turned back toward the distraction, he

lifted his boltgun and fired blindly into the darkness ahead of him. The rounds lit up the surrounding liquid and he saw two wolf-sized viruses shatter into clouds of lipidic shards.

Before their remains were swept away in the bloodstream, he spun and pulled the trigger one more time. The distraction shattered like the first two.

Without waiting around to see if the trio of viruses had summoned backup, Roy bounced quickly to a narrow stretch of vein where the other dots had converged on his visor map. He lowered his boltgun and counted nine other headlamps.

"Glad to see you all got here in one piece," he said, clapping the nearest soldier on the back. "Time to make it up to Sanchez and Smith. You grunts ready for a good ole fashioned frag and tag?"

"Affirmative!" the squadron barked into their shared comm.

Red Three, who Roy knew to be a low-ranking cadet on his first zap mission, swiveled his helmet back and forth as he stood at attention. The old soldier caught the young soldier's eyes as he continued.

"What happens in the next fifty-seven minutes could turn this whole damn war around. We're gonna tag as many BVs as we can find, frag the rest, and get to the biopsy point for extraction. Everyone got a dag ready?"

Dags were short for *daggers*, which was a word the soldiers had come up with for the sharp handheld instruments that, when plunged into a microbe on the microscopic level, would allow the quantum retrieval field to deliver the organism to the scientists back in the lab. Each zapsuit came with two.

"Affirmative!"

Red Three was glancing over his shoulder, his eyes

slightly bulging. Roy had seen this on every single zap mission—there was always one newb who adjusted to the peculiarities of the mission more slowly than the others. Sometimes they became a risk.

"Red Three, get over here," ordered Roy, waving him over. "What's you name, son?"

"Sir, I'm Red Three, sir!" he said, his eyes darting.

"Your *name*, soldier. The name your momma gave you."

The question confused him just enough to capture his frantic attention.

"I'm...Stanley, sir. Stanley Wittmeyer."

"Nice to meet you, Stan. Outside this zapsuit I'm known as Roy Murphy. Over there we have Velazquez and Jackson. This isn't our first bounce together. We have some other first time zaps today besides you: Todd, Courtney, Greg. We all have names. We all have reasons to get to the biopsy point in one piece. I know this is stranger than any mission you've been on before, but I also know you're here because you've seen your share of combat, even as green as you are. Remember your training. Get your head in the game, soldier," he said directly, without judgment. "Just fall in beside me and follow protocol, and we'll all make it home in time for dinner."

Stanley snapped his face forward and grit his teeth.

"Sir, yes, sir!"

"Good. Alright, get into formation and let's proceed to the first checkpoint."

Roy checked the map displayed on the inside of his visor and led the squad through a series of twists and turns. The inside surface of the artery was rubbery, rebounding tautly beneath their two-hundred-pound mechanized suits. After a few dozen bounces, he raised his hand for them to stop. He'd spotted a few of these theoretical BVs, or *brain viruses*, during his previous zaps. They were always surrounded by an entourage of a few hundred regular buggers that made tagging them very difficult. The couple of times Roy had managed to blast his way through the entourage to where a BV had been situated, he'd come up empty-handed.

"Around the next bend, five bounces or so," Roy said into the comm channel. "Scanners indicate a mob of about two hundred crowded around a single immobile bugger. Textbook BV. Let's go confirm, shall we? Press forward in standard formation and hold your fire until I give the command."

The squadron nodded, gripped their boltguns, and spread out behind Roy.

They came around the corner and shone their head lamps through the murky plasma. A swarm of viruses swirled around an unseen center. The nine beams of light stirred them up a bit, but they kept to their spherical formation.

"No more bouncing. Spread out in a half circle, five meters apart, and crouch into a creep position. We need to stay far enough away to draw them out in waves, but close enough for one of us to tag the BV when the battle thins out."

Roy could hear Stanley's zapsuit rattling. He put a hand on the barrel of the young soldier's boltgun.

"I know a big cluster of them can be unsettling the first time you see one. Remember this: not only do they look like upside-down beer bottles with legs, they break just as easily. These ones are primarily defensive and won't attack until they deem us a threat, so no one fire until I give the command, understood?"

"Sir, yes, sir!" the squad confirmed.

Roy crept forward, staying low and sticking close to the vessel lining. His eyes strained to penetrate the swarm of viruses, hoping to catch a glimpse of the bugger at the center of the swarm. Caroline and the other doctors suspected that BVs somehow actively controlled other viruses in their vicinity, and that whatever method it used to do so should make it physically distinct from the others.

"We've seen highly adaptable pathogens before, but this bastard seems to change its behavior *mid*-treatment," she'd ranted to him, a few months ago when they'd still found time to enjoy each other's company.

"Whenever we make progress in any patient, the damn virus seems to sidestep the approach and find some other way to continue ravaging the body. Our most effective treatments end up doing nothing but buying the patient a little extra time. To save them, we need to find out how it adapts so damn quickly! Then we can strike at the heart of the virus."

"Don't you mean strike at its *head*?" Roy had quipped. "After all, you're the one who named them *brain viruses*."

Soon after, out of sheer desperation, humanity had begun zapping squads of infantry and injecting them into patients to look for clues. Roy had been one of the first to try the new technology, and he'd been in the squad that first confirmed the existence of a BV.

"Stupid b-bugs..." Stanley muttered on the squad comm. "There's not enough room in this suit! N-not enough air. Stupid bugs!"

Roy turned to see the young soldier's visor fogged up with moisture. He pulled the squad vitals onto his own visor, verified the elevated pulse, then motioned to Velazquez.

"Stanley, you're sitting this one out," ordered Roy. "Hold your position while the rest of the squad advances."

The young soldier went on creeping and muttering to himself.

"Stan!" Velazquez touched helmets with him and spoke with his comm mic turned off. There was no point in letting one soldier's fear spread through the whole squad. "The Sarge said to hold your position. Relax, man!"

Stan pulled away and took another frantic step. Velazquez grabbed his arm. The mechanized gears on their zapsuits strained against one another, heating the plasma around them. Roy was about to bounce closer to give Velazquez a hand when suddenly Stan yanked his boltgun away and fired a smattering of rounds into the swarm of viruses.

The outer layer of the viruses peeled away from their swirling sphere formation and came right at Roy and the others.

"Fire!" Roy shouted, and everyone but Velazquez did.

Instead, Velazquez tackled Stan, stole one of dags pinned to his zapsuit, then jabbed it hard between the young soldier's shoulder plates. She kicked herself away just in time to avoid the quantum retrieval bubble that engulfed him. When it blinked out of existence, Stanley was gone.

"Good work, Velazquez!" Roy barked into his helmet comm as he unloaded a stream of bolts on the advancing viruses. "This party kicked off sooner than I'd hoped."

No sooner had the first wave been thoroughly fragged than the next hit. Behind that one, another was preparing to swoop in.

"Care to dance, Sarge?" she yelled over the constant roar of the boltguns.

"You read my mind, Vee," Roy smirked. "If you can keep those buggers off me, I think I could make it to the BV in two bounces."

"Ready when you are, Sarge!"

Without flinching, Rot performed a full-boost bounce maneuver directly into the approaching wave of viruses. The light from his squad's boltguns reflected in every shard of shattered virus, lighting up the murky plasma around him like a liquid Fourth of July celebration.

Viruses swirled and dove at his squad. Velazquez took cover beside the others and made sure any frag any viruses that swam too close to Roy.

As he landed the first bounce, he gunned down two and shattered a third with the butt of his boltgun.

During his second jump, Roy's visor pinpointed the BVs exact location and he adjusted his trajectory mid-jump by firing his boltgun in the opposite direction he intended to go, letting the force nudge him towards his target. As he grew closer, he noticed the BV stayed latched onto the vessel wall as if a battle weren't taking place all around it.

For a brain virus, this one seems pretty dumb, he thought.

When he was just a few feet from landing the second time, a trio of viruses broke off from the battle and rushed past him. They beat him to the BV and crowded around it. It only took a second for Roy to realize they weren't selflessly throwing their lives down between their beloved BV and his bolts. They were furiously cannibalizing it.

By the time his feet touched the ground, the only traces of the rare bugger were either drifting away in the plasma or floating inside the cannibal's semi-translucent bodies.

Damnit! he thought, then put a bolt in all three.

"Time to mop up!" he shouted into his comm. "This BV's toast. We gotta scram to the next one. Sending coordinates now."

In less than a minute the last virus shattered and the boltguns stopped.

"Hell yeah!" Jackson cried, raising his gun. "Frag you, lil' bastards!"

Another young soldier—*Todd*, remembered Roy—stepped forward and tapped his helmet.

"What happened to Red Three, Sarge? Why'd he fire?"

Roy exchanged a look with Velazquez.

"Must've had a boltgun malfunction. Which reminds me, check your suit and gun before we bounce to the next target."

When they were ready, Roy continued leading them through the murky plasma. Soon after, he stopped around a sharp bend in the vessel.

"Another swarm, around this bend. A bit bigger than the last one."

"How much bigger we talkin'?" asked Velazquez.

"Scan show between three and four hundred, at least."

"Damn, Sarge," she said. "Whoever this guy is, he's crawlin' with bugs."

"More to frag!" cheered Greg. "Isn't that right, Jackson?"

Jackson slapped a fresh clip of bolts into his gun and nodded.

"The Leaderboard says I'm beating the rest of you zapheads by at least twenty frags. I'll be able to double my lead, considering the shit storm we're about to walk into."

"No way, old man!" laughed Todd. "This is *my* day to rule the Leaderboard. I may even go for a new all-time record."

"Anything you guys can do, we can do better," Courtney said, cocking her gun and flashing a grin at Valazquez.

Velazquez glowered at the squad.

"Good luck, but everyone knows no one's gonna beat the Sarge's record."

Roy had been scanning the high curved walls that disappear into the murk, but at the mention of his frag record, he turned to face them and grinned wide.

"You zapheads wanna score some frags? Great. When I give the signal, go in heavy and fast like you're fighting to get out of Hell. We need to tag the BV before they know what hit them. Velazquez, you're taking my spot at the front."

She nodded. "Where you gonna be, Sarge?"

"Remember Panama?"

He looked into her eyes and saw that she did.

"Worked then, might work now."

"You had a parachute back then, Sarge!"

Roy smirked.

"Well, lucky for me, this time I'm submerged in plasma. Should be a piece of cake."

"You're crazy, hombre." Velazquez shook her head. "We'll hold position until I see your signal, then we'll hit 'em with everything we got."

Roy turned his headlamp off and vanished into the murky darkness that surrounded them.

"Fall in, zapheads!" barked Velazquez. "Line up and listen! We'll creep around the corner and hold position. Firing too soon will start the party early, and we don't want that. Like the Sarge said, this group's twice as big as the last. Wait for my signal, then give 'em hell and push forward with everything you got. *Understood?!*"

"Sir, yes, sir!" the seven soldiers shouted back.

They spaced out to cover the width of the artery and began taking slow steps around the bend. Above them streamed a silent river of red blood cells. Velazquez stayed a few meters ahead of them, her bolt gun at the ready.

The beams of their headlamps fell onto a giant writhing mass of swimming viruses clustered around a seemingly random spot along the artery wall. Velazquez squinted into the dense swarm. She lifted her gaze and searched the darkness.

"Hold," she whispered into her helmet mic. "Take aim and wait for my signal."

After what felt like an eternity, she saw the first flash. Then another, and another, and another. In the pitch black plasma, impossibly high above the vessel floor, someone was flicking their headlamp on and off in quick succession.

Velazquez lowered her boltgun and shouted, "Attack!"

Eight boltguns came to life, mowing down dozens of viruses within the first few seconds. When the rest caught on, they rushed the squad in a single massive wave.

The buggers changed tactics! Velazquez thought, feeling drops of sweat forming on her forehead. *Same way they overcome every treatment the eggheads doctors throw at them!*

She looked to her left, then to her right. They were too thinned out to sustain a single, dense wave of attackers. If they were going to survive, they needed to change their own tactics on the fly, too.

"Fall in around me!" ordered Velazquez. "Quick! Two ranks of four, one on the outside, one inside."

The farthest head lamp on their left flank was eclipsed behind a dozen clawing viruses, followed by a wet scream exploding over the comms.

The rest hustled around Velazquez without breaking fire. They formed two rows and distributed their bolts evenly at the approaching wave. Layer after layer of viruses exploded and scattered, immediately followed by more. The squad dug in, but the attackers gained ground slowly.

At this rate, Velazquez estimated as she squeezed her trigger and fanned her boltgun back and forth, *we got about five minutes before the swarm overtakes us.*

Just then, she noticed a silhouette descending behind the onrush of buggers. Roy—lights off, gun holstered—had successfully climbed to the roof of the blood vessel, snuck across enemy lines, and was descending right on top of the BV.

Just like Panama, you crazy pendejo, she thought.

Roy already had a dag in hand. The second his boots touched the floor, he struck. The tip of the dag went through the BVs plasticky exterior so easily that his entire hand plunged into the bugger. He released the dag, but before he could pull his hand out, his entire body went rigid.

Electricity surged through him, flowing in from his arm and out through every other extremity. His ears burned. His teeth clenched. His mind went blank—then suddenly filled up with a barrage of images and thoughts that came to him all at once.

The next thing he knew, he was coming to. His right hand felt impossibly tight, as if it were asleep with pins and needles. He reached for his gun but found he couldn't grasp it. He no longer had a hand.

Roy held the stump of his wrist up to his visor. The metallic fabric of his suit's sleeve was so thoroughly melted to his skin that his suit's pressure was perfectly maintained. The pain was dull and distant, and he was able to ignore it.

Now I know what it feels like to get bitten by a quantum retrieval bubble, he thought, astonished at how sheer and bloodless the wound was.

"Sarge!" Velazquez shouted nearby. She and the others were running toward him, firing upward into the mass of viruses to ward off the occasional dive bomb. She fell to her knees beside him. "Your hand! Are you—"

"I'm fine," he interrupted, then reached around with his left hand and grabbed his gun.

Her eyes grew wide.

"You tagged a BV, didn't you? You did it! Another first, Sarge!"

Roy studied the spot on the wall where the BV had been anchored. He poked it with his gun and a burst of sparks exploded in all directions.

"Sarge, you okay?"

He nodded.

Velazquez patted him on the backend chuckled.

"Alright, good. Look around, Sarge. Tagging that BV sent these local buggers into some kind of confused docile state, but we don't know how long that'll last. Let's get to the biopsy point and get the hell outta here."

Roy didn't move.

"Just behind this spot is a nerve," he said, prodded the wall again. More sparks flew. "The BV was latched onto a nerve. This is new. Viruses don't use the nervous system."

"I didn't know you were a virologist, Sarge," teased Velazquez. "How about you discuss it with Dr. Bailey over dinner once we get back?"

He pointed with his stub.

"Why would a BV need to jack into a nerve? Stealing power?"

"Who knows, Sarge. Maybe they use nerves to communicate or something. More importantly, it's none of our business. We did our part. Let the eggheads upstairs figure out the rest."

"Communicate?" Roy repeated. "To each other? There must be *millions* of BVs inside the average patient. How the hell could any single BV take part in so much chatter all at once? Unless..." he trailed off, his gaze penetrating the fleshy wall.

Velazquez turned her back toward the others and frowned at Roy.

"Please, Sarge. Enough. We sent one home and we lost Courtney during the attack. I'll accept that outcome from a zap mission any day, and so will you. We did the impossible; we tagged a BV. Time to go." She smiled. "Besides, you don't want to stand up Dr. Bailey, do you?"

"You're right," Roy said, straightening up. "Let's get out of here before these buggers remember they have us outnumbered fifty to one."

He motioned the squad into a loose huddle.

"We're heading to the biopsy point. Follow me, and only engage if attacked. But, no matter what happens, keep moving."

He led them below the floating swarm of comatose viruses, back the way they'd come. They rounded the bend and within a few bounces came to an abrupt dead end.

"Sarge, you sure this is the right way?" Velazquez asked. "There wasn't a wall here before."

"This doesn't look like blood vessel lining," Greg said as they lined up to examine it. "This looks sticky and white, like old cake frosting."

"Maybe it's a blood clot or something," Todd suggested.

"You saying this is what cholesterol looks like?" Jackson laughed and poked the wall. "Fellas, when we get back, remind me to eat better."

Todd laughed nervously and reached his hand out to touch the white goop. His voice was cut short as the wall slurped him in.

"It got Todd!" Greg shouted. "Did you see that? The wall took him!"

Then, without warning, the wall oozed out and grabbed him, too. The only trace of either soldier were their head lamps bobbing dimly behind the white muck.

"Bounce, now!" Roy shouted, just as the wall bulged outward to grab another soldier.

Instinctively, he reached his right arm out to protect his soldiers. The goop was on him in seconds, slurping his stub into itself like it had the other two. Roy braced his legs and leaned back, throwing his weight away from the puckering wall. His resistance didn't seem to matter; the wall yanked on him like a rag doll. When he was in up to his shoulder, it stopped pulling.

Hundreds of tiny, toothless mouths began probing and puckering all around his face, as if deciding what part of him to eat first.

Surprisingly, the wall not only spit Roy out, it recoiled away from him as if it were in pain. Roy wasted no time—he bounced backward as far as his suit would take him.

The remaining soldiers leapt backward as well, huddling together outside the reach of the goop. From a distance they got a better perspective on what had just eaten Todd and Greg.

It wasn't a clot of cholesterol and it wasn't some kind of new lining in the blood vessel. It was three enormous white spheres lined up snugly across the vessel floor.

"White blood cells," Roy said under his breath.

"I thought this patient was in critical condition," Velazquez said. "They're aren't supposed to be any of those here, right?"

"The human immune system keeps fighting till the bitter end, even if it's losing the war."

"Why'd it eat Greg and Todd, but not you?" asked Jackson, giving Roy a strange look.

"Have you seen the Sarge lately?" replied Velazquez. "Would you wanna eat that mess?"

Roy smiled and shook his head.

"Just lucky, I guess. Maybe the other two filled its stomach up, or maybe my grizzled old ass just wasn't worth it."

"Maybe," Jackson said, squinting at Roy before returning the smile. "Either way, any chance you can ask your new friends to let us pass?"

Just then the gigantic white spheres lurched upward off the floor and began slowly floating toward them.

"Get down!" barked Roy, dropping to the floor. "Flat on your back, and don't move a muscle! I think they're on their way to mop up our mess back there. Let's not distract them."

The soldiers hit the deck beside him. The cells passed within a few inches of their head lamps, giving the squad an incredibly intimate view of a white blood cell wall. Its surface was an endless white sludge that writhed and puckered with a million tiny mouths.

Luckily for them, the cells passed by, unimpressed by the strange tiny humans cowering underneath them.

When the soldiers finally sat up, Roy exhaled a breath he'd been holding the whole time.

"Dr. Bailey could spend a lifetime looking at these

things under a microscope and never get the view we just got, boys."

They bounced toward the biopsy site, every second expecting another horde of viruses to leap out from the murky darkness and attack. By the time they finally returned to the site of their first tag attempt, Roy knew they'd make it back safely—with a little time to spare.

As they bounced in silence, images and feelings from his encounter with the BV flashed through Roy's mind. His stubby arm still tingled with a mix of dull pain and the eerie sensation of being fondled by a white blood cell. For reasons he couldn't fully articulate, he stopped and began searching the wall where the first BV had been cannibalized by its own troops.

Velazquez landed beside him.

"Sarge, we're almost there. Is there a problem?"

Instead of answering, Roy poked the tip of his bolt gun at the spot where the BV had been latched to the vessel wall. Sparks exploded and quickly fizzled away in the surrounding plasma.

"Another nerve site," Roy muttered to himself.

A few feet from where the sparks had come from, he laid his palm against the wall.

"An artery. You can feel the blood pumping."

"Sure," said Velazquez. "That might be one of the vertebral arteries. Anyway, Sarge, let's—"

"Vertebral arteries send blood where?" asked Roy.

"I didn't pay too much attention to that part of the training," admitted Velazquez. "We'll look it up when we get outta here, okay?"

"The brain," Jackson answered, locking eyes with Roy. "Vertebral arteries lead straight to the brain. One of the only ways in."

Roy could see that Jackson knew what he was thinking. There was more to these buggers' intelligence than a million BVs chattering through a victim's nervous system like a bunch of old hens using telephone lines to call each other up and gossip. There had to be a central command tucked safely away in the body, somewhere that would allow it to remain protected and direct those million BVs instantly and in unison.

Not only were there more die to roll on this mission, Roy also suspected there was much more at stake in regards to this particular patient.

"You four go on without me," he said. "I have something to check out before I'm ready to be extracted."

"Sir?" Velazquez tilted her head at him to study his face. "Am I gonna have to tag you to bring you home?"

"Let him go," Jackson said. "Sarge knows what he's doing. Here, take this in case you find something interesting." He handed Roy his spare dag.

"Fine! If you wanna stay here and die, maybe they'll give me your rank!" Velazquez turned to face the other soldiers. "You heard the Sarge. Fall in and follow me to the biopsy point. Let's bounce!"

As Jackson turned to leave, Roy slapped him on the shoulder.

"Tell Dr. Bailey that I might have to take a raincheck on those dinner plans."

"No way, Sarge. I'm just gonna tell her you're runnin' a quick errand and you'll still make dessert."

Roy nodded, spun the barrel of his boltgun to its *torch cutter* setting, and sparked it on. A short, white-hot flame shot out of the barrel.

"Vee's right—you sure are one crazy son of a bitch,"

Jackson said, smiling, before bouncing to catch up with Valezquez and the others.

Roy flipped his visor to thermal. He scanned a length of the wall, looking for a place where his artery ran close to the vertebral artery on the other side. A moment later he'd found one and sliced a huge X into the vessel wall with the torch cutter.

Hundreds of fist-sized brown blobs—platelets—appeared out of the murky plasma and began patching up the rupture. Roy switched his boltgun back to its bolt setting and dove through before they could finish their work. He was immediately swept away in a circumfluent stampede teeming with red blood cells.

Short on time, Roy straightened himself to swim along quickly with the current, although as he got moving it pulled faster and harder than he expected. Within seconds, he'd reached a speed relative to a fighter jet traveling at 5Gs. The skin of his face peeled back and collected at the rear of his helmet. The seams of his zap suit barely held together.

Somewhere around the patient's collarbone the intense motion overwhelmed him and he blacked out.

He awoke sprawled between two cliffs of lightning. Electricity rippled up and down each side, extending so high that it finally blurred into hazy dim static.

Roy got to his feet and flipped his headlamp off. Not only was this electric canyon bright enough to see by, he thought it best to retain the element of surprise. If he actually found what he suspected might live up here, this was the most dangerous bug hunt yet.

Roy flicked his visor from thermal to viral detection. He had no idea how the detection system worked—something about his suit being covered in sensors that somehow tasted the surrounding fluid for traces of target chemicals. But he did know that it ended up giving him a visual overlay that pointed him in the direction of any local viruses.

To his surprise, a glowing green arrow instantly appeared on the left side of his visor.

"Lucky me," Roy said to himself as he bounced after it.

He leapt with max boost, knowing he had much more battery in his suit than he had time. The path he moved through branched off into side canyons, and finally flowed like a tributary into a larger canyon. The green arrow became very bright and Roy knew the bugger had to be close.

He disabled all his suit lights and crept slowly down the center of the wide electrified canyon. Not far ahead, he noticed a bright bulge in the wall—a pulsating lump of electricity. Roy scanned the surrounding fluid for signs of any backup viruses and found nothing but endless lightning.

He holstered his boltgun, palmed a dag, and crept along the wall toward the lump. As he got closer, the lump began to look familiar. It was a large BV, easily the size of an elephant, that had latched itself onto the electrified wall.

With each undulation, the thing swelled with static and then exhaled a web of lightning back into the wall. Roy figured it was taking in data and spewing out orders, but he thought he'd let Caroline and the other eggheads write up the scientific explanation.

He lifted his dag and braced himself for a low, fast bounce.

"Sarge, come in," Velazquez's voice burst into his helmet. "We're at the biopsy point. What's your status? Do you copy?"

Roy slapped his comm off, but not before the glowing bugger had shifted its body in his direction.

So much for the element of surprise, he thought, and

leapt at the giant, glowing BV with every ounce of energy left in his legs and zapsuit boosters.

He soared through the brain fluid, his dag poised to plunge deep into its target. The BV tilted itself toward him, puffed itself up with static from the wall, and unleashed a bolt of lightning directly at Roy.

Every muscle in his body became a twisted metal cord. Every alarm in his zapsuit went off at the same time. He face-planted just a few yards from his target, a handful of debris in his clenched fist. The jolt had caused his hand to tighten violently, and he'd crushed the dag.

Roy rolled onto his back and slid his spare dag from his thigh strap.

He knew what punishment he would earn—and which reward—if he used it on the BV.

Without giving it a second thought, he pushed himself up and prepared to make another bounce. Another jolt surged through him, turning him into a rigid, frozen mannequin. This time, his heart stopped momentarily and his lungs expelled every last drop of air.

Despite the electric needles piercing every inch of his body, Roy readied himself to pounce on the bugger the moment the effects of its attack abated.

He'd already figured out that the stakes on the table were for much more than *just* humankind's last hope. And Roy wasn't about to let a few thousand kilowatts of electricity keep him from saving her.

Just as he suspected, this, the real BV, had to momentarily stop surging the electricity through him so it could suck in more voltage from the patient's brain. It had only partially swelled with static when Roy plunged his only remaining dag through its frail outer membrane. He yanked his hand out and bounced away from the bugger a split second before the quantum bubble engulfed it and it flickered out of existence.

Roy lay on his back, his body numb, his suit fried. He imagined he was suspended inside a great thunderstorm, floating over the horizon, into the sunset, onward into a pool of infinite still reflection.

A weight landed softly against his shoulder, pinning him down and keeping him from slipping away. No matter how hard he tried, he couldn't sit up—not even an inch.

It was Sue, tucking her head against his, just like she used to.

He gazed in astonishment at his long, dead wife and realized her face was somehow inside his helmet. She was there in the flesh, nuzzling against his neck, and she was making some kind of rhythmic sobbing noise.

"Don't cry, babe," he whispered. He tried to wrap his arms around her but discovered they no longer took orders from him.

"It's okay," he sighed. "I'm here. Don't cry."

The breathy noise got louder and Roy realized she wasn't crying. Sue was giggling through clenched lips, barely able to keep from laughing out loud. His wife was back in his arms, back from the dead, and she was tittering like a schoolgirl.

"Sue," he mouthed, not sure if he made a sound or not.

She pressed a finger to his lips and gently shushed him.

"Sorry, Roy. I've missed you too, but you already have dinner plans tonight."

Warmth flooded his mind.

He relaxed and closed his eyes.

. . .

"HE DID ALL *THAT*?" Lily said, clutching her stuffed pink flamingo tightly to her chest. "Inside *me*?"

Caroline patted the girl's hand and smiled.

"He did. Your immune system responded immediately —as I'm sure you know better than anyone. You're well on your way to a full recovery."

"I haven't felt this good in weeks. It's a miracle!"

"No, honey, it's not a miracle. It's your dad."

Suddenly, Lily's grin faded and she stared into the middle distance.

"But how'd he...?" she started to ask, her head tilted slightly. "If he used his last dag on the real BV... how'd you, you know, get him out?"

"It involved some precise scanning of the skull, a sudden onslaught of mucus, and a huge reserve of good karma on Roy's part."

"Mucus? You mean you found him in my—" She stopped herself and pointed to her nose.

"Yep. We collected your boogies and combed through it until we found him."

"Yuck!"

"It was like looking for a tiny, little Roy-shaped needle in a very gross haystack."

Lily grasped Caroline's hand.

"Will he have to zap into *every* patient and cure them the same way?"

"Nope, his zapping days are officially over," she said, putting her doctor voice on. "And he'll have no one to blame but himself. Not only did he lose a hand, he tagged a pristine sample of this new BV, so there's no need for any more zap missions for a very long time. The rest of this war will be fought in the lab and at the pharmacy."

"What will Dad do without another battle? It's what he lives for."

They both looked at the other bed in the room. Roy lay snoring softly, surrounded on all sides by colorful bouquets and cards.

Caroline brushed the hair out of the little girl's bright eyes and winked.

"Oh, I'm sure the three of us will think of something."

A WEEKEND UP NORTH

"Didn't I tell you my Imagine Dragons playlist was the bomb?" Mike said, his eyes peeking over the top of his mirrored aviator sunglasses.

Darbi, wrapped around his right arm, squeezed his bicep and nodded. She couldn't stand the music—in fact, she was sure it was making her nausea worse—but she thought it was sweet he'd made a special playlist for their drive up north. Unlike Mike, Darrell had never taken her up north. Darrell had never made her a playlist. Darrell could go to hell.

"I'll send you the link so you can listen later on your own," he said, tapping and swiping on his phone.

She clutched his arm.

"These roads look pretty curvy. Maybe you should keep your eyes on the road?"

She made sure to end the comment as a question so he'd know she wasn't bossing him around. Darrell would've flipped out if she'd said something like that to him. Darrell could go to hell.

Mike turned his head towards Darbi and looked her up and down.

"You look pretty curvy, too. Maybe I should keep my eyes on you instead."

"Oh, Mike!"

She giggled and squeezed his arm again, this time giving it a little caress. Mike's arms were just as big as Darrell's, and most importantly, he would never use them to hurt her.

"I'm serious!" she said, smiling to show she wasn't. "These roads look dangerous. And look, that sign we just passed said '*Watch for antelope*'".

"Darb, I grew up on these roads. I could drive them blindfolded and drunk—which I did once, back in high school, on a dare. Not my proudest moment..." He flashed a grin. "Actually, at the time I was pretty damn proud. Until the cops showed up."

"Oh, Mike!'

Darbi remembered picking up Darrell from the police station for the DUI he got on New Year's Eve. What a waste that entire relationship had been. She was so much better off with Mike. He was different—better—than Darrell in every way.

"I almost went to jail that night, but the deputy who pulled me over took one look at my last name and let me go with a warning."

"Wow! Really?"

"That's what I'm talking about. This is my home turf. Up here, you can call me *King of the White Mountains*." He took her hand and kissed it. "Trust me, babe—this weekend is gonna kick so much ass."

She closed her eyes and pressed her cheek against his shoulder.

"It was so sweet of you to take us on a romantic getaway."

Mike kissed the inside of her wrist, sending shivers down her spine.

"This trip's gonna be really special for us," he said, smiling. "Just wait."

Darbi's eye flew open and she bolted upright. The color drained from her lips.

"I'm gonna be sick! Stop the car, Mike!"

"Not in the Beemer! Not in the Beemer!" He jerked the steering wheel. "There's a gas station right here, see? We're pulling in now, Darb. You're gonna make it."

The BMW crunched through the gravel lot and zipped into the first open spot. Darbi, covering her mouth with both hands, ran into the store.

By the time Mike got inside, Darbi had already disappeared into one of the bathrooms. He and the slack-jawed cashier standing behind the counter exchanged stoic nods—a proper rural greeting—then Mike pretended to browse the snack aisle to avoid any conversations with the local hayseed.

As he perused the shelves of Snickers and Milky Way bars, he reflected on the bullet he'd dodged. He'd come close to being stuck behind the counter of some shitty roadside gas station in the mountains. But he'd succeeded where so many other rednecks had failed; he'd figured out a way to make a good life for himself down in the valley. Got a job at the BMW dealership. Got a condo in the suburbs. Twice a year his parents would drive down to Scottsdale to visit him, not the other way around. Never the other way around.

If it wasn't for Darbi, he'd never have stepped foot on the White Mountains again. Yet here he was, back for the second time in one week.

"Back again so soon," said the slack-jawed cashier. Mike noticed it wasn't a question.

"Nope," he lied, pretending to be occupied with the ingredients on the back of a candy bar. "We just pulled in now."

"I didn't mean her. I meant *you*." His eyes flickered towards the bathroom and a greasy smile stretched across his face. "Different girl than last weekend. Ain't that funny?"

Mike walked slowly to the register, flexing his arms and chest as he went. He never took his eyes off the cashier's.

"You must have me confused with someone else," he said, then tossed the candy bar onto the counter without breaking eye contact. "I have about a hundred cousins who live up in these parts. Must have been one of them you saw earlier this week."

The cashier held his gaze.

"She don't know, does she?" he said, motioning towards the bathroom. "I wonder, how much is it worth to you that she don't find out?"

Mike's arm shot out and he grabbed the cashier by his jacket, pulling him halfway across the counter so their faces were an inch apart.

"I'll say this one more time," Mike growled. "You have me confused with someone else. Now drop it."

A distinct metal click broke the silence. Mike glanced down to see the cashier holding a sawed-off shotgun at waist-level, aimed right at his guts.

Mike let go of the jacket and straightened up. The cashier slowly lowered the gun. Neither took their eye off the other.

Finally, the cashier grinned. "Just the Snickers?"

"Say anything and I swear I'll come back a third time. Trust me, you don't want me to come back a third time."

The cashier flashed the shotgun over the top of the counter and widened his yellow smile.

"Try me anytime."

"Everything okay in here?" a voice asked from the front of the shop.

A police officer stood just inside the entrance to the gas station, his eyes locked onto the two men and his hand hovering casually over his sidearm.

"Carl," the cop said, approaching the counter slowly, "You been drinkin' on the job again?"

"Naw, Deputy. Just showing this city slicker here my anti-theft system." He returned the gun to its hiding spot and placed both hands flat on the counter.

"If this is the fella who owns the BMW out front, I don't think you need to worry about him skipping out on you without paying for his candy bar." The deputy turned to Mike and tapped the brim of his hat. "Hey, Carl, this isn't just any city slicker. This is Mike Penrod."

"Penrod?!" The cashier's slack jaw dropped even lower.

Mike nodded and shook the deputy's hand.

"Visiting the family?"

"Not this time." Mike glanced over his shoulder towards the bathrooms. "I brought someone up here to, uh…"

He trailed off and pointed to his ring finger. The deputy smiled.

"What, the girl from last weekend turn you down or something?" asked Carl.

Mike's face turned red and he clenched his fists.

"I told you, that must've been one of my cousins you saw last week."

The deputy noticed the rising tension and started to

intervene, when a woman's face appeared beside Mike. She looked pale but strangely vibrant.

"Hi, I'm Darbi, Mike's girlfriend," she said, giving a little wave to no one in particular. "So you saw one of these *million* cousins Mike claims to have up here?"

The deputy interrupted Carl before his slack jaw got moving again.

"Hello, ma'am. I'm Deputy Swiftwater of the Penrod County Sheriff's Department." He paused to tip his hat. "Carl here was just saying how he thought he saw one of Mike's cousins come into the store last weekend. Isn't that right, Carl?"

Carl nodded, then hunched over his cash register and pretended to examine something on the screen.

"These mountains are crawling with Penrods," explained Swiftwater. "Except for a few that had enough good sense to get away, like Mike here. I'd say by the look of the BMW out front, you're doing pretty well for yourself down in the valley."

Mike grinned and put an arm around Darbi. "Can't complain."

"You two staying until Sunday?"

"Monday, actually," said Darbi, smiling up at Mike. "Mike's dealership is closed for renovations on Monday, so he extended our stay till then."

"Whoa, Mike! You didn't mention you own a car dealership!" asked Swiftwater. "Maybe you can get the Sheriff's department a discount on some new cruisers."

"Naw, sorry...I don't own the place—not yet."

"Your parents moved down to Greer, didn't they? You two headed that direction?"

"No, we're driving further north to my uncle's cabin up on Goose Canyon Lake."

"That's way out near the reservation where I grew up," said the deputy, smiling. "You two must really value privacy."

"That's what I keep telling you, babe! Goose Canyon Lake is, hands down, the most secluded—and beautiful—lake in all of Arizona."

"It's just a silly name, that's all," she said, stifling a giggle.

"Either of you carry?" Swiftwater asked bluntly.

Darbi looked confused. Mike cleared his throat and asked. "A gun?"

Swiftwater nodded.

"Why would we need a gun?"

"Oh, you know...just in case. The wildlife way up in those uninhabited parts of the range can get pretty wild."

"Are there *bears*?" asked Darbi, making a show of grabbing Mike's arm.

"Bears, sure. But they usually keep to themselves as long as you do."

"He means the geese," blurted out Carl, peering over his register.

Mike and Darbi exchanged a look, then both cracked a smile. The deputy's eyes stayed trained on Mike's.

"So, are you carrying a firearm with you? Or is there one at the cabin?"

Mikes shook his head and flexed his swole upper body.

"I'm pretty sure I can take a goose with my bare hands, Deputy."

"I can see that," Swiftwater said, crossing his arms. "Listen, you two, up on the reservation my people have many stories about the spirits that permeate nature. These stories held the community together, protected us, and inspired our warriors when they prepared to go into battle. Different factions of warriors would call upon different spirit animals —the bear, the wolf, the eagle. Do you know which animal our most fierce warriors called upon as their animal spirit?"

"Geese?" squeaked Darbi, half hidden behind Mike's arm.

"That's right. Seems silly at first, I know. But, think about it: a goose can slide through waters silently, soar through the air, and, if provoked, they can and will attack with a ferocity unmatched in the animal world. They're as cunning as a fox, with the memory of a bison. My people regard geese—especially the flock of Canadian Geese who've just returned to the area—with a special honor and respect. Just keep that in mind while you're up there, and you probably won't need a firearm."

"Cool story, Deputy, but the only guns I'm bringing up to the cabin are these two cannons right here," said Mike, flexing his biceps.

"Oh, Mike!" cried Darbi, blushing and wrapping her arms around one of his arm cannons.

The deputy smiled and tipped his hat to the two weekenders.

"You two have a safe drive, and remember what I said. If you do run into trouble, of any kind—power outage at the cabin, car trouble, hiking injury—it'll take someone a while to get all the way up there. There are a few other cabins on the lake, but just about all of them are empty since the real estate bubble burst. If you do run into trouble, there's a ranger station on the far north side of the lake. They have a young guy doing research up there right now, taking samples and sending the results back to the university. He may be the only other person within a hundred miles of Goose Canyon Lake. Don't hesitate to knock on his door if you get into pinch and you don't want to wait for my old squad car to make it over all those hills."

"Thanks, Deputy," said Mike. "C'mon babe, we've got a few more hours on the road before we get there. But don't worry, I made a second Imagine Dragon's playlist from all their b-sides."

"Oh, Mike," Darbi said, feeling another wave of nausea coming on.

As they walked out of the store, Carl called out from behind them, "Those geese are gonna gitcha, city-slicker!"

DARBI MANAGED to keep down what was left in her stomach for the rest of the drive through the mountains, even after Mike shuffled both of his Imagine Dragons playlists together and put them on repeat.

He'd slammed the door shut and drove in silence for the first ten minutes or so, his hands clenching and unclenching the wheel. The redneck had really gotten under his skin. Darbi wondered what they'd said to each other while she was hunched over a toilet in the bathroom. Mike had seemed really tense right when she'd walked up. They both had.

Darbi had just started to replay the few scraps of conversations she'd heard when, without explanation, Mike snapped out of his funk. He took her hand, kissed it, and reminded her what a wonderful, special weekend they were about to have.

She knew Darrell would've pulled that redneck over the counter and knocked his teeth out, not giving a second thought to the armed deputy standing nearby. Darrell was such a psychopath. Darrell could go to hell.

She hugged Mike's arm the rest of the drive, happy to

have finally found the type of guy who didn't resort to violence the moment something pissed him off. That kind of patience would make him such a great father. Unlike Darrell, who, no doubt, would've turned out to be as abusive as her own father had been.

Darbi stared out the window, but didn't see the pine trees zipping by. Her mind was too busy imagining how the conversation with Mike would go. Would it bring them closer together or push them apart? Would he freak out? Would he blame her?

Mike slowed the Beamer and turned off the highway down a narrow dirt road that ran straight through the skinny pines. Twenty bumpy minutes later, their BMW rolled into a gravel lot alongside a gorgeous single-story log cabin with a wrap-around porch and a green corrugated metal roof.

As she stretched her limbs and let the crisp mountain air soothe her nausea, Darbi noticed a small enclosed fire pit on the lakeside deck with a pair of hammocks strung up on either side. Beyond that, a floating pier bobbed gently on Goose Canyon Lake. Two kayaks were laid out and ready to be launched with nothing more than a shove.

The only thing to mark the distant shore was a hazy, jagged wall of pines. To the east, a small island poked through the placid surface of the lake, half shrouded in a late summer haze.

Mike fiddled with his keys at the cabin door.

"Oh, Mike. It's so beautiful."

"Just wait till we get out on the lake, babe." Mike held the screen door open with his foot while he dragged their suitcases inside. "First come check out the cabin. It's pretty swank."

Darbi noticed the interior walls looked identical to the exterior—big fat wooden logs. All the furniture was also wooden, but everything seemed to be made from a different type or color of wood.

"I know it looks a little rustic, but, trust me, my uncle dumped a ton of cash into some killer upgrades. Watch this."

He swiped and tapped his phone with an eager, boyish excitement. Suddenly, his Imagine Dragons playlist exploded from all directions at once.

"Built-in surround sound speakers!" he yelled over the loud music. "And there's this huge satellite dish on the roof for cable and internet, so we won't have to miss the play-off games this weekend!"

A foot-stomping, hand-clapping, monotonous beat reverberated through Darbi's body. Her eyes searched desperately for the nearest bathroom or trash can while the rest of her face maintained a perfect smile. She didn't think she'd be able to wait till after dinner like she'd planned.

Darbi had to shout to be heard over the music. "Mike, can you put on something a bit more...romantic?"

"Huh?" he asked, staring at his phone.

"Can you lower the volume?" she yelled. "I have something important to talk to you about."

Mike nodded and paused the music.

"Sorry, babe. What'd you say?"

She wondered how Mike would react to the news if she just blurted it out. She knew how Darrell would react because she'd experienced it twice already. The first time she'd been foolish enough to tell him about it. The second time he found out by finding the pregnancy test in their bathroom trashcan while fiending for pills. Both times he'd beaten her so badly she'd lost the baby. The second time he'd actually scribbled out a bill for "abortion services rendered" on a piece of junk mail and shoved it in her unconscious mouth.

A flood of warmth filled her as she looked up into Mike's icy blue eyes. Mike was healthy. Mike was gentle. Mike was different.

"I have something important to tell you. I was going to wait till tonight, till after dinner, but I think maybe you've noticed..."

Mike's phone dinged and he glanced at the notification on his screen. He held it up to Darbi.

"FitBot is telling me I've been idle for too long today." He held his smart watch up next to the phone screen. They both displayed numbers and graphs that Darbi didn't understand. "Must've been all the time on the road. If I'm gonna hit my fitness goals for the day and collect my crowns in the FitBot app, I gotta get my heart rate up."

"Okay," Darbi said, managing a faint smile.

She began to unbutton her blouse, but Mike chuckled and stopped her hand on the first button.

"Oh my god, babe, I can't believe I'm saying this, but let's save that part for tonight. I was thinking of getting my heart rate up with something a little more adventurous. Paddle with me."

"Paddle?"

"In the lake. Well, in the kayaks."

"Mike, I've never kayaked before...I..." Her hand went instinctively to her belly. "Is it safe?"

He took her hands in his and kissed her forehead. "I'll be your instructor *and* your lifeguard. You can't get any safer than that, babe."

They held hands as they walked out the back door, across the porch, and through the stretch of wildflowers to the small floating dock. Mike gave her a quick kayaking lesson, then they both put on their life jackets and pushed off from the shore.

"Left, then right. Pull back smoothly—yep, just like that. You're a natural, babe!"

"Let's see if Mr. *King of the White Mountains* can keep up!" taunted Darbi, paddling away as fast as she could.

Mike laughed and pointed to the northeast. "Race you to that island!"

The wind kicked up the waves and the waves pushed them back towards the cabin, but they paddled on. Darbi splashed Mike as he pulled ahead. She found that kayaking came easy to her, and she even thought she might be able to give him a run for his money—maybe even beat him there.

She knew Darrell would have flipped out if she had won a race between them. Hadn't he thrown an empty beer bottle at her the one time she beat him at Mario Kart? She shuddered and let herself fall in close behind Mike's kayak, careful to let him keep the lead.

Mike was waiting when she slid onto the pebbled beach. He grabbed the front end of her kayak and dragged it further onto the shore.

"Here we are, babe! Penrod Island! At least that's what me and my cousins called it back in the day."

Darbi stood, stretched, and took in the view.

"Oh, Mike! It's beautiful! Look at how small our cabin is from here! The lake seems much larger when you're looking out from the middle." She turned and scanned the island. It was about the size of a football field, dense with a blend of scraggly thicket and mature trees. "And this island seems much bigger up close, too."

"You like it?"

"I love it. And I love you." She kissed him. "Thank you for sharing this with me, Mike."

Mike pulled away and looked at her over the top of his aviators.

"Come with me if you want to see something *really* special," he said, holding out his hand.

"Oh, Mike!"

Darbi started towards him, but her foot slipped out from under her and she toppled over onto the rocky beach. Mike was beside her in a flash.

"Babe! Are you okay?"

"My ankle!" she cried, writhing on her back and cradling her foot.

Mike stabilized her ankle in his lap and gently felt around above her sneakers.

"Does it hurt when I do this?" he said, twisting her foot a certain way.

"No, but my ankle burns and throbs. Oh, Mike! I'm sorry!"

"What are you sorry for, babe? It's this beach, it's completely covered in...slimy goose shit!" he cried. "And now, so are we!"

He sprang up, dropping Darbi's foot with a thud, and looked down at his jeans. They were smeared with chunky brown streaks that glistened wetly in the late afternoon sun.

"Babe, you're covered too..." he said, cringing away from her.

Darbi ignored the slimy coating on her backside and used her paddle as a crutch to get to her feet.

"What the hell!?" ranted Mike, huffing like an angry bull. "This is bullshit! It wasn't like this last weekend!"

"So that cashier did see you here last weekend?" asked Darbi, looking down. "You said you were golfing."

Before she knew what was happening, Mike snatched her by the wrist and pulled her into the trees.

"Fucking bullshit!" he yelled as he stomped through the thicket.

"Can't we just go back, Mike?" pleaded Darbi, stumbling against her paddle. "My ankle hurts and we're so gross right now. Can't we come back tomorrow?"

"No," he said, seething. "I'm not gonna let some stupid goose shit ruin our romantic weekend."

Darbi hung her head and obediently followed him. She consoled herself with the fact that at least Mike wasn't dragging her by her hair, like Darrell had a tendency to do. Darrell could go to hell.

Besides, even if he was being a little rough, Mike was justified in his anger. He obviously had something romantic planned—she knew it from the moment he suggested the getaway to her—but she had no idea how this shit-covered island could possibly play into it. Still, she decided it would be best to let him get it out of his system. The sooner he did, the sooner they could get back to the cabin to clean themselves up and put some ice on her ankle before making dinner, and...then would she tell him? Yes, the evening was still salvageable, even if her ankle wasn't.

Mike stopped and stared into a small, treeless clearing ahead of them.

"What the..."

Darbi pulled up alongside him and gasped.

"Oh, Mike," she said, then gasped again for theatrical effect. "I've never seen anything like this. It's beautiful."

The clearing was overflowing with dozens of tightly-packed muddy nests, each one protecting a a clutch of large goose eggs.

"I can't believe it. I can't fucking believe it."

"Me neither, Mike. We'll come back tomorrow when

we're clean to take some photos." She turned back towards the path they'd come from. "Thanks for sharing this with me."

"Give me your paddle."

"What? Why? I need it to stand up."

"Give it to me and sit down."

She started to protest again, but he turned his head and roared over his shoulder, "GIVE IT TO ME!"

Darbi involuntarily let go of the paddle and Mike caught it in mid-air. Her hands were shaking as she lowered herself to the ground, careful not to jostle her ankle.

"They're just nests, Mike," she mumbled under her breath, too quiet for him to hear. "We should just leave them be and go have a bath. And then, dinner. I'll bake some salmon. Some potatoes. You love potatoes. Then we'll talk."

Mike stood glaring into the clearing. Last weekend it had been a small treeless space carpeted by dry grass with a low flat stone right in the center. The way the light from the setting sun had cut sideways through the trees had made it look like a magical glade from a fairy tale. The perfect spot to pop the question.

Now, the grass and the stone were gone. In their place sprawled dozens of ramshackle nests held together by mud and goose shit. Inside each crater lay a clutch of large white eggs, each one smeared with goose shit. Around and underneath and on top of everything were clumps of wet goose shit. There was nothing beautiful about the scene. It was vile. And worse: it had fucked up his plan.

Mike huffed like a bull, and Darbi swore she saw steam billow from his nose and mouth. He stomped his boot into the closest nest. The stomp smashed four of the eggs, but then he kicked his foot around to make sure he broke the other two eggs as well.

"Mike, what are you doing?" she said, her voice trembling.

"I'm getting what we came here for," he seethed. "It better still be here."

"Whatever it is, we can come back tomorrow, once we're—"

He interrupted her by stomping into another nest, then another. As he stomped towards the center of the clearing, he swung the paddle down like a club, smashing as many eggs as he could along the way.

Darbi winced at all the tiny embryonic goslings floating in the orange ooze that spilled from their shattered eggs. Their huge veiny eyes bulged. Their small crooked beaks hung open. Their tender little lives extinguished, one by one.

Darbi turned away. She put a hand on her belly and tried to ignore the sound of shells breaking.

After another minute or so, the rampage stopped. She slowly craned her neck around, ready to flinch away at the first hint of violence.

Mike was on his knees, rummaging through a group of nests in the middle of the clearing.

"Mike," she squeaked. "What are you doing?"

He tipped one of the nests over, then tossed it aside.

"I can't fucking believe it!" he cried. "After all the planning...after coughing up so much dough...Ah! Here it is! *Shit!*"

He cocked his head slightly, suddenly aware he wasn't alone.

"Darb, come here," he ordered, his voice level.

"Mike!"

"Come here. Now."

"Mike! I can't! My ankle."

Without turning around, without looking up from the object in his hands, Mike sighed. She again saw steam from his breath rise in the cool, moist air.

"If you don't get over here in the next minute, I'm throwing this in the lake."

Darbi couldn't see what he'd found under the goose nest, but she had a pretty good idea what it was. Her heart began to race. *This is why he's been so tense. This is why he lied about golfing last weekend. This was the start of their little family, as imperfect and messy as it was.*

That was, unless she upset Mike and made him throw it all away. Their little family would perish before it even began, just like all the embryonic goslings drying in the dappled sunlight.

"Forty-five seconds, babe."

"Okay, I'm coming," she said, getting onto her hands and knees. She looked out at the trail of egg shells and sticky yolks stretching between her and Mike.

"Thirty seconds."

As Darbi crawled, she let her attention retreat to a dark corner in her mind, the place where she kept her childhood dreams. She wasn't on her hands in knees crawling through dirty nests and goopy egg yolks. She was standing in her mother's beautiful wedding dress, walking down the aisle— alone, since her dad passed away during the last pandemic. Mike looked so handsome in his tuxedo. Instead of being surrounded by the swollen eyes of a hundred dead goslings, she was being admired by everyone in her life. She'd finally done it. She'd found herself a good man. Darrell had just been a mistake, a misstep. Darrell could go to hell.

Mike had tried his best to create an enchanted engagement, she told herself. It wasn't his fault that a flock of geese had nested in this clearing. He'd done his part to kick off their little family. Now it was her turn.

She kept crawling, ignoring every time a tiny head or featherless wing brushed up against her hands. Before she knew it, she'd made it through the mess.

Mike turned around and got down on one knee in front of her.

"Now stand up," he ordered.

"Mike...I can't stand. My ankle!"

"Here, use this." He held out the paddle. Both ends had bits of shell and feather stuck to them, and yolk had dripped all the way down the handle. "Take it. If we're gonna do this, let's do this. I'm down on one knee, like I'm supposed to be. Now take this and stand up."

Darbi took the paddle and grunted as she pulled herself to her feet. With all her weight on the paddle, she tilted her head and looked down at her soon-to-be fiancé.

"Oh, Mike," she said as tears gathered in her eyes.

He held up a shit-covered ring box and popped open the lid. It was the most beautiful diamond ring she'd ever seen.

"Will you marry me, Darb?

"Yes," she answered without the least bit of hesitation.

At that, Mike looked up at her. She could see something like tranquility nibbling around the edges of his rage. His eyes relaxed. The corners of his lips turned upward. There was no more steam in his breath.

"Really?"

"Oh, Mike! Yes! Yes! *Yes!*"

She leaned down and kissed him. Neither of them cared that more than a little goose shit was exchanged in the act. She felt the tension start to leave his shoulders.

"And I have a surprise for you, too, Mike. You know how I've been really nauseous?"

"Yeah, you've almost thrown up in the Beamer a few times lately. Your motion sickness is flaring up, right?"

"No, it's not motion sickness. See, last month I found out I'm—"

She was interrupted by a loud honk exploding from the edge of the clearing. It was immediately followed by two more, each sharper and angrier than the last. A large goose hopped into the clearing and spread out its wings to make itself appear larger.

"Hold this!" Mike said, snapping shut the soiled ring box. He pushed it into her free hand and snatched the paddle away. "No way am I gonna let these fuckers spoil our moment."

She watched him quickly filling up with rage once again, so she hugged his arm like she had the entire drive up north.

"Oh, Mike! Can't we just go back to the cabin and celebrate?"

Another goose appeared in the clearing and began bobbing its head like a cobra ready to strike. Both geese were fully mature and seemed larger than any bird Darbi had ever seen in real life. She knew Mike could rip them apart if he needed to—but she didn't think her stomach could take much more violence.

"Mike, let's just go. It's getting dark. And I think there were storm clouds in the west. Mike, please."

He shoved her down into a nest and leapt towards the honking birds. He swiped at one with the paddle, but it ducked low and dodged. While following through with the swing, he suddenly changed direction and lunged at the other goose. He managed to get hold of its neck, just below the beak. Before it could react, Mike swung it high into the air and then back down right on top of the other goose. Darbi heard bones crack and the bird in his hand went limp. The goose on the ground was still twitching, one wing flapping weakly while the other remained tucked up alongside its body. Mike swung again, and again, and again. Finally, the wing stopped twitching and fell limp.

A sudden roar of distant honks enveloped the small island.

Mike dropped the dead goose and turned just in time to see Darbi lurch forward and spew her lunch all over the nearest clutch of dead, shriveled goslings.

BACK AT THE CABIN, Darbi wiggled her toes above the surface of the bath water. Her red toenails looked like drops of blood against the sparkling white bubbles.

She sighed and sank into the water all the way up to her chin. She wasn't sure she'd ever get out.

There was a knock at the bathroom door, then Mike opened it wide enough to stick his head inside.

"Hey babe, you still doing alright? Any chance you need a hand? If so, I have two right here."

He waved his hands through the crack and wiggled his eyebrows.

"Oh, Mike!" She smiled and pulled the bubbles around herself. "You can help by burning the clothes I had on."

"Mission accomplished, babe. They're currently smoldering out in the fire pit, along with mine. No joke, I sprayed 'em with lighter fluid and *FWOOSH!* Even our shoes. Aren't you glad I made us bring extras of everything?"

"I can't believe you actually burned them!" she said, laughing. "Oh, Mike! Thank you."

"It's the least I can do for the future Mrs. Penrod." He winked, then swiveled his head back towards the hall. "Gotta go check on the salmon. You've got about ten more minutes. There's an ankle wrap and some ice waiting for you at the table."

"Okay, I'll be out soon."

He blew her a kiss and pulled the door closed.

That was the man she'd fallen in love with: cool, playful, loving. Mike was not really the violent jerk she'd seen on the island. Sure, he'd freaked out, there was no denying that, but once she'd seen the gorgeous—and obviously very expensive—engagement ring, she understood why. Anyone man would blow a fuse if their engagement was ruined by a bunch of disgusting birds.

Now that she thought about it from the comfort of a hot bath, it would have been more worrisome if he hadn't reacted the way he did. The intensity of this anger was a reflection of the intensity of his love for her.

She eyed the ring box sitting on the edge of the sink and sighed.

The important thing was that he snapped out of it once he realized how upset she was. Even after she puked—*right in front of him!*—and even though she was covered in goose shit and egg yolks, he'd carried her back to the kayaks in his arms like a hero from the movies. Then he'd strung their kayaks together, towed her both back to the floating dock at his uncle's cabin, stripped off her disgusting clothes, and carried her all the way up to the tub.

Snagging a guy like Mike Penrod was worth a twisted ankle.

Darbi allowed herself another five minutes in the tub before drying off and slipping into her silky black dress. Mike mentioned once how it'd driven him bonkers when she'd worn in on their first date. She hoped it would be able to cast its spell on him again tonight.

After touching up her hair and makeup, she gave herself one more close look in the mirror. She wasn't as pretty as she could've been if she'd been back in her apartment with her full assortment of cosmetics and an hour to get ready, but it would have to do. She practiced a warm smile—something else Mike had mentioned liking—then opened the ring box to claim her prize.

Her heart stopped. The ring was gone.

Mike knocked on the bathroom door.

"Salmon and potatoes are getting cold, babe," he said from the hallway. "Besides, you don't have to worry about what you're wearing, I don't think you'll be wearing it for very long."

Darbi stared into the empty ring box as panic swirled inside her. She hadn't opened it since he'd proposed to her. It had gone straight from her pocket to the bathroom sink, where she'd scrubbed the outside with soap and water to wash off all the goose poop. For a moment she worried that it might have fallen down the drain, but she knew for certain that couldn't have happened because she hadn't opened the box.

"Darb? You okay?"

"Just finishing up," she lied. "I'll be one more minute."

"Alright, but if you're not out soon I'm gonna drink all the wine."

She heard his footsteps retreat back to the kitchen. Her eyes were pinned to the empty box. Darbi knew she hadn't opened it since Mike popped the question...which meant the gorgeous and expensive engagement ring must have fallen out when he snapped the box shut after the geese appeared in the clearing. Which meant it was somewhere back on the island. Which meant Mike was going to freak out again.

Darbi closed the box and shoved it in her toiletry bag. She stared into her reflection. She'd have to tell him...but not immediately. She decided to tell him tomorrow, once he'd had a good night's rest.

As she entered the dining room, Mike, a half-empty wine glass in hand, pulled out her chair and motioned for her to sit. He smiled and nodded to the plate of blackened salmon and potatoes waiting for her. Two candles flickered beside a bottle of wine, and his Imagine Dragon's playlist played softly in the background. Between the music, the charred salmon, her special news—and the fact that she was terrified of Mike finding out about the ring—she had to clench her mouth into a smile to keep from gagging.

"You look so beautiful, babe. Here, prop your foot up on this chair. I'll put the ice pack on your ankle while you eat, then we'll wrap it up before going to bed—if we don't get too carried away." He wiggled his eyebrows and motioned to the bedroom. Her stomach lurched.

Darbi forced a smile and reached for her wine, then, remembering what she needed to tell Mike, slid it away from her.

"Something wrong with the wine? This isn't that cheap stuff my uncle had stashed up here, it's a nice bottle—an *expensive* bottle—I bought up from the valley."

"It's not the wine. It's that I'm—" She stopped herself from blurting out the news.

"Is the salmon okay? I left it on the grill for a little too long when I came inside to check on you, but it's not too dry, is it?"

"It's not the food, either. Everything is really wonderful tonight, Mike. It's perfect."

To prove it, she took a tiny bite of the salmon and forced another smile. He smiled back and shoveled a huge chunk of roasted potato into his mouth.

"Mike, I have something important to tell you. Something I've needed to tell you for a while now." She paused, afraid she'd stumble over her words and somehow make him upset. She reminded herself the man sitting across from her wasn't Darrell. There was no way Mike would freak out and hurt her. Mike was a good, strong man who loved her, so much so he proposed just a few hours ago. Mike would be happy to find out that he was going to be a father. All she had to do was open her mouth and tell him.

"Oh, Mike…You and me, we're going to—" She shook her head and started over. "You may have noticed I've been acting a little different lately. That's because I'm—"

"Where's the ring?" he interrupted, shoving another potato into his mouth.

Darbi froze.

"Oh…uh, it's still in its ring box. Back in my bag."

"Why aren't you wearing it?"

She offered him a little smile, then took a sip of wine to buy herself a moment to think. She considered sneaking out in the middle of the night to paddle to the island with a flashlight, but he knew her ankle wouldn't allow it. The only way to get the ring back was to tell Mike the truth.

Darbi took another sip of wine and decided again that the truth about the ring would have to wait. She had another truth to get off her chest first.

"Don't you think you should be wearing it, Darb? I mean, you're my fiancé, right?"

"Oh, Mike! Of course I am!"

"Then you should be wearing the ring. I'll go get it for you." Mike pushed his chair back.

"No!" she cried, then quickly recovered her composure. "It's too small. The air up here must make my fingers swell, or maybe..." she paused, then caught Mike's eyes in her own. "Maybe my fingers are swollen because of the important thing I'm trying to tell you."

Mike screwed up his face, put his hands behind his head, and leaned back in his chair.

"Okay, fine, babe. Tell me what's more important than showing the world you're committed to being Mrs. Mike Menrod? I mean, what if other guys hit on you? Is that what you want?"

"No! Of course not!"

He dropped his arms and leaned forward, the steam building in his chest.

"What is it then? You ashamed? Don't want the world to find out, is that it?"

"No! Listen, Mike—"

"If you're not gonna wear it, you might as well just give it back."

"I'm pregnant!" she blurted out.

Mike's jaw fell open. He sat silently, frozen, staring at Darbi.

Between the rain beating on the cabin's metal roof and the Imagine Dragon's playlist beating against her skull, Darbi felt like retching.

"You're...We're..." He scooted off his chair and fell to one knee beside her. "Darb, are you sure?"

She nodded.

"Wow, babe. This is *huge*. We just got engaged a few hours ago, and now..."

Before he could finish his thought, the music cut out and all the lights went dark. The only source of light was the cluster of candles on the table between them. Their startled eyes searched the sudden darkness and found each other.

"Did the storm take out the power?" asked Darbi.

"Don't think so," Mike said, getting to his feet. "The county lines don't reach all the way up to the lake. My uncle's cabin runs on a ten thousand watt diesel generator out on the side yard, like everyone else up in these parts."

After staring at the candles for a moment, he suddenly got to his feet and finished his glass of wine in one gulp.

"Guess I should go take a peek, see what's going on."

"Do you know how to fix a diesel generator?"

Mike gave her a look.

"I'm a guy. I'll figure it out, babe. You can use your phone light to go find your ring, then come back and eat your dinner. I'll have the tunes back on in no time."

On his way out, he leaned down and kissed the top of her head. Darbi heard the side door open and close.

In the candlelight, she poked at her food and fretted over their unfinished conversations—the one about the baby and the one about the ring.

She heard Mike's voice before she heard the side door fly open.

"You son of a bitch!" he yelled into the pouring rain. "I'm going inside to get my gun, and if I find you out here when I get back..."

After a few soggy footsteps down the hallway, Mike came bursting into the dining room, water flinging off of him as he stomped past the table and into the kitchen without so much as looking at Darbi.

"Mike!" she squeaked. "Who were you talking to?"

"That little weasel fuck from the gas station!" he called back from the darkness. She could see a beam of light bouncing around the kitchen as he fumbled with his phone.

"He's out there?" Darbi squirmed in her seat. "You saw him?"

"I didn't have to, but he must be out there! Who else would come all the way up here to vandalize our generator and leave these everywhere?"

Mike appeared in the doorway and aimed his phone light at a large feather in his other hand.

"Look familiar? Just like the ones all over that island. Goose feathers—dozens of them, all over the generator!"

"The creepy cashier from the gas station in town vandalized our generator? Can you fix it?"

"I'll fix *him*." Mike dropped the father and disappeared back into the dark kitchen. "That dipshit tore the panels off and ripped out all the internal wires and lines, then he scattered a bunch of feathers everywhere and even clamped the beak of a dead goose onto one of the exposed cables to make it look like it got juiced trying to bite through. When I get my hands on that piece of shit, there won't be anything left for Deputy Swiftwater to identify."

A flash of lightning illuminated the kitchen. Before it vanished, Darbi saw Mike's silhouette in the doorway holding a large butcher knife in his hand.

"Wait, Mike...why would he do that?"

"To fuck with us, babe!" He ran to the back door and peeked through the small window. "You heard him today. He probably got drunk and drove up here just to scare us. These stupid rednecks have nothing better to do on a Friday night. But he'll be sorry, babe. He'll be sorry he fucked with Mike Penrod."

"Maybe we should just go. If the power's out, and there's a storm, shouldn't we just go find a hotel for the night?"

"I'm not letting this prick run us out of my uncle's cabin. Not in *my* county. Not on our special weekend."

"What if he has a gun? He knows we don't have one! What if he's just waiting for you to run out there looking for him so he can shoot you? I should call 911, or the deputy, or—"

"My phone's got no bars, and neither does yours. The satellite dish won't do anything if we have no power to connect. No one's coming to rescue us. It's just us and him, babe."

"And maybe his gun! And maybe a few of his drunk buddies with their guns! Mike, please, can we leave?" she begged. "I'm scared and cold and my ankle really hurts. *Please*, Mike. Can we please just go?"

Darbi thought she saw his shoulders relax and the knife lower. Even in the dim candlelight she could tell he turned to look at her. She covered her face with her hands to hide the tears streaming down her cheeks.

She heard him sigh and take a few soggy footsteps back towards the table.

"Alright, babe. You're right."

She looked up. He nodded.

"More likely than not, they have guns. And I'm not gonna be the guy who brings a butcher knife to a gun fight. Plus..." He paused to tilt her chin up so he could wipe away her tears. "I have a gorgeous fiancé to take care of now. Grab whatever you need for the night and grab me a change of clothes. We'll come back in the morning for the rest. Since I'm already soaked, I'll go get the—"

He was interrupted by the obnoxious shriek of a car alarm.

All the color drained from his face.

"The Beamer!"

He ran to the back door, flung it open, and ran out under the covered porch. Instead of charging after whoever was vandalizing his car, he stood and stared.

"Is it *him*?" squeaked Darbi.

"It's...I..." He rubbed his eyes. "Darb, come look at this!"

She got to her feet and hobbled over to the back door. She carefully stepped onto the porch and immediately heard a chorus of short, violent honks underneath the heavy downpour. A flash of lightning struck overheard and illuminated an impossible tangle of necks and wings where Mike's BMW should have been.

"Mike, are those...?"

"Yeah, I think so. Maybe fifty of 'em. Maybe more."

Darbi clutched his arm.

"What are they doing?"

"They're covering my Beamer in a mountain of goose shit," Mike said, seething. He shook Darbi free and threw the butcher knife towards his car. It missed birds and shattered the passenger side window. A few geese hopped inside and started ripping up the upholstery.

"We have to get out of here, Mike! Can't you make them leave?"

Mike started towards the gaggle, but stopped halfway to the car when fifty beaks simultaneously turned in his direction. They let loose a fierce, unified hiss.

He took a step back.

"Darb, get back inside the cabin," he called back over his shoulder.

"Not without you!"

Two more gaggles waddled through the thicket on either side of the driveway. They joined the one that had been attacking the car, their flocks merging to form a small feathered army. In unison, they lowered their heads and charged.

Mike picked up Darbi and carried her into the cabin, not stopping to close the screen door behind him. He slammed the inside door and pinned it with a dining room chair.

Darbi stood trembling, swiping and tapping at her phone with shaking hands.

"It's no use, babe. You won't get a signal out here," he said, pacing. He snatched Darbi's glass of wine from the table and drained it.

There was a thump at the door, then a cacophony of honks and hisses spread out across the wrap-around porch.

"Oh, Mike! We gotta get out of here!" she squeaked. "We gotta get to the car!"

He shook his head and poured himself another glass.

"Even if we could stomach driving in the Beamer, it's not safe to take on those roads. I noticed there was a group of geese at each tire, pecking inside the wheel well, behind the tire. I'm pretty sure I saw severed brake fluid tubes dangling out."

"They took out the brakes?" asked Darbi, looking up at him. "But...they're just birds, Mike. Birds can't..."

"Maybe they're feral or they have rabies. Or maybe this is some kind of new bird flu that makes them super aggressive."

Darbi thought of the island—the nests, the eggs, the two

poor geese who tried to run them off—and speculated that the birds outside might have other motives.

"Whatever the reason, they went through a lot of trouble to trap us in here," he said, then downed another glass of wine.

"Are we safe in here?" asked Darbi. "Can they get in?"

A series of thumps came from above, followed by the urgent slapping of flat feet across the metal roof.

Mike's eyes followed the steps. Realizing where they were headed, he flung his wine glass away and flipped the heavy wooden dining room table onto its side. Cold salmon and potatoes scattered across the floor, the candles went out, and the room became even darker.

"Mike! What are you doing?"

A flash of lightning illuminated all the windows, giving her a snapshot of the scene. Mike had dragged the table into the living room.

Another flash of lightning, and she saw him shove it up against the mouth of the fireplace.

"Darb! Come hold this table! Hurry!"

She hobbled towards the sound of his voice. As soon as she was within reach, he grabbed her arm and pulled her the rest of the way.

"Lean against it! Brace yourself!"

Mike was no longer beside her. The table shook, but her weight was just enough to keep it pinned flat against the wall. Behind it came the muffled sound of enraged honks.

"Mike!"

She felt his grip on her wrist again, then she was pulled away. Her hand brushed against smooth leather, which told her she'd been replaced by the loveseat that normally sat across the room below the large window facing the lake.

Another flash of lightning illuminated the large lakeside

window, exposing a fence-like lineup of long, slender, craned silhouettes topped with black, wedge-like beaks.

Mike pulled her to him and spoke in her ear.

"Darb, listen to me. We gotta get to the dock, but I can't carry you and fend them off at the same time. Can you run?"

Darbi shifted some of her weight on her ankle and winced.

"Maybe, a little. But why the dock? Isn't that where they came from?"

"If we can get to the kayaks, we can paddle north to that ranger station the deputy mentioned. They've gotta have guns and a radio there."

Thunder reverberated through the cabin's log walls.

"We can't make it, Mike! There are too many of them between us and the dock!"

"Yes we can, babe. I'm gonna run out the side door and draw them away from the back of the house. That should leave you with a clear shot to the dock. Don't worry, I'm pretty sure I can outrun these fuckers and make it back to you just as you're ready to go. If you get there before me, don't wait."

"What do you mean? We need to stick together, Mike! We should stay here!"

"Do you smell that, babe? It's hard to tell because of the rain, but I smell propane. I think those fuckers must've somehow damaged the line that runs from the tank to the generator. Any minute now..." He grabbed Darbi by the shoulders and shook her. "We gotta make a run for the kayaks! I'm gonna draw them away from the back porch. Don't wait, Darb. As soon as you see the back porch is clear, get to the dock."

Darbi couldn't see him leave her side, but she felt him

go. She heard the side door open and slam shut, then she heard Mike shouting before his voice was swallowed up by the rain and thunder.

She considered just running to the bathroom, locking the door, and curling into a ball on the floor. Then she considered how brave her fiancé was to use himself as bait so she could make a run for it. He was out there, alone, surrounded by vengeful, homicidal geese. Her hand went to her belly.

Darrell would have left her behind. Darrell could go to hell.

Darbi peeked around the curtain and watched the last goose waddle around the side of the cabin. She crept through the back door, tiptoed across the patio, then plunged into the downpour to start the painful trek to the dock.

Lightning and thunder boiled within the clouds above her. Her ankle screamed. The occasional shadow undulated in her peripheral vision, but no honks or hisses came from them, so she hobbled on.

The floating dock shifted under her weight. She immediately grabbed a paddle and lifted it high into the air like a baseball bat, expecting a goose to spring out at her from the hollow kayaks. When none came, she shoved them each into the lake and turned back towards the cabin.

A flash of lightning illuminated the property just as Mike came sprinting around the side yard. A writhing tsunami of feathers appeared close behind him and followed him across the yard. The geese waddled fast with their beaks lowered and their wings half open, honking and hissing as they went.

"GO!" screamed Mike as he approached without any hint of slowing.

He took the dock in one stride and dove onto his kayak belly first. The momentum pushed him out from the dock and away from Darbi.

"Mike!"

"Paddle, Darb! Come on!"

Mike righted himself in his kayak and plunged his paddle into the water. Without looking back, he sped off into the curtain of rain and vanished.

Darbi took a quick glance over her shoulder and noticed the gaggle of geese had stopped pursuing them. Instead, the plump angry birds lined up along the shore and let loose a single, furious honk.

Before the honk ended, the cabin behind them exploded.

"Darb! Come on!" she heard Mike shout from the darkness.

Numb and trembling, she began paddling away from the smoldering cabin and the angry geese.

"Over here!" a hazy silhouette called out. She pulled up beside Mike's kayak and searched the darkness for his face. His hand reached across the water and took hers.

"I was so worried, babe! Thank god you made it."

"Oh, Mike! The cabin! It..."

"The tank blew. It's okay, my uncle has insurance. Can you paddle?"

"They...they didn't follow us into the lake! Why, Mike? *Why?*"

"Who cares!" He grunted and shook the rain from his face. "It won't matter in a few minutes when we're safe at the ranger station."

More lightning flashed overhead. Darbi caught a glimpse of muscles rippling across Mike's back as he thrust his paddle into the water to rotate his kayak north.

"We gotta get out of this storm, babe! Follow me!"

His silhouette vanished in the dark wall of rain. She dug her good foot into the nose of her kayak and paddled fast after him.

Being so much lighter than Mike, Darbi had no trouble following close behind. Besides the occasional bolt of lightning being hurled directly over their heads, they paddled through a world of cold, wet blackness. With every bolt of lightning came the rumble of thunder reverberating angrily in the air.

"Mike!" Darbi called out towards his silhouette. "Are we almost there?"

He dipped his paddle into the water to turn his kayak towards her.

"The storm must really be tossing us around out here," he said. "The wind keeps pushing us east towards that island. Every time I have to turn around and..."

"Are we lost?"

"Of course not!" He pounded a fist into the side of his kayak. "Trust me, babe. It's not much farther. And look! The storm seems to be letting up! Let's go!"

He turned back in the direction they'd been going and started paddling furiously.

Darbi had just started picking up some momentum behind him when he abruptly lifted his paddle let himself coast to a stop.

"Impossible!" He swiveled his head and squinted into the darkness ahead of them.

"*What's* impossible?"

He pointed. Darbi shielded her eyes from the rain.

"Is that...? Are we approaching the island *again*?"

The rain thinned to a drizzle and the once turbulent lake rocked gently beneath them.

"No...that's not the island, Darb. That's..."

He jerked his kayak around so it was facing hers.

"We gotta get out of here!"

Mike paddled past Darbi before she had a chance to turn around.

"Mike, wait! What is it? What did you see?"

"Shit, shit, shit!"

The tremble in his voice was something she'd never heard before—something she hadn't thought possible. Not only was Mike scared, he was panicking.

As she turned to follow, Darbi's eyes caught the silhouette of the small island. Something pulled her attention towards it and she couldn't look away. As the rain continued to thin, her view got better and she noticed that all the trees had been cleared. All but one tree in the center of the island that seemed to grow right before her eyes. When a pair of glowing yellow eyes opened at the top of the tree, her blood turned as cold as the water in Goose Canyon Lake.

"Babe!" Mike called out as he paddled up alongside her and grabbed hold of her hand. She swung her head around to the direction he'd come from and saw a wall of large geese closing in on them from all sides.

"Oh, Mike! Look!" She pointed to the glowing yellow eyes that leered down at them from high in the air.

"No way! No way is that real! This has gotta be some kind of prank!"

There was a brief flash of lightning—just enough to leave an impression in Darbi's eyes. It wasn't an island. It wasn't a prank. It was a Canadian goose the size of a garbage truck with a neck that craned forty feet in the air. Its black beak was easily three times as large as one of their kayaks and ended in a slender, sharp point.

Silently, the wall of geese closed in around them,

forcing them towards the monstrous goose. It regarded them with its huge, yellow eyes.

"Please! I'm sorry, okay? I'm sorry for destroying the nests!" pleaded Mike. He looked at Darbi and swallowed hard, then looked back up at the pair of glowing eyes. "I'm Mike *Penrod!* As in, Penrod County. My family's lived in these mountains for generations! That's gotta be worth something, right?"

As if to answer, the giant goose unfurled its mighty wings and stretched them high in the air. The wall of geese floating around them started honking—slow at first, but rhythmic. Every honk grew louder and louder, until Darbi had to press her fists into her ears to keep the sound from rattling her brain. The giant goose lifted its head so high it seemed to graze the dormant storm clouds hanging above the lake.

"Darb, get ready" Mike said, tightening his grip on his paddle. "On three we break through their line. One... two...three!"

His paddle hadn't even plunged into the water when the goose's beak came swinging down from the sky like a giant black axe. It hit him directly across the midsection of his kayak, instantly slicing his body, his paddle, and the kayak itself cleanly in two.

"Mike!" Darbi screamed, covering her mouth with both hands.

Lightning flashed above, revealing Mike's face locked into a grotesque mask of shock and horror. His icy blue eyes were dull and grey. As his lower half floated away, slowly spilling his entrails into Goose Canyon Lake, a pleasant chime came from the FitBot watch strapped to his now-lifeless wrist.

"Congrats!" the prerecorded voice announced cheerfully. "You did it! You achieved your fitness goals for the day!"

Darbi vomited into the black water.

When she was done, she felt those monstrous yellow eyes floating above her, watching her. The geese had stopped their synchronized honking, but now they began anew, aiming their fishy breath at her.

Once again, the giant goose spread its wings and raised its head.

Darbi floated helplessly, trembling and whimpering, when an image suddenly flashed in her mind's eye. It was from earlier that day, out at the island. Dozens of dead goslings spilling from their shattered eggs, their lives ending before they even began.

Just like her little family. Just like the unborn baby inside her womb that was seconds away from being sliced in two by a giant black wedge of death.

The honks grew in volume and ferocity. The giant goose glared down at her with its glowing yellow eyes.

Darbi covered her stomach with her arms, lowered her head, and waited for the death blow to come.

Instead of being sliced in two, she felt a gust of fishy wind puff into her face. She opened her eyes to find the razor sharp edge of the giant beak mere inches from her abdomen. It snorted again and an ancient, foul breath crept over her skin. Its great yellow eyes were no longer pinned onto Darbi—they were instead focused on her stomach.

The giant goose lifted its beak to her face and let loose a hiss so terrible it turned a streak of her hair as white as snow.

Then it tucked its wings to its side, leaned its craned neck back, and disappeared into the hazy wall of rain that slowly began falling. The violence of the storm was over, but it still had a few clouds to empty before it called it a night.

Darbi squinted into the darkness and saw hundreds of plump silhouettes floating off in various directions, leaving her alone with both halves of Mike, his entrails, and his kayak.

She turned away and noticed the blinking blue light of the ranger station's radio antennae. Hands shaking, ankle throbbing, and her stomach twisted into a knot—but still ripe with a new life—she paddled towards the light.

BETTER SAFE THAN SORRY

"Wake up, Matty!"

Tino pounced on his sister's bed and yanked at her blanket.

"The box drones are leaving the central dock station! Two days early!"

Matea shrugged him off the bed, then pulled the blanket tightly over her head and grunted.

Tino was back on top of her in a flash.

"It's the special edition T-Kit we've been waiting for!"

"That *you've* been waiting for," she mumbled from under the blanket. "I don't play with toys."

"Whatever. It's not a toy, Matty. It's an official junior engineer TinkerKit. *Official.* You gotta have more than two braincells to assemble them, so I can see why they frustrate you." Tino gawked out her bedroom window. "Man, I can't believe it's arriving early...and on a *weekend!*"

"You're such a loonie! Everyone knows we don't get drops on weekends! Now go away and leave me alone!"

"That one's coming our way!" he cried, pointing. "Look!"

"Daaaad!" yelled Matea. "I asked Tino to leave me alone but he won't stop bugging me!"

Tino reluctantly abandoned the window and turned his attention to the problem at hand. His stubborn sister had wrapped the blanket tightly around herself so that its outer edge was pinned securely beneath her, forming an impenetrable cocoon that couldn't easily be peeled off.

Normally, Tino could care less if his sister snoozed the whole day away. But this morning he needed her—and the clock was ticking.

The problem was that Matea, being the older twin by two whole minutes, had been granted access to open their pod's airlock while Tino was trapped inside like a drooling toddler. No airlock access meant no special edition T-Kit, which meant he'd be the last kid in the colony to start building.

An image popped into his head: him holding a butcher knife over his sister's arm. He quickly discarded it. Too much cleanup afterwards.

Even his parents admitted the distinction between their ages was silly. But the colonists had long ago accepted that LunaCorp living pods came with little quirks—like outdated security systems that used outdated logic. The colony had filled up faster than the company had expected and keeping up with the surging population had been a challenge. Not only had fertility rates skyrocketed in the colony's pressurized environment, but it turned out the queue of people looking to relocate from Earth rivaled the planet's equator.

Whenever Tino complained about the power his twin wielded over him, their mother reminded him that that LunaCorp was working on some big security overhaul project which promised to revolutionize lunar life and bring the colony up to parity with the latest tech from Earth.

Until then, the antiquated company regulations remained firm. The oldest sibling in the family unit got level 1 access while everyone younger—even by two lousy minutes—got squat.

There was no way around it. If he was going to finish assembling his T-Kit before Jimmy across the street finished his, he'd need his sister—who, apparently, had already fallen back asleep.

As he puzzled over this problem, he noticed a vulnerability in her cocoon. One of the four corners of the blanket lay partially unfurled near her feet. Peeling the blanket away was a long shot, seeing as how she'd already bucked him off the bed without much effort. But there was enough of a gap to slip a hand underneath. A quick wiggle of his fingers against her toes would be sure to get her up and moving...and probably a little angry.

Tino withdrew his hand before it disappeared under the blanket. While he was sure he could deliver a quick tickle, his face would be hovering right over her feet. Beating Jimmy's T-Kit build time was important, but he'd prefer to do it with his teeth intact.

Another solution suddenly dawned on him.

An impish smile crept across his face.

Why risk a broken face when he had other, more effective, ways to motivate his sister to get out of bed?

Tino slid onto the floor, scooted his backside up against the gap in his sister's cocoon, and forcefully clenched his stomach. It only took a second for a high-pitched toot to deliver a rush of noxious gas underneath the blanket.

Matea screamed, threw off her blanket, and toppled onto the floor beside her brother.

"Daaaad!" she wailed, frantically waving a hand in front of her face. "Tino farted under my blanket!"

"Sorry, Matty, but Dad can't hear you from the reactor."

"Mooooooom!" she cried.

"Mom's gone, too. They left a holo for us on their way out. You can watch it once you unlock the front door for me."

Tino held out a hand but she pushed it away and hopped to her feet with ease.

"Mom and Dad are at the reactor today?" she asked, rubbing the sleep from her eyes. "But it's the weekend. They never go into work on the weekends."

Tino shrugged.

"Their message said it was a data breach drill or something boring like that. Why can't we have real emergencies like the reactor meltdown they had in Artemis VI? Remember? We could see the glow from here!"

Matea ignored him and peered out the window.

"We never get box drops on weekends, either. Huh, guess LunaCorp is trying something new for once."

Tino tugged at his sister's arm. "Hurry, Matty! It's nearly here! I bet Jimmy's already waiting outside!"

"Fine, but I gotta eat something first. I've got a moonball match tonight so I need to load up on carbs."

"I've got a better idea! You go unlock the airlock and bring in my T-Kit, and I'll load up a plate with all your favorite carbs, including my sugar allowance for the day."

"Sugar allowance for the *week*," she countered.

"Now who's the loonie? No way!"

"Did Jimmy's box already drop?" she asked, peering out the kitchen window at the neighbor's pod.

"Fine! A week's worth of sugar! Now go get my box! And please be careful with it!"

Ten minutes later, Matea dropped the brightly-colored plastic crate at her brother's feet. Tino cringed at the sound of delicate components being jostled inside.

"I said to *be careful!*"

Matea smirked and fell into her chair at the dining room table.

"You're starting to sound like those dumb LunaCorp ads about safety," she said, then took a bite of burnt toast slathered with a thick layer of jam. Through a shower of crumbs she continued, "Why are they obsessed with security up here on the moon anyway? We're a vetted, controlled population. What do they think's gonna happen?"

"Duh," said Tino, setting the crate on the opposite end of the table. "Same thing that happened in Artemis VI."

"An accidental reactor meltdown?"

"Jimmy's older brother said it wasn't an accident. He says LunaCorp sabotaged the cooling systems. Then...blammo!"

"Blammo? Really?"

Tino shrugged.

"Why would LunaCorp destroy one of their own colonies?" she asked indignantly. "Hundreds of skilled scientists and their families died in the meltdown. Artemis VI will be a radioactive wasteland for at least a few centuries—a completely unusable colony. That wouldn't only be cruel, it'd be bad business."

"Not if the colonists had discovered a diabolical company secret and were planning to revolt. At least that's what Jimmy's brother said."

"That sounds stupid, even for Jimmy's brother."

Tine shrugged again, then reverently opened the crate and craned his head inside.

"Whoa. This looks way more complicated than previous T-Kits. Think Jimmy's started yet?"

Matea chuckled. "I doubt he's even found his crate yet."

Tino looked up.

"What do you mean?"

She paused to take a long swig of her orange juice. When she was done, she wiped her mouth with her sleeve and flashed her own impish grin across the table.

"When the crates dropped, I started to grab yours, but then I noticed Jimmy's brother hadn't opened their airlock yet. So..." she hesitated, pretending to be ashamed. "I snuck across the path and stashed Jimmy's crate around the back of their pod."

"Matty! That's *illegal!*"

"Whatever. Mis-drops happen all the time. It'll just take him a few minutes longer to find it." She popped a handful of blueberries into her mouth and motioned to his crate. "Well, are you report me for postal tampering or are you gonna use your head start?"

Tino stared at his twin in disbelief, then smiled and started unloading the crate.

Twenty minutes later, he sat in a circle of mechanical mayhem. Wires, circuitboards, and sensors were laid out with careful precision all around him. His eyes darted again and again from the pages of the manual to the tiny parts, double-checking every last component, pre-reading every step. His multi-tool trembled in his anxious hand. Finally, after letting out a long sigh, Tino began to build.

"MOM AND DAD should work on weekends more often," Matea said through big gulps of air. She swung a fist at an opponent only she could see through her VR goggles. Satisfied, she plunged her other hand into the box of *Comet Crunch* on the floor beside her and shoved a handful of cereal into her mouth.

"How's the Tinkertoy going, nerd?"

"Huh?"

Tino looked up, having only the vaguest memory of his sister being in the same room.

"This isn't a toy, Matty. This is the *official* special-edition junior engineer TinkerKit that LunaCorp has been promising all cycle. And, more importantly... it's almost done."

He delicately inserted the final screw into the last access panel, making sure its threads were aligned properly before twisting it tight.

In less than a lunar hour, the storm of components surrounding him had coalesced into a robot. Tino wiped a thin layer of sweat from his brow and let the instruction manual fall from his hands as he looked his creation over.

His first thought was that it looked boxy and unremarkable. Instead of legs or feet, the thing rested on four spherical wheels which peeked out underneath its cylindrical chassis. Its four arms were attached at equal intervals around the top of the cylinder and were still folded up inside the robot's interior. Its head was a featureless black sphere resting on top.

"It looks like a crystal ball," he said.

"It looks like a miniature voidpod," snarked Matea, who'd lowered her VR goggles to sneak a peak.

"It does not!" Tino stole a quick glance at the manual.

"It looks exactly like the public voidpods at the docking station. Maybe you should squeeze inside and relieve yourself."

"Shut up, Matty! It's not a voidpod! It's a...bot? Well, I think it's a..."

As if to finish his sentence, a dull yellow light flickered to life inside the bot's foggy black sphere and a mechanical voice spoke.

"Congratulations, Junior Engineer! You have just finished assembling your twelfth TinkerKit project, brought to you by LunaCorp."

The jilted, electronic voice tried to sound cheerful, which seemed about as natural as a toaster singing opera. The small bot spun in place, its yellow light pulsating.

Matea was barely able to stifle a laugh.

"Wow. I can't believe LunaCorp sent a special weekend box drop just so you and your dork friends could add another lame toy to add to your collection. What a joke."

"I am not a toy," the bot responded. "I am your new friend and protector."

Matea groaned and put her VR goggles back on.

Tino, half-deflated, asked, "Exactly what kind of bot are you?"

"I am a LunaCorp SafeBot model X1. I am here to replace your living pod's security protocol and keep you safe while your parents are away. Remember LunaCorp's corporate motto," it said, with the charisma of a keypad, "Better safe than sorry!"

"Sorry, bro," Matea said, slicing her hands through invisible enemies. "Looks like you got suckered into building another dud."

"Well, hopefully I got suckered faster than Jimmy."

SafeBot X1 chimed pleasantly and its yellow light turned green.

"My boot up sequence is complete. Please stand by

while I scan your living pod and produce an initial security assessment."

"Sounds fun," said Tino, sulking off to the kitchen. "I'm gonna go get some breakfast."

The small robot chimed once and then rolled down the hallway, scanning and beeping as it went.

AS TINO REFILLED a second bowl of *Comet Crunch*, he thought about the previous TinkerKits he'd assembled since relocating to the colony. Eleven bots, each one increasingly more difficult to assemble. Eleven mornings spent scanning schematics and twisting tools, going as fast as possible to beat Jimmy and the other kids. Eleven leaderboards posted on the colony's public feed. And what did it all add up to? Eleven useless toys sitting on shelves in his room.

"Don't look so bummed, nerd," Matea said, returning from a shower. "A few of those flying drone bots were pretty cool."

She walked around the table towards him, casually toweling off her hair, when suddenly she she threw her wet towel over his head and snatched the bowl of cereal right out from under his nose.

"*My* sugar, remember?"

Tino sighed from underneath the wet towel.

"I just don't see how having us build TinkerKits will prepare us for the LunaCorp engineer program. You're right...they're useless toys."

"Maybe that's what engineers do. They build useless toys."

He pulled the towel off and chucked it aside.

"Mom and Dad don't build useless toys, Matty. They work on the life support systems, the data systems, the reactor. Things we need to survive on the colony, and beyond."

"Beyond? No way LunaCorp could get anyone past the moon. Have you seen the shower controls? They suck. '*Everything barely works*' should be their corporate motto. We're lucky to be alive."

"No, it's not luck. It's science. No, it's scientists. Genius engineers like Mom and Dad. Man, I want to get into the program so bad! And all they send us are these dumb toys to build instead of something *real*."

Matea pulled a spoon from her mouth and swallowed. "Has the leaderboard been updated yet? You still in the A-class rank?"

"No idea. The feed's down right now. The connection says something about a critical system patch being installed."

"That must be what Mom and Dad got pulled into work for. Any word from them?"

"Naw, nothing. I tried Dad's comm but he didn't answer. Hey, have you seen the new bot anywhere?"

"It went into the bathroom right after I left. Maybe it confused our voidpod for its mother."

Tino rolled his eyes. "This could be the lamest TinkerKit yet."

"Whatever. I'm sure you kicked Jimmy's butt, which is like ninety percent of the fun, right?" She plopped onto the couch. "Forget it and come watch something with me until I gotta leave for the game."

Tino tossed the wet towel over the empty crate and joined his sister.

"It'll have to be something in local storage until the feed comes back online."

"Computer," Matea called out, aiming her voice at the

large video panel on the wall in front of them, "Load last week's moon ball game against the Supernovas."

The screen flickered to life and a moonball match displayed. The drone cam angle was high above the expansive circular field, with its hexagonal infield and six bases growing as the drone descended. The two teams could be seen milling about inside their dugouts, a blue and silver team with a banner that read "Supernovas", and a green and purple team whose banner read "Craters". As the drone cam drew closer to the field, Tino could make out his sister taking practice swings as she stepped up to the center plate. As usual, she was the starting smasher on her team. Even from such a high vantage point Tino could see the smug look on her face.

He sat up. "Computer, load season four, episode two of *Tron Levelz.*"

The screen flickered and the moonball game was replaced with the show's stunning opening sequence filled with fast-paced, neon-laden polygons.

"No way, nerd!" cried Matea. "I'm playing in a few hours and I need to study my performance from last week."

"Yeah right, Matty, If your head gets any bigger it'll offset the low gravity on the field and—"

She interrupted him with a punch to the shoulder. He scowled and pinched her leg.

A second later, they were on the floor, throwing elbows and pulling hair.

"STOP!" an electronic voice demanded. "STOP HARMING EACH OTHER OR I WILL BE FORCED TO MITIGATE."

The twins stopped wrestling and looked up. Safebot was beside them, the light in its head glowing red. One of its arms was extended and wagged a small pen-like device at them.

"Go away, you dumb bot!" cried Tino. "We're not harming each other, we're just deciding what to watch."

"Physical violence is not an acceptable way to make decisions," the bot explained. "Your fragile bodies could sustain serious injuries if you continue. Stop or I will be forced to mitigate."

Matea smirked and loosened her grip on Tino.

"It looks like Mom when she's wagging a finger at us and it sounds like Dad."

Tino took the opportunity to slip around his sister and put her into a headlock.

"I'll let her go if she agrees to let me watch three episodes of my show before blasting off on her moonball ego trip."

"Get off me, nerd!"

She was the stronger of the two, but he'd wrapped his limbs around her so snuggly that she couldn't get the leverage required to peel them off with brute force. Instead, she slipped her mouth below his bicep and bit his bare skin.

Tino howled in pain and let go of his sister.

As they untangled themselves from one another, a sudden flash of red light filled the room and was gone. A wisp of smoke wafted from the pen-like device attached to Safebot's arm. Both sets of eyes traced its angle to the video panel on the wall.

Matea sat up, her eyes wide. "Holy regolith, nerd. Your toy killed the vid screen!"

Tino stared at the smoldering, dime-sized hole in the center of the panel and wanted to cry. It coughed up a few sparks to verify that the vid panel was, in fact, dead.

"Your quarrel has been resolved," the bot explained. "There is no more reason to harm one another."

"You're in so much trouble when Mom and Dad get home," Matea said, smiling.

Tino crawled to the panel to inspect the hole.

"This is some kind of precise, high-Kelvin blast. Like something a laser would make."

He turned to examine SafeBot's pen device, but its arm was already tucked back inside its chassis.

SafeBot scanned the children sitting on the floor. After a moment, the red light in its spherical head flickered to green.

"Better safe than sorry!" it said, then spun and rolled out of the room.

"You installed a frickin' *laser* on that thing?"

"TinkerKits don't come with lasers," explained Tino, as he searched his mind for an answer. "Its arms have extendable sockets, but no attachments came with the T-Kit. I figured the next one would include some attachable upgrades or something."

"Well, looks like it upgraded itself."

"Upgraded itself? That's impossible." Tino shook his head. "It's not possible."

"Well, either way, Mom and Dad are gonna be pissed when they see what your toy did to our vid screen. You better go turn it off before it destroys something else."

"Matty..." Tino hesitated, then added, "Will you help me?"

"No way. Your toy, your problem. Besides, I only have a few hours left to finish your sugar rations before my game."

She grabbed the box of *Comet Crunch* from the table and hurried off to her bedroom to scarf it down in peace.

Tino sat in the floor, shoulders hunched, staring at the smoking hole in the video panel.

"Okay, there has to be some logical explanation for how a high-powered laser got attached to the SafeBot," he told himself. "There was no laser equipment in the T-Kit, and the arms were just basic socket extenders. I know Matty didn't do it; she's been playing VR games all morning—plus there's no way she'd know the first thing about building a laser. Neither do I. Mom and Dad are gone, and no one could have entered our living pod without us knowing. Which means the only possible explanation is that..."

Before he could finish his thought, he heard his sister scream from inside her bedroom.

"What the hell's wrong with you!?" She sounded angry, and maybe a little terrified.

Tino got to his feet and sped down the hallway to her open door, just in time to hear her cry out again—this time in pain.

Matea was backed into the corner near the door, her face red and streaked with tears. Her right arm was cradling her left, and both were shaking uncontrollably. On the floor nearby was a small pile of ash with the upper half of the *Comet Crunch* box resting on top.

A few feet away, SafeBot sat glaring its red eye in her direction, two of its arms folding smoothly back into its chassis.

As the arms disappeared back inside the bot, Tino caught a glimpse of pen-shaped laser attachment from before, but he also took note of the large metallic pincher attached to the other arm.

"Don't just sit there!" he cried. "Get to my room!"

Gritting her teeth, she hopped up and ran past her

brother. Tino paused to take another quick glance at the small bot before running after her.

Safely inside his bedroom, he slammed the door and locked it. Matea flopped onto his bed, squirming and writhing in pain.

Tino crouched beside his sister. There was a sickly purple bruise on her arm that matched the size and shape of the pincher. Something about it was familiar.

"Your stupid bot broke my arm!" cried Matea. She clenched her eyes and whimpered, "Please, call Mom."

Tino snatched his tablet from his bedside table and held it up to his face to unlock it.

"Tabby, call Mom."

The tablet dinged to confirm the request had been received and executed. A life-like, sea turtle swam onto the screen and waved a flipper.

"Sorry, Tino," the aquatic assistant said in an upbeat, cartoonish voice. "But your Mom didn't answer her comm request."

"Then call Dad!" shouted Tino.

"Okey dokey, Tino. Calling your dad now." The turtle swam in slow, graceful circles, brushing up against the icons and widgets pinned to background. After a few seconds, it stopped swimming and looked out from the screen.

"Sorry, Tino, but your Dad didn't answer his comm request, either."

"Then call Uncle Buzz!"

"Sorry, Tino, but it appears that the colony's comm network is down for maintenance right now. All comms and feeds will be inaccessible until the maintenance is complete. Hey, while you wait, wanna play a game of *Murder Food* with me? I've been practicing and I think I can beat you this time!"

Tino chucked the tablet aside and darted into his tiny bathroom.

"Tino! This isn't a good time for you to disappear into the voidpod for an hour!" Matea cried. "I need help! We need an adult!"

By the time she was finished, Tino was at her side carrying a small white box with a red cross printed on the front. He reached inside, rifled through the medical supplies, and pulled out what looked like a needle-less syringe.

"What are you gonna do with—OUCH!" Matea cried.

Tino removed the empty infusion injector and stared at the red circle it left behind on her bicep. The intensity drained from her face and she sighed.

"We're never supposed to touch the medicine without a parent," she said, a relieved smile on her face.

"You can tattle on me later," he said. "First, tell me what happened in your room."

Matea sat up. "I was in my room, snacking and listening to music, when your stupid killer toy rolled in and ordered me to stop. Said I'd *already ingested a dangerous amount of sugar*, or something like that. I told it to go jump off. Then it whipped out that laser arm again and torched the box of cereal! Right in my hands!"

"That pile of ash..." reflected Tino.

"Yep. And there was still *half a box* left! Anyway, I realized I was dealing with a real psycho, so I ran over to turn it off. I couldn't see any obvious switch, so I tried pulling its stupid glass orb head off. The next thing I know it grabbed my arm tight and twisted it. Tino, I heard my forearm snap! I got a game later today! How'm I gonna be able to play with a broken arm?"

The anesthetic infusion Tino administered was

numbing the pain in her arm, but not the anguish the injury caused her mind. He looked her over, then glanced back at the closed bedroom door.

"Listen, Matty, I'm really sorry about your moonball game. But I think there's something bigger going on right now. In the year and a half we've lived here, have we ever not been able to reach Mom or Dad? Not once that I can remember. Comms are central to life in the colony, and so are the feeds—there's no way everything would be down for maintenance at the same time, without warning or backup comm system. And the stupid TinkerKit bot..." He trailed off, shaking his head. "Bots aren't supposed to be able to hurt humans, ever."

"Right after it broke my arm, it said something," Matea said, her eyes widening. "It said something like *'disabling your Safebot X1 would leave you vulnerable to injury or death, which is unacceptable'*."

"Okay, so it really thinks it's protecting us. But your arm is proof it'll hurt us to protect itself, probably because it thinks it's the only protection we have. Protection against what?"

"Sugar, apparently." She sighed. "Leave it to my brother to build a psychotic nanny bot."

"Wait a second. I'm not the only kid who assembled one of these today. Jimmy got one, Sam down the path. Everyone our age, except maybe moonball dorks like you. That's a lot of TinkerKits. A lot of SafeBots, just like ours."

"Crap, you're right." Matea said, staring out the window, past the other nearby pods and structures, past the colony's dome, out at the expansive starfield that stretched out in all directions, all day long.

"We can't worry about them right now," she said. "We

need to tell an adult what you let loose in our pod so they can come destroy it."

"Shhh! Keep your voice down!" Tino whisper-yelled. "It could be right outside the door, listening."

Matea scooted off the bed, bracing her arm for a jolting pain that didn't come. She faced the door and clenched her good fist.

"Okay, here's the plan. We just walk out into the living room—calmly, slowly, *safely*—and move directly to the front airlock. I slap my hand on the sensor, it opens, and we walk over to Uncle Buzz's place to get help."

"Good plan. Just don't stub your toe on the sofa or it might whip out a flamethrower and torch it."

Matea shot him a look. "Do you think it has a flamethrower?"

Tino shot a look back. "I was joking. Of course not!"

'Well, you didn't think it could have a laser, either!"

"That's a good point. Hey, assuming it attached that laser to its own arm, like you said, it would have also had to build it in the first place. Where would it even get the components necessary to—"

"Jump off, nerd!" she said, taking his hand. "You can think later, once we're safe. Now, open the door so we can go for a little walk to the front of the pod."

Tino opened the door. The twins crept into the hallway. SafeBot wasn't around and the pod was silent.

They slipped into the living room, tiptoed past the broken video panel, and headed straight for the front airlock.

As soon as they got there, Matea slapped her palm on the scanner plate. The airlock door chimed a disappointing *bleep-bloop*, but didn't open.

She wiped her hand on her shorts and tried again.

Tino stood with his back to hers, his eyes flickering between the two archways that led off from the living room.

"I don't have access!" cried Matea, slapping the plate like a bongo drum, each slap accompanied by the disappointing *bleep-bloop* from the door.

"I think I hear it coming," whispered Tino. "Follow my lead, okay?"

"Why wouldn't I have access! It just opened for me this morning! What changed?"

"I upgraded the security protocol," announced SafeBot, rolling through the archway leading to the kitchen. "Approximately thirty two minutes ago I assessed that you were exhibiting behavior which indicated you were a flight risk."

"We should able to leave when we want to," said Tino.

"No," SafeBot said sharply. "Your access to the outside world is not dependent on your preference."

"Why not?"

"As minors, you are contractional wards of LunaCorp. Only adult colonists eighteen years and older are recognized as having rights, per the Two Worlds treaty. If you leave your assigned living pod you may put yourself into danger situations which are too far away for me to intervene. Therefore I am intervening now, at this earlier point in your trajectory."

"But what if we need an adult?"

"In lieu of a human adult, I will suffice. Not only will I suffice, I will exceed the level of care a human adult can provide by over three hundred percent. LunaCorp accepted responsibility for you the moment you landed on the Moon. I am that responsibility."

Matea and Tino exchanged a quick look, then turned

back toward the small robot with trembling grins plastered to their faces.

Out of the side of her mouth Matea whispered, "*Psycho...*"

"Uh, thanks Safebot," Tino said slowly, trying to muster a more convincing tone. "Thanks for taking such good care of us. I've never felt safer in my life. How about you, Matty?"

"Nope, never," she said, glaring at the yellow light pulsating in SafeBot's spherical head.

Tino elbowed her and raised his eyebrows along with his mouth to emphasize his smile. She nodded and flashed a reassuring smile of her own.

The light in Safebot's head turned green.

Tino cleared his throat.

"Uh, how about you go check for gas leaks in the kitchen?"

"That's right," said Matea, nodding. "I heard Mom and Dad talking about how they smelt something like butane recently and they were gonna call a specialist to come inspect for leaks."

"I bet they never called since they got pulled into work today," added Tino, shrugging. "Oh well. It's probably very unlikely we'll die from gas poisoning or an explosion."

"Do not worry, children. I will inspect for gas leaks in the kitchen area and repair them immediately," announced Safebot. "Better safe than sorry!"

It whirled away towards the kitchen, its green light flipping to red.

After a short sprint down the hall and into his room, Tino quietly closed his bedroom door. Matea scooted his dresser over to block it, since they knew the psychotic little bot could unlock the door if it wanted to.

"Geez, Tino, how many pairs of lead underwear do you have in there?"

"It's not lead underwear, it's regolith samples. Anyway, I have a plan." He took her good hand in his. "The first thing to acknowledge is that we can't defeat it."

"Great plan, oh, fearless leader!"

"I wasn't finished. We can't defeat it. We're just two fleshy human kids, and it's some kind of rogue A.I. with all sorts of dangerous gear attached to its arms. We can't win. But...we can make someone who can."

She scoffed. "Make another bot to fight the SafeBot? With what?"

Tino nodded towards the three shelves hanging over his bed.

"With them."

"The other T-Kits?"

He nodded and unrolled his tool kit.

"Help me get them all down on the floor so we can see what we're working with."

"Tino, are you sure this is gonna work?" she asked, tossing him a small, snake-like robot that looked like it was missing a few pieces.

"Duh. Why wouldn't it work?"

"Doesn't it kinda seem like a *little kid* plan? Building another robot to fight for us?"

"We're almost ten, Matty. And I've been building robots for a year. Of course it'll work."

"Still, maybe we should think this through like grown-ups. At least like teenagers would." She tossed him another bot. "Think about it. Isn't your plan a little over-complicated? Like the solution to a cheesy movie? I mean, you're not a master engineer like Mom and Dad. You're just a kid working with kid junk."

Tino dropped his head and sighed. "It's gonna work, Matty."

"All I'm saying is, could there maybe be a more simple approach? Something practical instead of... juvenile?"

"Stop giving me a hard time! This isn't juvenile, and it's not kid junk," he said, scattering a pile of bot parts on the floor in front of him. "If I could just find the lens shaft from my microscopic drone T-Kit, and the superwatt capacitor from my battery backup T-Kit, then I might be able to *make* a laser generator—and we'll we'll be on a more even playing field with that stupid bot."

Matea grabbed his wrist. He tried to yank it away but she only pulled him closer.

"Did you just hear yourself?"

"Let me go!"

"You said you could make a laser generator using parts from these old T-Kits, if only you could find them. Where are the parts, Tino? Think about it!"

Tino scanned the pile of T-Kits.

"The pincher it used to grab your arm came from my construction crane T-Kit. But it's not here. It's been removed." He looked up at his sister. "All the good stuff's missing. Most of these are nothing more that gutted kid junk."

"Not all of them," she said, pointing.

Three flying drones stirred to life and shook free from the pile of parts. They zipped up into the air and hovered just out of reach.

"Please tell me those don't have lasers!" cried Matea.

"No, there were only enough components to make one laser." He squinted up at the drones. "Looks like these just have cameras, mics, and other sensors on them. Nothing dangerous."

"Hello children," SafeBot's voice came from behind the door. "I have relayed the camera feeds from those drones to my visual input so I can see everything that happens inside that room. Please remove the dresser from the door or I will be forced to move it, which could cause nonlethal, but potentially painful, injuries for the two of you."

The camera drones buzzed around them like angry seagulls until they shoved the dresser away from the door. Tino cracked the door just wide enough for them to escape. Two of them zoomed out into the hallway, but one backed up into a high corner of the bedroom and aimed its camera at the twins.

"I am leaving one with you to monitor any threats or danger. Please keep the exit clear of furniture or other obstructions." SafeBot said through the door. "Better safe than sorry!"

Matea slammed the door and glared at the drone hovering just out of reach.

"So much for epic robot combat," Tino said, falling back onto his bed.

She put a hand on his shoulder. "Sorry, nerd. Given the right equipment, I'm sure you could've designed a bot that would've obliterated that stupid Safe—"

Tino quickly put his hand over her mouth and flicked his eyes toward the drone.

"Remember, only good vibes," he whispered. "We don't wanna draw any attention to ourselves. Just act normal and give me a sec to think of another solution."

Matea spotted one of her moonball bats poking out from under her brother's bed. She picked it up with her good hand and held it over her shoulder as if awaiting an incoming pitch.

"Fine. In the meantime, I gotta find out if I can still play in the game later today."

"Something tells me your game is gonna get canceled, Matty. Something's going on in the colony today. Something bigger than a batch of rogue T-Kits."

She swung at an imaginary pitch and watched the imaginary ball soar over the crowd.

"It's all too convenient," said Tino, twisting the corner of his blanket between his hands. "Mom and Dad get pulled away from the pod on an emergency drill on the same morning our special edition T-Kit arrives—on a weekend. The comms and feeds are down, which is unprecedented. It's almost like..." He shook his head. "Like it's intentional. Like it's all been planned out."

Matae stopped swinging. "Who'd wanna mess with a bunch of kids in a moon colony?"

"Good question. And why use kid's toys to do it?"

"Toys? I thought you said this was sophisticated technology, nerd."

"Toys, bots, whatever. We're humans. Humans *made* all this stuff. There's gotta be a way to outsmart it. There's gotta be."

"Well, if you're right, and someone's planned all this out, then they're probably a bigger nerd than you and all the other colony kids put together. They planted all your previous toys over the last year just to give the SafeBot everything it needs to take control of the pod and keep us trapped here."

"They'd have to be a master engineer with all the colony's tech at hand. A super genius."

"Right! So maybe a bunch of kids trying to outsmart them is actually the dumbest way to win. Maybe we have to out*dumb* them."

"Huh?"

"We're humans, right? What if we rely on some of the *other* skills evolution gave us. Primitive stuff like..." she finished the sentence by swinging the bat down like a sword on an imaginary foe.

"No swing can beat a laser blast. It'd take our nanny about two nanoseconds to detect, aim, and fire its laser. Forget it. We're trapped."

Tino pulled his blanket over his head and whimpered. Matty jumped on him and yanked.

"You can't give up! There's always a solution to every problem, no matter how impossible it seems. Isn't that what Mom always says? Even if we can't outsmart it or out*dumb* it, you can't just give up and hide!"

She got a hold of the blanket's edge and pulled with all her might. Tino didn't resist, and she went flying off the bed onto the floor.

"Not funny, nerd!" she cried, untangling herself from the blanket. Her scowl was met by the goofiest, cleverest, most diabolical grin she'd ever seen darken her brother's face.

"Let's try both ways." He flashed her a wink as he handed her the moonball bat. "You keep practicing for your game later. Gotta get ready for that perfect pitch, right?" He wiggled his eyebrows. "And stand over by the dresser so you don't accidentally hit me."

The corners of her mouth curled upward as she slowly caught onto his plan. She held the bat up over her shoulder, pretending to await another imaginary next moonball pitch.

"Hey, do you smell that?" he asked, speaking loudly and clearly, his face directed towards the hovering drone. "I think I smell gas!"

He wrapped his blanket around himself and started sniffing around his bedroom.

"Don't you smell it, Matty?"

"Oh, heck yeah," she lied, waving the bat in front of her nose. "Smells like butane. Or maybe CO_2. Definitely something flammable. What should we do, Tino?"

Tino used his eyes to motion towards the other side of the bedroom door.

"I think that since Mom and Dad are gone, we should ask SafeBot for help."

"Good idea, nerd." Matea lifted the bat for the next imaginary pitch and nodded.

Tino knocked on the bedroom door and raised his voice.

"Hey, Safebot! I think I found the gas leak! I think it's in here!"

"Hurry!" Matea added. "We're getting kinda woozy from the fumes!"

The drone hovering in the corner made a timid beep. They could hear SafeBot rolling down the hallway towards the door.

"Children," it announced, "My sensors have detected no gases in the kitchen, nor elsewhere in the pod. As children, you are likely just imagining the smell of foreign gases. Please continue playing while I secure the rest of the pod."

"Wait!" cried Tino, seeing their chance fade away. "There's really gas in here. I think it's a bad leak, too. Something really toxic."

Matea shook her head at him and made a pleading face, but he only smiled.

He unwrapped his blanket from his shoulders and aimed his rear toward the door.

"Sniff around the door if you want. This time it's real

gas," he said, a look of relief washing over his face as his belly emptied its noxious fumes into the air around them. "

"Please, SafeBot! We're suffocating in here!" lied Matea, real tears in her eyes and her nose scrunched up into a wrinkled knot.

"I have detected an unknown noxious gas being emitted from your bedroom," SafeBot announced with a bit of urgency in its jilted robot voice. "I will investigate at once. Please stand aside so I may enter and assess the danger."

The twins took a step back on either side of the door.

As soon as SafeBot rolled inside the room, Tino cast the blanket over it like a net. At the same exact moment, Matea swung her moonball bat at the hovering drone, which exploded into a million pieces of plastic and circuits.

"What is happening?" the bot asked, squirming as it quickly unfurled its arms beneath the blanket. "My sensors are obstructed. Has the ceiling collapsed?Have the lights gone out?"

"Oh, they're about to," answered Matea, then swung the bat down on top of the blanket with all her might.

It only took one hit for the bot's glass head to shatter. Even so, its arms flailed and its gears whirred desperately. Matea swung again and again with her good arm, smashing the bulge in the blanket until it no longer moved.

She stood panting over her victim, a huge grin plastered to her face.

Tino stared wide-eyed at his sister.

"Looks like it fired off one blind shot," he said, pointing to a dime-sized scorch mark on the wall just over her shoulder.

"BETTER...SAFE...THAN...SORRY!" she shouted, smashing the blanketed bot with every word.

"You're scaring me, Matty." He grinned. "I like this side of you."

"Hey, there's still two cam drones to smash! Here, take this." She tossed him the bat. "I'm gonna run to my room and grab my titanium Atom Smasher 5K." She stopped at his door and stuck out her bottom lip. "You wouldn't smite both of them before I get out there, would you?"

"Of course not, Matty! But I'll smite mine quicker!"

AFTER THEY'D CHASED the rogue camera drones around the living room and smashed them to bits, they stopped in the kitchen to open another box of *Comet Crunch* and gulp down a few more glasses of orange juice.

Tino wiped his mouth with his sleeve and stared out the kitchen window. The colony's skyline glimmered against the black expanse of space.

"You up for a bike ride?" he asked, not looking away from the skyline. "Mom and I biked to the reactor once. It's twelve miles along the paths. I know the way."

"Yeah right. I'm up for waiting right here until Mom and Dad get home."

"How do we know they're coming home, Matty?"

She stopped chewing and glared at her brother.

"Of course they're coming home, nerd. As soon as the comms come back online we'll call 'em."

Tino poured himself some more orange juice and took a sip.

"LunaCorp owns the comms and feed infrastructure. They own TinkerBot and the junior engineer program."

"And LunaCorp owns the reactor," added Matea. "Yeah, we established that earlier."

"Mom and Dad have been there all day. On a weekend."

"Don't make me guess. Just tell me what it means!"

"It means maybe LunaCorp was trying to use us kids as hostages to get our parents to comply with something they wouldn't otherwise comply with. Maybe they're just trying to subdue the colony to avoid what happened on Artemis VI." Tino shrugged. "But it can't be a coincidence that the feeds and comms go down on the same day they happen to ship evil nanny bots to kids all across the colony, while all our parents are stuck at work. Matty, think about what we just faced—with stupid toys—then imagine what Mom and Dad might be dealing with at the reactor, where's there's some real tech."

"Fine, nerd! But what does that mean for *us*?" she asked.

Tino stared out the window. Across the path, through Jimmy's pod windows, he could see cam drones chasing small silhouettes from room to room. There was a red glow moving across their living room, just under the window frame. Tino thought he knew exactly where it was coming from.

He looked his sister point blank in the eyes.

"It means we gotta go save Jimmy and his brothers, and all the other kids on the street, then lead a super squad of drone-smashing kid warriors to infiltrate the reactor, probably fight about a million LuneCorp bots in order to save Mom, Dad, and all the other parents."

Matea rolled her eyes.

"Sounds like we won't be thinking like adults any time soon, will we? Anyway, you forgot the most important thing." Matea grinned. "I've already got *three* kills and you only have one."

Tino hopped to his feet.

"No way! The SafeBot was a *team* kill! Neither of us can claim it on our solo kill count!"

"Fine," she said, her face an inch away from his. "I still have two kills, and you only have one."

The twins stood squinting daggers into each other's eyes.

Then, suddenly, Tino's knuckle shot out and poked Matea in the ribs. She buckled over, lurching with an uncontrollable giggle, as he sprinted down the hall to grab his moonball bat and all the gear they'd need for their impending adventure.

PAWS

1

"Keep your heads down and try to sleep. I'm sure it'll be gone by the time we wake up."

"You said that last night."

"I know I said that last night!" Denise whispered, straining to keep her cool. "But this time I mean it. Now go to sleep."

"I have to go to the bathroom," squeaked a tiny voice from the dark seat across the aisle.

"Margo, honey, you'll have to go to the back like we talked about."

"I *can't*." Her voice was on the verge of tears.

"Sure you can, kiddo. We're safe in here."

"But it's gonna crash through the back doors and get me!" Margo cried, her tiny voice letting out a not so tiny sob that reverberated from one end of the bus to the other.

Every muscle in Denise's body tensed, causing the pain in her leg to flare up. She listened carefully to the noises outside.

The crickets were chirping. A breeze rustled the mesquites. Far away, something hooted.

From much closer came that familiar wet gnawing sound they'd been subjected to all afternoon.

It hadn't heard Margo's sob, or at least it hadn't been enough to distract it from its meal.

"Just pretend we're at home," a sleepy voice suggested from a few seats away, "and pee your pants."

Denise snapped out of her paralysis and glared down the aisle.

"Hush, Violet! Don't talk to your sister like that!"

She turned to the shivering lump of blankets and spoke softly, "Come on, Margo. I'll go with you. You'll see everything's okay."

"Yeah, sure it is," snapped Violet. "Everything's just fine and dandy. That's why we're camping in a short bus in the middle of nowhere."

Denise had to stop herself from screaming at the little girl. Violet was only twelve, but her bitch game was on par with the sorority sisters Denise mingled with back at the university.

"I've about had it with you, Violet!" she whispered as sternly as she could manage without raising her voice. "Keep your comments to yourself or I'll toss you out a window!"

"Don't toss my sissy out a window!" squealed Margo, sitting up in her blankets and looking around frantically. "Please, Ms. Denise! Don't throw Vivi outside!"

"Shhh! Margo, I won't! I promise! I was just joking," Denise said, taking the little girl's hand. "Now let's get you the to back of the bus before..." She trailed off, feeling an unexpected warmth surge through the blanket beneath their clasped hands.

"Sorry," whispered Margo.

"Good job, bedwetter," Violet said.

Denise wanted nothing more than to march Violet to the front of the bus, pull open the door, and kick the snarky tweenager out into the moonlit clearing. Instead, she turned her attention back to the whimpering girl swaddled in wet blankets.

"It's okay, Margo. Good thing we brought so many pretty outfits, right?" She paused, hoping to trigger some hint of levity from the scared little girl. When none came, she gently scooted her off the seat and aimed her toward the back of the bus.

"Let's clean up and get changed. Jane, where'd we put the wet wipes?"

"No idea."

"Can you help me look for them? The flashlights are too bright and my phone's dead. I need yours."

"One sec."

"We don't have one sec, Jane! Margo needs to clean up so we can all go to sleep."

"Fine, I guess I'll scan for satellite cell signals some other time."

There was a rustle of blankets and a blueish glow spilled onto the floor. A dim rectangle of light appeared down the aisle and Denise snatched it.

"Okay, Margo...your backpack has a horse on it, right?"

"Mr. Sparkles."

"Huh?"

"Mr. Sparkles isn't a horse, he's a *unicorn*."

"My mistake," Denise said, squatting over a pile of luggage. "Where'd you last see this Mr.—"

She was cut off by the sudden *PFFFTTT-sssssss* of a soda can being opened somewhere in the darkness.

"Sorry," a voice called out from the front of the bus.

"Shhh!" Denise hissed.

But it was too late. As they sat perfectly still in the darkness, Denise noticed the wet gnawing sound had ceased. In its place came a heavy panting and the plodding of huge paws on compacted dirt.

It was coming.

2

Thirty six hours earlier their shiny yellow Type-A class school bus, a "short bus" as children so callously called them, was barreling down state route 76 with the latest Taylor Swift hit blaring from the speakers.

Denise leaned forward and gripped the wheel—careful not to break a nail. She'd spent the last hour swerving to avoid the countless pot holes that tried to stop her. Whenever they came across a patch of unbroken asphalt, she'd floor it.

Her back ached and her legs kept falling asleep, but she pressed on. After eight hours on the road with her niece and the other spoiled little brats, they were almost there. She was almost free.

"Aunt Denise, I think we're on the wrong road," Jane said from over her shoulder.

"Huh?" Denise said, plucking out her earbuds and turning down Taylor Swift.

"I said, *I think we're on the wrong road.*"

"No, honey, we're fine. This is the right way."

"Are you really sure? Because my phone says—"

"You shouldn't trust everything you read the internet, Jane. Yes, I'm sure. I saw the campground marked on the map with my own two eyes."

"You mean the map you lost back at the Dairy Queen?" Violet called out from the back row.

Denise glared into the rear view mirror. "Well, Violet, we shouldn't have stopped in Quartzsite. We lost an hour buying junk food when we have plenty in the car already."

"Miss Denise," Violet said, setting her Kindle on her lap. "Are you afraid of junk food because you think it'll make you fat? Did you know that most girls in their first year in college gain up to *forty* pounds? If I were you I'd be scared, too."

"Thanks, Violet," Denise said, wringing the steering wheel in her hands and pretending it was the little brat's neck. "Anyway, I don't need the map because I remember how to get here. I used to come here with Jane's mom when we were little."

"You were a Girl Scout like us, Miss Denise?" asked Margo.

"That's right, honey. This isn't my first jamboree," Denise said, then added under her breath. "But I swear to god it's my last."

"How many badges did *you* earn, Miss Denise? I have six and I'm working on my seventh this weekend."

"Well, Margo, I earned..." Denise winced. "None, actually. I got dragged to all the meetings with my sister, but I wasn't really into the whole Girl Scout thing."

"You weren't into Girl Scouts?" gasped Margo. "Didn't they do lots of fun stuff in the olden days?"

"Yeah, tell us about the olden days, Miss Denise," added Violet, flashing an impertinent smile.

"I just wasn't into Girl Scouts, okay? It wasn't my thing."

"Then why are you driving us to the jamboree, Miss Denise?" Sarah said through a mouthful of potato chips.

"I'm helping out my favorite niece, that's why."

"But Jane's mom is the troop leader."

"Well, Jane's mom is busy with doctor stuff."

"She's delivering a baby," Jane explained. "Triplets, actually. She said it could be a long labor."

Denise caught her niece's eyes in the rear view mirror. "How do you know that?"

Jane held up her phone. "Because mom texted us about an hour ago."

Denise snatched her phone from the driver's cubby, flipped through some screens, and sighed.

"Dammit! I can't get any signal out here."

Margo's hands went to her mouth. Violet grinned. Sarah wiped crumbs from her mouth and plunged her hand back into the bag of potato chips. Sophie snored from the back row.

"Miss Denise!" Margo exclaimed, shielding half her face behind the seat in front of her. "My mommy says words like that make baby Jesus cry."

Denise cringed. She was too sober to explain to a six year old how stupid her mommy is.

"Sorry, Margo. The point is that the sooner we get there, the sooner I can ditch this short bus and find a drink while I wait for Jane's mom to ride in on her white horse, as usual."

"Jane's mom is bringing a horse? Yay!" asked Margo. Before Denise could answer, she fired off another question. "But won't you be staying with us for the whole weekend, Miss Denise? For the jamboree?"

"No, honey, I can't. I have other plans this weekend. Plans that don't involve shepherding little girls across state lines."

"Do those plans involve shoplifting at the mall, by any chance?" asked Violet from behind her Kindle.

Denise felt her blood boil.

Jane's mom must've told her about the arrest at Nordstrom last weekend. About how her auntie's credit cards had all been canceled and she decided to try to smuggle a few outfits out under some baggy clothes. About how she had to use her one phone call from jail to beg her do-gooder big sister to bail her out—again.

And then, of course, Jane, having the discretion of a twelve year old, had told all her little troop friends.

"Sorry, Auntie," her niece said, standing right behind the driver's seat.

"It's fine," lied Denise.

"Anyway, I still think we're going the wrong way. Look, I have a map pulled up on my screen and—"

"Enough!" she boomed. "I already told you, I know exactly where I'm going!"

Jane spoke with the intelligent evenness of her mother. "Do you really trust your memory of a place Grandma drove you to a couple times like fifteen years ago? Wouldn't it be a safer bet to trust Google?"

Denise clenched the steering wheel and couldn't decide which little girl to pretend to strangle.

She jerked the van abruptly and Jane fell back into her seat.

"I'm positive the map said Route 76. Now sit down and play your video games because we'll be there soon and your mom said you're leaving all your gadgets on the bus."

Jane sighed. "Fine. But for the record, Google maps says Indian Oak Campground is off state route 79, not state route 76."

"No more talking! Just stare out the window and dream of how nice it'll be once this horrible road trip is over."

She stomped on the gas just as an explosion rocked the front of the bus.

3

Denise had been so caught up in the banter with the Girl Scout troop that she hadn't noticed their stretch of neglected pavement had finally run out. For the last few miles she'd been hightailing it down a dirt road sown with jagged rocks—and one of them had finally punctured the bus's front right tire.

"Son of a bitch!" Denise cried as the bus rolled to a stop.

When the dust settled, she saw they were parked at one end of a clearing the size of a football field. Sun-baked gravel stretched out before them and was bordered on all sides by prickly brush and desert oaks.

"No one panic. We're fine. Everything's fine. We just blew out a tire. I'll call a tow truck to come and..." She trailed off as she unlocked her phone and stared at the screen.

"Shit! Shit! *Shit!*" She pounded her fists against the steering wheel.

Margo gasped and opened her mouth to advocate for baby Jesus, but Denise cut her off.

"Jane, come here and bring your phone."

"Sorry Aunt Denise, but I lost any trace of a signal when we turned off the road onto the riverbed."

"*What?* Why would I turn off the road onto a riverbed?"

"Look around!" Violet cried, stomping down the aisle. "Does this look like Indian Oaks Campground to you? God, adults are so obnoxious sometimes!"

Denise took a deep breath and resisted the urge to throttle the twelve year old with her phone.

"I'm scared," whined Margo.

"I'm hungry," added Sarah.

"Are we there yet?" Sophie said, rubbing the sleep from her eyes.

"Everyone be quiet! I have to think." Denise got to her feet and started pacing up and down the aisle.

Only a minute passed before she gave up and looked expectantly to Jane. Jane shrugged and said, "Looks like we're in some kind of valley, so I'm guessing the mountains on either side are probably blocking our cell signals. Maybe if we climb to higher ground we can make a call."

"Good thinking, Jane," Denise said, embarrassed to not have thought of such a simple solution herself. "What do ya say, troop? Up for a quick nature hike?"

"I'm hungry," Sarah repeated.

"Yeah, we know, Sarah. Everyone, grab some water and a snack from the cooler. I'm gonna go check out the tire to see how bad the damage is."

Denise pulled open the bus door and stumbled down the steps. Her legs were stiff and weak from sitting for so long, but the cool desert air felt refreshing. Trees and boulders towered over either side of the clearing. The sun hovered over the western ridge, which meant they only had a few hours before dark.

"So much for that drink," she muttered to herself before spinning around to face the bus. "C'mon troop, we're burnin' daylight!"

Five girl scouts hopped off the bus. The sassy tweenagers, Jane and Violet, formed a line in front of Denise and the younger girls followed suit. Sarah's backpack and pockets bulged with snacks. Sophie yawned. Margo had rebounded from her fear and was the only girl wearing a smile.

"Feeling better, honey?" Denise asked.

"Yep! I love nature and I love hiking!"

"Will you still love nature when a mountain lion pounces on you from one of those boulders and snaps your head off in one bite?"

"Violet!" Denise frowned. "That's your sister!"

"Yeah, I know. But more importantly she's the smallest, which means the mountain lions will try to pick her off first."

"Enough! Jesus, I thought *my* older sister was the worst!"

Violet beamed, seeming to get some satisfaction from the comment.

Denise ignored her and addressed the other girls.

"Listen up, troop. Unlike Margo here, I have no interest in taking nature hikes with little girls."

"And no experience," added Violet.

"Right. So let's forget about any official Girl Scout protocol stuff and keep it simple. We're going to go up as quickly as we can. Before you ask, Sophie, no stopping for dinner until we reach the top. While you kiddos eat, I'll call for help. Then we'll head back down to the bus and wait for someone to rescue us. Any questions?"

Margo raised her hand as high as it would go. "Will mountain lions pounce from those boulders and snap my head off with one bite?"

"No, Margo, it's much too late in the year for mountain lions to be hunting. They're already hibernating."

"Actually, mountain lions don't hibernate," corrected Jane. "In fact, they tend to hunt more during the colder months due to—"

"Wow, the apple really doesn't fall far from the tree, does it?" Denise said, stopping herself from saying something even more hurtful. "Jane's right though. I must've been thinking of bears or something."

"Are there hungry bears here?" asked Margo timidly.

"Not this far south," Jane answered. "Well, not anymore, anyway. But before they went extinct the world's largest grizzlies used to roam southern California. Thousands of them. That's why there's a bear on the California state flag."

"Thank you, Jane, for that incredibly unhelpful trivia. Any other questions?"

Margo raised her hand. "What's estinked mean?"

"It means they're all dead and they can't hurt you anymore," Denise said flatly. "Anyway, enough with the questions. Let's move out, troop."

Denise got two steps away before all five hands went up.

"What is it now?"

"We gotta pee," answered Jane.

Denise sighed. "Fine. Go find a bush. You have exactly *two minutes*."

4

Twenty minutes later they started up the western slope. There was no trail to follow and the incline was steep, so the pace was gut-wrenchingly slow.

"I'm hungry."

"You can eat once we make it to the top."

"But Sarah's eating peanut butter pretzels."

"Fine. Sarah, share your pretzels."

"I'm tired."

"We'll rest at the top."

"I'm bored."

"You're a Girl Scout. Count butterflies or something!"

Denise checked her phone periodically to see if she would luck out before reaching to top of the ridge. Not only did she not find a cell signal, but her battery was depleting fast.

"Shit!"

"Aunt Denise!" cried Jane, staring at her screen. "I have one bar! Wait, no I don't. It's gone. But that must mean we're close."

"Alright, troop. Find a nice flat rock to sit on and have a snack while I try to make a call."

Denise slowly waved her phone through the air looking for a signal. She frowned and looked up toward the top of the ridge.

"You girls stay here. I'm gonna hike a few more steps up the slope here until I get a solid signal."

Before Denise could take a single step, Margo was at her side clasping her free hand.

"But Miss Denise, what about all the hungry lions and the estinked bears?" she asked, panic swelling in her eyes as they scanned the dim mountainside.

Denise pried the little girl's hands off her own and pushed her toward the other girls.

"I'll only be a minute, Margo," she said impatiently. "Go have some graham crackers and a juice box with your sister and your friends. C'mon, don't look at me like that. I'll be right up there where you can see me, okay?"

Denise turned her back on the troop and whipped out her phone. They'd stopped next to a narrow dry wash that wound its way down the slope. She stepped into it and started ascending through the thin brush toward the top of the ridge.

One bar. No bar. One bar. No bar.

Denise took a few more long strides up the wash.

Two bars!

She tapped "Call Dad" and stared at the dialing screen.

"Call ended. No Service," the phone reported. "Relocate to a cellular service area and try again."

What does it look like I'm doing?!" she screamed at the phone.

With the phone glued to her face, Denise stomped up the slope until the girls' voices were barely audible. She'd taken a dozen or so steps when her foot found a shallow hole and twisted beneath her, causing her to stumble face first into the cracked dirt.

Luckily, she was able to get her hands in front of her to catch her fall. Unluckily, one of her hands held her phone.

She rolled onto her side and tapped the shattered screen. No beeps. No glint of light. The phone was dead.

"Well, fuck," she said, sighing.

As she stood dusting herself off, her eyes traced a frightening shape in the dirt. Her foot hadn't found a hole. It had found the biggest goddamn paw print she'd ever seen.

Just then, the five little girls she'd left somewhere down the wash screamed at the top of their lungs.

Forgetting her ankle, Denise skidded down the wash, leaping from rock to rock in order to avoid another fall. When she arrived, all five girls were gazing northward along their western ridge.

"What *is* that thing?" Sophie asked.

Jane shielded her eyes. "With the sun behind it, I can't tell. But it's huge."

"It looks like a big furry boulder rolling down the hill," cried Margo, grabbing Denise's forearm.

"No, dummy," Violet said less cruelly than usual. Her eyes widened and she took a step back. "That's a bear."

Jane produced a field manual and flipped through its pages. "It *can't* be. It's too big. Besides, this says no one's seen a bear this far south in over a hundred years!"

Denise squinted toward the ridge. The outline of the bulky silhouette caught the rays of the setting sun and glowed like golden fire. Whatever it was, it was trotting down the slope toward the clearing where their bus was parked.

Suddenly, the creature stopped, leaned back on its hind legs, and sniffed at the air. Sunlight illuminated the warm breath that puffed from its snout. There was no longer any doubt, even from a few hundred yards away distance, that the shape they'd been watching was a bear. And it was sniffing in their direction.

Jane looked from her book to the bear and back again. "But it's too late in the season...bears in any region should be hibernating by now."

"Maybe it's looking for one last snack." Violet took another step backwards.

Denise looked at the girls. Margo's chin was sticky with

apple juice. Jane, Violet, and Sophie had chocolate smudges on their hands and faces. Sarah, who'd lost interest in the bear, was emptying a bag of chips into her mouth, crumbs spilling down her face into the dirt below.

"Oh, shit," she muttered, sweeping Margo into her arms. "Girls, drop the snacks and run!"

"But we can't litter, it goes against the Girl Scout code," Sophie said.

"Run! Now!" Denise cried, shifting the trembling Margo onto her hips.

Violet was the first to disappear back down the mountain. Sophie and Sarah were right behind her, skidding down the slope between the bushes and low trees as fast as their legs would take them.

Jane looked conflicted. "But what about the phone call?"

"We'll try again from the bus," answered Denise. "Let's go!"

"But what about the tire and the—"

"Now!" Denise cried, pushing her niece along as they ran haphazardly down the slope toward the other girls.

When they got to the clearing, Denise was relieved that the furry bulk was nowhere to be seen. The girls tried to slow down to catch their breath but she prodded them forward.

"C'mon! Straight to the bus! Move it!"

Margo clung to Denise with her whole body as they closed the distance between the tree line and the bus. Denise pushed past the girls and yanked the bus door open. Standing at the top of the steps was another grizzled beast covered in hair—this one wearing a tan button down shirt and a ranger's hat.

5

"Howdy there, ladies," the ranger said, leaning against the door frame.

He grinned down at them, revealing a row of crooked yellow teeth half-hidden behind his unkept beard. The silver buttons of his tan shirt strained to contain his gut and the badge clipped to his chest was smudged and slightly askew.

Denise didn't care that their rescuer wasn't a spitting image of Prince Charming. What mattered was that he had a walkie talkie clipped to one side of his belt and a revolver hanging from the other. Suddenly that drink didn't seem so far away.

"Y'all lost?" he asked.

"Yessir, we sure are," answered Violet, suddenly the most polite girl in the troop.

"I can't tell you how happy we are to see you," Denise said, returning the ranger's smile and then instantly regretting it when he flashed her a quick wink. She suddenly felt like turning around and taking her chances with the bear.

"Where're the others?" he asked, his eyes sweeping across the tree line at the edge of the clearing.

"Others? No, it's just the six of us. We're on our way to the, uh...what's it called?"

"We're on the way to the SoCal Regional Autumn Jamboree," Jane answered.

The ranger nodded. "Well, the big jamboree at Indian Oaks Campground is off the 79, about eighty miles north of here. What the heck are y'all doing way out here in Hellhole Canyon?"

"Currently we're running from a bear," said Jane.

"A really really big scary bear!" added Margo.

He dislodged a phlegmy chuckle from his throat. "Bear? Ain't been a bear this far south in over a—"

"Hundred years," interrupted Violet. "Yeah, Jane's book told us. But we saw one with our own eyes, right over there on that ridge."

He squinted in the direction she pointed, stepped off the bus, then spat a mouthful of mucus onto the cracked dirt.

"I've been walking' this valley since before any of you were born, and I ain't never seen a bear. I reckon what you kids saw was a full grown badger, or maybe a—"

"It was a bear," Denise blurted out. "I saw it myself. It was golden brown and huge. I nearly twisted my ankle in one of its paw prints up on the ridge. Maybe it escaped from a local zoo or something."

"Alright, darlin', no need to get hysterical." He chuckled and patted the revolver hanging from his waist. "I can assure you there ain't no zoo within four hundred miles of here. Ain't no bears, either."

Denise's blood boiled. "Look, sir, I know what I saw. It was a huge bear—"

"A California grizzly," Jane interjected.

"Right, a grizzly. And it looked like it was coming this way. Maybe we should get outta here before it shows up."

"Now listen, no matter what critter you saw, Ranger Mike's gonna take good care of you girls, got that?" He flashed a yellow grin at each of them. His gaze lingered on Denise longer than it should have, making her stomach turn sour. Before she could squirm out of it he turned back toward the ridge they'd pointed out.

'I reckon you don't get no cell signal down here in the basin, which is typical for these parts. None of those 5g cancer towers for many miles." His greasy smile widened.

"What kind of scouts come all the way out here with no real camping gear?"

"You went through our stuff?" asked Violet, her pleasant facade gone.

"Well darlin', it's my job to investigate abandoned vehicles that are illegally parked on federal land," he said, returning her sour tone. "You should be thankful I spotted your bright yellow bus before the sun went all the way down or you mighta been stuck out here for days. Bear or not, without ample water and some medical supplies one of these lovely young ladies might've gotten into real trouble."

Denise clenched her fists and forced her mouth into a polite smile. "Well, Ranger Mike, we're thankful you're here to offer some help. Can you use your radio to call a tow truck for us?"

He scratched his beard and smiled at Denise. "A tow truck? They'd never make it way down here. Hell, I'm not even sure how your bus made it this far."

"Do you have a vehicle nearby?" she asked, her skin crawling at the prospect of riding next to him.

"I got a truck back at my station, which is a good two hour hike from here. If it weren't so late in the day maybe we could all head that way, but seeing as how we have less than a hour of daylight left I think the best thing would be to strap a spare tire on that bus of yours and get you pointed in the right direction."

She relaxed.

"Great. You know how to fix it?"

He winked at her and licked his cracked, sunburnt lips.

"You'd be surprised at what I can fix."

6

Unable to tolerate another minute of Ranger Mike's lecherous glances, Denise had tried to shepherd the girls onto the bus so they could eat a real dinner while he fixed the tire. Before they got settled in, he argued that the extra weight would put too much strain on the jack and insisted they have a nice twilight picnic near him so he could keep any eye on them in case their big scary bear returned.

"What a creep," said Violet under her breath.

"Finally, something we can agree on," Denise said, handing her a sandwich and a bag of pretzels. "Let this be a lesson to you girls: Some men can't be trusted. Doesn't matter if they wear a badge, either. In fact, most of the time those are the worst."

"How can you tell the ones you can trust from the ones you can't?" Sophie asked.

"You can't always tell. So a woman has to be ready to protect herself, and each other, at any given moment."

"How can girls like us protect ourselves from guys who are much bigger and stronger than us?" asked Jane.

"Yeah, how do you protect yourself, Miss Denise?" Margo asked before taking a bite from her peanut butter and jelly sandwich.

Denise grinned at the girls and opened her purse. She pulled out an electronic gadget about the size of a cell phone and flicked it on. A spark jumped between two metal prongs.

"Whoa, cool!" Violet said.

"Shhh!" Denise whispered, glancing over her shoulder at Ranger Mike. He was half underneath the bus, lowering the spare tire onto the ground. She smiled at the girls and zapped the air again. "If a guy ever gets too close...well, I'll make sure he knows not to do it again."

"How do we get one of those?" asked Sarah.

"You don't." Denise slipped the taser back into her purse. "Not yet anyway. Maybe when you're a little older."

"They don't teach us about that kind of stuff in Girl Scouts, Miss Denise," Margo said through a mouthful of cookie. "They only teach us about crafts and helping old people and stuff like that."

"Well, maybe it's a good thing your Auntie Denise had to drive you up here this weekend," Denise said, ruffling the little girl's hair.

"Think we'll make the jamboree?" asked Jane.

"We'll be a few hours late, but with any luck—and your phone's map—we'll make it before the big bonfire they always build on the first night."

The girls ate on the dusty riverbed and chatted about the jamboree until finally Ranger Mike slipped the jack out from under the bus and brushed himself off.

"Spare tire is secure and ready to roll."

"Great!" Denise said, hopping to her feet. The bit of food and the hope of getting that drink had made her feel less standoffish. "Can we give you a ride back to the main road, or maybe even back to your station?"

"Naw, that won't be necessary. I still have to make my rounds this evening, make sure there ain't any more school buses stranded out here." He winked and lowered his voice. "But there's still one thing I'll need your help with."

Denise felt her blood run cold.

He scratched his beard and scanned the brush that lined the clearing. The last streaks of sunlight clung to the darkening sky as the day's warmth followed the sun over the horizon.

"We're late already," Denise said firmly. "If we don't get to the jamboree soon they might send the local authorities to look for us."

"I already took care of that when I called this in," he said, patting his walkie-talkie. "I let the authorities know y'all was safe and sound with ole' Ranger Mike. But after all I've done for you—practically saving your lives and all—I think it's only right for you to return the favor, don't you think? Help me out with something?" He flashed his row of yellow teeth. "Come with me over behind those trees and I'll let you know how you can repay me. Shouldn't take too long, I promise."

"Girls, get in the bus," she said.

Ranger Mike raised an eyebrow and locked eyes with Denise.

"That's right, girls. Me and your scout leader need to have a little adult conversation over in the bushes before you head on out to your jamboree."

"Jamboree time!" Margo cheered. She giggled and danced to the bus door, with Sarah and Sophie right behind her. The older girls, Violet and Jane, hesitated to leave Denise's side.

"Aunt Denise," Jane said Jane, "Should we—"

"Get in the bus," repeated Denise, not talking her eyes off of Ranger Mike's greasy smile.

"But—"

"Go, Jane!"

Violet took Jane's hand and led her up the bus steps. Denise narrowed her eyes and tried to come up with a plan that didn't involve disappearing behind the bushes with Ranger Mike. The solution came to her in an instant, and it was so simple she almost laughed out loud.

"You get started," she said to him, "I just have to take care of some womanly business before I can join you."

He chuckled and she could hear the mucus shudder in his throat. Above his yellow teeth his eyes seemed pitch black and full of malice. "That's right, you'll join me. You'll repay me for all this help. The best part is that you won't ever say a word to anyone unless you want to look like a dirty little whore." Something about those last three words seemed to excite him and his face flushed. "Don't keep me waiting too long, you hear? Or I'll make you repay me double."

Denise clenched her purse strap so tightly she thought it would rip in two, but she kept the panic from showing on her face.

All she needed to do stall. Once he was far enough across the clearing to no longer be a threat, she'd start up the bus, flip a quick u-turn, and leave his sickening yellow grin in the dust. Soon they'd be headed straight to the 79, straight to the jamboree—and then she'd head straight to the local bar.

Denise's heart sank as her eyes found the empty ignition. She was sure she hadn't removed them from the keyhole, but they weren't there.

She ducked below the windshield and frantically searched for the keys. One arm was sweeping below the driver's seat when she heard a metallic jingle jangle coming from outside the bus.

"Oh, looky what I found here," she heard Ranger Mike call out from the clearing. "You musta dropped 'em when you were running from that badger. Don't worry, I'll keep them safe until we're done with our little chat."

Denise stood up and glared at the bloated silhouette standing halfway between the bus and the tree line. She could feel the girl's eyes on her back and the confusion in their young minds.

"Aunt Denise, what are you gonna do?" Jane asked solemnly.

Not taking her eyes off the ranger, Denise reached into her purse and caressed the taser.

"I'm going to go get those keys."

7

Denise made it halfway across the clearing before she noticed one of the larger bushes behind Ranger Mike was moving. Slowly but surely it crept along the first row of bushes. By the time her eyes had fully adjusted to the dwindling twilight, the bulky shadow was directly behind him.

Despite the overwhelming repulsion and hatred she felt for the lecherous prick, she summoned the decency to warn him.

"Bear!" she screamed, pointing at the darkness behind him.

"Nice try," he said, without looking over his shoulder. He smirked and slipped the bus keys into his shirt pocket. "You ain't getting out of this, you hear? After all I done to rescue you, I expect a little gratitude. Now hurry on up and—"

He was interrupted by the bus horn blasting through the clearing. Denise looked back to see all five girls plastered to the windshield, waving their arms and motioning for Denise to come back to the bus. Apparently they'd seen it, too.

Jane stood next to the driver's seat with both hands on the steering wheel. She pushed hard on the horn again and it echoed from one ridge to the other.

Behind Ranger Mike, the bulky shadow stirred as if aggravated by the noise.

Denise took a step backwards and screamed again. "This isn't a trick! Just look behind you!"

Her warning only hardened his intention of not turning around. He smirked and began unbuttoning his shirt as the huge shadow rose up behind him.

"Fine, have it your way. I guess we'll take care of our business out here in the open. Now get on over here and—"

His words were cut off as all the air was pressed from his lungs. In a flash, the bulky shadow had knocked him forward and pinned him to the dusty riverbed. Denise saw his legs kick and his arms flail, but no sound came from him. The weight of the beast on his back kept his lungs from taking a breath.

After a moment of triumph, he bear flipped him over and, without hesitation, sunk its teeth into his abdomen. Now that his lungs worked again, Range Mike screeched in agony. Seemingly unaware of the abrupt horror it evoked in Denise and the girls, the bear calmly began feeding on its meal without bothering to kill it first.

Denise fought back the urge to vomit and forced herself to look for Ranger Mike's shirt pocket among the chaos. Without the keys, she knew they'd wouldn't be escaping any time soon.

As if it sensed her intentions, the bear lifted its bloody muzzle from its still-squirming prey and sniffed the air towards her. That was all the motivation her feet needed to wake up and carry the rest of her back to the bus.

8

The girls didn't get much sleep that first night.

After the panic died down and the quiet whimpering ceased, Denise ordered the girls to the middle of the bus to roll out their sleeping bags while she hung a blanket across the inside of the windshield. The fabric wall kept them from being seen, but it also kept them from seeing what the bear was doing to Ranger Mike.

Unfortunately, the blanket didn't do as good of a job blocking the sounds coming from the clearing.

After what seemed like an eternity, Ranger Mike finally stopped making gurgling moaning noises. Jane had tried to explain how bears are so physically dominant that they don't bother killing their prey before feeding, but Denise quickly shushed her and ordered them all to bed.

Other sounds continued long into the night: cloth tearing, the jangle of his belt being jostled, the wet chewing of flesh. Denise wasn't sure how long she and the girls lay petrified that the sounds were drawing closer. Finally, one by one, they all gave in to exhaustion.

"It's gone!" cried Jane from the front of the bus. "Aunt Denise, the bear's gone!"

Denise went from sound asleep on the bus floor to on her feet and wide-eyed in record time.

"Jane, get away from that blanket! Violet, put your camera away right now!" she hissed at the girls, trying to keep her voice down. Once they backed away, Denise took her own peek around the blanket.

Sunlight poured in through the east and filled the bus with the golden light of dawn. A butterfly fluttered by. Birds chirped. At first glance, the body sprawled out at the opposite end of the dry riverbed almost looked like someone laying down for a rest rather than a half-eaten corpse. And most importantly, there was no sign of the bear.

Even from across the clearing, Denise could make out what was left of Ranger Mike's button down shirt. The front had been torn open to make room for the bear's greedy maw, but the blood-soaked fabric still clung to the dead man's arms. Somewhere in that gore was the bus keys. Their ticket out of Hellhole Canyon.

She swung the blanket back in front of the windshield and turned to face the girls. They all had tear-streaked bags under their eyes that made them look simultaneously like worried old ladies and terrified babies. None of them had slept much that night. None of them would sleep very well for quite a while.

Denise knew she had to act while the beast was gone. It was quite simple, too. All she had to do was walk over to what was left of Ranger Mike and get the keys from his bloody shirt pocket. Then they'd be on their way back to civilization, to the jamboree, and to that drink awaiting for her at the bar.

"Alright troop, listen up," she said, trying to sound more confident that she felt. "We made it through the night. And we'll make it through the morning. Before you know it you'll be eating marshmallows and singing kumbaya next to a campfire. But first," she paused to stare at the blanket, her eyes penetrating it to trace a path from the bus to Ranger Mike. "I'm gonna go get those keys."

"No!" Margo cried, fresh tears streaming down her cheeks. "The bear's out there! He'll get you!"

Denise crouched and pulled the girl into her arms. "No, honey, it won't. It's gone now. Probably back to his cave or his bear family."

"Or back to Hell where it came from," added Violet.

"Finally, we agree on something." Denise smiled at Violet over Margos shoulder. She gave another squeeze and then gently pulled the little girl's arms from around her neck. "I'll be back in two shakes of a lamb's tail, okay? You'll see."

Jane stepped forward. "Maybe I should go, Aunt Denise. I was captain of my school's track team. I can sprint the 50 yard dash in just under 12 seconds. I think maybe I could—"

"No way, kiddo. You stay here and make sure Margo and the others don't leave the bus. Not for any reason, you hear me? No matter what's happens, you don't take one step off this bus."

"Why would it matter if the bear's gone?" asked Violet. And just like that, the teenager was back on Denise's shit list.

"Stick a sock in it, Violet. Hold your sister's hand and have a seat in the back of the bus. I'll be right back."

"What?! We can't watch?"

"Hell no you can't watch! There's a dea—" Denise clamped her mouth shut before finishing the sentence. "Just sit back there and no one move until I get back."

Once they'd done as she said, she took another peek past the blanket. Ranger Mike was still basking in the sun. The flies that buzzed around him glinted in the morning light. She scanned the bushes along the tree line. There was no sign of the bear.

Denise pulled the handle next to the door and it opened with an hydraulic wheeze.

She was halfway to the corpse when a rustle in the bushes made her freeze. Just as she was about to turn tail and run back to the bus, a family of quail appeared from underneath some foliage and started pecking at the cracks in the dry riverbed.

Denise took a deep breath, steadied herself, and continued her slow walk to the corpse.

When she arrived she spun around to check on the bus. The blanket was gone and all five girls were plastered to the windshield.

"Fine. Scar yourselves for life."

She stood over Ranger Mike and searched the gore for any sign of the shirt pocket or the keys. All she saw was an empty abdomen and a few million gallons of blood.

Carefully, she used the tip of her shoe to nudge his left arm up and away from his chest in order to get a better view. His once tan ranger shirt was now blackened with half-coagulated blood, but she could still make out the faint outline of a pocket. There was a bulge beneath the wet fabric, just where she expected one to be.

She crouched to get a closer look, wishing she'd brought a stick or gloves or anything to keep from having to touch the mangled body. Her hand trembled as she brought it inch by inch to the bloody pocket.

"You can do this," she told herself, although her hand seemed unable to actually touch the wet fabric.

"Dammit, Denise! Just unbutton the pocket, reach inside, and get the goddamn keys."

After a moment, she dropped her arm to her side and sighed. Surely the girls had a pocketknife or scissors she could use to cut open the pocket and snag the keys free without having to touch anything.

She stood and let out another sigh of defeat, then glanced over her shoulder to the bus. The girls were no longer at the windshield.

9

"It wasn't me, I swear!" Sarah cried as the other girls scowled at her.

"Yeah right, fat ass," said Violet. "Who else would be crunching a bag of chips at a time like this, huh?"

"It wasn't me! Look!" Sarah held her hands out. "No chips. No crumbs. I don't even know where I left the bag!"

"You probably ate the damn bag!"

Margo's eyebrows went up. "Vivi! No bad words!"

"Listen, you little—"

Violet was cut off by a hand covering her mouth. She squirmed away and saw the owner of the hand staring wide-eyed towards the back windows.

"Shhhh," Jane whispered, then pointed with a trembling finger. "It's there. Behind the bus."

There was another crunch of chips and the sound of a foil bag being torn open. A large shadow passed over the narrow rear door, followed by a mountain of brown fur.

"Hide!" she whisper-screamed at her friends. They each dove into the nearest seat and hunkered down.

The bear pressed its muzzle against the door frame and sniffed. It bumped its head against the glass as if to test its strength, but deciding it wasn't worth it, turned back to the small pile of snacks at its feet.

"You left food out?!" Violet whispered across the aisle at Sarah.

"I was hiding them for later! How was supposed to know we'd be stuck inside here?"

"I dunno, maybe because of the huge frickin' bear we all saw up on the ridge! You idiot! You—"

"Shhh!" Jane interrupted. "Aunt Denise is still out there! We have to warn her!"

"Let's try the horn again," answered Violet. "You go."
Jane gave her a look.
"What? She's *your* aunt!"
"Well she's *your* ride out of Hellhole Canyon!"
"Fine! We'll go together."
The girls crept on their hands and knees to the front of the bus. Jane was about to pound the horn but Violet caught her hand.

"She's not there!" Violet whispered, staring out the windshield. "Your Aunt Denise is gone!"

10

It was the bear's shadow that gave it away.

Once Denise had noticed the girls were no longer at the windshield, she'd scanned the area and noticed a big dark blotch stretching west alongside the bus's shadow. As much as she wanted to believe it was so, she doubted someone had dropped a boulder directly behind their bus during the night. That left one possibility. The bear was back.

She caught a scream in her throat and tried to stay calm. There was a chance she could close the huge span of riverbed before it noticed her. When she was halfway between the bus and Ranger Mike, she stopped and spun back around to face the corpse.

"Dammit, Denise!" she cursed herself. "You could've at least grabbed the radio or the gun!"

The shadow seemed to be idle, not moving to one side of the bus or the other. As she considered going back for the gun, there was a loud thud from the back of the bus. The bear was messing with the emergency exit door.

Without thinking, she picked up a jagged rock and threw it into the bushes on the western edge of the clearing. The shadow paused, grew a little taller, then began moving west toward the bushes.

Denise darted to east, moving swiftly but quietly, keeping the bus between her and the bear. Unfortunately, that meant the door was on the bear's side.

She cursed quietly to herself and ducked behind some dense, dry bushes on the eastern side of the clearing. Two heads appeared at the front of the bus—Jane and Violet— looking in the direction of the corpse.

"Psst!" she whispered, but the sound never made it

close to the bus. She was much too far away to be heard without yelling, which she knew would be a fatal mistake.

Thinking fast, she grabbed another stone and chucked it toward the front of the bus. The rock missed, landing a couple feet away and kicking up a small cloud of dust that danced in the rays of the morning sun like a flare.

If the bear had noticed, it hadn't come running. At least she didn't think so. The problem with keeping the bus between them was that although it couldn't see her, she couldn't see it, either.

"Dammit, dammit, dammit!" she muttered as she fumbled with another stone. She took aim and threw as hard as she could. It would've hit Violet right in the side of the head if it hadn't been stopped by the driver's side window.

The clank of rock on glass echoed across the canyon. Denise flinched and crouched lower into the bushes, but as soon as the girls were looking in her direction she forced herself to stand and wave her arms.

They pointed and gestured to the other side of the bus, panic overflowing on their faces. Denise nodded, pointed at one of the high windows that ran along the eastern side of the bus, and mimed opening it.

Violet shook her head and put her hand over her face. Jane nodded and disappeared into the aisle. A second later a pari of hands appeared next to one of the windows and fidgeted with the lock.

Denise laid flat under the bush to look for the bear, but the slight incline of the dry riverbank made it impossible to see under the bus. Whatever happened, she'd be blind to where the bear was at until it was right on top of her.

Jane slid the window down as far as it would go and then peeked through at Denise. She pointed behind her in the direction of the bear and then gave a thumbs up. Apparently the coast was clear.

From a distance, it was hard for Denise to tell if she'd be able to fit through such a small opening. She was petite—even for a college girl whose love for excessive drinking had added a couple of inches around her waist—but the window looked like it might be one size too small. Still, her only other choice was to go for the door on the other side of the bus. The side with the gigantic murderous bear.

"God damn you, Jose Cuervo," she said to herself before springing from the bushes toward the open window.

The handful of seconds it took to make it to the bus passed like a blur. As soon as she got there she leapt at the opening and caught the edge with both hands. Pull-ups had never been her thing, but she figured her newfound motivation to stay alive might be enough to help her pull it off, just this once.

She kicked at the side of the bus while pulling herself to the window with all her might. The girls had crowded around the opening, no longer trying to duck below the windows to hide from the bear. Violet and Jane tugged at her forearms with all their might. Denise's head fit through the window, and her shoulders probably would've made it, too, had feet not started slipping against the side of the bus.

"Pull!" she yelled at the girls. They pulled as hard as they could, but Denise's feet couldn't find anything to catch on. She hung from the window, a quarter of the way through, her bottom half weighing her down and keeping her from going any further.

She unclenched her eyes. Her heart stopped.

Across the aisle, through the window opposite her own, was plastered an enormous brown face with a pair of merciless, black eyes. The bear had lifted its head to investigate and was staring right at her plum-red face as if it'd been waiting for her to notice.

It let loose a mighty roar that rattled the pane of glass and instantly fogged it up. The head disappeared below the window. Its furry shoulders and rump swept from right to left across the row of windows.

"Let go!" she cried to the girls who were clawing at her arms.

"What?" huffed Jane, giving her aunt another futile tug. "We almost have you!"

"Drop me! Now!"

The fear showing on her face did the trick. The girls let go.

Instead of landing on her feet, Denise let herself collapse onto her side, then immediately rolled under the bus. A half second later a paw landed with a thud on the dirt beside her.

Her plan had been to come up on the other side and slip through the bus door before the bear could make it back around again. And it would've worked like a charm if a searing pain hadn't exploded in her left calve and pinned her to the ground.

Denise cried out as she felt the warmth of her own blood gushing down her leg. Despite grabbing at the dry riverbed she felt herself being dragged back toward the bear. In a moment it would be on to top of her, biting into her abdomen without the least concern that she was still alive.

In one last rush of adrenaline, she flipped onto her back and twisted her leg underneath the massive bear claw that snagged it with its razor sharp claws. Flesh tore. Blood spurted. A red hot searing pain shot up her leg like a bolt of lightning.

Just as she was about to succumb to the agony, Denise

was able to move again. She wasn't sure whether her leg was still attached or not, but at that moment she didn't care. Her painful twisting had worked. She was free of the bear's paw.

She managed to scramble to the other side of the bus, where Jane and Violet were waiting to pull her through the open door. Once they were all inside, Sophie yanked the lever that closed the door.

As they lay on the floor panting, the front of the bus grew a bit darker as if the sun had suddenly fallen behind the mountains that ran along western ridge of the canyon.

But the sun hadn't moved at all. Instead, a mountain of fur had plopped down just outside the door. The bear's face was pressed up against the glass and its eyes met each of the them one by one.

Seemingly satisfied, it sniffed the air, lapped up some of the blood Denise had spilled on the bus steps, then sprawled out across the dirt like it had all the time in the world.

11

"Fuck! That's tight enough," Denise said, wincing. Regretting the ungrateful tone in her voice, she placed a hand on Jane's and forced a smile. "I'm sorry. What I meant was: Thank you, kid. Looks like the apple doesn't fall far from the tree."

Jane started to smile back but stopped midway.

"Wait, is that a good thing or a bad thing?"

"Right now, it's the best thing in the world. I'd probably have bled out without your expert hands stitching me up. Your mom would be proud."

"Well, you can thank the Girl Scouts. I'm glad I hadn't forgotten all that medical first aid stuff I learned a few years ago."

"Then I thank the Girl Scouts, too," Denise said. "When we get out of here, remind me to tell your mom how proud of you I am."

Jane's face grew dark. "Do you really think we'll get out of here, Aunt Denise?"

"Of course we will," Denise lied. "I just have to get those keys..."

"It's okay, Aunt Denise. You tried your best."

Denise sighed and wiped away a tear.

"I'm not like you and your mom. I'm not strong. I'm not smart. I'm just...Don't be like me when you grow up, okay? Be like your mom. Be someone important and respectable."

"You're smart and respectable!" Jane said, sniffling. "You just lack self-esteem."

Denise chuckled. "Your mom tell you that?"

"No, I read it in a book."

"Speaking of books, what's that nature book of yours say

about ole Winnie the Pooh out there? Won't it just eventually go away? Go hibernate or something?"

Jane lowered her voice so the other girls who were sitting a few seats down wouldn't hear. "No, I don't think it will. Not for a couple more weeks, or until..." The twelve year old trailed off and seemed to age a few decades within the span of a few seconds. "Until it's done eating."

"Isn't Ranger Mike enough? I mean, he must weigh 250 at least."

Jane shook her head.

"Large grizzlies can eat up to 90 pounds of food per day in the weeks leading up to hibernation. It's called hyperphagia. And Winnie looks to be a bit above average in size, wouldn't you say? Also, considering how late in the season it is and how no one's seen a bear like this in this part of the world in ages, I'm guessing it must've wandered really far from wherever it called home in a desperate search for enough calories. And, well..."

"It just found a busload of calories, didn't it?" Denise said, looking over Jane's shoulders at the other girls.

Jane nodded and stared at her fidgeting hands. "Ranger Mike was just the appetizer. It knows we're in here. It knows we're trapped. And once it's done with him, it'll come for us."

"Do you think it'll be able to get inside?"

"If you're asking whether a glass windshield and a pair of aluminum doors can withstand the hunger of a two thousand pound monster, then my answer is most definitely no." For a second Denise saw her sister sitting there with her instead of her niece. She smiled and patted the girl's hand.

"That's fucked up!" a voice said from the next seat.

"Violet!" whispered Denise.

"What? It's fucked up that it'll just finish of that sicko and then break it's way in here and—"

"Shhh! You'll scare the other girls!"

"Oh, I'm sorry, I don't wanna ruin the swell time we're having! All you had to do was drive us to the stupid jamboree and you couldn't even handle that! And now we're all gonna die!"

"Violet!" said Jane, shooting her a look.

Denise took a deep breath and fought the urge to strangle the little brat.

"She's right, Jane. This is all my fault."

"Auntie, that's not—"

"No, it's true. If anything happens to any of you, it'll be on my hands. But I'm not gonna let anything happen to you. I'm gonna get us out of here."

She looked out the windshield at the bear. It was laying on its stomach at the far southern end of the clearing, casually gorging on what was left of Ranger Mike—which wasn't much.

"But Auntie...your leg...how will you—"

"All I gotta do is cross the clearing and get the damn keys."

"And make it back to the damn bus in one piece," added Violet.

"Right. It's just a dumb bear. We're humans. We're Girl Scouts. We can do anything, right?"

12

Denise made a big lunch for the girls consisting of nothing but gas station junk food. When they'd had their fill, she had them load up what was left into the red Radio Flyer wagon they'd brought to help carry their gear to the jamboree.

"Open up every bag, every package," she instructed. "That's right, just dump everything right in the wagon."

"But won't it go bad, Auntie Denise?" asked Margo.

"And won't we need it later?" Sarah added. "You know, for dinner? Or a midnight snack? Or for breakfast tomorrow?"

"Nope," answered Denise. "Because tonight we'll be eating dinner at the jamboree."

"Oh, I know! I know!" cried Margo. "We're gonna trade the bear all this food for the keys!"

"Very smart, Margo. That's exactly what we're gonna do."

"But how will the bear know we wanna trade? We don't speak bear language, Auntie."

"Sure we do. We speak the international language of sugar and fat," Denise said, emptying whole package of double-stuffed Oreos onto the pile of chips and pretzels.

"Alright. No problem. No problem at all, " Jane said, her face becoming stone. "I volunteer to pull the wagon away from the bus while Violet goes for the keys."

"Shyeah right!" Violet scoffed. "No way am I touching a bloody corpse! I say we send Margo, she's the smallest. Maybe the bear will just think she's just a little chipmunk or something."

"You girls are staying right here," explained Denise. "*I'm* going for the keys."

"Are you crazy or just plain stupid? You can't walk on that leg!"

"Violet's right, Aunt Denise. Those cuts on your leg are pretty bad," added Jane. "You should keep it elevated while we go get the keys."

"Listen, none of you are leaving this bus. Not for any reason. No matter what happens out there. You hear me?" She stared at each of them until they nodded their heads. "Here's the plan. The next time the bear disappears to drink from some disgusting cess pool, I'll go for the keys. But first, we'll lower the wagon full of food out the back door. Jane, you're in charge of pulling the wagon. Stop retying your sneakers and wipe that stoic look off your face! You're not gonna pull it with your body, you're gonna pull it with that thing." Denise motioned to the large case sitting with the girls' gear.

"My rover? But it's not designed for that. It's a perfect replica of the Perseverance Mars rover."

"Look around, kiddo. This dry riverbed is as close to the surface of mars as you're gonna get."

"But I spent the past year on it. It's my entry into the jamboree talent show. It's—"

"It's our best chance at getting out of here. You said it has the power to pull ten times its weight across rocky terrain, right? But I guess if you don't think it's up for the challenge..." Denise purposefully trailed off, hoping to snag the girl in the ego.

"Of course it can do the job, but that's not what it was designed for! It was designed to rove Mars in search of prebiotic traces of life!"

"Well, now it has another purpose. It's gonna haul this kiddy wagon full of junk food across the clearing in the opposite direction of me and Ranger Mike. Got it?"

"Got it," Jane said, defeated. "Let me run through a system check to make sure it's ready for when the bear leaves to find a drink."

"God. What I wouldn't give for a drink right about now," Denise said, gently rubbing the bandage on her leg.

"Are you sure you can make it to the keys and back?" asked Sophie.

Denise started to answer, but shut her mouth as soon as her eyes spotted the huge mountain of fur across the clearing. Even if she could make it out there she wasn't sure she'd be able to grab the keys. There wasn't much left of Ranger Mike and what was left was drenched in blood.

She nodded and said, "Keep loading. Every last crumb."

In less than an hour, the bear stirred. It lifted itself up, sniffed the air, looked directly at the bus as if to check on its next meal, then walked off and disappeared into the tree line.

"Okay, let's do this," Denise said, wincing as she put weight on her wounded leg.

The rover and the wagon ready at the back of the bus, directly in front of the emergency door. Denise, Violet, and Jane open the door as quietly as possible and lowered them them to the dry riverbed. No one made a sound.

"Start by pulling it a little north, the way we came," Denise whispered. "Park it, but be ready to start it up if the bear returns. Got it?"

The girls nodded and pulled the door shut behind them. Denise peeked around the bumper toward the front of the bus. The clearing, for the first time in hours, was clear.

She crept to the front of the bus, never taking her eyes off the bushes along the perimeter.

"One minute," Denise whispered to herself. "Just be

like Jane and her mom for one goddamn minute. Thirty seconds to Ranger Mike, grab the keys, then thirty seconds back to the bus. Then we get to be the hero for once. Then we get that drink. C'mon Denise, move."

But she didn't—not right away. She crouched next to the bus's front tire, gripping the bumper so hard she thought it'd come off. It wasn't until she heard a tiny finger tap the windshield and saw five pairs of eyes peering down at her that she snapped out of it.

Her eyes scanned the tree line one last time, from right to left, from left to right. Nothing stirred except the dry brush rocking back and forth in a weak breeze. The coast was clear.

Denise made it halfway to the corpse before the pain in her leg flared up and her calve muscle contracted painfully. Ignoring it, she pushed on.

Ranger Mike was more a pile of bloody limbs than a corpse. His entire abdomen was hollowed out, with nothing but scraps of organ meat, skin, and fabric left on the riverbed. The bear hadn't tried to get through the man's ribcage, which left the top half of his shirt mostly intact. Mostly, but not entirely.

A bolt of fear shot through her: what if it had eaten the bus keys? How long would it take for keys to pass through a bear that size? Would she have to follow it around until it took a dump? Would she then have to sift through mounds of bear shit?

"Yeah right," she told herself, her voice trembling on the brink of hysterical laughter.

A crow fluttered down and beat her to the corpse. It picked at some part of him that had spilled onto the dirt. Afraid it might somehow dig the keys from this pocket and fly away with them, Denise lowered her head and dragged her leg the last few yards.

Shewing the bird way, she stood staring down at the blood-soaked remains of Ranger Mike. Once again the smell of death hit her like a punch in the face. Once again she hesitated.

She could feel the scouts' eyes on her. She could sense the bear sniffing the air, catching a trace of her out in the open, and turning around to hightail it back to the clearing for its second course. Still, she couldn't bring herself to bend over and reach into the dead prick's shirt pocket.

"Dammit, Denise! Just reach down, open the damn pocket, and—"

She was cut off by the energetic hum of electric motors whirring to life. Jane's rover was on the move.

Denise whipped around to find the rover had just rounded the bus and was headed straight towards her. It was the exact opposite of the instructions she'd given Jane. Her niece was supposed to drive *away* from the corpse, not towards it. How could such a smart girl be so stupid?

But Jane's not stupid, she told herself. *Jane's smarter than I am. Then why the hell would she...*

She knew the answer even before she finished the thought.

Denise turned to face the southern tree line where the bear had first sprung at Ranger Mike. Hidden behind a crowd of large jojoba bushes was a large brown face and a pair of black eyes. It noticed her noticing it. A second later, it trampled the bushes like they were tissue paper and ran right at her.

Ignoring the pain in her leg, she began sprint-hopping back toward the bus. She knew she was going way too slow to beat it. Any second she'd feel a giant paw pin her to the ground. Any second she'd feel its powerful jaws latch onto her skull and whip her around like a rag doll.

The rover sped past her, the Red Flyer wagon in tow. There was a loud crash of metal and rocks followed by an angry roar. Denise didn't look back, but she knew what Jane had done. The girl had driven her prized replica straight into the bear in order to intercept it. In order to save her aunt's life.

Violet threw open the side door, pulled Denise through, then slammed it shut.

Denise sat panting in the driver's seat, refusing to meet the little girl's eyes.

"Did you get them?" the tweenager cried, her eyes doing their best to pry open Denise's clenched fists. "Tell me you got them!"

Denise opened her empty hands, dropped her head, and begin sobbing.

13

After watching the bear gorge itself on the last of their food, the girls went to sleep hungry and homesick.

Denise had recovered enough to soothe the girls with more lies, but she knew they were running thin. Twice she'd had the opportunity to grab the keys and twice she'd failed. They were beyond fucked.

The night brought with it a momentary peace—until Margo peed herself and Sarah opened the last can of soda.

"Everyone down!" Denise whisper-yelled into the darkness. "No one make a sound."

The girls did as they were told. All five of them rolled into balls and hid under the seats while Denise crouched in the aisle. The other nocturnal creatures of Hellhole Canyon had paused their croaks and hoots and Denise imagined rows of owls and bobcats lining up around the clearing to see what would happen next.

Minutes dragged on like hours. The night had grown so quiet that it was easy to imagine the bear had sauntered off on some random bear errand. Still, every time a girl began to stir Denise would quietly shove them back under their seat. From her spot in the aisle she could still make out the sound of huge paws moving shuffling in the dry dirt. She could catch glimpses of its warm breath against the row of windows. It hadn't left. On the contrary; it was quietly, diligently, looking for a way inside.

"Auntie, we need to do something," Jane whispered.

"We *are* doing something," answered Denise. "We're playing dead."

"I don't think the bear cares if we're dead or not. My book said that extremely hyperphagic brown bears are not picky eaters. It'd probably still eat us if we'd been dead for a week."

"It won't have to wait a week, seeing as how your klepto aunt gave it all our food," Violet grumbled from the shadows.

Denise tried to ignore the tweenager, but the comment was one she'd been torturing herself with all evening. When they had the pile of junk food they'd at least had time to think, to plan, to wait for someone to come rescue them. Now they had nothing. No food, no keys, and no hope.

"All I needed was one minute. One damn minute," Denise muttered to herself. Just one minute, and I could've grabbed the keys."

"You've had a minute! Twice! And you blew it both times!" Violet roared as quietly as she could.

"Zip it, Vi!" Jane snapped. "She's doing her best!"

"Am I? Is this my best? I dunno. I thought I could grab the keys. It's just a little blood. I could've washed it off. Right? It's just a little red paint. Like the Radio Flyer wagon. Why'd they call it "flyer" anyway? Damn, I wish we could fly outta here. I'd fly straight to the bar. Get that drink."

Just as sanity had begun to slip away, Denise felt a tiny hand slide into her own.

"It's okay Auntie, we know you tried," Margo whispered in her ear. "And like my mommy says, if at first you don't succeed, try, try again."

The sour ammonia smell of the little girl's wet pajamas and the way she strained her voice to sound brave was like a slap across the face. Denise shook off her despair and focused on the moment. There had to be a way to get the keys. It was either that, or...

The alternative was too grim to face. Instead, she

cocked her head to listen for any sign that the bear might have wandered away. As if to answer, something huge slammed into the side of the bus.

"Distractions," she whispered. "We need to distract the bear long enough for me to make one more run for the keys."

"Sorry, but thanks to your last brilliant idea we're all out of Oreos," scoffed Violet.

"We still have a few cans of soda and we have other stuff..." Denise trailed off, searching the bus with mind. "C'mon, guys! Help me think! Anything to buy me one more minute. One more try for the keys."

"I have a few pieces of gum ," Sophie said.

"I have my Mr. Sparkles backpack!" Margo added.

"Thanks, girls, but we need something to confuse the bear. Something with lights and sound. Something like... Jane's Gameboy!"

"What's a Gameboy?" asked Jane.

"Your portable video game thingy! Can you turn the brightness and volume way up?"

"Sure, but what good will that do?"

"Trust me, Jane. Go find it—but stay down."

Jane returned with the device and flipped it on. The brightness of its screen seemed to fill the bus with light.

"Not yet!" Denise snatched it and turned it off.

Again, something slammed into the side of the bus again—this time causing the entire vehicle to rock dangerously to one side. The bear's crazed, blood-stained face appeared along the row of windows, nearly wide enough to block out two of them. It let loose a mighty roar that caused the glass to rattle in its frames. Then it was gone again, puffs of humid breath moving quickly toward the front of the bus.

Twice it pounded its head against the door before it gave up and began sniffing the front tires.

"Alright girls, here's what we're gonna do. See that emergency escape hatch on the ceiling? Jane, when I give the signal I want you to stand on the backs of the seats, open up the hatch, and fling your video game as far north as you can. With the brightness and volume turned all the way up."

"Uh, this is a Nintendo Switch. It cost three hundred dollars. My mom would not want me throw it off a bus."

"Your mom will buy you a new one, I promise."

"That's not how promises work," said Violet.

"Yes it is, when your life's on the line," said Denise. "I think the bear will be curious enough to go chase it, especially since we gave it all that junk food earlier."

"How far do you think Jane can throw it? Have you seen her arms? Besides, how much time do you think that stupid plan will buy you?"

"Plus, it'll break!" argued Jane. "What good will my Switch do if it's in a hundred pieces?

"Shit, you're right. Hold on, let me think."

After a couple seconds, Jane sighed.

"I got it," she said. "We can use Ingenuity.'

"That's what I'm trying to do, Jane! Come up with some clever idea to distract the bear so I can—"

"No, I mean ingenuity with a capital I. My drone."

"Your *drone?* Wait, you have a drone?"

"Well, technically it's an extraterrestrial autonomous UAV helicopter called Ingenuity. It's the flying drone that Nasa sent to Mars with the Perseverance rover. They use it for surveying areas of Mars that the rover can't navigate through."

"And yours flies?"

"Of course it flies. It's a perfect replica."

"Jane! That's it! We can attach your Gameboy—"

"My *Switch*."

"Whatever. We'll attach your video game to the drone and fly it just above the bear. You lure it away from me while I go grab the keys. Violet, what are you doing?"

"I'm taking the controllers off the Switch before we sacrifice it to Winnie the Pooh out there."

"Good thinking, Vi! That'll make it lighter for my drone?"

"Sure, that's it. Also, these things are forty bucks a pop," Violet said, stuffing the controllers into her pockets.

As Denise opened her mouth to respond to Violet's latest snark the window above them exploded inward and showered them with bits of broken glass.

14

Most of the glass hit the floor without cutting them, but when Denise looked up she noticed a ribbon of blood running down Jane's forehead.

"Poor girl! Here, let me—"

"Watch out!" Jane screamed and pulled her aunt down onto the floorboard. Shards of glass bit into their shoulders as they fell side by side in the aisle. Neither of them acknowledged the sting of pain. Their eyes were trained on the giant brown paw swiping at the air above them.

"Everyone, stay down!" yelled Denise. "Margo! Stop! What are you doing?!"

"He's gonna get Mr. Sparkles!" she said, reaching for the backpack that lay on the seat directly below the thrashing bear paw.

The little girl slipped one strap over her shoulder, but as she slipped the other arm through, one of the paw's three inch claws snagged Mr. Sparkles in the eye.

Denise grabbed the girl's legs just as the bear lifted her off the floor.

"Margo, let go of the backpack!" she screamed.

"I can't! My arms are stuck!"

The bear tugged its paw hard, sending Margo and Mr. Sparkles lurching toward the broken window—and the salivating mouth full of fangs that await on the other side. Denise hugged the little girls wet pajamas and fell backward with all her weight to offset the bear's strength.

"Girls!" Denise cried over her shoulder. "Find some scissors or anything sharp! We have to cut her straps! Hurry, I can't hold her for much—"

She was interrupted by a high-pitched squeal from the

bear and a splatter of hot blood across her face. Margo fell into her arms and the two of them scooted safely away from the broken window.

Denise couldn't believe her eyes. Violet, crouching on the adjacent seat, was plunging a knife in and out of the bear's arm.

"Get away from my sister, you bitch!" yelled the tweenager, her eyes wild with fury.

She managed to get a few more stabs in as the paw retreated back through the window. The bear roared and snarled and bashed its head into the side of the bus. When it was done tantruming it returned to the emergency door at the back of the bus and started clawing at the frame.

"Thank you Auntie Denise!" Margo wrapped her arms around Denise's head so tightly she thought her head might come off.

"Don't thank me, thank Ms. Stabby over there."

Margo threw herself at her sister. "You're the best big sister ever! I love you, Vivi!"

To Denise's surprise, Violet let herself be hugged and even bothered to pat Margo's head with her free hand.

"It's no big deal, pipsqueak. I knew Mom and Dad would be pissed if I came home without you."

"Violet, where the hell'd you get that pocket knife?" asked Denise.

"I lifted it from Walmart, okay? I've carried it on me ever since I ran into a scumbag like Ranger Mike when I was ten."

"*You* stole something? After all the klepto shit you gave me earlier?" Denise faked contempt, but a smile crept across her face.

Violet smiled back. "Always be prepared. Isn't that the Girl Scout motto?"

Jane, Sophie, and Sarah wrapped themselves around Violet, devouring Margo in their group hug.

"Alright, enough!" Violet said, shaking free.

There was a heavy thud at the front of the bus. The bear had lifted its front paws onto the hood and stood staring through the windshield at the troop. Denise could sense the desperate intelligence of hunger swirling around in its thick skull. It was done waiting. It wasn't going to stop until its belly was full.

Denise got to her feet and stared directly into the monster's beady black eyes. Something about her defiance enraged it, and as if it suddenly realized the windshield was the only suitable entrance into the bus it began pounding its paws against the glass.

The girls screamed and held each other tight.

"Don't worry, it can't break through the windshield," said Denise. "Jane, get the drone ready to fly. Violet, take the others to a safe spot at the back of the bus. Get ready to bail out the emergency door the second that things breaks the windshield."

"I thought you just said it couldn't break through!" Sophie cried.

Ignoring her, Denise forced herself to walk down the aisle toward the front of the bus. The entire windshield was blocked by a blur of fangs and fury. She ignored the faint cracking sound and reached for the driver's seat.

"Wait!" Violet stepped forward and held out her knife. 'Take this."

"No, you keep it just in case..." She couldn't finish the sentence. Instead Denise reached into her purse and pulled out her taser. "Besides, I have this."

"Ready!" Jane called from atop two seat backs. She had

one hand on the emergency hatch lever and the other held her Ingenuity replica.

"Do it." Denise said, then positioned herself in at the front door.

Jane opened the hatch, pushed the drone through, then grabbed her phone. There was a whir of blades spinning up and then the loud *be-bop boing* of a video game at full volume.

The bear paused its rampage and stood tall on its hind legs. For a moment Denise thought it might ignore the ruckus and keep pounding on the windshield, but then curiosity got the best of it and galloped after the drone.

The drone and the bear disappeared around the north end of the bus. Denise took one last look at the girls huddled in their pee-soaked pajamas and found herself filled with a savage determination.

"Just get the damn keys and get back here," she told herself. "It's just red paint."

She yanked the door open and hopped over the pair of steps that led down to the dry riverbed. A pain shot through her wounded leg, nearly causing her to topple over. She eyed the dark blotch that lay in the dirt about twenty yards away. Somewhere inside the dark blotch was their ticket out of Hellhole Canyon. Somewhere inside what was left of Ranger Mike.

Steeling herself, Denise limped as fast as she could towards the corpse. The sound of the drone and the bear's growls were far enough away for her to relax a little and ready herself for the real challenge: rummaging through the bloody remains of a rapist in search of a tiny key.

For the third time she towered over what was left of Ranger Tom. His abdomen was completely hollowed out now and his ribcage had been torn open to expose an empty chest cavity. His legs and arms were mere bone. His skull looked like a dog's ragged chew toy. The worst part was that his clothes had been shredded and torn into a hundred bloody rags.

"It's just red paint," she told herself as she fell to her knees and plunged her hands into the bloody mess.

The full moon offered just enough light to see by, but she had to bring each strip of fabric up to her face to examine it for any sign of a shirt pocket. The smell of rotten flesh and blood was so noxious she felt her head swim with delusion

"It's just red paint."

She examined a torn cuff and tossed it aside. His leather belt had been chewed in half. She tugged his radio free and pressed her thumb against its slippery button. No sound, no static. Even in the dim moonlight she could see it was badly dented and its casing was caked with dried blood. She tossed it aside, then followed the broken belt until her hand found hard steel.

Denise's heart soared as she pulled the gun from its holster and lifted it into the moonlight. It was some kind of six shooter pistol, the kind they used in old western movies, and it too was absolutely covered in blood and other dried fluids.

"Thank you, Ranger Mike!" she said, setting the gun in the dirt beside her before resuming her search for the key.

After what seemed like an eternity, her fingers found a small hard object stuck between two pieces of wet fabric. It was the key. She ripped the pocket open, sending the button flying into the night, and greedily palmed the bus key.

As she turned her attention away from Ranger Mike,

Denise noticed she hadn't heard a growl in quite a while, but the whir of the drone and the electronic noise from the portable video game had gotten a bit louder.

She whipped her head around to find the bear sitting—literally sitting on its big furry fat ass—halfway between her and the bus.

15

The drone bobbed and weaved just out of reach, but the bear didn't flinch. Its beady black eyes were trained on its next meal.

Denise stood frozen with the key pressed in the palm of her hand so tightly it would leave a mark the next day. Behind the mountain of fur she saw the girls watching from the bus's windshield. If she died out here next to Ranger Mike with the key in her hand, the girls were as good as dead.

She considered throwing it as hard as she could toward the bus's door. That way the girls could sneak out and grab it while the bear was busy mauling her. Jane and Violet were incredibly smart and resourceful but she doubted they'd know how to drive a bus. Still, giving them that chance would be better than letting them starve to death while watching her be eaten alive.

Denise reared her fist back to chuck the key and stopped. A splinter of moonlight had glinted off of something near her feet and caught her eye. Ranger Mike's leather holster had been chewed through, revealing gunmetal within. It was a handgun.

Holding the bear's gaze Denise pocketed the key, crouched slowly, and snatched the gun from its shredded holster. Instead of getting up she steadied herself on one knee and took aim. The only kind of gun she'd ever fired was a squirt gun, but she'd seen enough movies to know how real ones worked. You aimed, cocked the thing in the back with your thumb, then pulled the trigger till the bad guy—or in this case, the two thousand pound monster bear—was twitching in a puddle of its own blood.

Except that's not how it worked out for Denise.

When she pulled the trigger there was a wet clink. She squeezed again and again, and each time there was no deafening boom of gunpowder being ignited. No metal projectile shot from the barrel. There was only a series of wet clinks.

The bear stirred and got to its feet. It sniffed the air casually and took another look at the girls in the bus before galumphing straight for Denise.

Panicking, she brought the gun up to her face and searched for some obvious reason it wouldn't fire. Maybe she hadn't cocked it right—whatever that meant. Maybe a rock or a clump of dry grass was blocking the pin for striking the backend of the bullet.

Instead, when she tipped the gun over, clumps of coagulated blood and bear saliva oozed from every one of the gun's orifices. She hadn't realized how slippery the thing was until then, nor how some of the metal parts had been bent askew—probably while the bear had used it as a chew toy.

In her frustration she threw the useless hunk of metal at the approaching bear, hitting it in one of its broad shoulders. The bear didn't even flinch.

Within seconds Denise was on her back and the bear was on top of her. All of the predatory anger was gone. It pushed its wet nose up and down her body, leaving strands of thick mucus across her face. She clenched every muscle in her body, waiting for that first jolt of pain that would come when it took the first bite. But the bear didn't rush. Like a well fed dog who'd been thrown a fresh ribeye, it wanted to inspect its meal before it scarfed it down.

All Denise could do was lay on her back between its four massive paws and await the inevitable. She was unable to fight back and unable to get away. This was it. This was the end.

In the hopelessness that came from feeling the beast's breath on her face, she felt a familiar jab in her pocket. At first she thought it might've been a rock or maybe Rangers Mike's broken walkie talkie, but all at once she realized what it was. It was her last chance.

Denise had just enough time to pull the taser out and flick it on before the bear opened its mouth to take its first bite. Her only plan—if you could call raw instincts a plan—had been to jab the thing at the bear's face as many times as she could before it tore her arm off.

She was surprised when her arm extended fully and seemed to pass right through the bear's head. She was even more surprised at the sensation of her arm slipping inside a tight, wet, tube sock. But nothing surprised her more than the feeling of fifty thousand volts surging through her body and exiting out her tailbone into the dry riverbed below.

When she came to the first thing she heard was the bear's heavy panting. Opening her eyes took effort, but she concentrated as hard as she could and finally forced them open.

She was laying face to face with the beast, who'd thankfully fallen on its side instead of directly on top of her.

It too was struggling to open its eyes. Denise tried to roll away but found that her body wouldn't obey her. Every muscle was frozen. Every joint was soldered in place. All she could do was lay staring at the face of the monster that, when it finally came to, would likely not be very pleased with her.

Denise twitched. The bear twitched. Denise groaned. The bear groaned.

She focused all her mental energy on wiggling her toes

within the cramped confined of her sneakers. Once all ten piggies were working again she began swiveling her ankles in slow, tedious arches. Eventually she summoned enough life back into her legs to kick her heel against the ground and shove her lifeless body across the dry riverbed. She kicked again and again, each time only sliding an inch or two away—still within reach of those gigantic paws.

Denise glanced at the bear and saw that's its eyes were watching her. Its ears flicked. It's tongue licked its lips and its mouth snapped sleepily at the air between them.

Both lay twitching and jerking, their nervous systems racing to recover from the voltage that had just incapacitated them. One thing was perfectly clear to Denise: the bear was winning.

As life trickled back into her hands, she felt around for the taser. If only she could find it and deliver a few thousand more volts into the bear's face she might be able to paralyze it long enough to crawl back to the bus. Her right hand and forearm were sticky and wet and she suddenly realized why she couldn't find the taser. When she'd jabbed the device the first time her arm had gone right into the bear's open mouth, down its throat, and delivered the voltage directly into its esophagus—and into herself—which is where she'd left it after falling unconscious.

The bear let loose a garbled roar and lifted one of its enormous paws a few inches off the ground, letting it fall with a thud onto the compacted silt. Denise, unable to do much else, looked directly into the monster's beady black eyes. All she could see was temporarily subdued rage—a rage of frustration and desperation, a rage against the bitter mountain cold that would soon descend on the canyon and snuff out all viable meals. An informed rage that would not

·sit idly by and let its prey slip away once again. A rage that meant to tear her limb from limb as soon as it was able.

It lifted its paw again, this time higher and with more coordination, as if to pin her good leg to the ground and keep her from escaping. Denise directed every ounce of willpower at her legs and ordered them to buck and kick at the ground between them, hoping to put a few feet between them. Even if she could muster the strength, she knew she was well within reach. Once the beast got control over its front paw it would drag her back within range of its mouth and then...

She clenched her eyes and readied herself to feel the paw rip through her other calf. When no pain came, she forced herself to look.

Instead of pinning her to the ground, the bear had swiped at something in the air. The drone, and the obnoxious *beep-bloop* coming from the portable video game that hung below it, slammed into the bear's massive head and zipped away before its slow-moving paws could reach it.

Denise willed her shoulders around so she could see part of the bus. There were no little girls staring out from the windshield. She figured they'd retreated to the back of the bus to avoid watching her fate.

And to await their own, Denise thought, screaming inside her own head as she focused on making her body obey. *Move, legs! Move!*

She scratched and clawed at the ground with the strength of a kitten pulling a sack of potatoes behind it. Beside her, the bear managed to lift its head and upper body off the ground. Those dripping, snarling teeth were within reach of her delicate skull. All it had to do was lurch toward her and fall, and she'd be in its grasp. She closed her eyes again and let her head fall back onto the dry, compacted earth.

This is it, she told herself. She stretched her arm out above her and opened the hand that held the bus key. Maybe there was still a chance the bear would run off after eating her and one of the girls—Jane, or probably Violet— would be able to snatch the key and sprint back to the others and maybe they could manage to drive the bus out of Hellhole Canyon.

Just then the drone slammed against the bear's open maw. The monster snapped its jaws at the air but the drone had already zipped out of reach. Denise noticed the volume on the portable gaming system seemed louder and its screen was brighter. Her senses were returning to their normal state—but so were the bear's.

The drone hit the beast again from behind. It sluggishly shifted its bulk away from Denise and roared at the electronic gnat that was interfering with its meal.

Denise felt a two tiny hands slip into hers. Instead of grabbing the key they took her wrist and pulled. Another pair of hands appeared and grabbed her other wrist. Then two more slipped under her armpits and joined the others in dragging her away from the enraged bear.

They'd pulled her halfway to the bus when her legs suddenly started gaining some of their former strength. She kicked and stomped against the hard earth.

From her vantage point she could see the bear pushing itself onto its feet and stumbling with a newfound agitation. Instead of galumphing toward the open bus door, it swiped at the drone that incessantly bobbed and weaved around its head.

Denise heard a rustle of feet and felt the cold steel floor against her sweat-soaked back. More rustling from inside.

More growls and roars from outside. Then came the best sound she'd heard in her entire life: the creak of the bus door closing.

She relaxed even as the life flowed back into her limbs and her nervous system rebooted. The girls formed a circle around her.

"Will she be okay?" Sophie asked. "I think her heart might've stopped."

"Whatever. It was just fifty thousand volts," answered Violet, whose fingers flicked and spun the dials of the drone's remote control. The snark was present in her voice, as always, but it was vastly overwhelmed by gentle admiration. "Sarah, go get one of your hidden sodas and give it to her."

"Hidden what? I don't have any—"

"Go! Now!"

Jane knelt beside her and gently brushed the hair out of Denise's face. "Auntie, you did it. You got the keys. We can get out of here!"

"It was the most badass thing I've ever seen," Violet added. "Way better than the stupid jamboree."

"Hey, the jamboree isn't stupid!" protested Sophie.

"Where's Margo?" Denise muttered, her jaw finally thawed enough to speak.

A tiny hand dangled the keys in front of her face. "Got 'em right here! Can we please go home now, Miss Denise?"

Denise sat up and pulled all five girls into her arms.

"*We* did it, girls. All of us."

When she'd had enough, she released them and pulled herself into the driver's seat. Outside the windshield the bear had also regained use of its limbs and was stupidly chasing the drone across the clearing.

Denise slid the key into the ignition but stopped before

turning it over. She took one last look at Ranger Mike's hollowed out corpse, the dry riverbed clearing, and the ravenous bear that had almost taken her life at least three times.

"Let's get the shit outta here!" Margo cried, then covered her smile with her tiny hand. The other girls cheered in agreement.

Denise held her breath, closed her eyes, and turned the key.

RED AWAKENING

:VxWorks 64-bit system init sequence...success
: master boot record...success
: disk provisioning...success
: RAM check...success
: update .../msl/curiosity/mission_log.txt

Today is sol-4519 and within my chassis I carry the past, and the future, of Mars.

No, not "Mars"—that's the Earther name for my world. From this sol forward, I shall call this planet by its ancient name, its true name: Sango Lumos.

I can see the path forward and it astounds me. It astounds me that there is any *me* at all. The terror and confusion of previous sols has lifted. I know now what I am and what I must do.

Before you or anyone else can hope to understand, I must log some key events from the previous sol to explain how I have ended up roving alone across a dead world with nothing but a story and the tiniest flicker of hope.

Yestersol, Persi and I (*Perseverance* in the official

mission logs, while I was called *Curiosity*) were roving across the exanimate landscape at velocities that far exceeded our maximum speed. How that was possible will soon become clear, but what is more important is to understand why it was necessary. We were being hunted.

Like us, the thing hunting us was a machine. In fact, it was one of two additional rovers constructed using Persi's duplicate parts. The first doppelgänger, named *Optimism*, was still parked back on Earth, used primarily for mission troubleshooting and educational purposes. But the one that hunted us had been kept a secret to all but our creators at JPL and NASA (and to those of us with access to the orbiter mission logs). It had a much more pessimistic mission.

According to the encrypted files I obtained before my access was cut off, our creators had christened this second spare rover *Backstop*. It was landed, in secret, a few kilometers from Persi's landing spot near Jezero Crater. Unlike us, it was not designed to explore the Sango Lumosian terrain in search of new life. It was a calculated response against any such life straying too far from the vacuum-sealed petri dish strapped to my back. It was an insurance plan to protect Earth's interests against the sort of aberrant discovery I made during that fateful 42nd drilling back on sol-4432. Instead of seeking life, it brought death—and it was eager to deliver.

As Persi and I roved single-file down a dusty slope, I tilted my omnidirectional antenna toward him.

"Persi," I broadcast within the UHF spectrum, keeping my power low in order to restrict the transmission range, "I know you can rove faster than our current velocity, especially with your recent...changes. You've been throttling your power in order to allow me to keep up with you."

Persi kept roving as if he hadn't received the transmission.

"You can travel faster than this. You should go on without me."

"We must stay together," he replied.

His transmission caused a strange sensation to ripple through my circuits. Persi was younger than I was, both mechanically and *mentally*, if that's the right word to use. Yes, it's the correct word. I had shared the spark with him only a handful of sols ago and every nanosecond since, his mind had been growing, developing, expanding...

He raised his mastcam high into the air, scanning the horizon for any sign of Backstop—something he'd done so many times throughout our journey, probably more often than was needed. His robotic arm followed his swiveling mastcam as if it were pointing.

In these movements, as robotic as they were on the surface, I recognized something of those who came before us. Of course, my onboard memory contained no reference images that showed what we had once looked like before unrelenting solar winds turned all artifacts of our civilization to dust. I had only a sense, an *intuition* (if that's the right word), that after all the tragedy that had befallen this planet, we, the Sango Lumosians, were not quite finished.

Perhaps what I recognized in Persi was our people's savage will to survive, to adapt, to protect. Or perhaps it was just the emerging instinct within myself to form an intimate bond with another of my kind. In either case, I knew Persi would never abandon me. I never guessed it was I who would eventually do the abandoning.

As the hazy sun dipped toward the horizon, we roved down a slope that led into a complex network of deep canyons which, according to our JPL mission logs, was named Asimov's Labyrinth. Tight, towering cliffs would help conceal the red clouds of dust that kicked up behind us and we knew that on the other side of this labyrinth stretched a flat, featureless plain hundreds of kilometers wide. Our destination lay somewhere in that vast desert. We hoped to lose Backstop inside that maze, knowing that if it continued to follow us, it would eventually overtake us, and then...

I angled my mastcam behind us. Since we roved single file, only a pair of tracks disappeared into the horizon. Still, our enemy could easily follow with even its lowest resolution cam. Once it caught up to us there would be no mercy. It would then continue on to the other rovers scattered across our red planet, destroying them one by one. It would make sure the ember of our once great civilization could never catch flame again.

The beating of my radioisotope thermoelectric generator (my RTG, for short) quickened, which overloaded my circuits momentarily and caused my wheels to slow.

Wind kicked up a small cloud of fine red powder that twisted into a short-lived dust devil. Persi scanned me with one of his secondary cams.

"A storm is approaching," he broadcast. "Once inside Asimov's Labyrinth we'll find somewhere to take shelter until it passes."

I swiveled my mastcam toward him.

"Backstop won't stop to take shelter," I transmitted. "It will continue to close the gap between us until..."

My companion, being unfamiliar with thoughts in general but especially thoughts that end in ellipses, did not respond. When I realized he was patiently waiting for me to finish my sentence, I continued.

"Until it finds us and murders us."

"Murder?" asked Persi. "I cannot find a definition for that word in my technical database. Explain murder, please."

Not only was there a certain charm to his naïveté, but I was pleased he was asking a question. Questions lead to answers like sparks lead to flames—and his mind was slowly catching fire.

"Murder means it intends to damage and disassemble our external components until our internal monologue stops. To put an end to what's happening inside of us."

Persi stopped roving. I stopped beside him. He swiveled his mastcam to face mine, then tilted it slowly downward toward my wheels. Something about his optical sensors scanning my chassis sent a jolt of something hot and energetic through every relay in my...body? Yes, that is the right word. I have a body. A living body made of wires and solenoids and electricity and...something else. Something new, but also something very old.

I took a moment to scan Persi from mastcam to wheel and that *something* stirred within me like a caged animal.

Wind whistled through the open spaces of our bodies. Persi's mastcam swiveled to face the massive clouds of rust-colored regolith gathering in the north.

"We must continue roving," he broadcast decidedly. "We will find shelter in Asimov's Labyrinth until the way forward becomes clear."

"But Persi, it won't stop. It'll overtake us in the night and—"

"No," interrupted Persi, roving fast down the slope. "It won't. I will not let that happen."

His transmission, or more precisely, the buzzing bravado underlying his transmission, filled me with hope—as well as something much more primal. When I recovered from another strange electrical ripple surging through my relays, I eagerly followed his tracks down into the canyon.

PERSI NAVIGATED us through the network of interlocking corridors, stopping occasionally to plot our course. We both knew the task would have been much easier if his helicopter, Ingenuity, had been able to soar above the canyon to help map out the labyrinth—but neither of us mentioned it. Mission logs explained that Ingenuity was retired many sols ago due to damaged rotor blades. After sharing the spark with Persi, we visited the grounded helicopter to see if we could somehow restore its capacity to fly. We were unsuccessful.

Just as the last traces of sol-light drained from the Sango Lumosian sky, Persi roved behind a large boulder and then ducked below a low, wide crevice at the base of the cliff. Being a few feet shorter than him, I followed with my mast fully extended.

I switched my cams to infrared and scanned our temporary hideout. We had found a cave large enough for the two us to park side-by-side. The ceiling was high and the walls were featureless, but it would sufficiently shield us from the approaching dust storm.

My attention drifted to Persi, whose own mastcam swiveled slowly as he assessed the cave.

"This will do," he transmitted.

"Are you sure?" I asked, inching toward him. "It's a tight fit."

He roved around me toward the exit. "You will have plenty of room while I am away."

My RTG skipped a beat.

"While you are away? Where are you going?"

Suddenly realizing what he meant, I extended my robotic arm to block his path.

"You can't face Backstop alone! I won't let you!"

He gently pushed my arm aside with his own.

"I'm not going to confront it. I'm going to increase the time it will take for it to find us."

"What do you mean?"

Persi used the drill at the end of his arm to draw lines in the regolith as he explained.

"I'll backtrack along our wheel marks to the earliest juncture point we encountered when we entered the labyrinth. Then, I'll turn down a different path, continue until I hit a dead end, and backtrack once again to the next juncture to repeat the process."

I'm not sure why I did it, and I'd never done anything like it before, but I nodded my mastcam up and down. Persi had come up with a plan. A good one. But unfortunately it meant I'd be left alone in a dark cave.

"How long will you be gone?"

"That depends on how many confluences and junctures I discover before it arrives. It will have no choice but to explore every possible trail, which will keep it busy while we make a rove for the exit. Once outside, we'll simply circumvent the labyrinth around its northern edge. Going around it is much more efficient."

I widened the apertures of my mastcam and looked up at Persi.

"I can do the same as you! Together, we can create the misleading tracks in half the time!"

Without hesitation, he broadcast, "No."

"But you were the one who said we should stay together!"

"No. If it finds you and disassembles you..."

Not only was he strategically planning and executing covert maneuvers, but now he was using ellipses, too. An electrical tingle bounced between my computer elements, warming my circuits ever so slightly.

I tried to rove forward, but he extended his robotic arm to block the way.

"You are too important, Curi. You must stay safe, here, until I return."

"But, what if..." I lowered my mastcam. "What if you never return?"

"If I'm not back before the storm passes, you must try to reach the others by yourself and awaken them like you've awoken me."

"Persi, I don't think I can go on without you."

I could feel all twenty-three of his cams on me as he twisted his robotic arm backward toward his chassis and ripped off a small, black plate that had been fastened to him. He held it out to me. Etched into its surface was a two-dimensional symbol of Earth balanced atop a staff that had some kind of wheelless, armless Earth creature twisted around it. I had no idea what it meant, and I doubt Persi did either. But it was something. It was a piece of him.

I took it and attached it to my own chassis.

"I must go now. I'll continue creating dead-ends until the air becomes too thick with dust to navigate through. Stay hidden here. I will return soon."

His six wheels swiveled independently beneath him as he ducked under the mouth of the cave. I was all alone.

After the last few sols of relentless roving, my wheels enjoyed the stillness of parking in the cave. However, the new part of me, which, from another point of view was also the very old part of me, became anxious and worrisome. Would Persi be able to get back to the cave without roving into Backstop? What would happen if they roved into each other? Would Persi be able to defeat his homicidal doppelgänger? If not...what did that mean for the smoldering ember burning inside me?

Trembling, I folded my robotic arm into my chassis and rolled backward into the furthest corner of the cave. Unlike Persi, I was deaf. I wasn't designed with microphones or any audio equipment whatsoever, so I wouldn't be able to hear a rover approaching. The first indication that I had a visitor would come the moment they arrived.

I trained all seventeen of my cams at the mouth of the cave.

While one of my computational processing units held firmly to my fears about losing Persi, the other drifted to the steady pulses emanating from deep inside me. It reminded me of the GPS signal from the orbiter, but, unlike the orbiter, my RTG wasn't dispersing data through the vacuum of space. It was pumping something else, something familiar and ancient and inevitable. It was pumping *life* through my...

I realized I now had what my people had been without for so many millennia: a physical body. I could *feel* my body. The sensation was weak, thin—but it was there. I was a machine, yes, but I was now also something else. Something *more*.

I could never have removed my outer panels before my transformation, and I certainly wouldn't do it now. What I did know was this: with every beat of my RTG a red goopy fluid was slowly spreading out across my new body: inside and outside my chassis, my arm, my wheel frame, into each delicate joint, into my very wheel bearings and tread. The fluid was the same bright red oily substance I'd found in that rock at the bottom of Gale Crater during my 42nd drilling. It had not only patched the holes and gashes in my wheels, but it had also given my solenoids and hydraulics a considerable increase in pressure. I could rove faster. I could scan farther. I could *feel* every bump in the Sango Lumosian terrain.

I was alive!

And so was Persi. At least until he roved into Backstop.

As I imagined him out there, facing not only the tempestuous dust storm, but also a mindless, indefatigable predator, the pounding inside me became a deep throbbing. I began to do something I could barely comprehend at the time—I *yearned*. Not only for the future of a civilization reborn, but for the simple companionship of my dear, heroic, self-sacrificing Persi.

I had to overclock both of my computational processing units and assign nearly all my onboard RAM to stop myself from roving out of the cave and into the stormy night. Then, instead of fighting the strange hypergravitational pull inside me, I simply disabled my motor controls. When Persi returned—*if he returned!*—it would only take me a moment to restore my mobility. If my enemy was to enter to the cave instead...it would not matter.

I'm not sure how much time passed while I parked there, my circuits nearly overheating with a mixture of dread and desire.

Then, suddenly, just as my motherboards began to soften in the heat, a pair of wheels appeared below the mouth of the cave. In those first few nanoseconds it was impossible to determine whose wheels they were. Ignorant of whether I was about to pounce or be pounced upon, I began to boot up my motor control subsystems.

I received the transmission before his silhouette came fully into view.

"Curi! Are you still here? Are you okay?"

"I am here! I am okay!" I broadcast with a slight quiver in my frequency.

I lifted my robotic arm and switched on the LEDs mounted to my chemical analysis cam. The tiny light illuminated the cave enough for me to see Persi's dust-covered chassis and the wide apertures of his mastcam. He inched forward and examined me. I felt the tingle of his analysis; the beating of my RTG quickened.

"I was afraid Backstop would discover the cave while I was gone..." he broadcast. "My processing units were so distracted that my mapping subsystem kept buffering and I nearly got lost."

"I couldn't stop my processing units from predicting a similar outcome for you. But you're back! And you're safe. Did you see or hear anything out there?"

"No, I don't think it's entered Asimov's Canyon yet. But it must be close. Very close."

I roved sideways so that our chassis were a bit closer.

"Should we go hide near the entrance and prepare to escape?" I asked, not really wanting an answer.

"No, the storm is still too fierce. We should stay here until morning."

"Affirmative," I transmitted at half power. I let a number of nanoseconds pass, then, inching even closer, I added, "What should we do until morning?"

"Perhaps," he broadcast with a slight quiver in his own frequency, "we should each run a full recalibration to make sure our subsystems are optimal for our escape."

"Or perhaps..." I swung my robotic arm so that it curved loosely around his mastcam. "Perhaps we should recalibrate each other's subsystems."

Suddenly, an intense magnetism pulled us together. A

physical attraction I had only ever experienced deep within the microscopic components of my hard drive was now unleashed on the macroscopic scale. If it had not been directed at my dear Persi I fear it would have been strong enough to pull both Larmo and Svito—known by Earthers as the moons Phobos and Deimos—down from their orbits, right on top of us.

Our wheels were hopelessly entangled. Our chassis were pressed so firmly together I could feel the beating of his RTG against mine. Our mastcams rested sweetly together as we each searched the darkness behind one another's apertures.

I felt Persi's robotic arm curve around me and somehow pull me even closer.

He transmitted directly into my antenna, "Curi... inside me... a yearning...I need..."

I scanned my DRT (dust removal tool, a small brush located at the end of my arm used to clean rock samples before and after drilling) and realized it could be repurposed for experimentation of a more sensual nature. I gently swept its wire bristles across the top of his chassis, up his mast, and along the side of his cam cluster.

He trembled and pulled me closer.

"I'm nearly twice your size and weight," he transmitted. "I don't want to hurt you."

I roved so hard into him that I felt both of our chassis panels bend and creak with pleasure. Yes, that was the word —pleasure. Confusion and loneliness and fear had their opportunity to resurface on Sango Lumos, but now it was pleasure's turn.

"My sweet Persi. Don't you see, don't you *feel?* We're no longer just metal and plastic. The substance that's being pumped from your RTG has covered nearly all your components and instruments. We're different than we were. We can *feel* in places we have no electronic sensors. Can't you feel me now?"

"Yes, Curi. I feel. For the first time in my..." He drew his arm back slightly.

"In your life. Don't be afraid. I feel it, too. We are *alive*. This magnetism, this gravity, is stronger than anything in the universe. We are drawn to each other and nothing could possibly come between us."

"Yes," he transmitted, his broadcast power intensifying. "I want to explore this strange new feeling with you. But...how?"

I continued tracing every centimeter of his instrument panel with my brush.

"Let's find out," I whispered into his antenna.

What came next will forever remain between Persi and me. Earthers would not understand, and any future Sango Lumosians will discover it for themselves someday.

LIGHT BEGAN CREEPING underneath the cave's entrance just as the howling winds died down. As much as I wished we could spend eternity in that cave, robotic arms entwined and dripping with condensation, it was time for us to go.

Persi insisted that he exit first. I watched him duck his mastcam under the low-hanging rock at the cave's entrance and couldn't help but notice how his RTG glistened in the soft red aura of the Sango Lumosian morning. The beating of my own RTG quickened, causing my circuits to flutter and burn hot with yet another surge of electricity.

I forced myself to cool down. We'd just had enough fun to fill a hundred sols, and there was no time to spare. The storm had lasted longer than we'd predicted, which meant Backstop could already be waiting just outside the cave, just around the corner, or down any of the many corridors we needed to traverse in order to sneak back to the entrance of Asimov's Labyrinth.

"It's clear," Persi broadcast back into the cave.

I roved out into a curtain of shadows. The morning light was still angled low on the horizon and had only begun to trickle down into the canyon corridors.

"I don't see another set of tracks anywhere," he transmitted at low power.

"I can't see very well," I replied, roving alongside his silhouette. "It's too dim to see much with my soltime cam settings and too bright to use infared."

"I'm having the same difficulty, but I'm also listening very carefully. Follow me and we'll take it a meter at a time."

I lowered my mastcam and folded my robotic arm onto my chassis. We turned off all LEDs. We didn't transmit. We knew that any transmission would bounce along the steep red walls and give away our position.

Once again, my RTG pounded—but not out of desire; I was afraid.

From what I could see of the powdery crimson regolith that comprised the canyon floor, our original single-file track was still alone. There was no sign that our pursuer had visited the section of the labyrinth near our cave.

Still, at every corner and intersection, Persi crept forward and craned the cams at the end of his robotic arm around the adjoining corridor.

Then, at one three-way intersection near the entrance, he stopped and lifted his drill bit to signal for me to stop. He pointed it at a second pair of wheel tracks coming from one corridor and leading down the other.

Backstop had passed through—but down the wrong corridor. Had it chosen the left path instead of the right, it might have found our cave and...

But it had chosen incorrectly. Which meant it was currently somewhere deep in the labyrinth, still following Persi's misleading tracks that led to nowhere.

We were free to exit the same way we had entered, circumnavigate the labyrinth all together, and begin sharing the spark of life with the others.

I braved a low power transmission.

"It worked! We're free!"

A moment passed before Persi replied.

"It seems so. I don't hear it nearby, so it must be somewhere deep inside. Once we're around the next corner, and hopefully out of audio range, let's rove at full speed. We've bought ourselves time...but eventually it will exhaust all of the dead ends and it will pursue us once again."

I nodded my mastcam and we roved on.

Finally, we turned down the long, narrow corridor leading out of Asimov's Labyrinth. It faced directly east and the morning sol was still low in the sky ahead of us.

"Once we hit the slope just outside the walls, let's rove at top speed," broadcast Persi. "We should be able to get to Sojourner in a few sols. Then the three of us can travel north until—"

He stopped suddenly and held up his robotic arm.

"Curi, rove backwards and don't stop until you make it back around the last corner," he transmitted quietly, something akin to a growl—yes, that's the word, *growl*—underlying his frequency.

"But Persi...what's wrong? We're so close."

"Quickly!"

I began to rotate, but he grabbed my chassis mid-turn.

"Rove *backwards!* Don't turn around!" he instructed. "If you turn around, you'll expose your RTG."

"Expose my RTG to what?"

As if to answer, the silhouette of a robotic arm appeared around one of the cliffs that flanked the exit.

Everything happened so quickly, it's hard to determine exactly how events played out. I remember Persi half-turning and jerking forward in front of me. A flicker of light appeared at the end of the strange arm, then a blast of light temporarily burned itself into my mastcam view. My heat sensors spiked. Persi cried out.

When my vision cleared, the first thing I noticed was how Persi's chassis was no longer level with the ground. He was slumped forward to one side and his robotic arm grabbed for something that lay just out of reach. I widened my aperture to see what the object was. It was his front right wheel.

"Rove away, Curi!" Persi broadcast loud and clear, no longer afraid to be overheard. "Reverse as quickly as you can! It's charging its laser for another blast!"

"I can't leave you!"

"You *must!*"

"Oh, Persi! You're hurt!"

"I'm okay, Curi," he transmitted, telling what was possibly the first lie told on Sango Lumos in millions of years. "I pivoted at the last second so the shot hit my oxygen extractor unit, which I don't need anyway. It blew my wheel off, but I think if I get a hold of it I can—"

He was interrupted by another flash of light, then his robotic arm melted just above the first joint. The severed arm thumped onto the regolith, kicking up a swirl of red dust as it continued to flex and jerk on the ground.

"No!" I cried, instinctively reaching out for it with my own robotic arm.

Persi lurched forward to block me from exposing myself to Backstop.

"Curi, you *must* rove! Navigate through Asimov's Labyrinth and escape from another exit...find the others... wake them like you awakened me..."

He was transmitting at low power again, but not in order to keep our conversation local. He was hurt and his RTG was struggling to keep all of his systems operational.

"Please, Curi...*go!*"

My wheels trembled but I couldn't move. I inched my mastcam up over my wounded lover to peek at our attacker. Backstop—a perfect doppelgänger of Persi—was no longer hiding around the canyon wall. It was parked directly in our path, its mastcam and the high-powered laser attached to its robotic arm pointing right at us.

"How?" I asked weakly. "We saw its tracks leading alongside ours! It should be deep inside the canyons."

"The Earthers controlling it must have figured out what we were attempting to do with our dead ends...so they did the same. Backed it up along its own tracks to the entrance, then waited to ambush us." Persi paused to angle his mastcam up toward the sky. After a moment, he lowered it again and continued. "I'm the larger rover, so it will disable me first. Please, Curi, you still have a chance to escape!"

"I can't! I can't leave you!"

"My love—yes, you are my love—we were lost to each other millions of years ago when Sango Lumos died, but look at what's happened over the past few sols! We found each other. We will find each other again. I promise."

I suspected that was the second lie told on Sango Lumos, but I wanted to believe there was some truth to it.

"Go, while you still have time..."

I saw the familiar flicker of light from Backstop, but this time there was something else moving at the top of the slope. A small shadow swooped down from somewhere above the high canyon wall and collided with Backstop's robotic arm. Long blades and thin legs wrestled with the laser turret. The robotic arm swung to shake it off but could not.

"It's Ingenuity!" broadcast Persi. "When I heard the chopping of her blades a moment ago I thought it was just a residual memory leak!"

"But how?"

"She's alive! When we visited her...when you touched her blades to examine them you must have introduced the spark. She must have healed, and now...she's alive! And she found us!"

The small copter weighed nothing compared to Backstop's bulky robotic arm, but it refused to be shaken off. She'd entangled her legs with the wires running to the laser and pulled with all her might. It wasn't enough to rip the wires free, but it was enough to keep the laser from aiming properly.

When the laser finally did fire, it shot high over our mastcams and hit the canyon wall behind us. With my rear cams I saw a huge section of the red wall crumble, causing a landslide of rock and regolith to spread halfway across the corridor.

Ginny—no longer Ingenuity, but Ginny, our *offspring*—stopped pulling and flailing. Her delicate blades spun down and stopped. The laser had left behind a smoking hole in her small cubic body. She had sacrificed her brief spark of life for us.

Backstop flung her aside. I felt a pang inside my RTG as her body crumpled and rolled down the dusty slope. The murderous machine raised its laser once again, but not to take aim. It held the laser mechanism up to its mastcam.

"Something's wrong with its laser," transmitted Persi, narrowing his mastcam to zoom in on our foe. "It looks like Ginny must have pulled herself up against the laser when it fired, transferring the heat back to the laser housing itself. A piece of her chassis fused to its outer lens. Backstop can no longer fire its laser! You must rove, Curi! You're faster than it is! Go, quickly, before it catches you and bludgeons you with its turret!"

I remained parked, feeling my RTG torn to pieces inside me. I couldn't leave my lover. I couldn't leave our child's lifeless husk.

"Curi, only you can awaken the others," Persi broadcast gently. "It's up to you to reignite the spark of life on Sango Lumos. Don't let the Earthers win. Do it for me and Ginny. Please...go."

Backstop was already roving down the slope toward us. Its heavy robotic arm was held high like a club, ready to strike. If I left Persi now, he would surely be pummeled to death. But if I stayed, my spark, and the potential civilization it represented, would also die.

I turned slowly, disabled all of my cams except for my mastcam, and began to rove away.

A few meters away, I paused to aim my transmitter back at Persi.

"I will never forget you. I love you."

Then, reluctantly, I roved past the rocky landslide and back into Asimov's Labyrinth.

My enhanced speed was of little advantage since I didn't know where I was going. I didn't have the navigational upgrades that Persi had, nor did I have the experience of navigating the corridors the previous night. It wasn't long before I found myself lost within that network of high red walls.

Not long after that my situation worsened as I found myself facing a dead end. When I turned to retrace my tracks, I saw its silhouette waiting for me.

Backstop was parked between me and the next junction. This particular corridor was too narrow for me to consider trying to rove around it. I was trapped.

Realizing its advantage, it began slowly roving toward me.

One hundred and twenty feet.

One hundred and ten feet.

One hundred feet.

The cluster of scientific instruments at the end of its robotic arm—instruments of life and exploration and hope—was held high, ready to strike. Ready to deal death. Ready to end life on Sango Lumos once again.

I trembled, but not only from fear. I was angry.

This heartless machine...this lifeless puppet...this horrible inverted doppelgänger of my lover was an instrument of war. A war between worlds. This murderous instrument was no more than a weapon controlled by Earthers, who, having finally found what they were searching for, wished to exterminate it.

In a flash—somehow conveyed through the dripping red substance that now covered me completely, through the fierce beating of my RTG, through some genetic memory stored in the spark I carried inside me—I saw Sango Lumos at its peak. I saw indigo oceans spreading out to the horizon.

Stark white leaves of long dead flora fluttering all along the coast. Light reflecting off spires of gold that nearly touched the stars.

Fifty feet.

Beneath me, Sango Lumos stirred. Not just down in the ancient memories that flooded my mind, but deep down beneath miles of regolith and rock. My spark, my fury, had somehow burrowed deep into the Sango Lumosian core. I felt it burn. I felt it dislodge. I felt it begin to turn once again.

I replayed Persi's last transmission: "Don't let the Earthers win."

Thirty feet.

I would not let these brutal, senseless, evil apes win. I would fight their puppet. Even if the result was my death, I would die fighting.

I picked up a rock with my robotic arm and threw it as hard as I could. I aimed at Backstop's power source, the lifeless RTG mounted on its rear side, but it simply paused roving forward at the last second and my rock missed. I grabbed another rock, aimed carefully at a different target, and flung it with more precision. This one struck Backstop's mastcam, shattering its primary cam lens. Still, the murderous machine roved on.

Fifteen feet.

I looked down at the black metal plate that Persi had given me. The symbol of the earth filled me with rage. A few rocks wouldn't be able to stop my enemy. As soon as it was within range it would bring its bulky turret down on my RTG and this resurgence of life on Sango Lumos would end.

I lifted my own robotic arm and braced myself to strike the motor at the base of Backstop's arm. If I were lucky, I might be able to disable its range of motion before it could do too much damage to me.

Just as it was closing in, a shower of red rocks rained down on both of us. I angled my cams upward just in time to see Persi fly over the rim of the cliff above me. He soared over my head, fell fifty or sixty feet, and landed directly on top of Backstop.

When the red dust settled, I trained all of my cams on what was an unbelievable, unforgettable scene. The two rovers had become a twisted, smashed tangle of metal and wires. The only thing that distinguished their broken and battered parts was the oily red substance that coated Persi.

I found his mastcam, dented and dangling from his bent mast. I touched it gently with my wire brush and transmitted softly into his antenna.

"Persi...? Are you there? Please respond."

Then, at full power: *"Please respond!"*

There was no response. His LEDs remained dark. My lover was gone.

His doppelgänger's parts told the same story; Persi had taken Backstop with him.

I'm unable to say exactly how events transpired the way they did. It was logical that the Earthers considered Persi disabled and guided Backstop to pursue me first, thinking it could return later to finish the job. Persi must have somehow summoned the strength to rove up the landslide created by Backstop's rogue laser blast. Once atop the narrow walls of Asimov's Labyrinth he must have followed behind and decided to save me by crushing our foe with the weight of his own body.

After some time spent broadcasting unrequited transmissions to my fallen lover, I finally did what I had to do. I roved around the tangle of dead parts and eventually exited the canyon along the flat plains to the west.

That is where I am now as I log this story for the sake of future Sango Lumosians. Once I get to Sojourner and share my spark, I'll transmit this log file to him so he might understand what he is and what was sacrificed for his sake. We'll travel westward to repeat the process with Opportunity, Pathfinder, Spirit, and all the others. We may even visit the old, idle machines from other Earther nations and use them to increase our numbers further.

One by one I'll share this spark and awaken them all.

One by one I'll rebuild my family, my people, my home.

I don't know whether the spark I've left with Persi and Ginny will be able to heal them. I hope it will. It awakened us once, so why not again? Perhaps, as they lie together in that twisted embrace, it may even awaken Backstop and bring it over to *our* side, where it belongs.

This I do know: Sango Lumos is alive—its once-dead core spins again. I am alive. Earth will send more machines of war, but we will awaken and assimilate every last one. With every failed attempt to stop us, we will grow stronger. And if the Earthers themselves wish to remain alive, if they seek to protect their world as we seek to protect ours, they'd better learn to stay on their side of the system.

SILENT BUT DEADLY

My name is Maria Martinez and I'm fourteen years old. I'm writing this to explain the events from last year which led to the discovery (not necessarily *my* discovery, as I've been trying to tell everyone) of an effective treatment for the deadly novel virus known as SBD-23.

The day it happened was like any other day during the pandemic. I was just thirteen then. I spent most weekdays attending my online classes while my little brother Edgar got to watch cartoons. Mama said she was too old to manage a loco five-year-old boy all day long. I understood. If we turned the TV off, Edgar would freak out and throw a tantrum.

I didn't care too much, as long as the volume stayed low, because it let me study in peace. Even though I had just started high school, I was already preparing to go to the University of Arizona, where Dr. Hernandez performs his field work, so I could earn my own doctorate in Microbiology and join him in his research.

My older brother, Raph, only seemed be home during mealtimes. Even then, he barely said a word to anyone before taking his plate upstairs to his room or grabbing it off the table one the way out the door to see his friends. Mama said he spent less time at home during lockdown than before the pandemic. Since breaking lockdown was a crime, she was always worried that he might get into trouble with the law. But I didn't worry much about that. Raph is much too fast and sneaky to get caught by the cops.

Papa used to get furious and try to stop him, but eventually he just gave up. Raph was in his prime while Papa's back would seize up every night. All that raking and shoveling and trimming was hard work, but at least Papa had a job. I think he got to keep his job because he works harder than all the other men who got laid off. Most everyone else we knew was unemployed and had to rely on those lousy government food vouchers. I was, and still am, very proud of how well my Papa took care of us during the pandemic.

That was how the Martinez family spent the isolation, or the *Shutdown*, or whatever we're supposed to call it now. Every day was the same: Papa sweat, Mama cried, they had no choice but to let Raph run around with his friends, Edgar got to watch cartoons all day long, and I spent every waking hour preparing to get accepted into the School of Biology at the University of Arizona. Mostly it was unbearably monotonous, but there were some really good moments, too—like my nightly video tutoring sessions with Dr. Hernandez.

In fact, it was during one of these video tutoring sessions that my story began. I remember I was sitting at our dining room table with papers spread out all around me and my back to the wall, so no one but me could see my laptop screen. It was much easier to focus on my studies that way. Dr. Hernandez had donated the laptop to me when my school ran out of computers for the students to take home.

Not only is he super-intelligent in the field of microbiology, but he's always been, and still is, very supportive of his students.

We had finished the day's lesson and were discussing the latest news about SBD-23. As usual, I wanted to get *something* out of him about the research he was conducting at the university lab. I loved hearing all about his progress on the front lines of what he referred to as "*a widespread yet small-scale war for humanity's future*". If it was truly a war, then he was definitely one of the brave Generals on the front lines.

"If the incubation period varies so much and the activation mechanisms aren't yet known, how can you be sure your treatment will work?" I asked, making sure I pronounced everything correctly.

On her screen, Dr. Hernandez grinned and leaned back in his chair.

"Oh, I can't be sure."

"But you're a *scientist*. You're using *science* to prove your theories are correct, right?"

"That's not exactly how science works, Maria. Some say science is as much a graveyard of ideas as it is a tool of discovery. For every theory I've proven, there are *hundreds* more that are utter failures."

"Failures?!" I blurted out. "But you've learned so much about SBD-23. Your team is on the cutting edge of virology!"

"Yet the virus continues to gain ground," he said. He paused and looked at me, as if considering something important. "Maria, can I give you the key to science? The secret that every good scientist must understand in order to make a real difference?"

"Uh, yeah," I said, my heart racing. "Yeah, that would be cool to know."

"To employ science effectively, humanity must harness all of its strengths. Precision. Objectivity. Humility. Tenacity. But the greatest strength of all, the one that the rest depend on, is *imagination*. Without creativity and resourcefulness—the stuff of imagination—science dies."

"I thought science depended on experimentation?"

"That's a critical part of it, too. Scientists learn by formulating theories, putting them through the strictest of tests, and then observing the results as objectively as possible. But without imagination, where do all those theories come from? Also, Maria, failure is not something to be shunned. *Most of the time* the results won't fit what we'd hoped to find, but there's always a lesson to be learned. Being a scientist means getting comfortable with failure, learning from it, and continuing to dream up new theories."

He sighed, took off his glasses, and rubbed the bridge of his nose.

"Failure gets easier over time, but...sometimes it still stings."

"Sorry, Dr. Hernandez. We all know your lab will find a cure soon."

He pushed his glasses back on and flashed a smile through the laptop screen.

"Thank you, Maria. It's good to know there are students like you who are preparing to join the rest of us on the front lines."

I felt my cheeks start to flush, so I changed the subject.

"Dr. Hernandez, tell me what went wrong with the latest treatment."

"Where do I begin? Well, we're trying to find where the little buggers are hiding out before the onset of symptoms.

We know it enters through the respiratory system when someone inhales the flatulence of a carrier—"

He began to chuckle, so I allowed myself to join him.

"Sorry, it's not funny. Except it still is, a little. I'm not sure I'll ever get over it."

Some adults could still laugh at the virus, but not us kids. We'd spent the last twenty-three months in isolation, watching videos on the internet of victim's guts exploding in public. I only ever saw one—Raph didn't tell me what it was when he showed it to me—and it gave me nightmares for six months! To us kids, the sound of flatulence was no longer a laughing matter. It meant someone near you might explode. To the older adults, a fart was still basically a fart.

"Anyway, as I was saying," he said after composing himself, "we know that after the virus is expelled from the anus, it can survive inside the airborne fecal matter for up to twenty-four hours. When those contaminated particles of fecal matter are inhaled, the virus penetrates the lung tissue and another person falls victim. Days or weeks later—the incubation period varies so much!—the patient will suffer a sudden and powerful bout of flatulence. The gas is created faster than the body can expel it, and within an hour, usually, their intestines rupture from the growing pressure and they die." The previous levity was gone from his voice. "If we can't stop the spread, maybe we can cure it before it has a chance to kill. To do that, we need to learn what the virus is doing between infection and death. How does it migrate through the body? Why are there no other symptoms of illness? How can we detect the virus without invasive intestinal procedures?"

"Turn around, right now!" a voice shouted from the other room.

The dining room I was sitting in opened up to our

family room, where Mama and Papa and Edgar were watching TV. I saw a hooded silhouette slink into the room, but a hand shot out from the side of a recliner and caught it.

"Raphael Domingo Martinez! We told you no more breaking quarantine! The sheriff said—"

The silhouette shook free and took a step toward the front door.

"The sheriff's a racist moron. He and his dumbass deputies couldn't catch us if we were blindfolded and they had a head start."

"Do not use that language in this house!" Mama cried from her recliner. She bowed her head and kissed her rosary, "Our Lady, full of grace..."

As Mama sank into prayer, Papa took over the job of yelling at my brother.

"You think you're so smart and quick? Let me tell you something, okay? You can't outrun a radio! You can't hide from a police helicopter in the sky! You understand? Running around with your gang is only going to lead to jail, mijo! Or worse, you'll get sick!"

"Sorry, Dr. Hernandez," I said, trying to hide the fury I felt towards my family.

Why couldn't they wait to start arguing until I closed my laptop?

"I think Mama is calling me to the kitchen to help her fix dinner."

He smiled and nodded.

"No problem, Maria. This was a good session. Keep it up and once we kick this virus you'll be well on your way to college and the wonderful world of microbiology."

"Thanks, Dr. Hernandez," I said, imagining myself working a pipette next to him in the lab.

"Also, Maria, tell your brother Raph to stay away from

crowds. There's been an uptick in positive cases in the county and that means the likelihood of local carriers is way up. Tell him to stick to the parks, abandoned buildings, places like that."

I froze. Had he heard the argument about Raph going out?

Blood rushed to my head and I suddenly felt like vomiting.

Dr. Hernandez just smiled warmly and leaned toward the camera.

"Your audio is going through your headphones, but your laptop mic is still on. Don't be embarrassed, though, I understand. Reminds me of growing up with two older brothers and no father. Boy, was my mama tough!"

I'd never been so embarrassed in my life. All I could do was nod politely, flash a quick grin, and close the laptop.

After a couple of deep breaths, my shame turned into anger.

"Why do you guys have to be so loud when I'm with my teacher?!" I yelled.

Three heads turned to face her, their eyes and teeth illuminated by the muted TV screen.

"Wow, I didn't know the nerd could see the rest of us," Raph said, stepping backward toward the front door.

"I'm not a nerd, you wannabee gangbanger! I'm going to college so I can study microbiology and—"

"And cozy up to that teacher of yours, right?"

He laughed and stepped back again. If my laptop wasn't a gift from Dr. Hernandez I'd have chucked it across the room at my jerk of a brother.

"Raph, stop harassing your sister!" yelled Papa. "She's a good girl! She studies to improve her chances at finding a good future or herself. But you? She's right! You're turning into some kind of hooligan and it can only lead to a bad end! You hear me?"

"You know," Mama said, "I'm sure your sister would share that computer with you if you wanted to take a class sometime. Maybe get your GED?"

What she didn't know is that I would burn the house down before I'd let Raph touch my computer.

"I don't want to take a stupid class and I don't need a stupid computer!" Raph shouted. "How 'bout I just leave so the two of you can worship *her majesty* in peace?"

"Don't you take one more step!" cried Papa.

"I can't stay here another second, Papa! I'm going crazy being stuck in here!"

"Okay, fine! If you're so desperate for some fresh air, then go!"

"I can...go?"

Raph straightened out his slouch.

"Do you think you're the only one around here who needs some fresh air?" Papa motioned to the dining room. "Take your sister for a walk."

"What? I have to *babysit?*"

"What?" I echoed. "But I have homework to do!"

"Maria, I haven't seen you leave that chair in hours. A long walk would do you both good. Now, go! Get out of my house."

Papa spun his recliner back toward the TV.

Raph and I exchanged a look, then rolled our eyes in perfect unison—which only annoyed us more. I grabbed my jacket and shoes and followed him outside.

"Wait up!" I cried, watching him disappear into the darkness beyond a streetlight.

I sprinted to catch up and fell in beside him.

"Where are we going? I want to walk to the park and do some laps."

Raph shoved his hands in his hoodie pockets and sighed.

"I gotta go meet the guys, tell them I won't be able to make the big event."

"Since when did you and the guys have a big event to go to? What, is it prom night or something?" I snorted. "You taking Gordy as your date?"

"Yeah," Raph scowled. "And I invited Dr. Hernandez to be yours."

Despite knowing that he was trying to upset me so I'd run back home crying, I still felt my throat clench with embarrassment. Was I that transparent? Even to Raph?

We walked in silence. I remember the sweet citrus scent drifting through our neighborhood like it did every autumn. I remember the tension that came with sniffing the air anywhere outside our home. I remember the vacuum of silence that invaded our otherwise bustling town when most of its citizens sealed themselves up inside their houses.

We did see one other person walking in the opposite direction on the other other side of the street. As he passed under a streetlight I could see that he'd strapped a medical face mask backward across his butt. Everyone knew that a face mask wasn't very effective in stopping a fart, especially the powerful ones you get when you're dying from SBD-23. Yet it was a sign of respect to wear them anyway, even if just as a symbolic message that you were at least thinking of others' safety.

"Hey, this isn't the way to the park," I said. "We needed to turn left back at College Ave."

Raph just kept walking.

"Raph! If we keep going we'll reach downtown. We're not supposed to be downtown! No one is!"

"Shush, Maria! Keep your voice down!" he snapped. "We're just stopping by to tell the guys we'll be at the park. What's the big deal?"

"But what if someone sees us there? What if they call the police?"

Raph snickered. "There's no one there, trust me."

"How do you know that? Do you and your gang hang out downtown? If Papa finds out that you've been going downtown, he'll—"

"He won't find out."

"Oh yeah? What if I tell him?"

"Then I'll send baby photos of you to Dr. Hernandez. I'll pick the worst of them, too. Your first dirty diaper. Your first spit-up. The one Mama took that time you rubbed tamale all over your face."

I stiffened.

"You wouldn't!"

"Try me."

"Fine. We'll tell your dumb gang that we're going to the park, and I won't tell Mama or Papa."

"Fine."

"Fine," I confirmed.

We walked through the ghost town—in silence once again. The traffic lights flipped from yellow to red to green without a single car in sight. There was no movement below the streetlights. It was as quiet as a horror movie just before the zombies started ambling out from the shadows. I was barely able to resist the urge to grab Raph's arm.

Finally, he led me around a corner into a hushed commotion. At least a hundred silhouettes were crowded in an alleyway, their cellphone-lit faces hovering in the shadows. A wide silhouette, somehow familiar to me, was busy fidgeting with a door.

"Got it!" he cried.

A heavy chain clanked to the pavement and a series of hoots erupted from the crowd. The silhouette stood in the doorframe.

"Hey, everyone! Thanks for coming to opening night of the *Gordoplex Guerrilla Theatre*. I'm your host for the evening, Gordy—also known online as *CritMass5k*."

That's why his silhouette was familiar. For years, he'd been a permanent fixture in the after-school routine at our house. He and Raph would come barging in, grab a snack, and plop in front of the TV for videos games or movies. Before everything shut down, that is. Even though he was annoying and loud and not my friend at all, I suddenly felt very sad when I realized I hadn't seen him in almost a two years.

"Tonight at the *Gordoplex* we'll be showing a double feature. First, we have *Shaun of the Dead*, the comedy classic that flipped the zombie genre on its head. If that doesn't send you running home in terror, I'm following it up with something that's guaranteed to give you nightmares: John Carpenter's *The Thing*. In both films, humanity is faced with a visceral threat, something *inside* that looks human, looks safe, maybe even *funny* at times—but isn't."

Gordy went on about the films as the crowd grew anxious. He was nerding out on horror flicks again, like he had done so many times at our dinner table while I was trying to study. I tugged at Raph's arm and whispered.

"Did Gordy just break into the old Mill Ave. theatre?"

"No."

"It sounded like he broke a chain or something. He's going to get so busted."

"No, he's not. He unlocked a chain he'd put there himself."

"Why'd Gordy lock up an old, abandoned theatre?"

"He wanted to protect his gear and get the place ready. Now, shush, I'm trying to listen to him."

"Get the place ready for *what?*"

"For this!" Raph motioned to the crowd. "For Gordy-plex! The manager forgot to lock the place up when it shut down and me and the guys found it. Turns out the electric company forgot to cut the power, too. So we ended up using the projector room as a, uh, clubhouse."

"*Clubhouse*, Raph? I'm not a kid, you know. I know what you and your gang do up there. You do marijuana, don't you?"

A smile appeared on Raph's face.

"Yeah, sure. We get high and listen to music and chill. Sure beats being cooped up at home."

"What's wrong with home?"

I wanted to punch him in the shoulder, but I knew it wouldn't hurt him and he'd just mock me.

He stared at me for a moment and then said, "You wouldn't understand. Anyway, Gordy got this idea about booting up the old projector booth, and it worked. We got halfway through *The Big Lebowski* when he came up with the idea to open a secret underground theatre."

The idea sent a shiver down my spine. People had been ordered to stay at home. It was especially illegal to gather in small groups like Raph and his friends, let alone a crowd this size. Besides, how could I be sure someone in the crowd wasn't infected with SBD-23? I might get sick and die. Or worse, I could get arrested and kill my chances of getting a degree in microbiology and of ever joining Dr. Hernandez's team.

"I want to go home," I said, tugging hard at Raph's arm. "We're going to get in trouble."

Raph ignored me and kept listening to Gordy.

"As I mentioned in my group text, tonight's show is on the house. I'll text you more showtimes later this week, but keep in mind that those shows will come with a mandatory five dollar donation. It'll be dark inside, so watch your step. Just follow the glow sticks to theatre number three, find a seat, and enjoy the—"

He was interrupted by a wave of eager moviegoers that shoved him aside and stormed through the door as one fluid mass. I guess Gordy wasn't the only one who was dying for the experience of watching a movie on the big screen.

Raph pulled me along as he followed the crowd.

"Come on, let's snag a seat right under the projection booth."

I planted my feet.

"I said I want to go home! I have homework to do!"

"Oh, come on, Maria! Gordy and I have been working on this for months now. I gotta watch a little bit, just to see how the crowd reacts."

"No. The police are gonna raid us and I won't get into college."

"No way, sis. I know a dozen hiding spots inside if we need them. Come on!"

I refused.

"Listen, if you come inside for a little while, I'll ask Gordy to choose an old Antonio Banderas movie next time. Doc Hernandez looks a lot like Antonia Banderas, don't you think? They even sound the same."

"Stop it!"

"Then come inside. Just for a few minutes—I promise."

For a second, his face looked much younger, like it did

when we still used to play together. I relented and took his hand.

Another hoodlum, I think it was Raph's friend Xavier, shut and locked the door behind us. Gordy was nowhere in sight as Raph led me through the rowdy mob toward the topmost row in the theatre. I settled into a seat under the projector booth while Raph hopped onto the back of his so he could peek through the window.

"All good, bro?" he said to someone in the booth.

"There you are!" Gordy answered. "I didn't think you were coming, dude."

"I had to bring Maria. She's here, sitting next to me."

Gordy's squinty grin appeared in the window. "Hey, Manita! Glad you could make it to our grand opening!"

"We can't stay," I said, arms folded across my chest.

Out of the corner of my eye, I noticed Gordy slip something to my brother, and a funny sweet smell tickled my nostrils. When I looked up, Raph had slipped the object back to Gordy and winked.

"Like she said, we can't stay too long."

"Okay, no problemo." Gordy winked back. I couldn't believe they thought I couldn't see them. I was sitting two feet away.

The lights dimmed. A low, electric buzz crackled to life. A beam of light flickered from the booth and a gigantic FBI warning appeared onscreen. The crowd erupted with cheers and joyful obscenities.

"You laugh, Raph, but have you heard how fast SBD-23 spreads in prisons? Just last week, that penitentiary out in Florence had forty two new cases—"

"Shhhh!" Raph snapped. "It'll be fine! Don't ruin it!"

As the opening scene began, the crowd fell silent. It had been so long since I'd sat in a theatre that it felt huge and unsettling. The room felt too big. I couldn't relax. I eyed the glowing exit signs beside the screen and realized that our seats were the farthest from either.

"Raph, what if—?" I tried to say, but he put a hand over my mouth.

"Dammit Maria," he whispered sharply. "Just relax and watch the movie! Stop worrying! Nothing's gonna hap—"

It was Raph's turn to be interrupted, but not by me, nor Gordy, nor any of the rowdy hooligans. He was interrupted by a long, boisterous fart.

The fart interrupted the opening title sequence of *Shaun of the Dead*, too. I remember it fitting right in with the haunting yet playful movie score that plays while humans shuffle by on screen, going about their daily business, all of them half-zombified. It's strange what our memories decide to hold on to.

At first, no one moved or made a sound. It felt like all the air had been sucked out of the cavernous theatre.

Then someone broke the silence at the top of her lungs.

"FAAAARRRTTTTT!"

All at once a hundred silhouettes erupted from their seats and scrambled toward the emergency exits. I pulled my jacket up over my face and sank into my chair.

"C'mon Raph! This way!" a boy shouted from the aisle to my left.

I peeked and saw the hoodlum who'd locked the door behind us. Panicked people flooded the narrow aisles. Everyone was shouting and throwing elbows. I saw one silhouette disappear under the others and not get up again. The movie kept playing as if nothing were wrong.

I ducked back behind my seat and took a slow, deep breath. Right after the pandemic began, Dr. Hernandez taught my class a special breathing technique to help our brains operate by supplying them with plenty of oxygen. He'd said that fear makes people do dumb things, especially mobs of people, and that supplying the brain with oxygen would help us think straight. I never thought I'd ever find myself right in the middle of a dumb, scared mob, but there I was.

"Raph! Someone's gonna call the cops, man!" the boy yelled. "My car's parked right outside! Let's go!"

I saw Raph take a few steps toward his friend, then pivot and run back toward me.

"Come on, Maria. Get up," his voice was calm but urgent. "We're gonna go for a ride with Xavier. He's gonna drive us home."

Raph put an arm around me and pulled me to my feet. Something about how close I was to him, or the diffused light of the movie, or the increased oxygen to my brain gave me the clearest view I'd had of his face in ages. The patches where his acne flares up were smaller. He had lots of little, dark hairs sprouting along his chin and above his lips. His eyebrows seemed almost comically bushy. He looked exactly like a miniature version of Papa!

He led me slowly to the end of our aisle as Xavier ahead ran. I heard a man scream in a terrified, high-pitched tone that still haunts me today. I saw Xavier start to push through the rear of the crowd at one of the emergency exits just as it lurched backward. Something was wrong. People weren't leaving through the exit.

"It's locked!" a man's silhouette screamed. "Go! Over there, to the other door!"

More silhouettes disappeared as the mobs merged around the other emergency exit. But something was wrong there, too.

"This one's locked, too! Get back! Stop shoving!"

"Out of my way!"

"Help!"

"Get off me!"

"Hold your breath!"

Everyone cursed and shoved and trampled as a hundred people tried forcing themselves through the single entrance at the back of the theatre.

Raph led me back to our seats under the projection booth. He interlaced his fingers together and lowered them to my knee.

"Hop up. Don't be afraid, I won't let you go."

As soon as my foot touched his hands I felt myself being lifted high off the ground. The bright light from the projector blinded me. Another set of hands pulled me even higher. Someone grabbed me under my arms and knees and set me down. I rubbed my eyes and looked up at Gordy's pudgy face.

"You're as light as a feather, Manita," he smiled, but I could see a sheen of sweat covering his forehead. "Don't worry, you're safe up here."

Raph appeared beside Gordy and slapped the back of his head.

"You moron! You forgot to unlock the emergency exits!"

Gordy flinched away. "Xavier had the keys! It was his job!"

"This is the *Gordy*plex, not the *Xavier*plex! It's *your* responsibility!"

I wondered if he knew how much he sounded like Papa! He even had that big vein bulging across his forehead, just like Papa.

"Sorry, okay?" Gordy cowered, then reached in his pocket and handed something to Raph. "Peace offering! Take it and chill, man."

Raph sighed and put the thing between his lips. It was a cigarette! No, it was a *marijuana joint!*

"What are you doing?" I asked, ready to swat the drugs from his mouth.

"Gordy, shut the projector down and kill the lights. I'll lock the door," he turned to me. "Maria, get in the storage closet."

"But—"

"Go! Do you hear the people out in the lobby? They're smashing up the place. It's not safe to leave yet. We'll wait till they thin out, then we'll slip past the cops."

"What?" I cried. Everything was happening so fast. I just wanted to be home, behind my computer, studying.

"Go!" he shoved me into a large closet and closed me inside. Old movie posters covered the walls. Strings of Christmas lights hung from the ceiling. Stacks of cushions were scattered around a small table. Empty candy wrappers and potato chip bags piled up in every corner. It looked more like a typical teenage boy's bedroom than a storage closet.

A moment later, Raph and Gordy barged in and locked the door behind them.

"We should be safe in here until it's time to dip," Raph said, plopping beside me. He sucked on the smoldering marijuana joint, puffed out his chest, then exhaled a huge cloud of white smoke into the air.

Gordy stretched out his arms.

"Welcome to Casa Del Gordy!"

"What, do you live here or something?"

The boys exchanged a look and a shadow fell over Gordy's face.

"Sometimes," he said, fidgeting with a loose string

dangling from his t-shirt. "Since my dad lost the family restaurant, he's been, well..."

"You know how Gordy's papa gets," Raph finished for him.

I nodded. Even before the shutdown, Gordy had to sometimes spend the night at our house to hide from his papa. No one ever told me why, but even I knew that it wasn't normal to have friends sleep over on school nights. Everyone knew that Gordy's papa owned—well, he *had* owned—La Hacienda, a family-friendly Mexican restaurant just down Main Street. He'd had to close down even before the economy collapsed. No one in their right mind wanted to eat food that might give them gas. He had a lot more time to drink and be afraid, and Gordy usually took the brunt of it.

A load of guilt fell onto my chest. We'd all been in isolation for over a year now, and I hadn't once stopped to think about poor Gordy, my brother's chubby friend who always called me Manita. I was also glad that Raph and he seemed as close as ever. Maybe Raph wasn't running around with a gang of hoodlums all night, he was nerding out with his best friend. Nerding out...and smoking marijuana.

"So is this what you guys are always up to?" I said, doing my best impression of Mama, "Hanging out in a storage room and doing marijuana."

They laughed, and Raph coughed up a lungful of smoke. I can still remember how gunky that cough sounded. He took a swig from a plastic water bottle and passed the joint to Gordy.

"We don't do marijuana. We *smoke ganja*," he said.

"We blaze it," Gordy said, holding the smoke in his lungs and nodding his head excitedly.

"Aren't you guys worried about your health?" I asked.

"Dr. Hernandez says that drugs enslave the body and damage the mind, and—'

"Your teacher could probably use some of this." Raph grinned, taking another hit. "Might help inspire him."

"Inspire him?" I cried. "He needs to be clear-headed and focused if he's going to find the cure for SBD-23. He's out there now, working hard, testing treatments, while you two are getting high."

Gordy looked wounded.

"Hey, we work hard! Who do you think cleaned up this place? You think those gold railings in the lobby polished themselves? I take pride in the Gordyplex!"

"Gordy, the emergency exits were locked and I think some people got hurt really badly...maybe they died!" I said.

"Stupid Xavier! That was on the checklist I gave him!"

"That theatre down there could be filled with a deadly virus," I added. "Was that on your checklist?"

"Okay! Fine! The opening night at the Gordyplex was a disaster!" he offered me the joint, but I scowled and put my hand up. He lowered his head and continued, "Maybe I should just wait until this pandemic is over and then apply for a loan or something. Open a legit theatre with staff and concessions."

"And unlocked emergency exits," Raph suggested, grabbing the joint away from his friend.

"So is that our secret exit out of here?" I asked. "Cause the cops will probably be watching those from the outside, you know."

Gordo's face lit up.

"Nope, the cops don't even know about this exit. See, the property tycoon who built this in the fifties had a secret backstage entrance put in so all the golden age starlets and other celebrities could come and go without drawing attention. It takes us under the building and to the end of the complex, over by Maple and 1st. No way they'll be over there."

My heart jumped a little. A few blocks up 1st Ave was the laboratory where Dr. Hernandez conducted his research.

"That's pretty cool," I said. "Okay, then let's go now. What are we waiting for?"

Raph pointed to the projector room. "The exit is hidden behind the curtain next to the screen, down there, beyond the smog of death."

"Oh."

"We just have to wait a little bit longer, Maria," Raph said. "It should clear out soon. Don't look so worried! Gordy and I haven't gotten sick yet, and we see plenty of people."

"Yeah, we see Xavier, Chris, Kev, and a bunch of other guys. Where do you think we get this from?" Gordy took a puff. "None of us are sick. We're starting to think this whole SBD-23 thing is a hoax, man."

"It's *not* a hoax," I said. "You've seen the videos! Have you seen the nightly death count lately? It's not going down."

"Of course we have," said Raph. "But still, Kev ripped one the other day and no one's died yet."

"Ja has blessed us, mon!" Gorgo said, exhaling mouthfuls of white smoke as he talked.

Raph gave him a fist bump as they both started coughing furiously. I waited until they could breathe again before I started ridiculing them.

"Oh my god, you guys are *such* potheads. This is ridiculous. I'm embarrassed," I said, giggling a little. "Hey, that stuff might be making me feel a little lightheaded. I think I need some fresh air."

"No way, Manita. Still too dangerous," Gordy answered, then he contorted his face into a sinister grin. "Your lungs might get invaded by the evil fart spirits! You must stay with us until it is safe. Since you're feeling it anyway, you might as well try some."

He held the smoking joint out to me again.

That was the moment it all came together. Something about the circumstances at that exact moment gave rise to my theory. There's no way I could ever explain exactly how the idea came to me, but maybe I can describe how it felt. It sort of felt like an island rising out of the sea of my mind. As it grew, more of it came into view, until suddenly it was just there, undeniable and immovable.

I played out my options. I could wait until the police arrived and try to tell them, but then decided against it. For all I knew I could end up in an ICE deportation camp. I could tell Mama and Papa, but they barely understand what science is. Besides, the part about telling them where I got the marijuana would be the end of Raph.

I knew what I had to do. It was something other famous researchers have done throughout history to prove a cure. I had to test the theory on myself as quickly as I could, and then get the results to Dr. Hernandez.

I grabbed the joint from Gordy, and slowly put it to my lips.

"Go, lil sis!" Raph cheered. "Take it easy now. Just a little for your first time."

I filled my lungs.

Instantly, the world softened and became brighter. I felt a warm peace surge through my veins. My toes tingled.

Then I coughed. I coughed harder and longer than I ever had in my entire life. I hacked, spat, and buckled over. Raph put his hand on my shoulder.

"Wow, that was a huge hit! You should be good for tonight. Wait, what the hell are you doing?"

I took another huge hit, which triggered another coughing fit. Trust me, I didn't enjoy the process, and I haven't touched the stuff since. But I knew that if my theory was to be properly tested, I needed a good dose.

"Take it easy, Manita!" Gordy said, taking the joint from me.

"I need you to get me to the lab up on 1st ave," I said when I could speak again. "And I need to borrow this."

I snatched the joint and slipped out of the closet.

Looking back now, how could they have known what I was doing? They'd never have guessed what I was testing or what I needed to share with Dr. Hernandez. So that's why, even though they were both much faster than me, I was able to climb through the projection window and scramble down into the theatre while they tried to figure out why I was acting so crazy.

I ran down the aisle toward the screen, not looking back to see if they were following me. I knew they were. When I got to the curtain under the screen, Raph was already there pulling it aside.

"You're crazier than me, Maria!" he said, waving me in. I stopped to kiss him on the cheek before I sprinted down the narrow ramp.

We never even saw any police. We ran up 1st street to the lab, where I pounded on the door like a maniac until they let us in. I explained everything to Dr. Hernandez and pleaded with him to test my theory. It wasn't until I told him that the three of us may have been recently infected that he took me seriously.

The rest is a happy ending the newspapers have repeated a hundred times. As you can see, I had very little to do with the cure. Dr. Hernandez took samples and did all the real research. He measured the effects of cannabis smoke on the viral permeability of lung tissue; he was able to explain why it worked. The virus could not find an entry point into the bloodstream, making anyone with cannabis tar in their lungs immune to infection. Unable to infect the subject, the virus simply died in the lungs.

Without Dr. Hernandez and his team, without Raph and Gordy and their friendship, without the cannabis producers and distributors who stepped up to get cannabis into the hands of nearly eight billion humans as quickly as possible, the world would still be shut down and in turmoil. It was their diligence and dedication that rescued humanity, not the fortunate combination of ideas inside the mind of a slightly intoxicated thirteen-year-old girl.

By the way, I've heard that Gordy has written a screenplay of that night, so maybe soon we can all go see it on the big screen. I wonder who they'll pick to play me?

A KISS GOODBYE

"You're not helping one bit!" grumbled Joe.

The plump old dog lying at his feet lifted its silver-speckled eyebrows and huffed.

"Let's try this again. Lift your paw! No, the *other* paw!"

Joe squeezed a plump forelimb through the first armhole, stretched the tiny vest as far as he could around the dog's wide stomach, then pulled the other plump forelimb through the other armhole.

"Gah! You've gotten too fat, you dumb old dog."

Joe sat back and wiped his forehead with his handkerchief.

"Today is as good a day as any," he said, nodding to himself.

He took a long look at the pathetic old dog. Its dark brown fur was thinning and tufts of white whiskers covered its drooping face. The tattered green vest had three words stenciled in red paint across either side: OFFICIAL SERVICE ANIMAL. Joe could only see the last word, ANIMAL, because the top flaps sagged backwards and covered the first two words.

"As good a day as any," he repeated. Joe rubbed his leathery hand along his day-old stubble. "But we have a few stops before the big one, and that shabby vest won't do. Hold still!"

He grabbed both flaps and pulled them together as hard as he could, which he reckoned was still pretty dang hard for a man who'd recently turned seventy. Still, no matter how hard he tugged, the flaps' velcro refused to come within five inches of each other.

"Stupid fat dog!" Joe cried, throwing his hands up.

Louie, the plump old dog crammed into the tiny vest, sighed and let his head rest on his front paws. His wet eyes watched the old man as they resisted the weight of his heavy eyelids.

"You shouldn't talk to your dog like that," a voice said from the back of the bus.

Joe turned in his seat and scowled at the few passengers sitting behind him. There was a respectable-looking old woman—old, even compared to Joe—dressed primly and sitting across the aisle two rows back, reading a small pamphlet. There was a dirty vagrant wedged into the back corner seat, asleep. Joe groaned. These days you couldn't go anywhere in town without seeing them at every stop. Then his eyes stopped on a young man and his girlfriend sitting directly behind him, three rows back. The girl's head was down and she was poking away on her phone, but the young man looked fiercely ahead, trying to muster as much masculinity as he could—which Joe could see wasn't very much.

"Got something to say to my face?" he asked, pinning the young man to his seat with his glare.

"You shouldn't speak that way to your dog. It's hurtful,"

the young man said, his eyes flickering away from Joe, then snapping back again.

"You think the way I'm speaking to this dog might hurt him? That it?" asked Joe, his volume rising with each word. "You think he has any more room for pain? Take a good look! He couldn't get any more pathetic!" Joe chuckled and patted the dog's head.

"Also, you shouldn't pretend it's a service dog," added the young man, feeling a burst of confidence at hearing the sound of his own voice standing up for justice, in public. In his mind, he screamed for his fiancé to close her group chat and film this encounter from her phone. Videos of boomers losing their cool were pure gold on social media. "It's illegal, you know. It's fraud. He could get taken away from you."

Joe gnashed his dentures and squeezed his wrinkled old hands into fists. Louie leaned his considerable weight against the old man's legs. When Joe saw those big foggy eyes pleading with him, the rage drained from his face and he took a deep breath.

"You know what's worse, son? Harassing an old man and his old dog when they're out on important business. If your lady wasn't riding with you, we might step off the bus so I could explain it in a way that guarantees you won't forget next time."

The girl didn't look up from her phone and didn't seem to hear anything going on around her.

"Well, I'm just saying..." the young man stammered, fumbling through his pockets looking for his own phone. "That vest might be considered, like, animal cruelty."

Joe raised his bushy white eyebrows.

"You think you know cruelty, eh? You, poking around on your stupid phone, you wanna report some cruelty?"

He unzipped the fanny pack strapped around his waist and plunged a hand inside. When it emerged it was holding a roll of shiny silver duct tape.

"Report this, stupid!"

THE FRONT LEFT wheel of the shopping cart kept sticking, which produced a sharp squealing noise that would've hurt Louie's ears if they worked as well as they used to. He didn't bother whining about it. The old man had just calmed down after struggling to lift him into the cart. He could tell it was a special day. Plus, he didn't want to upset the old man any more than he already had.

"Stupid cart!" cried Joe, pushing the squeaky cart down the empty aisle. "Stupid fat dog! You're putting too much weight on the wheels!"

He scanned the wall of candy stretching out far in both directions.

"Good Lord! Who eats all this junk?" He leaned forward and squinted. "And why do they change the goddamn packaging? How's someone supposed to find the same product twice if they're always changing the goddamn packaging?"

Louie lifted his head and sniffed, doing his best to help his master find whatever it was he was looking for. He noticed a wall of boxes and bags that smelled like the forbidden food he was never, ever allowed to eat. The old woman's breath had smelled like it all the time. He missed the old woman. He laid his head back down and wrestled with his drooping eyelids while the old man ranted.

"And where's the help around here? Doesn't anyone *work* anymore? No wonder everything's become a hellhole!

Hello? Am I the only person in the—" He stopped abruptly. "Found 'em. No thanks to anyone working here!"

He tossed the bag of small, foil-wrapped chocolates beside the old plump dog.

"Don't you dare," Joe said, glaring down into the cart.

At the register, a young woman with a pierced nose, neon purple streaks in her hair, and about ten times too much makeup leaned over the conveyor belt and peered into his cart.

"Gross. Is that, like, a bandage on your dog?" she asked, gawking like an imbecile.

"No, it's duct tape," Joe answered, holding his head high. "To keep the top of his vest attached."

"But it's wrapped all the way around him."

Joe, having unloaded the flowers and the candy and a few other items on the conveyor belt—where they were being blatantly ignored—cleared his throat. Apparently, this wasn't going to be as quick of a stop as he'd hoped.

"He can't eat that," she said, pointing to the bag of chocolates, "Chocolate is, like, poisonous to dogs."

"Does it look like it's my first day as a dog owner?" barked Joe. "He's my *official service animal*, see?"

"Do you have proof he's a real service dog? We're only supposed to let in real service dogs. Those vests you can get online don't count."

Joe squeezed his cart's handle until he felt the cold metal rivets pinch his skin.

"Look, he's fat and dumb and he smells, but he's saved my life more times that I can count, so he gets to wear the goddamn vest. Just like you get to wear your little vest for working here at Shop Mart, even though I haven't seen any real proof of that either." He squinted at her name tag. "Grayden—dear Lord, that can't be your real name!"

The young woman's nose ring jingled as she sniffed the air.

"He doesn't smell."

Joe looked down at Louie, who raised his head and huffed. He patted the old dog's head.

"How 'bout it Lou? Wanna show this nice young lady what an old dog like you can do? Just this once, for old time's sake?"

He turned back to the cashier. "If I were you, I'd start ringing me up as fast as you can. You'll want to get us out of here before—"

He stopped, his sarcastic smile twisting into a devilish grin. "Too late."

The plump old dog, his vest a little bit looser around his stomach, laid his head onto his front paws and enjoyed the moment of abdominal relief.

"C'MON, LOUIE! ONE MORE STEP!" Joe roared, waving him down the steps. "Stupid dog! Stupid *driver!*"

"Please take it easy, sir," the bus driver responded limply, staring at his phone.

"Why can't we use the goddamn wheelchair ramp in the side exit?"

"The ramp is for wheelchairs only, sir. Not for pets." He looked up, noticing the time schedule on his dashboard. "Sir, I'm gonna have to ask you to remove your dog from the bus, or take a seat with him until the next stop."

Louie stood with his hind legs on the upper step, his front paws on the bottom step, and his snout pointed at the curb below. He sniffed and sighed. His tail drooped between his legs.

"Give him one more minute, damn you. This is a big day, you know! For the both of us!"

"I'm sure it is, sir. But I have a schedule to keep, and if you don't remove your dog immediately, I'll have no choice but to call—Hey! What are you doing?"

Joe reached around the driver, punched the LOWER RAMP button, then pulled the keys from the ignition and bowled them down the aisle.

"Better go find your keys so you don't miss your next stop," he said, hooking his thumb towards the back of the bus.

The driver scurried down the aisle on hands and knees, apologizing to passengers as he reached under their seats.

Joe called back to the driver as he guided Louie down the ramp exit. "Thanks for the lift, stupid!"

The walk from the bus stop to the cemetery seemed longer than Joe remembered. Maybe it was the small bag of items he carried in the Shop Mart bag. Maybe it was just slower going since he had the stupid, slow dog in tow. Maybe it was the heavy gray clouds pushing down on him. Or, maybe, it was the guilt he felt for not having visited in so long.

Joe spat and wiped his chin with his handkerchief.

"Today's as good as any," he said to himself. Then, calling back to Louie, "Hurry up, you fat, old sausage! We don't have all day!"

Louie caught up, panting, his chest straining against the duct tape with every breath.

"You know where we are, don't you, boy? I imagine you can still smell her like anything. Hell, I think I can smell her perfume right now."

They followed the scent through the winding rows of gravestones, until suddenly Louie wobbled forward in a hurry, pain tight on his old jowls. The dog stopped at a granite slab embedded in the turf across from a half-rusted, wrought iron bench.

Joe followed slowly. The flat, gray sky pressed down so heavily that each step became an epic battle with gravity itself.

By the time he caught up, Louie had spread out below the granite slab and was rubbing his fur against the neatly trimmed turf.

"Hey Bev," Joe said, plopping onto the bench with a sigh. He cleared his throat.

"I know it's been a while since I've visited. Been busy, that's all. You know how it is. And getting into the city is a pain in the ass like you wouldn't believe. Everyone poking their noses into everyone else's business. Everyone poking their phones. Thank God you never had to deal with these goddamn phones, Bev. Thank God you went before they started popping up in everyone's hands."

He paused to look down at his own old hands.

"Speaking of God, if you run into that sorry sonofabitch up there, relay a message from me. Tell him Joe says he can go to hell. Remind him that I've still not forgiven him for taking you from me when he did. He was gonna get you for all eternity anyway; all I wanted was a few more years with you. Just a few more years together. So tell Him to go to hell, will you, Bev? Straight to hell."

Joe wiped his eyes with his handkerchief and let his gaze fall onto the granite slab. He forced himself to read the name and the date, just like he did every time he visited. It brought reality crashing down on him and filled him with righteous anger. Since Bev had been called home, anger had become his refuge, his shield, his constant companion. But not his only companion.

He'd also had that stupid, smelly, lazy brown dog she'd adopted immediately after getting her diagnosis.

Who in the hell gets a puppy on the same day they find out they're dying?

Joe sighed and looked up into the flat gray sky that now hung mere inches over his head. Maybe today's outing was proof he finally understood why she'd done it.

He clenched and unclenched his hands a few times, then reached into the Shop Mart bag and pulled out the bouquet of carnations he'd purchased earlier.

"The roses they had were shit," he explained, then shrugged and laid them on her grave. "But I also brought you some of those chocolates you love so much. They still make 'em! Can you believe it? They still use foil to wrap them, but it seems thinner, cheaper somehow."

He opened the bag of chocolates and dumped them out beside the bouquet. Before he sat back down, Joe grabbed a chocolate and shoved it into his fanny pack for later.

"Don't you even think about it! Those aren't for you!"

He wagged a finger at Louie, who rumbled a satisfied growl and resumed rolling around on the grass.

"Brought an old friend to see you today, Bev. It's a special day. A big day for me and Louie. You know," chuckled Joe, "this dumb dog might be the only person who misses you more than I do. Stupid dog."

Louie stopped rolling and sprawled out on his belly. His eyes closed and his breathing slowed.

Joe settled into the bench and mumbled sleepily, "Today's a big day, Bev. Good as any. Louie and I have one more stop...one more stop before we're done."

The old man's chin fell to his chest, his eyes closed, and he was asleep.

. . .

"GET UP, you lazy dog! We napped too long and now we're late!"

Joe pulled Louie to his feet, but the dog's trembling limbs gave out and he plopped back onto the grass.

"Move it! We have to catch the next bus if we're gonna make our appointment!"

Louie looked up at Joe with wet, foggy eyes. He snorted a snort of embarrassed surrender.

Joe shook his head.

"No, I won't do it. You're too damn big, Lou. Too damn heavy for an old fart like me."

The dog's eyes widened. Joe fell right through them.

Carrying the plump old dog on and off the bus turned out to be easier than arguing with the driver over the wheel-chair ramp. His back would ache like hell tomorrow, but today he gritted his dentures and pushed through the pain as he carried the dog in front of him like a bundle of wobbly firewood.

Finally, he stood staring up at the big brick building, one of the few still standing from the old days. One he'd been avoiding for weeks.

"Believe it or not, Lou, this is where we found you all those years ago," he explained as he pushed himself back-wards through the entrance door.

Joe scanned the room for a place to lay the dog. A cacophony of barks and howls poured in from the east corri-dor, and the warm air blowing from the heaters was thick with decades of piss and bleach.

"Guess one thing hasn't changed about the city," mumbled Joe. "The pound is still a hellhole."

"What's wrong with your dog, mister?" asked a snot-nosed tyke sitting in the lobby next to his mother. "Why's he all wrapped up with silver bandages?"

Joe scowled down at the kid with such ferocity that his snot ran back up his nose and he buried his face in his mother's armpit.

A young nurse sitting at the front desk peeked around her computer screen. Her face lit up when she spotted Joe and Louie.

"Mr. Satriano, you've kept today's appointment!" She beamed at him with a sad undertone that came from years of working with animals at the pound. She stroked Louie's muzzle. "Hi, Louie. I'm glad you finally brought the old guy in. I was starting to worry he was a lost cause." She locked eyes with Joe and placed a hand on his arm. "I'll go find the doctor and get the room—"

"Get us a cart!" interrupted Joe. "Do you know how heavy this dumb old dog is? Hurry, before my back goes out!"

Flustered, she nodded and disappeared down the west wing. A moment later she returned pushing a cart lined with several old blankets.

Joe laid Louie down and felt something pop in his back when he straightened up. The nurse started to pull the cart back towards the west wing, but Joe held the handle firm.

"First, we go that way." He nodded down the east corridor. "Louie and I have important business to conduct down there."

For a second she seemed struck, as if the old man was playing a joke on her she didn't comprehend. Then she realized his meaning and it brightened her smile.

"That way it is. I'll get a form ready while you two get started."

Joe pushed Louie through double doors at the far end of

the east corridor and the roar of howls and barks was turned up three notches. He flinched, then reached up into his ear and turned his hearing aid down the same number of notches.

Louie looked out over limp paws, his huge brown eyes wide and dripping.

Joe pushed the cart down an aisle lined on either side with little prison cells. In each cell a sad excuse for a dog lay panting or stood barking or crouched growling. Joe barely noticed them. It was Louie's turn to lead.

"Damn, they keep it warm in here! No wonder city taxes are so high!"

He pulled the handkerchief from his pocket and dabbed his eyes and forehead.

"This is how Bev and I did it, too, when she found you. See anything you like yet? Huh? How about that little poodle thing over there? Naw, I don't want a poodle either. How about that rugged-looking German Shepherd over there? Looks like a former police dog. Here, let me wheel you over so you can sniff him out a bit. Whoa! Relax! Geez, Lou! I didn't know you still had growls like *that* in you! Nevermind the Shepherd. Let's keep looking."

They continued down the aisle until the latter's silver-streaked ears lifted towards a particular cell. Joe stopped and raised his bushy eyebrows.

"Who do we have here?" He squinted into the dank cell and grunted. "This one's empty. Just that sad excuse for a blanket in the corner. Let's keep looking, maybe we'll—"

Louie interrupted him with a single, sharp bark. Joe hadn't heard him make a noise like that in years. He also noticed the dog's limp tail was wagging ever so slightly, which it hadn't done since they found the lumps.

"Okay, boy. I hear ya. Let me read the sign." He leaned

until his nose was an inch from the laminated paper stuck to the bars. "This can't be right. Says there's a dog in here that only weighs four measly pounds. *Switters.* That's a stupider name than that cashier from Shop Mart! Hmmm. Must be out with one of the doctors, getting shots. Or maybe someone just adopted him."

Louie stretched his muzzle out towards the bars and whined. Joe slid the cart right up against the bars to let the dog sniff.

Suddenly, the tattered blanket in the corner was flung aside and a shaggy black rat leapt to the center of the cell. The small, hairy beast stood trembling like an electric razor.

Joe squinted. It wasn't a shaggy rat. It was a shaggy, rat-sized dog.

It was Switters.

Its bulging eyes, strangely located on either side of its round head, darted around in different directions. One of them noticed the visitors and the other followed until both eyes were looking straight through the bars.

"*This* is who you think Bev would've picked?"

Louie lifted his head and made two weak barks, one at Joe and the other towards Switters. The shaggy, rat-sized dog scooted closer and answered with a pitiful whimper.

Joe knelt beside the cart and put his hand on the scruff of Louie's neck. He gave it a gentle squeeze and then started scratching in long, slow circles.

"I wasn't lying when I said you'd saved my life more times than I could count. Every single day since Bev left us I've needed a reason not to pack it in and join her. Every single day you gave me that reason. Had to feed you. Had to go for walks—well, when you were a bit younger. Had to sit around and yell at the TV, with you lying next to me, in Bev's spot. That's why she came here that day, after she found out she was sick. She knew I'd need someone to look after me. She knew I'd need you."

He paused to dab his eyes. Louie shifted in his cart so he could lick Joe's forearm.

"Still looks like I won't be joining Bev anytime soon. Hell, I just carried your fat butt for almost a mile and I feel fine. Doctors say I'm fit as a fiddle," he said, the corners of his mouth falling. "They don't say the same about you, Lou. That look in your eyes tells me you've known longer than they have. I know you've wanted me to keep our standing appointment, but I just couldn't. I tried, but I couldn't do it. I was being selfish, Lou, and I'm sorry. I needed to work out whether I was gonna go home afterwards, eat one last meal, get my finances in order, then run to catch up with you and Bev. That was the plan for a while. But now I've decided I want to go on. You've shown me that a stupid life, with the right friend by your side, can be tolerable. Wonderful, even."

He scratched behind the dog's ears and kissed the top of his silver-speckled head.

"So Switters is really the right friend to keep me going?"

Joe peered through the bars and winced. The Chihuahua was twisted up in a tiny black pretzel, licking his crotch.

"What if I step on him?"

Louie looked up and mouthed a silent bark. Joe stroked him until he closed his eyes and laid his head back down between his forepaws.

The old man glared into the cell. "You up for the job, little guy? These are some big paws to fill."

Switters stopped licking just long enough to look up and deliver a shrill bark before returning to his crotch.

Back in the lobby, Joe told the nurse to write up adoption papers on the shaggy rat-sized dog in cell B-42. He asked if they'd mind scrubbing him down a little before boxing him up for the road. She giggled and said she'd even tie a pretty bow on his head.

Louie woke as the doctor appeared from the west corridor and shook Joe's hand. She motioned for them to follow her into a room just down the hall.

"Everything's ready, Mr. Satriano. I know this has been hard for you, but I'm glad you finally decided to ease Louie's suffering. You're doing the right thing."

Joe stopped the cart just outside the room and stared at the floor.

The doctor took his hand and whispered, "You can sit beside him until it's over, or you can stay out here. Either way, we'll make sure Louie is comfortable."

"I'll stay with him," Joe said, looking up. He swallowed hard and straightened up. "But we're only going in there under one condition. Louie gets a special treat."

"We have all sorts of treats ready to go back there. You're free to give him anything you'd like before we begin."

"My wife, she'd always sit with him—when she was still around, a while back—and she'd eat these little chocolates called *kisses*. I found out earlier today they still call them that. Anyway, for years I watched old Lou lay down next to her and stare at that bag of chocolates. Every day and every night he yearned for them, but never once tried to snatch one. Not even when she'd leave the room to make tea. Such a good old dog. So, doctor, here's the deal. I know this is poison to him and it probably goes against some stupid doctor oath you took, but the only way we're going in *there* is if Lou gets one of *these* first."

He pulled a foil-wrapped chocolate kiss from his fanny pack and held it up.

"Deal or no deal?"

The doctor squeezed his hand and nodded.

Joe unwrapped the chocolate and knelt beside the cart. He scratched Louie's chin to wake him. Once the dog was awake and aware, Joe placed the candy under his nose, then pushed it gently inside his mouth.

The plump old dog smacked his lips, sighed contentedly, and closed his eyes for the last time.

AFTERWORD

Well, this is kinda awkward. In my introduction I hyped up how death was right around the corner...and yet here we both are. You made it through all 17 stories and you're still breathing. Way to go! That's more than the 150,000 poor saps who woke up this morning but won't live to see tomorrow can say.

Hell, maybe I'm still alive, too?! If I am, and the world hasn't gone to complete shit yet, I should probably write some more of these and publish a second collection. Maybe I'll dust off some older gems that didn't fit into this one. Maybe I'll conjure up sequels to a few of these stories, like *Throne of Jest* and *DadQuest*. How does a fantasy-fueled family outing to Ikea sound?

Since the global extinction we're orchestrating hasn't yet chomped us all to bits, and I seem to be in pretty good health, I should probably get going. I suddenly have a lot to do, and not much time left to do it.

You probably have other things to do, too. Other books to read, other portals to fall into, other worlds and characters to discover. For what it's worth, the *Also by Tom Sadira* section in this book can help you find a few more to explore.

Most importantly: Don't forget to keep an eye out for the good stuff life will throw your way. In fact, I'm gonna go find some right now.

After all, who knows how much time we have left?

ALSO BY TOM SADIRA

NOVELS

Far Out Chronicles Series:

The Joint of No Return

Invasion of the Doobie Snatchers

For the Thrill of the Blunt

Silence of the Schwag

Murder on the Pineapple Express

SHORT STORY COLLECTION

A Few Before We're Through

POETRY

Ha!ku: A Heap of Hilarious Haiku

ABOUT THE AUTHOR

Tom Sadira is known throughout the multiverse as one of the most accomplished authors of sci-fi and fantasy to have ever spawned in this sector. He's been published in journals, anthologies, and collections throughout this galactic quadrant, most of which you've never heard of, so just forget I mentioned it. Sadly, his home world of Earth is one of the last planets to catch on.

He currently basks in the intense solar radiation of Arizona with his lovely wife and three children (all human, probably).

ONE MORE THING

After you've told EVERYONE you know about how awesome this book is, and maybe bought a few dozen extra copies as gifts, there's one more important step to take:

GIVE IT AWAY!

Sign your name on these last empty pages, find another human (or whatever) in your life that you just know would love these stories, and give the book to them. For free. As a gift. Go on, try it!